BLACK TIDE

Color Mage Book One

ANNE MARIE LUTZ

BLACK TIDE

Second Edition
ISBN 978-1-937979-58-4 (Paperback)
Hydra Publications Goshen, Kentucky 40026 HydraPublications.com

To my mom, who always knew she'd hold a book of mine in her hands. And to Steve, for his love and support through draft after draft of this novel.

Acknowledgments

I've had a lot of help from family members (some of whom also double as first readers). Thanks to all of you! Also, thanks are due to the members of the North Columbus Fantasy/SciFi Writers group— I've learned a lot from all of you, and no doubt will learn more in the future. Good luck to all of you in your writing.

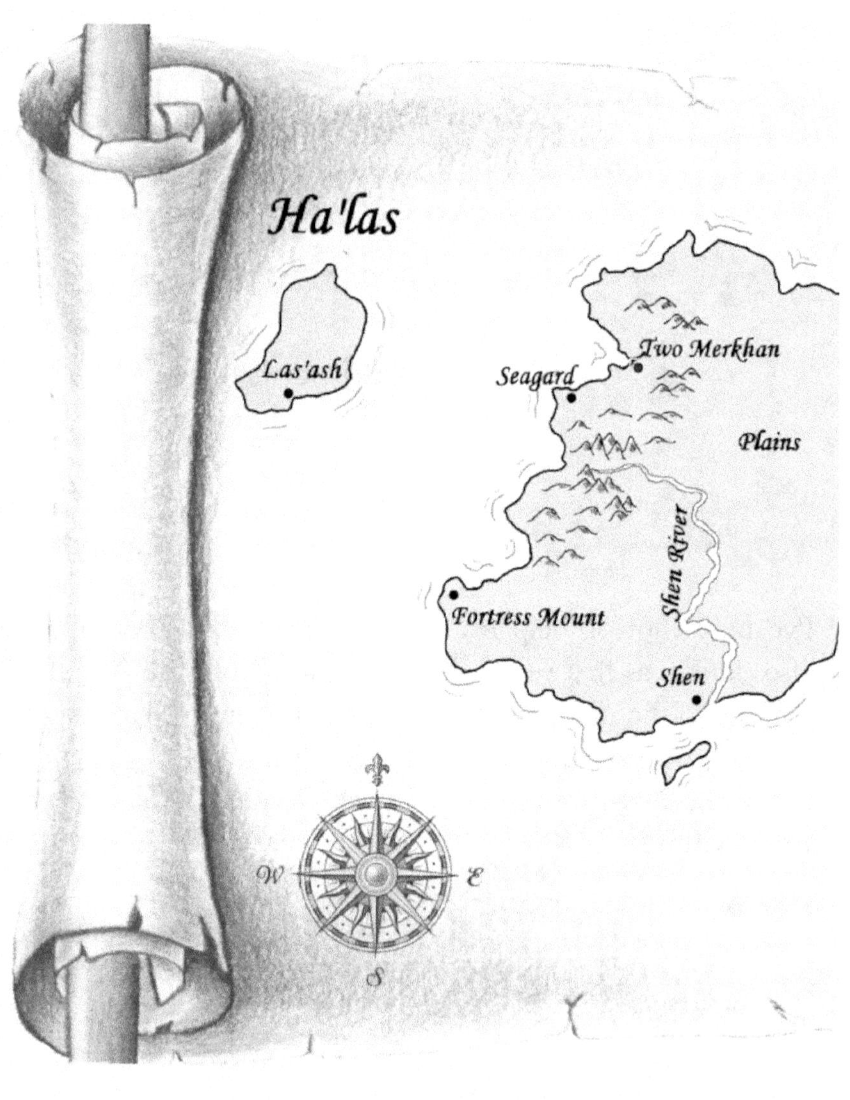
Ha'las
Las'ash
Seagard
Two Merkhan
Plains
Shen River
Fortress Mount
Shen
W
E
N
S

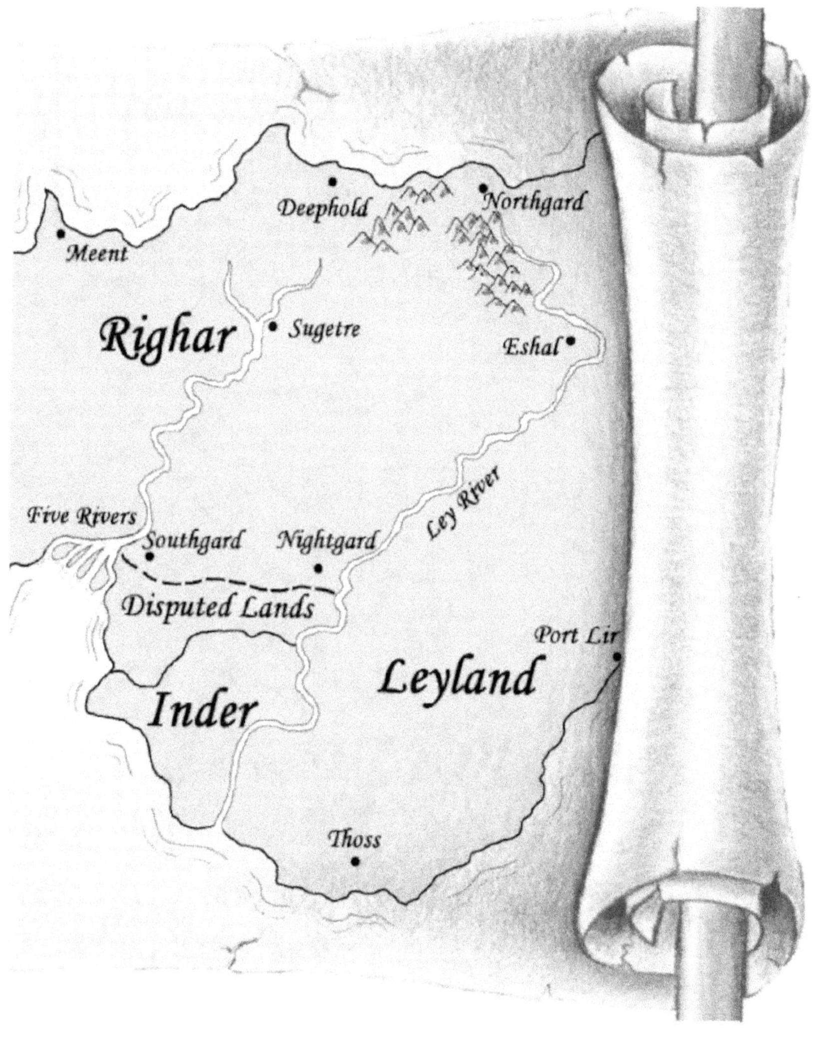

Meent
Deephold
Northgard
Righar
Sugetre
Eshal
Five Rivers
Ley River
Southgard
Nightgard
Disputed Lands
Port Lir
Inder
Leyland
Thoss

Chapter One

Kirian stepped down the dusty wooden steps of the caravan and looked around. The road to Seagard Village dropped off precipitously from the wagon road on the ridge. A medley of rocky outcroppings and scrubby bushes, leading to a distant slate-colored sea foaming against wet rocks, spilled out below.

The caravan master shouted to someone inside the baggage wagon to hurry with the Healer's bags.

"Kirian, let me come with you!"

She turned and smiled at the young man who stood there staring at her. Everything Inmay did was intense; it made her only more anxious to leave him behind.

"You know you can't come with me. I want to focus on learning from the old Healer, and I won't have any time for you. Besides, Inmay, you have your own posting." She let the smile vanish as she spoke; there was no point in encouraging him.

"I didn't choose my posting any more than you did yours."

Inmay brushed his hair back with nervous fingers. A gleam of premature gray showed in the pale yellow strands.

"You agreed to go."

"I had no choice! They would have exiled me."

Kirian sighed. The man refused to understand how dangerous he was perceived to be in the homes of the powerful. "You're lucky, Inmay. The last person who helped a slave escape was publicly beheaded. If you hadn't been who you are—now, here come my bags! I have to go."

The caravan master placed her bag in the dirt next to her. He bowed. Dust clung to his hair and to his sweaty face.

"Good journey, good luck," he said with spurious goodwill. "Thank you. Good journey to you as well," Kirian said. She had no money for a tip, but good wishes were free.

The caravan master shook his head at her and waved to his lead driver. "Let's move!" he said, swinging onto the wagon. The driver snapped the reins against the sweated flanks of the horses. Inmay, in the third wagon back, called good luck to her. His head vanished inside the limp hangings that protected the passengers from the dust of the road. Kirian had no such protection; the horses' hooves kicked up the dirt of the ridge road into a gritty cloud as the caravan groaned into motion.

The dirt track of the Seagard road dribbled down to the distant village, which Kirian could barely make out. She sighed, hoisted her Healer's bag over one shoulder and secured her heavier bag in her right hand, and set out. The way was rough, with rocks sticking out of the track here and there, but the breeze was cool and carried the taste of the nearby sea. The mountains were shadowed by an early dusk and struck a warning chill. Sea birds called and complained along the cliff edges. As dusk came, the sky was a cobalt blue, like a gem, a color Kirian had never before seen. If she were not so weary, she would have enjoyed the walk.

But she had come from Sugetre that day, coughing up the dust on the wagon road, and she was not used to the mountain terrain. Her bags grew heavier, and she discovered that her shoes were all wrong. She fell once, scraping her knees and doing further damage to her already irritable temper. When she finally reached the foot of the track and walked into Seagard, she was not at all in the correct frame of mind for a Healer newly come to her town.

A woman, bent with age or with the weight of the wooden bucket she carried, stood near a gray shed with a half-open door. Kirian knew what was in the bucket—she had been smelling fish for the last five minutes.

"Hello!" Kirian said. "I bring greetings from Sugetre, from the Healer's College."

"Welcome, child!" the old woman said. "Come in, come in! I know who you be, the healer Ruthan's been waiting for this last week."

Kirian was disarmed by the old woman's friendliness. In Sugetre one was never welcomed with such pleasure—in fact, in Sugetre people were often glad to see the back of you, unless they were in immediate need of your skills as a Healer. This old one looked to be in reasonably good health, and Kirian was a perfect stranger to her, but she set down the stinking bucket and escorted Kirian inside.

Kirian looked around the cramped space. There was a wooden bench and an overstuffed chair that had seen better days. A long table filled the center of the room. The remains of a meal for three littered the table—dirty plates, frayed cloth napkins, fish bones and a half- empty dish of turnips.

"Sit, sit!" demanded the old woman. "I be Marka, Ruthan's friend. I'll send my daughter Missa for her as soon as can be." She set down the bucket and bustled around the little house, speaking to someone in the back room. A younger woman brought a mug of bitter ale, and Kirian sipped it gratefully. In a few more minutes, Kirian heard a door close in the kitchen. The young woman ushered in a very tiny, bent woman cloaked against the night sea mist.

Kirian stood. "Hon Ruthan, I am Kirian. I am sent to help you and learn from you by Master Raiko at the Healer's College. I am very glad to meet you."

The old woman looked up with eyes as blank as boiled eggs. Kirian stopped, taken aback. There were no pupils to the old woman's eyes, only endless whites. She hesitated with her hand out, feeling stupid for her instinctive reaction. How could a blind Healer work?

"She can see you just fine," Missa said gently.

Ruthan took Kirian's hand with perfect ease. Her blank eyes stared into Kirian's. Kirian looked away.

"My eyes are all colors instead of just one," the old woman said. "I can see perfectly well your lovely face and your bright eyes, young Kirian. That hair will be the talk of Seagard by tomorrow morning. Is that a new style in Sugetre?"

Kirian relaxed a little. "No, Hon Ruthan, it's my own choice." Her hair was cut very short, like that of a boy who studied arms and wanted to keep his locks out of his face. Sometimes, when it was humid, it spiked.

Ruthan grinned. "I like it. Elder Hame won't, and Lord Alkiran won't, so be prepared. But don't change it."

"I won't."

By this time they were all seated again. Ruthan looked small and frail in the place of honor in the overstuffed chair, but Kirian recalled the grip of the old Healer's hand. She was stronger than she looked.

"Forgive me," Kirian said. "But how——?"

"Healer Ruthan was gifted with her Sight by them up at the Castle," old Marka said.

"Now I can truly see, young woman," Ruthan said. "With the Sight I can see if sickness lies still in the blood after I think I have purged it out. I can see if the bones in a broken leg lie together just right, before I bind them up. I can see how the babe lies when a woman is ready to give birth. Ah, they are a blessing, these eyes of all colors. I'll never regret the day I asked Lord Alkiran for them."

The old Healer must have done some significant service to the old lord to receive such a blessing. Far from being blind, Ruthan could see better than anyone Healer Kirian had ever known. Kirian sipped her ale to gain a moment to gather her thoughts; in one short hour she had lost her arrogance. What could Kirian, a twenty-six year old with a few years' book-learning, bring to this village that an experienced woman with Ruthan's gift could not?

Ruthan stood, leaning on Missa's arm. "Ah, I am glad to see you, young woman. I look forward to long talks about what you have learned from old Raiko. You will be a freshening sea breeze around here, I can tell, especially with that assertive hair. Will you come? I have a room set up for you, and a place for you to put your things."

"Gladly," Kirian said sincerely. "I am honored to be here." Nodding to Marka, she hauled the baggage to her shoulder and followed the old Healer as she led the way out of Marka's house and down a stony lane to the Healer's house.

"Missa and Marka are the roots of this village," Ruthan told her. "They're the ones you'll see at all the festivals, setting up games for the little ones, and at all the houses when some-one's ill, bringing fish soup and bread. You'll see them often."

Kirian nodded. Missa and Marka were the mothers of this village. She did hope, however, that she would not have to eat fish soup anytime soon.

Ruthan's house was a wooden structure from which any

traces of paint had been stripped by the salt breeze. Its siding blended with the dusk in a monochromatic gray. Inside, two cramped outer rooms were clearly dedicated to Ruthan's work, containing simple cots, shelves of labeled jars, blankets, earthenware bowls, and a tray of bandages at the ready. She had sacrificed a parlor for her healer's rooms; farther in were her kitchen, crammed with a table still spread with her interrupted dinner, a small pantry, and two bedrooms. Ruthan directed Kirian to one of these with a tired gesture.

"Is there anything I can help with here tonight, Hon Ruthan?" Kirian asked. The old Healer looked weary; so was Kirian, but she was young and strong, and she couldn't bear to start out life in this little village resting in Ruthan's spare room while the old woman scraped plates and did dishes.

But the old lady shook her head and waved Kirian away. Kirian was relieved. The dust from the road still coated her throat, in spite of the ale, and her knee throbbed where she had fallen on it. Most of all she was feeling overcome with the strangeness of everything. She closed the door, took off her cloak and shoes, and lay down fully clothed on the neatly made bed.

She let her eyes drift closed and calmed herself with images of home—images of the students in the dormitories; of her roommate Sindar laughing; of Mistress Urasha in the supply room laying out stacks of brown blankets, vials of remedies, and bags of fragrant herbs for the Healers who traveled; and of the warm stone of the College itself, that drew the day's heat in and then threw it back in the evenings, toasting the students' backs as they sat against the stone walls. She thought of Inmay, on his way to his new posting while wishing he was back in the capital with the slave woman he had tried to free. Thoughts of her noble classmates, with their thinly-veiled scorn for her, intruded only briefly before she swept them away.

After a while, thought faded. Only the soothing roll of waves lapping up to the shore broke the darkness. Kirian listened for a while, and then smiled before she let sleep draw her away.

In the next sennight, Kirian learned the village. She saw the men and a few of the women go out to sea in their boats in the gray mornings, rocking on the water below the strip of beach Seagard owned. They brought home fish of various colors and sizes, most of which Kirian was unfamiliar with, and they brought lobsters once, several of which were sent to the lord and his family up in the castle.

Some of the villagers who did not go out to sea tended sparse gardens, from which they coaxed greens and other produce to fill the stew pot. Some had a goat or a pig, and everyone, including the livestock, ate fish. Marka wove jewel-toned blankets from the wool of sheep that were kept somewhere high up in the mountains. The blankets were sent out on the monthly caravan to be sold at a shop in the city.

Kirian helped Ruthan augment her income by packaging a remedy or two when a particular herb was abundant. She gathered the herbs on long walks up the cliff path into the brush, and along the Two Merkhan road.

"Give me some more gidroot, young Kirian," Ruthan said as they sat outside the door on a sunny day. Kirian collected a handful from the drying rack, feeling the bristly leaves brush against her skin. They stripped the dried stems from the fragrant leaves, and then they put the leaves into a mortar. A few grinds reduced the leaves to powder, which was then put into colorful glass vials.

"These are beautiful, Ruthan," Kirian said, turning an

amethyst- colored vial back and forth in the sunlight. "Where do these come from?"

"These? From the south. They make them to hold perfumes. There was a chest of them on board a ship that wrecked on the rocks in a storm a few years ago."

"Why is it so dangerous?"

"There are rocks that are only exposed in the low tides. There's a warning light on the High Rocks, but they don't always see it."

"So these sell well at Two Merkhan?"

Ruthan chuckled. "Very well! And gidroot is the most popular of all, though I've told them it won't do a thing to make a woman fertile."

"I suppose they're desperate," Kirian said, filling another jar.

"Kin and Rashiri take these to Two Merkhan every month or so, when I have them. They fish and then sell at the market there—about the only ones around here who do."

Ruthan spent a lot of time that first sennight telling Kirian about the people who lived in the village. In a full month, Kirian did not set foot in the castle. After a while, she thought this was odd; the Healer's first duty was to attend the nobility up at the castle, and the presence of the Alkirani was the only reason a little village like Seagard rated a college-trained Healer at all. Kirian had inquired about the Alkirani before she left Sugetre, so she knew the Alkirani were friends of the King, related by marriage. The current Lady Alkiran was sister to the King.

"Oh, they're busy," Ruthan said, when asked about this omission. "They've company this sennight or two. We'll go up and introduce you after the party from the city has gone."

"Do you like them, the Alkirani?" Kirian asked. "What are they like?"

"I like some of them," she replied, "And that's the best any Healer will be doing with any noble *righ* patrons, my dear, so don't be expecting to be invited to dinner with them. We are servants to them. They'll call when they need us, and dismiss us without a thought, seeing we have done our job. Lord Forell won't listen to you at all and will complain of you to his father, Lord Alkiran, when he falls ill from the overindulgence you warned him about. Shala Si, the concubine, will ask for potions that we don't provide, the ones they use in the heathen city she comes from. But Lady Alkiran is pleasant enough, and so is the girl, Litha Sira."

"What about Lord Alkiran?"

"He is a Collared Mage, and requires what's due him. That's all. Best not to talk to him more than you have to. I don't."

"He's dangerous then?"

Ruthan snorted. "They all are, the *righ* lords. He's no exception. He has a temper. Wants what he wants, when he wants it, and has the power to get it."

"What happens when he's displeased?" Kirian asked.

"He'll throw sparks," Ruthan said quite seriously. "There's not a one of them who can keep the color magic under control when he's put out."

"I meant…"

Ruthan shook her head, her white eyes catching the firelight and gleaming ocher. "Never forget that, unlike me, you are a college Healer. You are under the protection of the Lord Healer. What would Lord Alkiran do to such a one?"

"That's the question," she said, dropping her eyes to her work. Kirian didn't know how much protection she could expect from the college. She had been a rescued street-child, admitted to the college as one of their required acts of charity, and trained along with the children of the merchant and noble classes who were the other students. She had no wealthy patron or family to argue her case if she felt she was unfairly treated at school. She had been raised to thank the Unknown God for rescuing her from the slavery that would have been her lot as an unclaimed girl-child in Sugetre. Then the College had sent her here. Inmay was right; she had no choice in her posting.

Kirian knew she was fortunate; however, she thought that Lord Alkiran could probably get away with any kind of treatment of her that he wished, without any risk of reprimand from the College.

Now that she was posted here and the noble family had access to a Healer, the College's duty was done. They had probably forgotten she existed.

The next day Kirian heard a knock on the door. She opened it to a middle-aged man wearing a brown jacket and breeches.

"There you are!" he said. "You must be this new Healer my lord wants to see. Hon Kirian, is it? Lord Alkiran wants you. I'm Tabe, the second groom."

Kirian felt a gust of wind grab at the door she held open. She looked west; the sky was a foreboding shade of gray. A few people were dragging boats up onto the rocks, away from the foaming surf.

"There's going to be a storm," she told the groom. "It looks like it could be pretty bad. Is it safe to go up the cliff in the storm?"

"Whether it is or not, we're going all the same," he said. "Hon Ruthan, you in there? My lord wants you too."

"Lord Alkiran's timing is just as good as it always is," Ruthan grumbled. "Hurry, young Tabe, and maybe we can get up the cliff before it hits. Kirian, your cloak, girl!"

Kirian grabbed the cloaks and her bag and pulled the door

tight as they left. An old coach and four nervous horses waited around the corner. A village boy dropped the reins into Tabe's hands as the groom climbed into the coachman's seat. Kirian helped Ruthan into the coach and climbed in herself.

The coach started off immediately. "Come on, old horse, come on," Tabe's voice urged from the coachman's seat. Kirian looked out at the village moving past her window, and a few minutes later felt the lurch as the horses pulled the coach onto the cliff path.

The wind picked up force. Kirian felt it shoving at the coach as they ascended the path. Looking out the window and down, she could see the gray sea swirling around rocks below. The coach jolted, and her hand grabbed for the strap.

Ruthan cackled. "Great fun, isn't it, my girl? I'll wager my lord didn't look out the window before he summoned us."

Kirian wondered why they hadn't invited Tabe into the house, sent the horses to shelter in Marka's shed, and waited out the storm before going up the cliff. Instead, she asked: "Is it safe to take the cliff path with four horses like this?"

"Two horses can't pull the coach up," Ruthan said. "Though I'll agree it seems narrow for four. Tabe knows what he's doing, Kirian."

Kirian risked another look out the window. The path came perilously close to the edge of the cliff, she thought. Below, the sea crashed against the rocks. In the distant slate-gray sky, thunder rolled. The coach bumped up the path; Kirian wondered if it was always this rough, or if Tabe was rushing his horses to beat the storm. She held on to the strap to keep herself from sliding across the seat into Ruthan.

The coach pulled to a stop before a stone arch. The door was yanked open. Kirian saw a boy dressed in groom's brown. "Hurry," he said, and helped Ruthan down the coach steps. Kirian grabbed her bag and followed Ruthan under the arch just as the curtain of rain reached them. The wind pushed it under the arch and soaked the edge of Kirian's cloak in just a few seconds.

"That's a wild one," the servant boy said, grinning up at the healers. "Here, I'll take you to someone who will show you where to go. I gotta help Tabe with the horses."

Kirian waved thanks to Tabe, who held the horses' heads. As they entered the castle, thunder crashed above them, and Kirian heard the frightened neigh of one of the coach horses.

A liveried servant led them up two flights of stone stairs to a comfortable room. Kirian took off her wet cloak and took Ruthan's as well, holding them since no one offered to hang them for her.

"This is Lord Alkiran's study," Ruthan said, while settling into a chair near the fire. The chair next to hers was a tall, engraved affair that was clearly meant for Lord Alkiran. Kirian remained standing and looked around at the room, which was warmed by a large fire and lit against the darkness of the storm by several oil lamps. There was a large mirror, a tool of the color mage's art, in a corner of the room; a corner of it gleamed from under the red hanging that draped it. A large window dominated the sea-side of the room; it was made of the faintly green, thick glass that was used in fancy goblets. It was an unimaginable luxury in such an expanse of window.

Lord Alkiran strode into the room a moment later and sat in the ornate chair by the fire. He surveyed Kirian with dark, hawk-like eyes in a face that had aged into lines of severity. His black and silver hair fell to the top of his shoulders, almost hiding the golden gleam of the Collar around his neck.

Remembering Ruthan's instructions, Kirian bowed. Ruthan, remaining seated with the allowance due her old age, bowed from the neck.

"So," Lord Alkiran said. "This is the new Healer."

"Yes, Lord Alkiran. My name is Kirian. I graduated from the Healer's College a year ago. Master Raiko sent me to complete my journeyman's time with Hon Ruthan and to be the Healer to Seagard Castle."

"Of what quality is this Healer?" Alkiran asked, turning toward Ruthan. "I have had word from Raiko that she is one of their best, despite her lowly origins."

"Lord Alkiran, I have no complaint of her. She should meet your needs well. She has knowledge of the body, illnesses and injuries, as well as the needful herbs and medicines. She relates well to all those she has met, which is a valuable thing in a Healer." Ruthan coughed a little, behind her hand.

"Relate to whom? Villagers and fishermen?" Alkiran's brows drew together as he transferred his gaze to Kirian. "You are engaged to treat our ills, not relate to us, Healer."

"Yes, my lord."

Alkiran stared at her. "I was told you have no family so that there is nothing to keep you from serving us as Healer permanently."

Kirian felt a spark of anger that he should be pleased about her charity origins. "Yes, Lord Alkiran. I'm free to make this posting my first priority, as all Healers do, regardless of their families."

His eyes narrowed. "You may remain in the village while you are completing your training with Ruthan. Then you must move up to the Castle. It is important that you are close in case there is need."

"My lord," Kirian said, still standing with the wet cloaks soaking through her sleeve. "As you just saw, I can be here from the village in twenty minutes, even in a thunderstorm." Ruthan coughed again.

"Nevertheless." Alkiran turned to look at Ruthan for a moment. The fire glinted off the gold of his Collar. Kirian thought it appeared uncomfortably tight. The skin of his neck stretched into wrinkles above and below its smooth expanse.

Kirian bit back her first urge for a swift retort. The man was a despot, but she would endeavor to begin their association on a favorable note. "I assume that I may also serve as Healer to Seagard Village while residing at the castle?"

"Second to your duties here, yes. It is to our benefit that you stay skillful in your craft, and also that the villagers stay healthy enough to provide fish for our needs."

"My lord." She bowed.

"You will find, Hon Kirian, that you will be treated with a respect commensurate with your position, if you show you understand where your duty lies. You may ask your mentor for a clarification later. Ruthan will acquaint you with the residents of the Castle, both *righ* and otherwise, and our medical needs. I must speak with her now, however. In the meantime, you may begin by seeing Lord Forell's concubine. I am informed she has need of a Healer."

She bowed again to Lord Alkiran, said something polite, and left the study. In the hall a manservant awaited. She followed him down wood-paneled corridors that merged into older stone halls with foot- hollowed troughs in the center. The servant announced her at a plain wooden door.

The door opened, and nothing else was plain. Gold and red hangings draped the window, which was shuttered against the storm. A trailing plant hung from a hook in the ceiling, its long branches adorned with bright green leaves of an almost circular shape. A bed took up most of the middle of the room, but there was a side table covered with many small glass jars and pots, some with jeweled brushes stuck into them. The concubine's cosmetics and perfumes, no doubt. Kirian turned to ask the manservant where the woman was, but he had vanished.

"Hon Healer, I am here." A low voice spoke from the curtained alcove. "I am Shala Si, the Lord Forell's concubine."

Kirian saw a young woman of middle height, with dark hair and eyes and the golden skin of the southern provinces. Instead of the revealing costume that Kirian had expected, Shala Si was completely covered in several colorful robes of a very thin, shimmering fabric. The effect was exotic and brightened the room even further.

The woman raised her hand in a gesture of welcome, and Kirian saw the thin golden chain that circled Shala Si's wrist, connected by fragile links to the concubine's necklace. Kirian realized this woman was a slave, and the decorative chain, fashioned to be similar to chains worn by slave laborers, was an unsubtle reminder of the fact. Kirian wondered who had given her the chain; it was someone with a nasty sense of humor, no doubt—her noble master, perhaps.

"I am pleased to meet you, Shala Si," Kirian said. "I am Kirian from the Healer's College, Hon Ruthan's new assistant. How can I help you?"

Shala Si leaned very close to Kirian, so close that her flowery fragrance enveloped Kirian. "I am glad you have come, and not that old bitch. She would not do as I asked. She gave me an herb to prevent me from conceiving a child. I stopped taking it months ago, but still there is no sign of a child!"

Kirian said, "Shala Si, you must know I cannot give you any herbs for fertility without the consent of Lord Forell."

"Because I am a slave! Yes, that is so. But you can tell me what to do, can you not, to make it happen? My lord is with me almost every night; indeed, he thinks highly of me. Still I bleed every month and there is no child!"

Kirian sighed. The young slave seemed desperate. If this were any other person seeking her aid, she would tell them the best time to conceive. She might even make up for them some of the powdered herbs that would – no, not ensure pregnancy, but make the womb softer, safer, more ready to nurture any child that might be ordained by the Unknown God. But not this woman. In fact, by the Healer's code she ought to inform Lord Forell immediately of his concubine's attempt to get fertility herbs.

"I cannot do it," she said. "Not without your master's consent, Shala Si. Indeed I sympathize, but I am new here, and to do this without Lord Forell's consent—well, I would lose my posting at the least."

Shala Si picked up one of her cosmetic pots with her delicate chained hands and flung it at Kirian. It struck Kirian on the shoulder. The lid flew off, leaving a smear of some honey-colored cream on Kirian's tunic.

Kirian said, "I am sorry, Shala Si. Is there anything else?"

"No, there is nothing else!" Shala Si hissed. "I will tell my lord that I am ill and you refused to help me. He will tell Lord Alkiran to send you back where you came from. Now get out of my room!"

The concubine reached for another bottle, this one of glass.

Kirian bowed, grabbed her bag, and left the room, feeling wretched.

A servant led Kirian to the stone arch where Ruthan awaited her. The old woman looked at Kirian's downcast expression and the smear of cream on her tunic.

"You needn't fear," Ruthan said. "She won't do what she says."

"How do you know?"

The coach drew up to the arch. Tabe sat on the box again, the horses much calmer now. The storm had subsided to a steady rain that would have been relaxing if Kirian had been in her own room back in the College. Now, its chill seemed to soak through her skin into her heart.

"She's threatened me before," Ruthan said. "The silly chit. She thinks she can scare us into doing as she asks. When she calms down, she'll remember that Forell may not ask questions, but Lord Alkiran will."

"What questions?"

"Like why she called for us in the first place. Mikati is a color mage, Kirian—cruel, but sharp as a tack. If he found that his son's slave mistress—who has no mage talent either—was plotting to have an illegitimate child . . ." Ruthan snorted. "Well, I wouldn't give a fishtail for her chances of living until the next caravan came by."

"I know the Collared Lords are supposed to keep the blood pure, to breed the mage talent true. But he would kill her?"

Ruthan coughed again, and Kirian wished she had a blanket for the old woman. "Mikati is a *Collared Lord*, Kirian. The only ruler in Seagard Province. Even the King won't thwart him."

Kirian looked down at the sea. It had calmed considerably. The sky was dark with rain and with the nearing of night. She hoped Tabe could see his way down the rain-slick path.

She had heard about the supreme powers of the Collared Lords, but somehow she had never thought through what that might mean. The Collared Lords were bound by the King's magic to Watch endlessly for incursions from Righar's enemies—in this case, on the western coast, from the island nation of Ha'las and its psychic mages. From the time they were Collared, they could not leave the Watch, but in return they and their families had wealth, influence and real power greater than anyone but the King's. The *righ* families were raised to consider the Collar a great honor, for which they alone were suited; they had their male children

Collared too, as soon as they were old enough, to serve the King.

"I hadn't thought," Kirian confessed. "What if Shala Si just happens to conceive? Will they blame me?"

Ruthan coughed. "It cannot happen. She stopped taking the preparation I made for her, but I ordered the cook to add it to her tea. She has tea every morning."

Kirian felt a vague guilt. Surely the woman should be allowed to have a child if she wanted. Only her slave status and Lord Alkiran prevented her. But Kirian didn't feel courageous enough to defy her new *righ* Lord. At least, not as a student that arrived less than a month ago at Seagard village.

"Until I found myself here and under his power, I didn't understand anything about Collared Lords." Ruthan hesitated. "I must warn you, young one . . . ." She broke into a fit of coughing so hard that she bent over, unable to speak.

"Later," Kirian said. "Are we almost there? Here, I have a sugar drop in my bag; perhaps that will help."

She felt the coach level off, leaving the path at last. It was dark now, but lamplight shone in the windows of the houses they passed. The smell of fish rose up from someone's shed as they passed, strong, homey and welcome. Kirian determined to get the old woman a cup of hot tea and then into bed as soon as they arrived. The rest would wait until later.

After she helped Ruthan into bed, she thought again about Mikati. He reminded her most unpleasantly of some of the noble students who had been her bane at College—those who looked down on her because of her common origins. Dramin in particular, the third son of an impoverished lord, had been brutal to the charity students when he was drunk. She did not suspect Lord Mikati Alkiran of getting drunk and beating his servants; the man was too secure in his power for that. But he would not hesitate to punish when he did not get his way.

The rain that followed the first violence of the storm had eased off. She could no longer hear the steady drizzle on the roof of Ruthan's house. She was comfortable in her shapeless old robe, curled up in her bed, with the sounds of the rain and the sea in the back of her consciousness. She decided she could find a way to work with Lord Mikati. She liked it too well here to fail so soon.

Chapter Two

Callo ran Alkiran entered the palace through a side door and ran down the servants' stairs, adjusting his gold-trimmed dress tunic as he went. The residential part of the palace was nearly empty; only an occasional lamp cast a glow around the halls, and there was no sign of life at all. Everyone was downstairs at the ball.

As he emerged from the back of the main hall and approached the reception rooms, a murmur that had been registering on his subconscious for some minutes expanded into a roar. Callo grimaced. Most of Sugetre must be here, talking at full volume. He could not even hear the musicians above the racket. The two liveried servants who flanked the reception room looked at him and made no attempt to announce his entrance.

The room was almost unrecognizable in its finery. Rose-colored hangings draped the walls; the Queen's conceit no doubt. The hangings sometimes shifted in a draft, adding a surreal air to the festivities. The ancient chandelier, a treasure of the royal Monteni house, blazed with candles, dripping wax on the shoulders of the dancers below. The room was jammed with the most prominent nobles and soldiers in Sugetre. Lords and ladies in their evening finery glittered in the light of the amazing chandelier and numerous other candles and lamps, clustered carefully away from the silken wall hangings. Guardsmen dotted the room, immediately visible in their dress surcoats and medals. Sweating slaves squirmed between the guests, trying to offer food and drink without bumping into anyone.

Callo searched the room, but could see no sign of the King or Queen. Perhaps they had not yet entered the room.

"Callo! Here at last, are you?"

Callo turned to see Lord Arias Alkiran, his half-brother and oldest friend, grinning at him. Lord Arias Alkiran was the heir to Lord Mikati Alkiran, who held Seagard castle, but instead of the gold- trimmed tunic of a nobleman, Arias wore the black cloak of a color mage. Swirls of color rose and then dissipated in the cloak, as if sinking into liquid. It was disconcerting; Callo had never liked it.

"I forgot the time," Callo said.

Arias snorted. "You just didn't want to come. Well, now that you're here, I want you to meet someone. Come!"

Arias took Callo's arm and pulled him through the crowd. His half-brother apologized to those they brushed past, but did not alter his path to wind around and between the shifting groups as Callo would have done. Behind him, the mage's cloak appeared woven with sinuous bands of color. People made way, sometimes bowing, sometimes grinning. Callo gave a crooked grin; Arias had that effect on people.

Callo nodded his own apology as he was pulled through the throng. His bows met with indifference, and an occasional look of scorn. He could feel his brows tighten into a frown at that reaction, though he should have been well accustomed to it after all these years as King Martan's bastard—but neverthe-less royal—nephew.

At last Arias stopped. Callo saw his brother bow before a vision of beauty in a gown that seemed but lightly dusted onto a voluptuous body. Lady Fiora had been the talk of the young men in the guard for a sennight now. She was the new widow of an ancient lord to whom she had been betrothed by her parents. She had shown no sign, in her short time in the capital city, of mourning his loss.

Lady Fiora paid Callo no attention, but she smiled at Lord Arias. "My lord!" she said. "I didn't think to see you again so soon."

"My lady, I want you to meet my half brother, Lord Callo ran Alkiran" Arias said, drawing Callo forward. "Callo, this is Lady Fiora Eshal."

"I'm delighted," Callo said. Arias, looking much younger than his thirty-two years, grinned at him.

Lady Fiora's smile vanished. She stared at Callo with huge blue eyes and withdrew her hand, which had been extended to greet him. "Lord Arias," she protested, transferring her gaze to his face.

"What?" Arias turned and saw her expression. The grin dropped away. Arias suddenly bore a strong resemblance to his grim old father. Callo felt his own temper rise; he stifled it.

"Let it go," Callo said to his brother.

Arias ignored him. "My lady, this is my half brother. If you cannot welcome him, then my presence must not be welcome either."

Lady Fiora blushed. "But, my lord, I have been told…"

"Told what? By what idiot?" Arias' voice rose. His dark Alkirani eyes glittered in a way that Callo knew well, and wasn't prepared to deal with here in the middle of the King's ball. Around them, the curious were turning to look in their direction.

"Arias, let it go," Callo said again, frustrated.

Lady Fiora stared at Arias for a moment. Callo could almost see the calculations whirling in her head; this one was not as shallow as she pretended to be. Then Lady Fiora smiled at Callo. He knew the smile was false, but it was so sweet that he felt himself smile back.

This one, he thought, is dangerous.

"Lord Callo," Lady Fiora said. "I beg your pardon. Whoever Lord Arias introduces must be a welcome acquaintance." She held out her hand.

Arias relaxed as Callo took the lady's scented fingers and bowed over them. Callo uttered a few meaningless social phrases, an odd premonition of misfortune stirring within him. The crowd returned to its own gossip. In a few seconds a gray-haired woman in a jeweled gown came to draw Lady Fiora away. The intervention was so prompt that Callo wondered if it was really a rescue.

"Isn't she beautiful?" Arias asked, pleased with life again. He took two glasses of wine from a passing slave's tray and gave one to Callo.

"They're all beautiful," Callo returned. He sipped the wine. It tasted like berries on his tongue, clearly the finest Southern wine available.

"They are," Arias returned, smiling after Lady Fiora. On the other side of the room, a group of very young men surrounded her, laughing and vying to entertain the lady.

"You're ten years too old for her, Brother. She's just a flighty child, let off the hook by Eshal's death. She wants a young guardsman, or maybe a musician. What would you do with her, haul her off to Seagard Castle and keep her locked away?"

"I think I could convince her to stay without any need for lock and key."

"Ha!" said Callo. "One thing on your mind as usual."

Arias laughed. The colors in his cloak swirled like a gentle sunset, colors of pleasure. He slapped Callo on the back and hailed a guardsman he knew. Callo dropped away from his side and went to find something to eat.

The musicians began to play the Royal March. Callo stepped out of the way as the crowd swirled left or right to make a path into the room. King Martan Alghasi Monteni entered, his keen gray eyes scanning the crowd, passing over Callo without stopping. Nevertheless, Callo knew the King had marked his presence among the other bowing nobles; he was not known as Sharpeyes without good reason. Queen Efalla entered behind the King, her arm draped over that of the Mage Lord; she was resplendent in her silk gown and glittering jewels.

Behind them came the representatives of the Collared Lords, seven leaders of the *righ* class trusted by their lords to plan and confer in their names. Since the Collared Lords never left their holds, these men spoke for them here in the Capital. The crowd bowed to them, almost as deeply as they had for the King and Queen. Callo wondered what matters they had discussed, up in the King's rooms while the rest of the crowd danced. He looked for and found Sopharin, Lord Alkiran's representative, a whip-thin man wearing a valus-fur trimmed tunic and brocade leggings, as well as boots that appeared to be set with jewels. Sopharin loved finery, and his rewards from Lord Alkiran allowed him to indulge his passion. Callo found him sycophantic; he knew Arias did not care for the man either.

The music resumed. A young girl, her hair dressed with flowers in the traditional way, smiled at him. He smiled back.

Her chaperone leaned over to whisper in her ear. The girl turned away.

Callo made his way to the silk-clad wall to sip his wine. In only a few moments, a distinctive, scratchy voice interrupted his thoughts.

"Lord Callo, are you trying to avoid me?"

Callo turned to see a heavyset lady, tightly gowned in puce and red velvet that clashed with the wall hangings. The lady held out her hand and Callo grinned, grasping it.

"I am always happy to see you, Lady Phoire." It was true; Phoire was one of the few in the nobility who not only accepted his presence among them but actually seemed to enjoy it, regardless of his uncertain status as the King's bastard nephew. He looked around for a chair for Lady Phoire, who tended to run out of breath due to her girth and tight clothing. The weight of her jewelry probably did not help either.

"No, no," Phoire said. "I've just come to drop a word in your ear. A word regarding your handsome half-brother, in fact. I've always had a soft spot for him, in spite of his likeness to his father."

"Arias? He's here somewhere . . ." Callo looked around.

"It's where he is that should be *your* concern."

Callo finally spotted Arias, dancing with Lady Fiora. They made a striking couple. Arias smiled down at Fiora, who chattered at him as the dance carried them around the room.

"With Lady Fiora? Arias knows what she is, I think."

"Of course he does. No fool he, when it comes to women. But, maybe, when it comes to men, he does not see so clearly, friend Callo. Look at His Majesty Sharpeyes." She turned away for a moment. "Yes, I will take that seat after all, if the ridiculous thing will hold me." Phoire motioned to a passing slave who brought a cushioned bench over and set it near the wall, out of the way of the crowd. She let her considerable weight down onto the bench, sighing with relief.

"Sharpeyes, you say? Surely . . ." Callo stopped short, his eyes on his uncle. The King sat on the dais, paying no attention to any of the courtiers and ladies that awaited his attention. His shrewd gray eyes were riveted to Arias and Fiora as they passed in the dance. Callo frowned, noting this for a moment. The King did not take his eyes from the lady as the dance ended, and Arias relinquished Lady Fiora into the care of her companion.

"The lady is beautiful," Callo said, turning back to Phoire with a raised eyebrow. "She draws many eyes."

"That she does, and her chaperone is thanking the gods for it. I understand Eshal's estate did not amount to much and so the girl must remarry soon," Phoire said. "But I have never seen the King so fascinated by a woman."

Callo shrugged. "He does not stray from the Queen. I have never known him to."

"He wants that young woman. I have never marked it better. You tell me, Lord Callo, from your experience, which I know is unique— what does his Majesty do when he sees something he wants?"

"Hm." Callo turned back to the King. Martan was still fixated on Fiora, who seemed to light up her vicinity with her enjoyment of the ball. The sheen of perspiration on the young woman's face only added to her attraction; she was very alive. Across the room, the Queen moved in the stately patterns of the dance with the graying Sea Commander, barely smiling. She moved with such dignity that the dance did not disturb the smallest lock of her hair.

"I will tell Arias," Callo said. "I think you are right."

He found Arias much later in the evening just as his half-brother was taking his leave of two of his drinking companions. Callo touched Arias' arm to gain his attention.

"A word with you, Arias," he said.

"Tomorrow," Arias said. His dark eyes were slightly blurry with drink. He turned to leave.

"Arias, wait. Look at Sharpeyes."

Arias' eyes went to the King and stayed there. He frowned.

"The King is greatly interested in your lady. Lady Phoire marked it, and bade me give you a word of warning."

"I will thank her for her concern," Arias said lightly. "As I thank you for yours, no matter how misguided you are."

"Just take care, Arias. You know as well as I do that Sharpeyes is not to be trifled with."

"Yes, I do. Now let me go, Callo; I am tired and not in any immediate danger, after all!"

Callo smiled and released Arias' sleeve, watching his half-brother make his way to the stairs and vanish upstairs. He cast a last look at Sharpeyes and headed for his own quarters, which were in the commanders' housing near the guard barracks.

The next days were busy, and Callo gave no thought to Arias and his infatuation with Lady Fiora. On the morning of the third day after the ball, there was a knock on the door. Callo had just finished tying his fair hair back in his usual warrior's tail. His manservant Chiss was straightening the room. Chiss answered the knock and bowed as a gray-bearded man entered. The man's mage cloak swirled silver in its depths.

"Mage Oron!" greeted Callo in considerable surprise. The lord of the mages was a stern man who, in spite of his severity, had a soft spot for the mercurial Lord Arias. Callo had always thought Oron disapproved of himself, like most of society here in the capital.

"Lord Callo," returned Oron with a nod. He waved away the chair that Chiss drew out for him. The mage's eyes, as gray as his beard, traveled around the small room. It was a room consistent with Callo's status as a commander in the Guard, providing privacy and some comfort, but no luxury. Callo's unanswered correspondence was scattered over the small table, along with the remains of a simple breakfast and an earthenware mug. His sword was in its leather scabbard, slung over a wooden hook near the bed.

"I am surprised to find your quarters in this section of the complex. I was under the impression your rooms were near those of your half-brother."

Callo felt his mouth twist a little. Oron had expected to find him in the main palace, in rooms considerably more luxurious than this one. His influence with the King would not have reached so far. "I have no need for more than one room," he said.

"Indeed." The lord of mages nodded, Callo thought in approval. "I have come on a matter of concern to us both, Lord Callo." He turned to Chiss. "You, my man —"

"Chiss, my lord."

"Chiss, then. Please leave us."

"Wine, my lord?" Callo asked.

Oron shook his head. "I have no time. I come about something that is none of my business, you will no doubt say, and you would be correct—your half brother, and this Lady Fiora who is leading him around by her skirts." Oron paused, as if waiting for a response, then continued. "The King has taken an interest in the woman, and quite plainly, I must say I fear for Arias' safety. I have dropped a word in Arias' ear… "

"Unsuccessfully, I take it."

"Perhaps you would not believe it, but he laughed at me." Oron's mouth twitched.

Callo grinned. "That's just like him, my lord. What do you want me to do? I must tell you I've already warned him of this, with no more success than you."

"Use whatever influence you have," said Mage Oron. "Use up any credit you have with him. He's infatuated, I know, but it isn't worth the loss of his life."

"Surely the King would not…"

"Who knows what Sharpeyes might do?"

"I have very little influence over Arias," Callo said.

"I am sure you underrate yourself," Oron replied. "Do what you can. He is in more danger than he knows."

After Oron took his leave, Callo stood staring out his small window, seeing nothing. Oron's concern about this matter troubled him. If the Mage Lord had interrupted his schedule to call upon a minor noble of uncertain status, of whom he did not really approve— he must consider the matter serious.

Callo's duties that day took him to the guardhouse, where he heard several of the younger guardsmen laughing over Lord Arias' attraction for the young widow. He grew more and more worried. He did not see Arias all day, either in the practice circle or the guardhouse, so before dinner he walked by Arias' suite of rooms and knocked on the door. The lone servant who answered the knock informed him that Arias was at a private party, and was not expected back until very late.

The next morning, Callo was dragged out of a deep sleep by Chiss' hand shaking his shoulder. There was only a sliver of pale light visible under the shutters. The fire had burned down to ashes and had not yet been built up for the morning.

"What's wrong?" Callo mumbled.

"I have urgent news for you, my lord," Chiss said. "Here, get up. I brought you tea."

Callo put his feet out of the bed. His mind felt groggy. He reached for the tea and sipped it.

"My lord," Chiss said. "I beg your pardon for awakening you at such an hour. There is news I thought you should know immediately."

"It must be Arias," Callo said, putting down the teacup. "What now?"

"Servants' chatter, my lord. The talk is that Lord Arias took the young lady away from the King at a gathering last night."

"He did *what*?"

"The young lady was speaking with His Majesty, my lord. Apparently Lord Arias simply smiled at her, and she left His Majesty's side and went with Lord Arias. The King was much enraged, they say."

"The cursed idiot!" Callo said, reaching for his clothes. "Chiss, you have my gratitude and Arias' also as soon as he gets his hide out of the capital. Where is he, do you know? What time is it?"

"Still not dawn, my lord. Here is your tunic. Will you wear the riding leathers?"

"My sword, too. Gods know I may need it before I get that fool out of the city. Thanks to you, Chiss!"

In a very few minutes Callo stood before Arias' door. A sleepy- eyed guardsman answered Callo's knock.

"Lord Callo? Sir, my lord is sleeping. You must come back later."

"I'll see him now," Callo grunted, and shouldered the guard aside. "If he has a woman with him, tell her to get out." Familiar with Callo's close relationship with their lord, the guard did nothing other than to utter a useless protest and follow him through the outer room and into Arias' chamber.

Arias' chamber was lit only by the embers of a fire, which cast red reflections on the few items of metal or glass in the chamber. The bed and its occupant were only a darker shadow on one side of the room.

"Arias! Get up!"

"What the hell?" Arias voice was thick with sleep.

"My lord, I am sorry for the disturbance. It is Lord Callo," the guard said to Arias.

"Stir that fire up," Callo ordered the guard, "And then get yourself out of here."

The guard obeyed. The fire leapt up enough to illuminate Arias' face. Callo shoved a chair out of the way and stalked over to his half- brother, who was alone in the big bed.

Arias sat up, rubbed his hands over his face and yawned. "All right, I know why you are here. Get it out of your system and let me go back to sleep."

"Sleep, hell. You'll get your hide out of the city and to Seagard before the King is out of bed if you have any sense. What do you think you are doing, Arias?"

Arias lay back and crossed his arms behind his head, studying Callo with an unreadable expression. "I did nothing."

"That's not what I heard. You are the talk of the servants' hall, and you'll be the talk of the whole palace before luncheon."

"Chiss!" Arias sighed. "I must remember to thank him for this."

"You should," Callo said, calming down a little. "You jest, Arias, but you should. The King was enraged, Chiss said."

"He was not pleased. I swear I did nothing, Callo. She took it into her head to bear me company for a while—that is all. She is young, and naive. But, yes, the King was angry. Sit down, will you? You are making me nervous."

"I should be making you fear for your life. Arias, you idiot, whether you deserve it or not the King will be sending guards for you by noon. Go to Seagard!"

"There is no need," Arias said. "Here, there is wine on the table. Have some. You seem to need it more than I do."

Callo scowled at his half-brother, then sat down at one of the heavily-carved chairs and poured wine into a cup. He sipped it, still frowning at Arias. "What do you propose to do then?"

"I don't know yet. His Majesty is not likely to imprison me for a meaningless flirtation. The man is too shrewd to alienate my father for such a reason. Yes, he is angry, but he will not endanger his own peace because of a silly girl. You are as anxious as an old woman, Callo, barging in here to tell me run for my life!"

"I know well what the King is capable of, having lived my life subject to his will. If he does not arrest you, he will find some other way." Callo felt his temper rise and quelled it again, ruthlessly, as he had been forced to do all his life. "I'll go then. Your fate is on your own head."

"It would be anyway," Arias murmured. "Tomorrow," he said, lying back and closing his eyes.

Callo spent the day in an unsettled state of mind. He felt it affecting his performance during his shift, making him irritable with his men and with Chiss. That evening he went to the practice ring alone and spent a hard candlemark practicing his forms. When he was finished and stood, sweating and bone-weary in the center circle, with his sword lifted to the dusky sky, he felt centered again. He thanked Jashan for it; when properly worshiped in the ancient forms, the god always restored his self-control and kept his temper from causing trouble.

The day passed with worry hanging over him like a constant ache. No word came from Arias, which he accounted good news. No gossip came through Chiss, as if the subject had been shut down by a higher authority; that was probably not good news, not at all. Callo noticed that Chiss, too, seemed on edge. Chiss had been with him in the capacity of manservant, guide and partner, since he was nine, and Callo could not help but be attuned to the man's moods. Chiss was also experienced in dealing with the king, since he had been responsible for Callo's conduct during his early training. If Chiss was worried, there was good reason for Callo to be as well. Callo stood his watches and dealt with the minor matters of his command and determined that he had warned Arias, and now it was the fool's own responsibility to take some action; but he could not concentrate. Even his second in command Drale commented on his distraction.

He returned to his room after his watch to find Chiss packing his belongings. For a moment he stared in surprise at the stack of clothing.

"What is this?" he asked.

"I have been told to pack your belongings for a journey to Seagard Castle," Chiss said. Chiss' long fingers folded a gilt sash; there was a glint of gold thread in the pile of tunics prepared for the journey.

"Who…"

Chiss said, "His Majesty, of course, my lord. I think you'll find some correspondence on the table."

Callo found the letter on the table and broke the seal. In the ornate script of His Majesty's scribe, it commanded him to prepare himself and a small unit of the guard he commanded to journey to Seagard Castle with His Majesty King Martan Alghasi Monteni. There was no indication of the reason for the journey.

"I'll send to the men," Callo said. He sat down to scribble orders to his second. Hon Drale was an eager young man newly returned from the Leyish border who had been assigned to Callo's troop. He signed and sealed it, then went to a drawer and pulled out his *righ* ring on its gold chain. "Chiss, please pack this as well." On this trip, it might be necessary for even the King's bastard nephew to show off his rank.

Callo added it to the pile, just as there was a drumming on his door.

"Come in," he called.

The door swung open to admit Arias. He was smiling. Once again he wore his mage's cloak, just now vibrant with peach and red amid the blackness that eclipsed even Arias' dark Alkirani hair. No sword hung at his side; though Arias was competent with the weapon, color mages had their own means of self-defense.

"Callo!" Arias said. "Why so grim? It's only a visit to the family."

"In the company of His Majesty Sharpeyes," Callo said. "You go as well?"

"Indeed. I was summoned this morning."

"Well?"

"You're thinking of that thing with the Lady Fiora. I was a little concerned about it myself. His Majesty asked about the lady's health, and I told him I had no idea about the state of her health, since I hadn't seen her since the party."

Callo looked up, searching Arias' eyes.

"You're perfectly right," Arias said. "I have decided I am better off far away from Lady Fiora."

"Poor Fiora!" said Callo lightly. But the tension began to leave his shoulders.

"Well, I don't know about that," Arias said. "She will be triumphant to have attached His Majesty himself."

"That won't last."

"True—but in the meantime Fiora will be second only to the Queen, and I will escape from this mess with my neck unbroken." Arias paced around the room, stopping for a moment by Callo's window to look out at the fortifications that were his only view.

"It seems so. You were not as unconscious of the danger as you appeared, then."

"How could I be? Every friend has been warning me for a sennight." Arias laughed, and a spark of green showed in his eyes as he released his tension in the form of some minor color magic.

"I've been remembering poor Husholt." Callo knew Arias would remember Husholt, who had been hanged for daring to cross King Martan in some matter of property.

"I thought of him myself." Arias sighed. "I will see you on the road, I suppose. You will be with your unit?"

Callo nodded.

"I ride with the king and Sopharin." Arias grimaced. "I will need patience to put up with that fop all the way to Seagard."

———

It was a tiresome journey to Seagard with Arias and King Martan's ponderous retinue. Martan kept to himself and his family during the journey, occasionally hosting the nobles and mages for an evening drink or an impromptu concert by Queen Efalla, who had brought her lyre with her. Queen Efalla was a technically accomplished musician, but her playing lacked energy and emotion. Arias returned from these evenings exhausted and sometimes inebriated, since the guests had nothing better to do during the interminable concerts than drink the fine wine and brandy that was offered. At those times Callo grinned and sent for Arias' manservant Rosh to put Arias to bed, rejoicing that he was not expected to attend the royal concerts by reason of his unusual status with the royal family.

Never was there a hint of any royal displeasure. Callo began to think Lord Arias had escaped.

At Seagard Castle, Arias settled into the luxurious rooms he had enjoyed on previous visits to his family's holding. Though he had not spent his youth there, Arias had made brief visits to Seagard to see his father, Lord Mikati Moran Alkiran, his mother Lady Sira Joah Alkiran, and his brother and sister. Callo never joined him on these visits. Now, Callo beheld the fortress with a frown, put off by the atmosphere of grim watchfulness that pervaded the place. The Watch Tower itself stood like a fist against the sky.

Callo was pointedly not invited to the family dinners, and but for a sly comment or two from one of the servants, would have thought the noble family was unaware of his presence. Lady Sira Joah, it seemed, had been spending most evenings alone in her suite of rooms, possibly embarrassed to face the bastard son who had turned out to be her legitimate son's best friend. Unoffended and a little amused by the studied ignorance of his presence, Callo whiled away his free time with books, riding out when the weather permitted, and, once, exploring all the way to the fishing village down the mountainside. Lord Arias kept him company in the evenings when he was not engaged by his family or the king. King Martan did not require Callo's presence before the Alkiran family.

Then on the sixth night of their stay, he received a message from one of King Martan's slaves.

"Lord Arias is in the upper solar. He needs you."

This was so strange that Callo did not hesitate even to close the door to his apartments. He followed the slave to the upper solar, a lofty room with windows open to the sky.

Tonight, the stars shone through sporadic cloud cover. There, he found Arias.

Arias stood perilously close to the open window, leaning heavily on his arms as he stared down at the booming surf far below. A chill wind whipped Arias' cloak around him and sent the few candles on the mantle guttering.

"Arias?" Callo said cautiously.

There was no response, but a glimmer of color traced Arias' hands where they lay on the stone. Arias seemed disturbed, then.

Callo drew closer. "Arias?"

Arias' back was still turned. Callo reached out and grasped Arias' arm just as his friend swayed toward the yawning window.

"Arias!" Callo grabbed him hard, dispensing with politeness. "What the hell are you doing? What's wrong?"

Arias wrenched away, but not before Callo had time to see the glitter of the new Collar on his friend's neck.

"Jashan!" Callo swore. He pulled Arias forcibly toward him, away from the window.

"Callo," Arias said weakly, seeming to finally realize his friend was there. "I'm Collared."

"I see," Callo said grimly, "And I can warrant why, too. Curse him, King or not, for a jealous old fool! Come with me, Arias; I'll get you to your room."

It was almost criminal to leave a newly-Collared mage alone. New bindings had a way of taking hold with an unexpected force; it had been known for persons newly bound to a place to be so strongly attracted to it that they jumped out of windows or leaped from the decks of ships to be closer to the place of binding. And sometimes a person fought the Collar. Bindings worked best on the young, where they lay as a powerful framework upon the person's mind; but an individual as old as Arias had his own framework, his own ingrained habits and loyalties. Callo had heard of a case where someone Arias' age died from an attempted binding.

Callo stuck his head out the door and called the first slave he saw. "Get my lord's manservant Rosh! I need him here now! And then come back yourself. We may need you."

The slave ran off and Callo turned his full attention to Lord Arias. Arias leaned on Callo, seeming only half aware of his surroundings. As soon as Rosh arrived, he allowed them to help him down the corridor. Arias seemed sluggish, and he stumbled often on the hollowed stone steps down to the residential level. From time to time he shook his head as if trying to clear it. His eyes showed red under drooping lids. Callo grew angrier the farther they went.

Callo and Rosh guided Arias through his dressing room and into the bedchamber. There, Arias slumped on the bed while Rosh, mumbling to himself in distress at his master's condition, removed his boots and cloak.

"Arias, how are you feeling now?" Callo asked as Rosh helped his master lie down, still clothed in breeches and loose tunic. "Are you any better?"

"I feel hot," Arias said. Callo reached out the back of his hand to check Arias' forehead. He drew his hand away fast, shocked at the heat.

"Gods!" he said. "I'll get a Healer. Stay put, will you? Just for a moment. I will expect you to be here when I return, Arias!" Callo had no confidence that middle-aged, plump Rosh could restrain Lord Arias if it came to that.

Arias lifted a hand in acknowledgment, so Callo felt fairly safe in leaving him for a few minutes. He pulled the door closed behind him. A footman loitered in the corridor.

"You!" called Callo. "I need a Healer called, right now. There is a Healer?"

"In the village, lord," the footman said. "Hon Ruthan."

"Get her, now!" Callo ordered. "Lord Arias is becoming very ill. Tell the Healer she may be up here for some time. Tell her it is a binding fever."

The footman's eyes widened and he turned to go at a run down the corridor. Callo remembered the rocky cliff path and hoped it would not take candlemarks for the Healer to arrive. The fever had come upon Arias so quickly, and seemed so high, that he feared for his friend's life.

He returned to the room and ordered Rosh to do what he could to make Arias comfortable. He sent for wine and ice from the cellars, but Arias would not touch them. Rosh stripped the covers off the bed so Arias could lie on cool sheets, but his fever still raged.

Arias began to mumble to himself, his words thick. He seemed only sporadically aware of the presence of others. Soon his fever began burning away his control on his magery, and a cocoon of disturbed color began wrapping his restless hands. Callo was forced to retreat to the door as the occasional sparks of magery glimmered from the bed hangings and washed violently up the walls in a churning sea of hues. He dreaded that he would soon feel the subtle graying of the world that would indicate that Arias was pulling strength from the living things around him, but at least so far Arias retained enough control to resist.

Rosh edged farther and farther away from the bed. He finally begged leave to go. "It's dangerous, sir!"

"You're needed," Callo responded shortly.

"Sir!" Rosh pleaded. His eyes fixed on the shifting energies pooling around the feverish mage.

"He won't hurt you," Callo said, although he was far from sure of that.

"He won't hurt *you*, my lord. He has no idea I am even here. May I wait outside, sir?"

"Oh, go ahead!" snapped Callo.

Then the door swept open and Lord Mikati Alkiran, Arias' father, walked in without waiting for permission. Lord Mikati had dark hair and a lined, handsome face. His own Collar, set there many years ago by the King, shone on his neck. He stared at his son for a moment and then caught sight of Callo, leaning against the wall.

"You!" Lord Mikati said.

Callo gave a slight bow. "Yes, my lord," he said. "How is Lord Arias doing?"

"Very ill, so far. It would be much better if this Healer could be hurried along, my lord," Callo said. "A Collar, at Arias' age . . ."

Mikati shrugged. "It is his duty, after all," he said. "He should have been Collared long ago."

Callo nodded. "Is there anything you can do, my lord? Can you suppress this magery? It will make it hard for the healer to work."

"No. Arias is strong, and I can't risk depleting my own energy to control him. I must Watch tonight."

It was an Alkiran's prime duty—Lord Mikati's bound duty, in fact—to Watch toward Ha'las for the Black Tide. Nothing would stay him from it. That was the nature of the binding put upon the Seagard Alkirani by King Martan Sharpeyes. From now on, if he survived this violent binding, Lord Arias would also let nothing stop him from the task of the Watch for the Black Tide. Arias' life had changed for good.

"Lord Forell? Perhaps Lord Eamon?" Callo asked, naming Arias' brother and uncle, who had spent their lives here and been bound to the same service as Mikati.

"I'll thank you not to disturb either of them. The Healer

will manage. Stay with him. Call some servants—Borin will help."

Lord Mikati swept out, leaving Callo fighting a rush of anger. On his heels came a slave leading an ancient woman with ruined eyes and a young woman with defiantly cropped hair. Both wore cloaks beaded with water from the sea spray and carried bulky bags.

"The Healers, Lord Callo," the slave said.

"Thank you. Stay close for a while, in case we need you," Callo ordered.

"I am Ruthan, and this is the new Healer from the college, Hon Kirian," said the old woman. She ignored the flashes of color magic around the man on the bed and walked right up to touch his forehead. "This man is very hot. A binding fever, you say?"

"He is newly Collared," Callo said. "He was not expecting it. It was in the nature of an attack."

The younger woman's brown eyes searched his. "Is this his first binding, my lord?"

Callo nodded. "He went into this fever almost immediately, Healer. I warn you, he is a color mage, and in this fever he will be dangerous."

"We will reduce the fever," Ruthan said to the young Healer. "Bitterwood."

"Do you want me to bring in Lord Arias' manservant to help you?" Callo asked.

"Is that who was huddling out there?" the younger woman asked. "He's not doing much good. He is afraid of the magery?"

Callo nodded. "He's not wrong to be afraid, Hon Kirian."

The old woman interrupted, her hand on Arias' wrist as she measured his pulse. "Mix me some mellweed too, young Kirian; he looks to need it."

"But . . ." Callo stopped.

"Mellweed," Ruthan repeated. Her blank eyes looked in Callo's direction. "It will send his mind elsewhere, into dream or vision. He might be fortunate enough to have a true dream, sent by one of the gods. But he will no longer have the focus to fight the Collar."

Callo nodded, understanding. It was a sad thing to conspire to thwart his friend's will to fight against this binding that he clearly had no wish for. If asked right now, Lord Arias might even refuse the drug, choosing to struggle against the King's binding with every bit of his strength. But Callo knew such a fight would kill Arias; he had no hope of succeeding. And he wanted Lord Arias alive, even if it meant his half-brother's submission to the King's vengeful binding.

"Go ahead," he said.

The younger Healer mixed the bitterwood in an earthen jar. The familiar odor wrinkled Callo's nose even where he stood. The mellweed, mixed with cold tea in another jar, looked innocuous and soothing; it was difficult to understand the power the thick substance had. Arias seemed to smell the mixtures as well; he paused in his restless movements and took a deep breath, as if inhaling the healing mixtures. The wild colors momentarily ebbed.

"That's right, my lord," Ruthan said. "You know this is what you need. You'll take it without any need to get that manservant in here to help, I think."

The old woman lifted the earthenware jar to Arias' lips. She tilted the mixture down his throat and he swallowed, but then he struck out with a flash of red power that shattered the jar and the nearby window, throwing the old woman back onto the floor.

Callo leaped to the bedside and pinned his friend's arms to

the bed. Kirian helped the old woman up. Hon Ruthan cradled her right wrist in her other hand.

"Ruthan!" Kirian said. "Are you all right?"

"No," Ruthan gasped as she allowed herself to be helped to a chair. "When he broke that jar, he got my wrist, too. It's broken; there's no doubt."

"Oh, no!"

"We'll deal with that in due course," Ruthan said. "Here's a task for you, my new assistant! Get that mellweed down him, and the sooner the better for all concerned."

Kirian picked up the cup and nodded to Callo, who tightened his grip on his friend's arms. She tilted the mixture down my lord's throat and leaped back out of immediate reach.

Arias swallowed and opened his eyes, looking for a moment aware and bewildered.

"Callo!" he said. "Why are you holding me down?" As soon as the words were out, his eyes closed again, and he slumped into Callo's hold, unconscious. The color magic receded in a glorious ebbing tide back through his hands and into nonexistence.

Callo let go. He and Kirian stared at Arias' still form until they were sure he was no more threat.

"At last!" said Callo.

Kirian went to Arias' side to check his pulse and breathing. She worked with a cool professional calm, eventually straightening the sick man's pillow and pulling a silk sheet over him.

"He'll do, for now," she said. "Now, Hon Ruthan needs me."

Ruthan sat hunched over, in obvious pain. Kirian examined the injured wrist.

"What does it look like?" she asked Ruthan.

"Broken," Ruthan said. "I looked at it while you were busy

with Lord Arias there. We'll need a stiff splint for now, more when we return home."

"How does she know?" Callo asked, puzzled. The wrist looked normal to him. There were no bones poking out, and the wrist showed no swelling yet.

"She knows, my lord," Kirian said. "She can see it. Here, Ruthan, let me take care of it."

Callo left the young woman to the task of splinting and binding up the old Healer's wrist. He stood over Lord Arias for a moment, noting his friend's even breathing and the flicker of his eyelids as the mellweed took effect. Then he stepped outside, beckoning Rosh back into the room.

"It's safe," he said. "Find out what he'll need from the Healers. You'll stay with him first, and get help to keep watch through the night. I'll send Chiss, too."

"Yes, sir," Rosh said, and re-entered the room.

Callo sighed, closed his eyes as he leaned up against the wall, and finally relaxed his shoulders. They did not want to ease after the hours spent in tension. Callo looked down the hall toward his own chamber, wishing for rest. He yawned, then startled when a deep voice interrupted him. It was the steward Borin, finally showing up when all the hard work was done. Callo ordered accommodations for the Healers, and the man faded away down the hallway to a servants' pantry. Callo heard the clink of pottery from the little room. He felt as if he would fall asleep where he stood.

Chapter Three

Kirian finished binding Ruthan's wrist. She walked over to the bedside. Lord Arias looked peaceful now, no longer feverish and wild as he had been when she walked into the room. She wondered how he would feel if he knew he had broken Ruthan's wrist. It was hard to say with nobles; most cared for no one but themselves and their riches. Inmay would have it that all *righ* were selfish fools.

Perhaps that was why King Martan had to bind them to the Watch, unable to count on his *righ* mages to serve the land of their own free will. Kirian shrugged. Whatever the reason, this had been a brutal binding, and the man in the bed had almost died from it. She didn't envy those who were bound, no matter how rich and privileged they were.

She thought he looked rather handsome, even lying there with his mouth open.

"Now young Kirian," Ruthan said, "Those sweets aren't for you." Kirian grinned. "I know it," she said.

"Besides, you have to work for him," Ruthan said more seriously. "He is a noble and a mage, and thinks no more of you than his father does of the beggars in the street in Sugetre."

"I was just looking at him," she said. Just then the lord's manservant came back into the room, and Kirian busied herself for the next few minutes giving instructions to the man. Then she and Ruthan took their leave and walked out into the drafty stone hall.

The nobleman who had been in the room when they arrived leaned against the wall. When he looked up, Kirian took note of him for the first time since her arrival. He was tall, and broad of shoulder, with long fair hair drawn back in a warrior's tail, and he had unusual eyes, like clear amber. He looked nothing at all like a member of the Alkirani clan. He saw her examining him and smiled at her. It was a nice smile, she thought; she couldn't picture such on the lean dark face of an Alkiran.

"Where are you going?" he asked. "Is it safe to leave him?"

"We are staying here overnight, and will be returning to the village in the morning," Ruthan said. "His man in there has all our instructions."

"Well, let me find Borin. He can show you to your room and order you something to eat." He led them to a little room at the end of the corridor where a servant worked, collecting cups of wine on a lacquered tray. "Borin, please attend to them. Thank you for your assistance—however belated." He spoke with a flash of irritation that the steward did not react to, undoubtedly being used to such treatment from the *righ* he served. Then Callo bowed to Ruthan and Kirian, an unexpected courtesy, and left them.

In the small room that had been allotted them, Kirian asked about Callo.

"What was he doing there, taking care of Lord Arias,

instead of a member of the noble family?" she asked as she changed into the night robe she kept in her healer's bag.

"I expect Lord Mikati was too wrapped up in the Watch to care what was happening down here."

"What about the brother and sister? What about his lady mother?"

"Brother and sister—well, I have no idea, young one. But as for the mother…" Ruthan chuckled. "She will not be seen outside her rooms until this Callo goes, no matter if divine Jashan himself comes to call."

"What does she have against Lord Callo?" Kirian mumbled through the sting of her tooth cleaner.

Ruthan sat down on one of the beds. "This Callo, you see, is Lady Sira Joah's bastard son."

Kirian's mouth dropped open. "But she is the King's sister!"

"The King's sister, Lord Mikati's wife. She had an affair with some minor dignitary who visited here one year. Of course, Lord Mikati can't stand the bastard son, but the boy is the son of the King's sister after all, and he has rank in spite of the circumstances of his birth. And just to spite them all, Lord Arias and Lord Callo are great friends."

"Then I think the better of Lord Arias," Kirian said. "How is your wrist?"

Ruthan complained that it was sore and swelling, but then smiled and said, "You did a good job on it, sweet."

"My thanks," Kirian said, and slid under the covers. When Ruthan was settled she blew out the single candle and darkness claimed the room. In only a few minutes, she fell into a dreamless sleep.

She opened her eyes to see faint gray light along the edges of the shutters and was surprised she had awakened so early. In the next bed, Ruthan snored in the light sleep of the elderly.

Kirian rose and dressed as quietly as possible, dragged a comb through her hair, and eased out the door.

The corridor was empty but for one early-rising manservant carrying a jug of water, who went silently along without a glance at Kirian. She reversed her steps from last night, ending up at Lord Arias' door. The door opened to show the broad, weary face of Arias' servant Rosh.

"Good morning," Kirian whispered. "I thought I would check on his lordship. How is he doing?"

Rosh stepped to the side, allowing her to enter. "No change," he said. "He sleeps as if he has not slept for days."

Kirian went to the bed and rested a hand on Arias' forehead. It was cool, and the mage did not stir at her touch. His breathing was deep and even. She smiled.

"He seems well," she told Rosh. "Do not allow him to be disturbed until he wakes of his own accord. Then, if he complains of headache, or if the fever begins rising again, give him the dose Hon Ruthan provided you."

"Yes, Hon Healer."

"Have you been here all night by yourself?"

Rosh shook his head. "No. Lord Callo sent his manservant to help, and the servants brought us food and drink. We are well."

Kirian nodded and left, pleased with the progress of her patient. She found herself at loose ends and began walking through the corridor, looking at the tapestries which covered the old stone walls. Many of them had clearly been there for a very long time, as they showed the fading colors and occasional frayed strands of age; but they were all clean, and apparently cared for with some attention. She descended the corner stairs, her shoes scraping against the stone, and found her way through a maze of formal rooms to a corner room which was a sort of conservatory, with tall unshuttered windows along the eastern and southern walls. The room held low benches, a marvel of a tiny fountain, and pots of greenery. There she sat; looking at the gracious space around her while the morning sun grew stronger and began to take the chill from the room.

The peace of the room sank into her, first pleasing her eyes, then radiating to her muscles. She relaxed.

"Who the hell are you?"

She started. A heavy young man stood at the door, staring at her with the hawk-like eyes of the Alkirani but oddly surrounded in folds of fat. The Collar gleamed on his thick neck. This must be Lord Forell, Lord Alkiran's second son.

Kirian flushed and stood. "I am Hon Kirian, sir, the healer from Seagard. I was up early and thought to enjoy the room."

The man smiled, showing brownish teeth. His tunic was gathered at his bulging belly by a sash which he caressed with one hand as he approached her. He walked slowly, but did not seem to want to stop. When he came close enough to make Kirian uncomfortable at his nearness, she stood and faced him. She smelled the fragrance he used; it was some exotic scent she had not experienced before.

"Look at this hair!" he said, taking a short strand of it between thumb and forefinger. "What kind of statement were you intending to make, with this hair?"

Kirian flushed. "Statement, my lord?"

His hand dropped to caress the line of her neck, then dropped as she stepped back, startled. "You are like a gazelle," he murmured.

"My lord, stop."

"Don't be afraid," he said. "I am Lord Forell Alkiran. You were tending my older brother last night, or so I hear. Perhaps now you can tend me. I have been feeling faint and easily tired. Come with me, gazelle, and tend my hurts."

"My lord!" she said coldly. "I will be happy to see you as a Healer. Hon Ruthan is with me. Only let me summon her . . ."

"Not the old one?" Forell said, disappointed. "She does nothing but prescribe abstinence, and she is not sympathetic at all. Perhaps you can examine me alone, Hon Gazelle." His hand reached for her breast, but Kirian stepped away.

"It would not be right, my lord. I am learning from Hon Ruthan. Also, I must insist that you not touch me, my lord."

"What is the point," Forell said to the ceiling, "Of sending to us such an oddity, a young woman skilled in the arts of the body, a woman with the face and hair of a boy, the limbs of a gazelle, the breast of a . . ."

"My lord!"

"And forbidding me to touch her?" Forell reached out again, grasping Kirian's slender hand in his plump one. "There is little to entertain us here in Seagard Castle, my oddity. Perhaps you will let me entertain you. Otherwise, by Jashan it grows dull here!"

"My lord," Kirian said, withdrawing her hand, "I cannot accept your very, uh, interesting offer. Do you require Hon Ruthan's services?"

"Ah, curse the old one. There's nothing I need so badly I will listen to her. Go, then—but don't think you can always count on my forbearance."

Kirian bowed and made her escape, grateful that she had won out of that one without antagonizing one of her important noble clients. She strode back through the maze of rooms and up the stairs, passing many more people now, including a set of armed guardsmen who frowned at her as she left the family's common areas and regained her own floor. Back in the room she shared with Hon Ruthan, she turned her back to the door and leaned against it.

Ruthan sat fully clothed on the edge of the bed, closing her healer's bag. She looked up at Kirian with her blank white eyes and grinned.

"Now," she wondered, "What member of the noble Alkiran clan is chasing you into your room so early in the morning?"

"Lord Forell," Kirian said. "Hon Ruthan, how will I ever be able to treat him or examine him alone?"

"You will take me with you, when possible," Ruthan said. "Best to never see him alone. He's known for his eye for the village women too. But to be safe, I will have a word with Shala Si. She can make Lord Forell aware—without saying a straight word to him!—that if you are touched, she will take her vengeance. Also, it would not do for Lord Mikati to know that Forell had mistreated you."

"Why should Shala Si care? She certainly doesn't like me."

Ruthan shrugged. "Everything to do with her master is of concern to her. Her lot is much better here than it would be anywhere else, Kirian. She will want to protect her place."

"Her place is not in danger. He was only bored, I presume." Kirian wished, sharply and suddenly, that Inmay was here; then, just as quickly, she knew that Inmay would be of no use to her. He would probably fall in love with Shala Si anyway; the concubine had soft dark eyes and a rounded body and was bound to appeal to him. Attractive slaves were Inmay's weakness.

"Come, Hon Ruthan," she said. "I have checked on Lord Arias and he's doing well. Can we get out of here before I do something to get us both in trouble?"

———

Back in Seagard an hour later, Kirian went walking on the shore, spending an hour or so in the crystal morning air and returning to the house windblown and red-cheeked. Sitting before the hearth sorting herbs that had dried on the wooden rack, she mulled over what had happened the night before.

"Why," she asked Ruthan, "wasn't that mage bound already? Surely he's too old for a first binding?"

"Arias has always been different, living in Sugetre and all. He is in line to inherit the throne, after some cousin or other, so he was not Collared. His majesty usually binds all mages when they take the cloak," Ruthan agreed. "After all, if he does not Collar them or bind them to a task, they end up self-binding to their art, and the King doesn't want that."

"Why not?"

"Because mages that are bound to their art care not for kings or lords. All they care about is magery. Mages are too powerful to leave running around with no loyalties but to themselves."

"It was cruel," Kirian said. "I know it is the *righ* mages' duty to protect us from Ha'las, but it was cruel. The man almost died, and now he is virtually a slave to the Watch."

Ruthan cackled. "I knew you cared more about him than you should. Why does it matter if a spoiled noble is finally forced to his duty? He has enough privileges, so let him do his duty! Don't let his face charm you, young Kirian. He's no better than the rest of them, I'm sure."

"I don't even know the man, and he will never notice me." In fact, as she continued sorting the herbs, she wondered more about the amber-eyed warrior than about Lord Arias. Lord Callo had smiled directly into her eyes that morning, which was more than any other of them had done, except Lord Forell who was bent on manipulating her into his bed. She had felt an answering smile and a friendly connection to the man. But Lord Callo was a *righ* too, in spite of his questionable parentage; she could admire him, but it would be unwise to try to make a friend of him.

———

A sennight later, Kirian left Ruthan's house early to see a village woman in her ninth month of pregnancy. She reassured the woman that her time was not yet, was offered hot tea and berry cakes, and left the house with a smile on her face.

Kirian walked down the rocky strand with the sea breeze in her hair, noticing that the air had grown colder in the last week or so. The villagers were salting extra catches in preparation for the winter, and Marka had butchered a pig. The children who played tag between the gray houses wore cloaks. Ruthan had warned Kirian that she would not like the village so much after she had experienced a Seagard winter.

As Kirian passed Marka's house, a small boy ran up to her with an excited grin on his face.

"Hon Kirian, come and see! There is a horse!"

Kirian laughed. "Indeed, Cam! I know how you love horses. But whose horse could it be?"

"A warrior came from the Castle to talk to Elder Hame. He left his horse tied to the line. Come with me, Hon Kirian!" Cam grabbed her hand and pulled her toward the Elder's house.

It was not just any carthorse that stood tied loosely to Hame's clothesline. The mare was a beauty, with clean, delicate lines—a nobleman's mount. The mare turned her head to look at them as they approached. Cam was charmed.

"Can I pat her, Hon Kirian?"

"I don't know, Cam—this mare may not want to be bothered, and it is not your horse."

Before she could finish her thought, the mare bobbed her

head at Cam as though inviting him nearer. The boy approached and gently rubbed her chestnut neck.

"I wish this was my horse," Cam said.

Running footsteps sounded behind them. There was a rattle of flung gravel, and a few of the small stones struck the mare. She startled and pulled at her tether.

Cam drew back. "Hey!"

Kirian turned, but the offender had hidden around the corner of another house. "Who is that? Is that you, young Peak?"

There came another rattle of stones, thrown from the other corner of the house. Kirian saw a grinning face—Peak, one of the older boys known for his sometimes mean pranks. This time a stone struck the mare's nose. She neighed and reared, twisting, and one of her hooves struck Cam's shoulder, knocking him to the ground. Cam yelled in pain.

Booted footsteps sounded on Elder Hame's wooden walkway. A deep voice, vaguely familiar, said: "What's going on here?"

Kirian fell to her knees next to Cam. He clutched his left shoulder, blood leaking from between his fingers. His hand shook.

The man went to his horse's head. The mare was still shaken, her eyes showing white. "Calm down now, Miri, my sweet. Nothing threatens you."

Elder Hame stomped out onto his walkway. "I saw you, young Peak!" he roared at a figure fleeing down the beach. He came up behind Kirian. "Is he all right?"

"Send someone for his mother, if you please, Elder Hame," said Kirian. Cam was crying hysterically, trying to scramble farther away from the mare. "Stop now, little one. You must let me look at your shoulder. Your mother is on her way."

Cam paid her no attention. He shoved her hands away, sobbing. "Cam! Let me look, little one. I can help you."

Someone crouched down beside her. "Who is this? Cam, did you say? Cam, my mare did not mean to hurt you. She was frightened." Kirian looked up to see Lord Callo, the amber-eyed lord from Seagard Castle. His voice was deep and calm. "Let the Healer see to your shoulder, and then you can come with me and meet Miri properly."

Cam's teary eyes looked up. He stopped shaking. Gently, Kirian took his hand and moved it from the bleeding shoulder.

"Good, that's the trick," Kirian said. "I think your Mama is coming, Cam—let's show her you're brave, shall we?"

A small crowd approached, led by Cam's anxious mother. Lord Callo went on talking, about nothing very much. His deep voice carried a soothing vibration Kirian could not identify. She felt calmer, listening to it. It held Cam still like a bug pinned to paper.

Cam remained unnaturally still as Kirian examined the injured shoulder. His fixed stare remained on Lord Callo's face. Kirian knew she was hurting the boy, but Callo's voice talked on, calm and relaxing like mellweed, and did not stop until she had finished.

Then Cam moved, staring at Kirian, his eyes wide.

"All is well, Cam," she said. "The bleeding has almost stopped by itself, and no bones are broken. Go and reassure your mother, and then come to Ruthan's house so I can tend to the wound."

Cam stood, not even wobbly any more. "But he said…"

"Yes, just a moment, Healer." Callo took the boy's hand and led him to the mare. Cam stood taller as they walked. Miri snorted and tossed her head. Callo laid a hand on the mare's neck and stroked her. "Cam, this is Miri. She is descended from a long line of Leyish purebreds, so she is strong and fast, but sometimes she is nervous as well. I'm sorry she hurt you."

Cam hesitated. Then he stroked the mare's neck. Miri looked at him with her soft brown eyes and whickered. The boy broke into a smile.

"See, she feels friendly to you now," Callo said.

Cam held out his palm, and Miri snuffled it with her soft nose. "Come up to the Castle stable sometime, and ask one of the grooms to let you see her. You can look around at the other horses, as well. I'll leave word it's all right. Would you like that?"

Cam nodded, speechless. Then he gave a hurried bow and ran off to his waiting mother.

Lord Callo loosed Miri's rein and turned her away from the small crowd that had gathered. He bade his goodbyes to Elder Hame and began to lead the mare away.

"Lord Callo!" Kirian said, impelled by some odd attraction to draw his attention again. "Thank you for your help."

"It would have been simpler had you kept that boy from throwing rocks at my mare. No wonder she startled." Kirian heard the snap of temper in his voice.

"Elder Hame will deal with Peak," she said.

"Or I will," Callo said.

"It will not happen again, I am sure."

"And what were you thinking, Healer, to let that child touch a strange animal anyway?"

"Is your mare dangerous, then, my lord?"

"Well." Callo paused. "She is not a dangerous animal. You are a sweet-tempered lady, aren't you, my good one?" His hand stroked Miri's neck. They began walking down the strand toward the path.

"How is Lord Arias?" Kirian asked, taking advantage of the change in his tone.

Callo's amber eyes met hers. There was a glint of humor behind them. "He is fine. But he speaks of nothing but the Watch. It is hard to get away from the subject."

Kirian laughed. "So he is well. I am glad. And thank you for your invitation to Cam. He does love horses. And he is in awe of you, I saw that. He was like a statue as I checked his arm, and I know it was painful." She remembered the boy's odd stillness.

Callo shrugged. "Perhaps he did not wish to weep in front of a stranger from the Castle." He glanced up at the Castle Watch Tower. Kirian thought he must be eager to be on his way.

"Thank you, my lord. Now I must go to Ruthan's. The boy will be coming to have his shoulder bandaged under better conditions."

Callo nodded. "It is good to see you again, Hon Kirian," he said. He swung up into the saddle and smiled down at her. "Tell the boy to come up tomorrow."

She nodded and inclined her head in an informal bow. Lord Alkiran would have upbraided her in his bitter voice for such disrespect; however, Lord Callo just made a gesture of farewell and turned Miri toward the cliff path. Kirian stared after him. His long hair shone in the morning sun, and she had the oddest impression that there was a slight glow about him. She shook her head, disgusted with herself. The man was attractive, surely, but no god. She turned and went back to tell Ruthan about young Cam's misadventure.

Ruthan sat near her window; she had seen Lord Callo take his leave. When Kirian came in, the old woman grinned at her, showing yellowed teeth. "You are letting that lordling get to you, young Kirian—I can see it."

Kirian laughed. "I suppose so. He is very handsome."

"And a *righ*, remember that. Oh, by all means indulge your

eye — you're young, after all. But never forget who they spring from, the *righ*, and what they care about. It's not us; that's certain."

Kirian unwrapped her cloak. Her face stung as her chilled skin began to warm in the heat of Ruthan's crackling fire. "You sound like someone I knew at College. He cursed all nobles."

"I have reason. Look, do you see Gru on the docks sometimes, doing naught much of anything?"

Kirian nodded. Gru was a man of middle years whom she guessed had once been able and energetic. Now the man spent all day sitting on the docks, in the sun or hooded and cloaked in the wind, sometimes drinking, sometimes just dreaming. His face was weathered, but there were remnants of beauty there. He was married with two children, yet Kirian noticed that his wife and children mostly ignored him.

"Lord Alkiran punished Gru for interfering between himself and Gru's wife."

"Gru's wife? I thought the *righ* were forbidden to father half- breed children?" That made her think of Lord Callo, and she frowned. Perhaps he was a different case, due to his rank. It seemed unfair.

"Sure, they are forbidden to father children on a commoner. That does not mean they can't take their pleasure where they will. Gru's wife was young and very lovely, and Mikati saw her once—gods know where; it's not like he spends time down here with us fisherfolk. Gru raged and cried to me, but said not a word to Alkiran. Afraid for his life, he was. I gave her herbs, but they did not work. When she quickened, and then bore the child to term and it was *his…* "

Kirian was riveted, sitting on the floor at Ruthan's feet. "How did they know it was Lord Alkiran's?"

"I knew. My eyes could tell. But it mattered not. If Alkiran had been unsure, he would have acted the same."

"What did he do?"

"Sent his men to take the babe as soon as it was born. Gru tried to hide it, but he was no match for warriors. They stole the babe and left Gru and his wife screaming for it."

"What—what did he do with the child?"

"He slew it. Himself, with his own sword, and ordered the guards to set the body out on the rocks for Jashan."

"By the Unknown God! How could he?"

"We're not human to him, you see. Only the *righ* are human. And when Gru came raging up the mountain with a fishing knife in his hand, Lord Alkiran used his color magery on the man, and Gru came back confused. He's never been the same."

"I wonder he didn't kill him."

Ruthan cackled. "That was his idea of mercy, to leave the man alive but so empty-minded he sits in the weather and leaves his family to be fed by his brother."

———

Ruthan confirmed that Cam's shoulder was not broken, but scolded Kirian for growing to depend too much on Ruthan's sight. Kirian sent Cam away, the boy skipping and babbling some song as he headed for the cliff path to see Miri in the Alkiran stables.

Later that week, Kirian made a point of stopping along the docks where Gru sat in the sun. The man was wrapped in cloak and blanket against the chill sea wind. His hood was drawn down over his eyes. He stared out to sea even though the sun on the waves was so bright Kirian could stand it for only a few seconds. But Gru looked, and did not waver.

Perhaps it was not as bright as the color magery that had stolen his wits. After a few moments he looked up at her, his eyes in his once-handsome face now blank and incurious. She asked him if he needed anything, and he did not respond; instead, he just stared at her with the same lack of intensity he had given to the ocean. She waited a while, then wished him well and left him. She knew no healing that could help a man whose mind had been taken by magery.

Walking along the strand, she spoke to Elder Hame. The old man told her he had been sending boys out to the High Rocks to look for a ship. "My Lord Alkiran wants word as soon as she passes the rocks," he told her. "Lord Callo said she is a Leyish ship. They're heathen brutes, the Leyish. Breed good horses though."

Thinking of Miri, she looked up and saw riders on the strand. From a distance she could not distinguish who they might be, but she caught a gleam of gold and thought it might be the sun on Lord Callo's hair. He rode with others, perhaps men of his command. The sun struck answering reflections from metal on their tack and weapons. They turned and galloped closer, on their way to the cliff path to take them upward to the Castle. It was indeed Lord Callo, graceful in the saddle, and two other men. Lord Callo's eyes were on the way up the cliff path, and he did not glance toward Kirian.

———

The sea sparkled as a brilliant sun shone upon the little craft. Kirian, sitting near the bow, unpinned her brooch and let her cloak slide down her shoulders. It was simply too hot to wear a cloak, though there was a chill in the salt spray. The recent cold snap had given way to a series of warm days, a last reminder of summer before winter's final bite. Kirian had taken advantage of the sultry weather to ask Kin and Rashiri to take her out on their boat.

Kin and Rashiri hauled up the nets. Water streamed from the squirming catch and caught the light in glorious rainbows. A flopping, silvery mass of fish spilled out onto the deck of the *Homebound*.

"And she is bound to home, too," Rashiri had told Kirian. "We paid for a color mage from Two Merkhan to come and do a binding on her. She is bound to Seagard. So fear not, city girl! You are safe with us."

Kirian had never before been in a boat, not even the little mage-powered sailcraft that drifted in circles around Lake Heart in Sugetre. There, the sailcrafts were rented by the hour to those who were willing to pay a few coins for the pleasure, and never had a sailcraft been lost or even capsized on the calm little lake. So Kirian had boarded the *Homebound* with some trepidation. But after a few hours of sitting at her ease on deck, soaking up the sun and delighting in the vast beauty of the smiling sea, she was reconciled. She loved the feel of the sun, and the shouts and calls of the fish merchants at Two Merkhan were a pleasure to hear after the quiet of little Seagard. After the pair had sold their catch, the *Homebound* turned south again, heading for home.

"I envy you," she told Rashiri when the other woman took a break from her work to sip a jar of cold, honeyed tea with Kirian, both in the bow. "You're surrounded by such amazing beauty here."

"We are very lucky to be able to do this together," Rashiri said. Her face was creased and deeply tanned from exposure to the sun and wind. Her uncomplicated smile showed strong white teeth. "But don't think it's all like this."

"There must be storms, and rain, and wind."

"Those are bitter cold days, indeed," Rashiri said. "And

there are days with no fish, and days when one of us gets sliced by one of our own knives or the teeth on some unexpected catch." She held out one arm to show Kirian the frightening white scar that ran around her forearm in an arc. "That's a bite!" she said.

"I see," Kirian said faintly.

"Spilled right out of the net with the catch and bit me before I could say aye. Kin got it off me, but Ruthan was busy that day and a few after, I can tell you."

"Fishing isn't so peaceful then."

"It's hard work. But I love it, Hon Kirian, and it's the blessing from the Unknown God that I can be out on the bright sea every day with my love. How many can do that? Here, have some more tea."

Kirian held out her mug and let the other woman splash some of the caramel-colored liquid into it. The *Homebound* was approaching port now, steered by Kin in his stained and fishy tunic. Kirian looked straight ahead, to the clutter of houses on the shore that was Seagard Village, then up and up, to the castle that looked out like a hawk on the promontory. She wondered how the newly-bound Lord Arias was progressing, and remembered Lord Callo's amber eyes.

Behind them, the sun sank hotly to the edge of the sea.

Out on the far horizon, like a pencil line drawn by an artist to delineate the calm sea, lay a mark between sea and sky.

"Rashiri! What is that?"

Rashiri stood and craned her neck, then cried out to her husband in the bow. "Kin! Black Tide!"

The line grew thicker, as if the artist inked it, a black border lying on the surface of the ocean. Kirian stared as the line widened, broad as a brush now, and felt her breath torn away by a freshening wind, or by fear; she could not tell which.

Then it seemed to rush toward them, speeding towards the

craft as Kin and Rashiri raced to push all possible speed from the *Homebound.*

"Gods! We're in its path!" shouted Kin, and the sheet of black drawn over the ocean sped closer.

Kin shouted orders, and the wind rushed louder. Kirian, trying to stay out of the way, felt the boat surge forward under their expert handling. But the dock was too far away, and there was no way to beat the accelerating darkness. She gazed in paralyzed shock as the whole western sea turned black. A tumble of stunned and helpless fish was washed along in the front of the blackness, those creatures already experiencing the deadening effects of the Black Tide. The Tide was so close she could see its odd matte surface, which did not reflect the rays of the setting sun.

Out of the corner of her eye, she saw a flare of brilliance from the Castle. Someone there, one of the Alkirani mages, was on duty. A wave of energy swept off the shore and onto the sea—glorious reds, blues, greens, and golds. The colors overtook the *Homebound* and swept her with radiance before meeting the Black Tide in an inaudible crash. A vibrant shield rose into the sky. Through the translucent colors, Kirian saw the Black Tide curling back, retreating against the strength of the defense.

"Jashan and all the gods," whispered Kirian.

The *Homebound* reached dock. Helping hands grabbed ropes to moor the boat, and hustled all three of them to shore. They left the *Homebound* bobbing, at the mercy of the stiffening wind, but not even Kin and Rashiri dared to wait outside to put her properly away.

"Did you see that?" cried Elder Hame, his white hair whipped in the sudden gale. "Did you see that?"

"Couldn't help seeing it, old one. We were almost eaten by it!" Kin said. He sat down abruptly on a stool in the house they had been ushered into. He put his head in his hands. Rashiri stood behind him and placed her calloused hands gently on his shoulders.

"I take it," Kirian said carefully, "That doesn't happen, uh, often?"

Hame laughed. "Never seen it, though they say it happened once ten years ago. What power! My lord mage was brilliant! That'll teach those Ha'lasi not to sneak up on us that way!"

"It was too close," Rashiri said.

"I need to go back to Ruthan," Kirian said. "Kin, Rashiri, you get yourselves home and have a warm mug of wine. That's from your Healer, now!"

"We have to tend to the *Homebound*," Kin said.

"Leave her. Someone else will take care of her for you this time. You've had a shock, you know." Two men nodded at her and went out to take care of the *Homebound*.

Rashiri nodded, hands still on Kin's shoulders as he slumped on the stool. "I'll get us home, Hon Healer," she said. "We're fine though. Get to Ruthan, or she'll be worried about you."

Kirian backed away, her eyes still on Kin, torn between her duty to old Ruthan and the possible need for her here. The door opened and there stood Ruthan, bent with age and the struggle against the wind, cloaked for a journey.

"Young Kirian!" she said. "Come! They will be calling for us at the castle."

"We're fine," Rashiri said. "Go."

Kirian waited only to grab her cloak, and she was gone.

Chapter Four

Callo unbuckled his sword belt and handed it to the guard at the door. The guard gestured to him and he removed his cloak, letting the man see that he had no other weapons slung about his person. The guard opened the door.

King Martan Alghasi Monteni sat on an ornately carved chair, one of the prizes of the Alkirani, who lived in a land with few trees. His clothing was fit for the throne room in Sugetre, from the light silver crown around his graying head to the valus fur trimming his cloak. A few courtiers lounged around him, equally well-dressed. A clerk sat at a nearby desk, writing instructions. Callo glanced around for Arias, who sometimes graced this crowd between his Watches, but saw no sign of his half brother.

Callo bowed.

King Martan paid Callo no heed until he finished the conversation he was having with one of his guardsmen. As soon as that man bowed and went about his affairs, His Majesty turned to Callo.

"Where have you been?" the King asked.

Callo felt irritation stir at the King's brusque question, but forced it down. He thanked Jashan for the calm the god had granted him during the sword forms he had just completed in the ring. It had always been critical that he keep a calm mind, since unpleasant things seemed to happen around him when he did not. Chiss had introduced him to a Jashanite warrior-priest when he was ten; the man had taught him everything he knew about the sword, and initiated him into the discipline of the ritual forms.

"Your Majesty, I have been in the training ring. Did you require my presence earlier?"

"I have not heard from the village. The Leyish ship is overdue. Send down to the village to see what is going on. Also, you'd better send a man to Two Merkhan—if the ship has already arrived, I'll have some heads."

"Sire, Elder Hame assured me they would keep constant watch. The ship must round the High Rocks to make port at Two Merkhan, and when it passes them, it will be visible from the village. I believe the Elder is actually sending boys out to the High Rocks to check. But of course I will send to make sure."

"Do that. I will be departing immediately for Sugetre. As one of my Guard captains, I require you to make your men ready. Leave a man here to meet the ship and send word to Sugetre when it arrives. Alkiran will have to do the honors when the delegation arrives."

"Your Majesty!" Callo said. He paused, his thoughts spinning. He wanted to remain here a little longer; something about the place drew him, and he was reluctant to leave Arias just yet. "I respectfully request to remain and await the Leyish delegation."

King Martan's eyes grew even colder. "Why do you not

wish to accompany me, Lord Callo? Have you forgotten where your living derives?"

"No, your Majesty, and as always I appreciate your generosity." Callo fought down the twist of anger; he should be used to Sharpeyes' manipulative techniques by now. When King Martan had taken him on as a child, out of family obligation since his sister Lady Sira Joah refused to have the boy in her house, he had gifted Callo with the title and income from a small manor near the Leyish border. That was what allowed Callo to dress and live like the hereditary noble he was, in spite of his shameful birth.

King Martan stared at Callo as if trying to figure him out. "You are not ready to depart?"

"With your permission, I will await the delegation and give them an appropriate welcome."

King Martan was silent for a moment. "Granted," he said. "Bring me news out of this place when you come. I will start you out by telling you that our hasty departure is due to an attack on us by the Ha'lasi. Not a candlemark ago there was a Black Tide, turned just in time by the alertness of Lord Mikati and Lord Arias. See, that binding pays its due already! I must depart. My safety is paramount. But I want news out of this place as we prepare for hostilities."

"Yes, Sire!" Callo was shocked. He had been unaware of any such momentous events, practicing his forms in the training room all alone. If there had been a magical attack from Ha'las, the enemy fleet would be waiting behind the Black Tide. The Ha'lasi warriors would be planning to take the Castle with a minimum of trouble, easily slaying the defenders who would have been struck into a state of torpor by the psychic deadening of the Tide.

"A sennight," King Martan said. "No longer, Nephew."

"Absolutely, Sire." Callo left the King to his conferences

and preparations and left the royal chambers, retrieving his sword at the door and returning to the floor where he and Arias had their guest rooms. Midway down the hall, he saw Rosh carrying newly-cleaned clothing to his lord's rooms.

"Hai, Rosh!" Callo called, and the manservant turned.

"Sir?"

"Where is Lord Arias?"

"In the Tower Watch room, sir. He keeps Watch with Lord Mikati."

Callo made haste to go up to the tower room. There, he entered the outer chamber, a sort of luxurious sitting room for the comfort of the noble family, and a hubbub of many voices speaking at once fell on his ears.

Lord Mikati sat in the center of a sofa, head thrown back on its crimson cushions. He seemed pale and weary, and the lines on his face seemed deeper than they had the day before. A servant stood close with a jar of wine, and the old Healer from Seagard Village held Lord Mikati's wrist and spoke to him softly.

Two men at arms escorted Lord Forell into the tower room, apparently to stand the next Watch. The plump young lord was speaking constantly, complaining that this was not his assigned time for the Watch and someone was going to have to go to his rooms and inform his concubine that he would not be with her.

"And you can take the consequences," he told one of the guards grumpily. He spun around, wafting some exotic scent into the small room as he took in the scene. "Better in there than out here, I suppose," he said, and vanished into the tower chamber.

In the center of the room stood Lord Arias, his dark eyes very bright, speaking to Healer Kirian. He clutched his cloak about him, although the room was quite warm. Callo went immediately to his half-brother, who smiled.

"Cal! Have you heard? There was a Black Tide." Arias' face was flushed. Callo saw his hand tremble as he gathered his cloak closer. A spray of color spun around his hands, and Arias grimaced, frowning.

"My lord, come sit down," said Kirian. "You are newly Collared, and this exertion has tired you more than you realize."

Arias allowed Callo to pull him to a nearby soft chair. Now he was shaking all over, but he ignored this and began telling Callo about the attack as the young Healer began checking her patient's pulse, breathing and condition. Arias paid her no attention, indeed almost seemed unaware of her, as he told Callo about the attack, and about the ships that were mobilized from Two Merkhan as soon as the attack was turned back in case Ha'lasi troops waited behind the Tide.

Callo looked at the spiky bent head tending to Arias and felt an unexpected flash of impatience. Was the Healer a slave to be ignored like this? Then Arias paused, gasping a little for breath, and Callo forgot his irritation.

"Quiet for a while, you idiot!" he said with the full license permitted a friend. "Let this Healer tell you what you can do to regain your strength. I have never heard what happens when a mage turns back a Black Tide, but I've seen your friend Mikalion after he puts on the fireworks for the graduating mages, and you'd best rest for a while, my friend!"

Arias laughed and put his head back on the cushions, closing his eyes. "Yes, Mikalion needs a sennight's rest after the graduation party, but that's not because of the fireworks. That's because he dearly loves the wine and the mellweed. I'll be fine, Cal." But he shivered as more magery escaped his control.

"Why did they attack now?" Callo said abruptly.

"Who knows? There have been reports out of Ha'las of desertions. The boy King is feared, and this new Ku'an'an…"

"Later, then," Callo interrupted, remembering the presence of the Healers and two guardsmen who didn't need to know the state of affairs between Righar and Ha'las. He looked at the young woman as she stood. "How is he?"

"It seems you just asked me that a sennight ago," she said, and Arias grinned with his eyes closed. "He will be fine, my lord. Lord Arias, you must avoid exerting yourself, physically or—using your talent—for a few days."

"Forell will love that," murmured Arias.

"You run the risk of depleting yourself for far longer if you do," Kirian said sharply. "Your lord father seems to be in a more serious condition. I will go help Hon Ruthan with him."

Callo turned to see Lord Mikati being helped onto a litter. Callo looked down and saw the old lord looking drawn and pale. He was breathing oddly, almost panting as they carried him by.

"Possibly his heart," Ruthan murmured to Kirian as they followed, but Callo caught the words and raised his brows in surprise.

"What?" Arias said to Callo.

"Nothing. Your father is not so strong."

"No wonder. It was amazing, Callo—half exhilarating, half like being pounded with a mace. I doubt he could have turned it alone. Jashan, I doubt I could have turned it alone! Why is there only one on Watch at any time? I wonder why there is not someone standing by, at least."

"Let that wait for later," Callo said. "It is your new binding, you know, making you think about the Watch constantly. Rest. And as for other matters…"

Arias stood up, shrugging his cloak closer about him. "It is cursed cold in this room. Odd I never noticed it before. What is Sharpeyes doing about this? I assume that's why you're here?" There was no sign of more magery escaping Arias' control. He had years of training, much of it devoted to helping a color mage keep the magery where it belonged, instead of letting the energy escape to wreak havoc. Forcing it back after a major working was supposed to be a considerable challenge. Callo kept his eyes on his half-brother, relieved to see that Arias was coping with his usual grace.

"Indirectly. He's leaving, before nightfall."

"You, too, then?" Arias began walking toward the door, and Callo followed.

"I have asked to remain and await the Leyish ship."

Arias glanced over at him as they began walking down the stairs. "It's just a diplomatic delegation. You needn't wait. I am here, and my father."

"I must have time to consider things. It won't be the same at Sugetre. You will be staying here now."

"I have no choice anymore."

Callo noticed his half-brother didn't seem distressed about that fact, as he would have been had this been suggested to him a few days ago. The Collar did that; nothing was as important as the Watch now, or ever would be. Callo felt a twinge of irritation that Arias would not miss his friendship, and then shook himself free of that. It wasn't Arias' fault, far from it.

"Does Sharpeyes know what you're considering, that jealous fool?" The question had a bite to it. Callo felt better.

"Sharpeyes has ordered me to bring him intelligence, and I will do as he commands. In the meantime, Brother, our lady mother will be less than thrilled that I am staying, and I doubt she will be able to hide in her chambers the whole time I am here. Must I skulk about avoiding everyone as I have been doing? For a couple of sennights it was bearable, but I would much rather face her and have it done."

"Of course," Arias said, but Callo thought he sounded distracted.

Callo snapped his fingers, a sound which brought Arias' surprised eyes back around to his face again. "Don't fade off, Brother," Callo said, growing angry. "Fight that binding a little, will you? It's me here. We fought in the south together, remember?"

Arias flushed. "You need not remind me," he said. "It's because of you I'm here today."

"Well, then?"

"The damned Collar is new. It is everything I can do to—well, enough of that. I will support you as I can. You know that. I suppose I can send a message off to Sugetre with Rosh, to tell the Guardmaster I will not be returning? And to inform those at my lodgings?"

"If you're quick. I really think you'll have no need to tell anyone. Unfortunately, the story of your binding is common knowledge."

Unexpectedly and charmingly, Arias grinned. "I had no idea I was such a threat to Sharpeyes. The stories of my prowess go before me. Poor Lady Fiora! I hope she's happy with the old man."

Callo grinned too, glad to see his friend returning to his old self, relieved to see the cloak loosened about Arias' shoulders as his friend lost the strange chill that had gripped him after the attack.

"You'll do," he said. "Now let's just work on my future."

But any decisions about Callo's future were delayed as Lord Mikati, who had trouble with his heart and was now further weakened by the battle against the Black Tide, fell ill. The old lord would not stand for the new Healer to see him, so

Ruthan attended him at all hours, staying in a guest room in the Castle while Kirian tended to the needs of the villagers in Seagard Village.

"How's he doing?" Callo asked Arias as he passed his friend in the hall two days later.

Arias shrugged. "The Healer requested audience with all of us last night. She says there is not much she can do for this kind of heart condition. She says he needs good food and rest, and Jashan will decide." He paused for a moment, looking at his friend with tired eyes. "I have sent a messenger to try to inform Sharpeyes before he gets back to Sugetre."

"That close, is it?" Callo said. "That will be a burden for you and Forell and Eamon, to be alone on the Watch."

"They did it without me, remember. Besides, the old man wants to Watch."

"He's been taking a Watch? Hon Ruthan lets him?"

"You should know nothing stops my father from doing what he wants, especially when it has to do with the Watch. His binding won't let him rest if he hasn't Watched. He gets upset, and Hon Ruthan finally said to give him some time in the tower each day." Arias yawned. "He falls asleep, though. One of us needs to be there too."

"You look like you're about to fall asleep. Get some rest!" Callo put a hand on his brother's shoulder and pushed him off in the direction of his room. Then he continued on to the family breakfast room.

Lady Sira Joah looked up from her plate, her eyes wide as she saw him.

Callo paused. "Lady Alkiran!" he said. He bowed, then hesitated. "Would you like me to . . . I will return later."

"Stay. I understand you are lodging here for a while, and I am sick of my chamber walls. I suppose I had better greet you here and now." She did not sound happy to see him. Her eyes swept over him then fell to her plate. He had expected her eyes to be his own shade of amber, and was surprised they were the same pale gray as the King's. Her embroidered head veil, which had been pushed back behind her shoulders, drooped forward to shade her face.

"Greetings to you as well, Lady Mother." Callo looked at her for a moment, seeing the fine lines on the clear skin, the hands showing the signs of age. He could see a few strands of her hair under her veil, hair the same color as his, but sparked now with strands of white. Lady Sira Joah was only a year or two older than her husband Lord Mikati Alkiran, but she looked a decade older now.

A servant brought him tea and bread. The man's eyes were sharp and curious.

"I am sorry to hear about Lord Alkiran," Callo said. He sat and buttered his bread and spooned fish from the covered dish on the table. "How does he do?"

She shook her head. "Not well. He is very weak." She looked away from him and sipped her tea. The silence between the two of them filled up the room. Callo shifted in his chair.

"I will be civil to you," Lady Sira Joah finally said as she stood and pulled her cloak around her against the pervading chill in the room. "I do not expect to have to be friendly. Martan went against my wishes when he took you in. Arias did the same when he chose to have you as a friend. But it would not do for me to have to remain in my rooms the whole time you are here, and I know that Arias will not send you away as long as you wish to stay. The best for both of us would be for you to stay out of my way."

Callo could feel his mouth twist. "As you wish, Lady Mother," he acknowledged bitterly. He stood and bowed as she left the room. He supposed he should count it as a great improvement that she should be willing to see him at all. He had long known she couldn't stand the memory of her youthful indiscretion. But it was still strange to have her reinforce her hatred at the breakfast table, and in such an unemotional voice. He left his food uneaten and headed for the guardroom.

———

There was no guard duty for Callo to stand at Seagard Castle. With his men under the command of Drale, his second, now gone to Sugetre with the king, Callo found too little to do. Arias occupied himself with the Watch most of the day; with Mikati gravely ill, he had been taking on some of the old lord's duties as well. Callo rarely saw him, unless for an hour or so after the evening meal, when they would meet for wine and dice in the castle guard commanders' quarters.

Callo spent time in the ring, honing his skills, occasionally doing the Jashanite ritual when he felt his irritation threatening to escape his control. He knew others watched him. They always did, wherever he practiced the sword; his skill was well known. But he was surprised when one day he came sweating out of the ring to find Sopharin, Lord Mikati's representative to Sugetre, sitting on a bench with his legs crossed, watching him.

Sopharin rose when Callo neared him. The man wore garb completely unsuited to the ring—a gold-trimmed tunic and surcoat with green silk lining showing through artful slashes, and silk breeches. His boots were coated with the dust of the ring.

"My lord Callo!" Sopharin bent in an elegant bow. Callo eyed him with a slight frown. He never had much to do with the representative, and Sopharin was always scornful of him when they chanced to meet.

"Hon Sopharin." Callo bowed in return. Behind him he could hear the shouts of two combatants as they began their contest in the ring. "Have you come to speak with me?"

"I was told you were here each morning." Sopharin fell into step with him as Callo began walking back to the changing room. "I thought we must speak soon, with events in such turmoil."

"Turmoil? Oh—you refer to Lord Mikati's illness. Surely you should rather speak with Lord Arias? I have little familiarity with Lord Mikati. As you know well."

"You have given it little thought, it seems. It will indeed involve you, my lord." Callo could almost hear *my lord bastard* from the sneering lips. Nevertheless, in spite of his past disdain, the man had troubled to speak with him in private.

"It is most regrettable that Lord Mikati Alkiran is likely to go to the gods quite soon. I have the utmost sympathy for all his relatives— however incidental—and how they must feel on this occasion." Sophiran gave a sigh. "But reality must be faced, my lord. Great families such as this cannot go long without continuity in their representation in the capital. It may seem callous of me to be discussing such issues at such a time "

Callo made an impatient gesture. "You know well my connection to Lord Alkiran is slight. Spare me this delicacy. You wish to discuss your position? Arias is the one you should be speaking to, Hon Sophiran."

"At such a time it is difficult."

Callo doubted that. This thin man with a penchant for rich clothing had the sensibilities of an ox. Callo's stomach growled, eager for food after his exercise. Chiss stood in the shadows of the changing room, waiting for him. He shifted his weight from one foot to the other, certain that Sophiran caught his restlessness.

"Lord Callo, let me be blunt. Lord Arias has not had the

opportunity to get to know me. I dare say he thinks he does not like me. When Lord Mikati dies, Lord Arias is likely to ask you to become his representative to the capital."

"Me?" That surprised him.

"I think so. He trusts you greatly, my lord, a trust of which you are more than worthy. I myself have often been impressed by… "

"Hon Sophiran, please. You and I have not had occasion to speak much. What you know of me, I am sure, is what is spread about in Sugetre. There is no need to throw compliments in my face. So, you think Arias would choose me for his representative. And of this, you wish to say…?"

"Do not do it, my lord. If you were to try to accomplish the role of Seagard's representative, you would put the aims and directives of Lord Arias at risk. Simply because of something that is beyond your control, by which I mean the circumstances of your birth."

"Yes?" Callo looked at Sophiran's face, untrusting of its sincerity. He realized that Sophiran must feel his own position was greatly at risk, to warn Callo face to face like this.

"I have years of dealing with the King and other powers in the capital. I urge you, my lord, to ask Lord Arias to reconsider what is best for Seagard, not to decide based on shallow personal preference."

"Lord Arias has said nothing of this. I will bear it in mind. It is, uh, conscientious of you to mention this, Hon Sophiran." Callo bowed, politely dismissing the other man. Sophiran made a most ornate bow and left him. Callo looked after him for a moment, then turned and strode back towards the changing area. Chiss awaited him.

"My lord," he said. "Was that Hon Sophiran?"

"Amazing, isn't it? Yes, it was. Anticipating Arias' ascension to the lordship, and safeguarding his position."

"The man is a fop, Lord Callo, but dangerous."

"By proxy, like a poisoner."

"*Exactly* like that," Chiss said. "He is still someone to beware of."

"Thank you, Mother," Callo said. He grinned at Chiss, who simply shook his head at his employer.

"My lord, do not dismiss these concerns. Perhaps you have not thought—but since Lord Arias is now Collared and out of consideration for the throne—"

Callo made an impatient gesture. "Ander is the heir. I will never ascend to the throne. I have not the wish for it, nor the training for it, nor the power base for it. And if I ever tried, the assassins' guild would be swamped with business immediately."

"I am well aware of this. But, my lord, it puts you in a position of some power."

Callo shifted his shoulders, restless. He was still sweaty from the ring and hungry as well. "Enough of this. What do you have for me?"

"A messenger has arrived from the king. He is turning back, expecting to hear of Lord Mikati's death. Lord Arias asked me to find you and tell you the messenger has also asked about the Leyish ship. I told Lord Arias you had no word, but he said the messenger was most demanding."

It was time to send another man to Elder Hame, to ask about the delayed Leyish ship. He wondered if some trouble had befallen the Leyish emissaries the King had been awaiting. With Ha'las showing signs of aggression again, he only hoped the emissaries had not been taken prisoner. He took his leave of Chiss, cleaned up, and changed his clothing. He was only part of the way to the guardroom when the huge horn, usually sounded only for battle, reverberated through the air in the low note used for mourning. The sound throbbed like a living thing through the hall, and everyone stopped while it ebbed away. After a moment, it sounded again.

Lord Mikati Moran Alkiran was dead.

———

Jashan's temple shone with white, the color of rejoicing, the color of mourning. White symbolized the wholeness of all things. For a color mage such as Mikati Alkiran had been, it symbolized the unattainable.

The funeral chamber, with the dead lord on a bier in the front of the room, was blinding as the Alkiran family, neighboring lords and King Martan Alghasi Monteni, and Queen Efalla gathered to release Mikati from his earthly bindings, of which Callo knew there were several. There was not only the overriding binding placed on him by his overlord, to faithfully keep the Watch and defend against the Black Tide, but also a lesser binding to his wife, and there were others as well. The Collared lords and their families were webs of bindings. Lord Mikati's soul would not rest until he had been formally released.

In the midst of the chamber, behind those of greater rank, sat the solemn merchants and tradesmen of Two Merkhan who wished to mark his lordship's passing. The back of the chamber was crowded with the lowborn visitors from Seagard village, including the two Healers and the village elders.

Callo hesitated for a moment as he entered, one of the last to arrive. The guards at the door looked at him curiously as he paused in the doorway. It was only a moment until Callo caught Lord Arias' eye, and his brother gestured him inside the chamber to a place between the family and the King.

Callo took a deep breath and bowed as he took a place in the highest rank. He felt sure he would be sorry for this later.

Right now he didn't care; Arias' face was tight with strain in the middle of this gathering of vultures, and he was glad to be near enough to support him.

Lady Sira Joah's personal cleric, a pinched-looking man in spotless white, led the prayer and lit the ritual candles and lamps until Callo thought there was not a shadow in the place. Everything stood out in stark clarity as jewels blazed with the light. The unforgiving light exposed every line and blemish on the faces of the gathered mourners. It grew hot in the room; Callo, cursing his choice of the valus fur cloak, began to sweat.

The cleric began the story that was recited at every birth, and death of one of the *righ* class. Callo knew the story was pounded into the *righ* from the time they were born to make sure they internalized the pride due their class and accepted its obligation. Callo did not think this necessary; the *righ* he knew were altogether too enamored of their own status already. He sat back and listened to the story he had heard many times before.

It was the story of an early Righar, a land consisting of little states each ruled by a king or lord. The rulers raided each other, looking for riches in the form of cattle, cloth, gold, and sometimes slaves. They hired color mages to help them. The people who lived near borders wore themselves out in the constant watch for incursions, and they bore the brunt of the raids through the deaths of their men and the loss of their women, as well as through starvation when their crops or live-stock were stolen. The rulers of the lands, impoverished since they could not wring taxes from a starving people, struggled to end the constant warfare through marriage alliances, magery, and deceit, but failed. The wars grew more brutal.

Then Jashan made himself known to the man who eventually became the first King of Righar—Valotnor the Great.

Valotnor, ruler of a tiny plains kingdom in mid-Righar,

first saw Jashan when Valotnor was on the battlefield. A spear had been driven through his mail and into his chest. Blood bubbled out in his breaths and flowed from his mouth and nose. His enemy stood back, watching him die.

A warrior Valotnor did not know slew his attacker with a spear of color magery, before revealing himself to be the god Jashan. Then Jashan showed him what would happen to his land in the future because of this war.

Valotnor was not a compassionate man. Like his contemporaries, he did not hesitate to rape and pillage. Nonetheless, Valotnor wept as he saw his newborn son disemboweled by an enemy warrior, his wife raped, and his castle inhabited by his enemy. He felt the life leaving him, and asked the god to save him.

Jashan extracted oaths from him, and, to ensure that he followed them, the god bound him with a mighty spell and sealed it with a Collar, which he placed on Valotnor's neck as a symbol of his duty to his people, and a sign that he was favored by Jashan. Then he healed Valotnor and began an intimidating display of color magery that stopped the battle immediately, stealing all the power from the color mages involved.

Thus, this story provided the seed of the legend.

"Jashan is god of color magery, fire, light," the cleric said. "But first and foremost he is the god of discipline. This noble member of the *righ* who lies dead before us has dedicated his life to that discipline, for his god and King. Let us ask His Majesty to cut his binding, and we will send him to his god."

King Martan went to the front of the chamber. As Mikati's overlord, and a color mage, it fell to him to release the dead lord. Flashes of light began to etch his still form as he stood there and reached for his color magery. Green and blue, violet and gold, tendrils of color began escaping his control as he stretched his hands over the body of Lord Mikati. In the sudden glare, Callo fancied he could actually see the binding constricting Mikati, a veritable cable of light that wrapped the dead man and held him to the earth.

With a sharp movement, King Martan speared light at the bindings, and they split. The light dimmed; some of the candles in the room guttered and died. Two or three lamps were extinguished. Shadow reappeared, blessedly marking a return to the real world, and Callo released a breath he hadn't realized he had been holding. King Martan bowed to the dead lord and then took his seat. The cleric gestured to the slaves who were responsible for lifting the body onto the pyre that had been prepared on the cliffs.

As Mikati's body was carried out, the family followed. Callo decided not to follow. He had not liked the stern old lord, but he had no desire to watch him burn. Instead, he watched the mourners as they chattered their way out of the funeral chamber. Most of them had come just for the spectacle, and he couldn't blame them. He saw a few people he knew, including the two Healers from Seagard village, and nodded a greeting to them. Healer Kirian smiled at him with a glint in her eye, pretending to no sorrow, and he liked her better for it. The family saw Lord Mikati placed on the pyre and prayed over before they retreated to the Castle to wait out the burning. After the guests filed out, Callo joined the family and His Majesty King Martan in the upper solar.

As he entered, Lady Sira Joah pointed at him, her eyes bright with anger. "I have put up with his presence in this castle for sennights, but I will not have it now. Why should I have to have him here in the room, even as my husband burns on the cliff?"

Lord Arias' jaw clenched. Callo knew his half-brother had always been quick to defend him. But this was not the time.

"I'll go," Callo said. He bowed to them all, somewhat relieved.

"Stay," King Martan said. "Sira, Jashan knows Lord Callo cannot help being here. Ha, that was all your doing, remember? My nephew shall remain here. I wish to speak with him."

Lady Sira Joah pushed her luminous white head veil back and glared at the king. "It is not all my doing! If it were not for that demon of Ha'las and his evil, there would have been no half-*righ* bastard. And if it were not for you, Your Majesty, he would not have been allowed to live beyond his first day!"

Callo stopped short and stared at her. All other talk in the chamber ceased.

Lord Arias stepped nearer with narrowed eyes. "A ku'an from Ha'las, mother? Only now you tell him this, after all these years?"

The King grinned. "It is just like you, Sira, to let the secret out as soon as Mikati is no longer here to stop your tongue. Well, you'd best go on now, and tell the rest of it. You see they all wait with bated breath."

Arias' eyes sparked a little green. Callo saw him take a deep breath. "Mother—please continue!"

Lady Sira Joah turned away. "It was merely a slip of the tongue. I have no wish to go further into the matter."

"Lady Alkiran!" Callo said dangerously.

She stiffened but did not look at him. Her daughter, Litha Sira, took her mother's hand and clasped it in both of her own. The girl looked very pale, and her eyes darted to Callo's face as he spoke.

"My lady, I have never asked questions of you. Even when His Majesty required me to be here I have stayed out of your sight. But now that you have seen fit to announce the news in front of the whole family, I must know the rest."

The room seemed to wait in breathless silence, just for one

moment, and the sounds of the pyre and the crowd drifted up to the windows from far below and down by the sea. Arias, frowning, stared at his mother and said, "You must tell him now. Take him to the conservatory if you want privacy. You will be alone there—Eamon is Watching, and everyone else is here."

"I will not go with him alone, and I can't tell him here," Sira Joah said, head held high again.

"Tell him in private," said Queen Efalla, who was nibbling on sugared nuts at the table. "Sira, my dear, there is no taking back those words spoken without consideration."

"By Jashan and all the gods! I am glad every one concurs!" the King snapped. "I have had enough of this gentle coaxing. Go away, Sira. In fact, everyone out! Except for you, Lord Alkiran, since you are now Collared Lord. I'll speak to Lord Callo here. After all, I've work for him, which is why I had him come up here to talk to me in the first place. I am sick of all this wretched whining!"

The family members went quietly, respecting the temper of the king. Lady Sira Joah looked away from Callo's face as she continued out the door. Only King Martan, Lord Arias, and Callo were left in the drafty solar.

"Your Majesty," Callo said. "I must know the whole truth." He could feel his shoulders knot with tension.

"Yes, yes, yes," said King Martan irritably. "Well, then, you must both know. It was a traveling mage who stayed here at the castle a month or so."

"What do you mean, a traveling mage?" Arias said angrily. "My mother just said he was a ku'an, from Ha'las—" Callo knew his half- brother's dislike of the Ha'lasi would have been sharpened by the new binding which bade him bear constant guard against them, but he wished Arias would calm down.

"Your Majesty," Callo said.

"You are impatient. I am aware. As you have been told, the man was really a ku'an from Ha'las, but then we thought him a simple traveling mage. He was young and good-looking, claimed to be third son of some rural *righ* family. Lady Sira Joah was infatuated with him, and he favored her. She claims he manipulated her into his bed with his psychic magery . . ."

"And how do we know he did not?" Arias growled.

"What happened to the mage?" Callo asked.

"Long gone. Back in Ha'las, no doubt, and my spies could discover nothing of him in the capital. What he wanted, we never found out."

"You think it was part of a plan, then," Callo said.

"Of course I do. Why else would a ku'an be within our borders? Why, apparently, target the wife of a Collared Lord? No one was able to trace him when he left. He didn't go to Seagard Village or Two Merkhan or Sugetre or any other place we could find. We asked about him at all the ports and even sent spies to Ha'las. If he had been an innocent traveler, he would have been found."

"How did you learn he was ku'an?" Callo asked.

"The mage told her himself, when he left Seagard."

"But she never told my father!" Arias bit out. Callo wondered through his stunned confusion why Arias was so concerned about his father's honor now, when he had never cared before.

King Martan shrugged. His eyes dwelled with amusement on Callo, who felt as if his feet stood on shifting sand instead of the worn stone floors of the upper solar.

"To what point? The man was Collared; he couldn't leave and attack the Ha'lasi."

But you could have. The thought burned in Callo's mind, and he saw Arias' eyes drop and knew he was thinking the same thing. It would be worth their heads to ask why King Martan

Sharpeyes had failed to move the earth and sea to avenge his sister's lost innocence.

"Why did you take him in then?" Arias asked, as if Callo wasn't there. "Why did you feed him and educate him and even gift him with a holding, when my lady mother wished never to see him again?"

"It is better," said King Martan Sharpeyes, "To keep one's enemies—and their tools—under one's eye."

The King's tone was cold—absolutely bitter, with none of the malicious humor he had shown as he watched all their reactions to the news spilled by Sira Joah. Callo's gut clenched. There was no affection here, no sense of duty, as he had often imagined. Here was only a King, watching with his sharp eye over the future of his throne.

Arias walked over to one of the tall windows. The breeze came in, carrying with it the smoky odor from the pyre on the cliffs, but Arias seemed not to notice as he stared out over the sea in the direction of Ha'las. King Martan eyed his newest Collared Lord for a moment as if gauging his reaction, then turned to stare at Callo.

"I have work for you," he said.

"Your Majesty," Callo said, going on one knee. "With your permission, I claim leave."

"What? You have not been your brother's guest long enough?"

Callo did not need to look up to know that King Martan's cold gray eyes were on his face. Callo was not good at hiding his feelings. He could feel his shock and shame flooding his expression. His legs felt unsteady as he knelt. He had known, of course, that he was a bastard, but his Ha'lasi ancestry was a shock, as was Arias' cold reaction to the news. He had never thought he would hear Arias' scorn and anger directed at himself.

The King's eyes narrowed as Callo fought back the strength of his reaction, as if he could feel his nephew's turmoil.

"Where would you go?" asked the king.

"I am not sure yet, Sire. I could go to Ha'las."

"You should get back to Sugetre, away from the border," Arias said from the window.

King Martan ignored Lord Arias. "You would seek him out?"

"Perhaps. I do not know."

"Your chances of success are small."

"No doubt. I may try anyway. The attempts you made, years ago, were defeated while they were on guard against pursuit. And they say the ku'an have means to cloud the intellect."

"There are many rumors about the ku'an," King Martan said. "Their power over emotion is profound. But I never yet heard they could cast illusions or dreams over the mind. This is what Lady Sira Joah claims, that this mage tricked her with illusion and manipulation."

"Jashan!" cursed Arias, growing angry again.

King Martan was amused. "Calm down, Nephew. It has been thirty years, you know—far past time for rage. Callo, the truth is none of us know the limits of the power of the Ha'lasi mages. But then we had help. We had spies; we had mages. If she could find nothing, then you certainly won't succeed now."

"Nevertheless, Sire. I would like to clear this up."

"You must deal with that yourself. I grow weary of all this. The story's out; there is no more to say. Your leave is denied, Nephew. You will await those damned Leyish, if they haven't foundered in the journey. You have official status and your own troop to escort them to Sugetre. I need them before there is another Tide, by Jashan!"

There was no arguing with that. King Martan turned away as Callo bowed, then left the solar preceded by the guards who had been outside the door. His white finery flashed in the sunlight behind him. Lord Arias had bowed too, but he rose as the king left and looked at his half-brother. His face was unusually grim.

"Yes, I can see you don't like this a bit," Callo said. "How do you think I feel? But you'll have me out of your hair as soon as the Leyish ship arrives, Arias."

Arias shrugged, but his eyes were angry. He said nothing, just stalked out of the room after the King.

Callo sighed. The brisk sea wind changed direction and blew briefly straight into the room, carrying with it the unmistakable smell of the pyre. He looked down as his valus fur and saw the dark smudges of ash across his sleeve. Shock froze him where he stood for a moment, but he could feel the emotion pushing at his control, trying to escape. The wall he had built, with Jashan's help, to contain such a powerful feeling was trembling.

Chapter Five

Kirian scrambled up the slope between leafless bushes, her basket slung over one shoulder. She felt a tug on her cloak and reached back to pull it clear of the branch on which it had snagged. It was a good thing Ruthan had lent her this old, moss-stained cloak; it wouldn't win any prizes for beauty, but it was a veteran of herb gathering expeditions, and another hole wouldn't matter at all.

She rattled the rueberries in the basket, disappointed at the small pile. For some unknown reason—perhaps a trick of the late-arriving winter or the unusually large numbers of hungry migrating birds—the rueberries were scarce. The villagers and the Castle residents swore by Ruthan's headache remedy, but it required several baskets of rueberries, crushed and infused with other ingredients, to make enough for a typical year. This year, most of the rueberry bushes were already stripped of their fruit. Kirian had been searching most of the morning, climbing up the overgrown slope near the cliff path, until her hands were raw from holding onto rough branches, and the skin of her face felt stiff with cold.

Kirian stood to look out over the bushes. The wintry sun glared out of a cloudless sky. She thought she saw an untouched group of red-tinged bushes a little farther up. Perhaps there were still a few berries on those bushes. She sighed, pulled the cloak tighter about her, and leaned into the climb.

A flash of light caught her eye.

Kirian stopped. The flash had come from an area just off her intended path, where she knew there was a tiny clearing. As she scanned the area, she saw it again—sunlight glancing off metal.

She walked forward. She pushed aside branches and stepped between a group of tall, brown weeds—and stopped, gasping in shock.

There was a sword at her throat.

For an endless moment, Kirian stopped breathing and stared into the narrowed eyes of the swordsman. Then Lord Callo dropped his sword-point and stepped back.

Kirian caught her breath. The shock made her feel a little weak. "Lord Callo, I didn't know it was you."

Lord Callo dragged his forearm across his forehead. He was sweating and breathing hard. He said, "I didn't know anyone came up here."

With no apology from him for scaring the breath out of her, Kirian felt a twinge of disappointment. She had thought he was different from other nobles, but perhaps not after all.

"I was picking rueberries, although there are not many. Ruthan uses it for her headache tea. I'm sorry I startled you, my lord."

Callo moved his weight from one foot to the other, as if he was anxious to resume his practice. The sword was a splinter of deadly steel, balanced in one hand. She felt as if she had interrupted him at some religious rite. Puzzled, she backed off. "I will leave you, my lord. Good morning."

He nodded. The sun shone on those golden eyes, giving him a disconcerting, glowing look. She backed away, watching him. He lifted his face to the sky, briefly closing his eyes, seeming almost unaware of her, then stepped into his form again. Self-protective and a little frightened of his strange mood, Kirian decided to forego further berry-picking today. As she walked along an animal trail toward the cliff path, she heard a whicker and saw Miri, tethered loosely to a scrawny tree-branch.

"Hello, Miri," she whispered, not wanting Lord Callo to hear her. "How are you, pretty girl? And better yet, how is your master?" Lord Callo had the look of a man in trouble. She remembered the old lord's funeral, two days before. Surely Lord Callo was not mourning?

Well, Kirian told herself, what was it to her if some nobleman felt distressed? It was no concern of hers. But as she negotiated the cliff path toward the village, the memory of Callo's eyes stayed with her.

She had reached a steeper section of the path when she heard the jingle of harness and the thud of hooves approaching. With the caution this trail demanded, she stepped off the path to allow the horsemen to pass. They came into her sight, four of them, wrapped in fur cloaks, climbing two abreast. Instead of ignoring her on their way to the Castle, the lead horseman pulled his horse to a halt. His companions followed suit. The smells of horse and leather enveloped her.

"Would you be Hon Kirian, Healer to the castlefolk?" asked the man on the lead horse. He was a burly man with a thick black beard, and the tone of his voice showed he expected to be obeyed.

"I am," Kirian said. "Who are you?" She eyed the four horses nervously as they stood a little too close to the drop.

"I am Hon Jiriman, Captain of the Guard for Lady Mia Lon at Fortress Mount. I have been sent to look for an associate of yours. Come with me, Healer!" Jiriman wheeled his horse about with negligent disregard for the edge of the cliff and beckoned her up the trail, toward the Castle on the ridge.

Kirian's temper sparked at this rude summons. "I am returning to Hon Ruthan, the village Healer. I don't see any reason why I should follow you. If Lord Alkiran wants me to talk to you then I…"

"Insolence!" said one of the other men. "I'll take her up, Captain." Kirian stepped further back as the man grabbed for her arm. There was a rattle of displaced stones and a fifth horse made its appearance on the steep and crowded trail. Miri neighed and tossed her head as she was pulled to a stop. Lord Callo blocked the way, his face grim. His sword remained in its sheath.

"Who are you men?" he asked. "What is your business with this Healer?"

Kirian saw Jiriman evaluating the quality of Lord Callo's horse, his sword, and his accent. Jiriman's tone was somewhat more respectful when he spoke, but still allowed no dissent.

"Sir, I am Hon Jiriman, Captain of the Guard for Lady Mia Lon at Fortress Mount. A friend of this Healer's who was posted at Fortress is being sought for a crime. I must take this Healer up to the Castle to be questioned."

Kirian didn't like the feel she was getting from Lord Callo; the man seemed angry, unsettled. She remembered his demeanor as he practiced his sword forms in the clearing, and decided to end this confrontation.

"I will come," she said.

"You need not," Lord Callo said. "You, Jiriman, must speak to Lord Alkiran before seizing any of his people." Miri fidgeted and tossed her head as if the hand on her reins was impatient.

"Who do you think you are?" retorted Jiriman, his face flushing.

"My name is Callo ran Alkiran."

"Ah, I have heard of you. You are the Royal Bastard." Jiriman showed his teeth. "Let us by, Bastard."

Kirian was shocked at his tone. What was wrong with the man, who clearly knew Callo's identity as the King's nephew, yet mocked him in this way? The other horsemen had an ugly look about them too; what was wrong with all of them?

"By Jashan!" swore Callo, flushing in anger. His hand gripped his sword hilt. "You will have some respect for Lord Alkiran's authority, if not mine!" Miri's rear hooves were a few inches from the edge of the cliff. They displaced small stones as Callo urged her in toward the men. One of the guardsmen shoved forward, and Callo half-drew his sword.

"Stop!" Kirian demanded. She held up her hands as she stepped between the horses. "All of you, there is a wider part of the path a little way down. Take your quarrel there before someone ends up on the rocks!"

Lord Callo didn't move, but Jiriman cast a quick look down the cliff at the sea churning away at the rocks. He paled a little, and pulled back. With a sidelong look at Callo, he said, "Let us take this advice. Show us the way, Healer."

Kirian pushed her way between the knot of horses and walked a few minutes until the path curled to one side, into a small level area away from the steep edge. The horsemen followed her. She damped the strange irritation she felt under her skin—so strange, for her to feel so on edge, just like the men whose quarrel had blown up out of nothing.

She took a deep breath of the cleansing sea air and felt better.

The little walk to the level area had cooled the men's tensions.

Lord Callo sheathed his sword. He looked tired; the coiling tension was gone from his shoulders.

Jiriman still looked rather red in the face. "I apologize to you, Healer, and to you, Lord Callo. I don't know what—well, I will indeed speak with Lord Mikati before requesting your cooperation, Healer Kirian."

"Lord Mikati is dead," Callo said. "It is Lord Arias who is Lord Alkiran now."

"Indeed!" Jiriman said. "Then Lord Arias. I saw him once at Fortress Mount. He will not remember me, but he will remember Lady Mia Lon."

Now that it appeared that there would not be a battle on the cliff trail, Kirian was curious. "Captain, who are you searching for?"

"His name is Inmay, a Healer from the College. He is known to be a friend of yours, and it is thought he might have sought shelter here."

"I will tell you freely that I have not seen him at all, not since we parted on the way to our postings. What . . ." she cleared her throat, suddenly afraid. "May I ask, what is he accused of?"

"He has stolen a valuable slave. And he is accused of attempted murder against a lord of the land."

Callo was alert again, eyes narrowed. "Whom did he attempt to kill?"

"Lord Tilonar, Lady Mia Lon's lord husband. He is the slave's master. We will want to conduct a search—with Lord Alkiran's permission." Jiriman cast a placating glance at Lord Callo.

"I am sure Lord Alkiran will conduct the proper searches. I will take you up to him. Hon Kirian, you may return home with my own apology, and I'm sure that of these men as well."

She looked up at him with a rueful smile. It had been a disturbing morning, what with swords at her throat and near-battles on the cliff path. Callo smiled back at her, the sun gleaming on his fair hair, once again human and terribly attractive. She was glad to see the demons had fled his mind, at least for now.

"I do apologize, Hon Kirian," Jiriman said. "But I will be back in the village to see you later."

She nodded and turned her back on all of them. The few rueberries, somehow previously undisturbed by all the fuss, now rattled in her basket. She wished she could ask the men to make it up to her by getting her a few more baskets of berries, but, of course, that was inappropriate, though the idea made her grin. She heard them resume climbing the path, saddles creaking. Inmay was somewhere in the open with his slave girl, running from Fortress Mount's guards. She had no doubt he had committed the crime he was accused of; it was in his pattern, after all. She reached the end of the cliff path, came out onto blessedly level ground, and looked around at the village, brightened by the winter sun. She prayed to the Unknown God that Inmay didn't come here.

Tired, cold, and disconcerted by the morning's high emotion—Kirian still wondered, a little shocked at herself, why she had felt so angry on the bluff—she decided to return directly to Ruthan's house. She could put the berries in the window, where they would stay chilled until she felt able to make another excursion.

No sooner had she closed the door of Ruthan's house behind her than she knew something was amiss. Ruthan sat in the battered old chair facing the door as if she were awaiting

Kirian. The doors to both of the outer rooms were closed. Ruthan did not greet her. Kirian set the basket of berries on the kitchen table and returned to Ruthan's side.

"Well, child," Ruthan said. "You have visitors." The old woman's voice creaked, and her hands were clenched on the woolen shawl she wore.

"Who?"

"I fear it is that young Healer and the slave the guardsmen were searching for, not an hour ago. They knocked on the door immediately after the guards were gone up the cliff path."

"You mean they searched here already? Without telling Lord Arias?"

"We didn't encourage them, but yes. Lord Mikati would have clapped them into the cells for such presumption. I expect this new lord will be no different—he has a temper too, after all."

Kirian turned and stared at the two closed rooms where Ruthan saw those who needed her aid. "They are in there? Are they hurt?"

"No, just cautious. We didn't know who was at the door. I told the young man to leave, but he would wait for you."

As she spoke, a door cracked open and a pale face peered out. It was crowned by a thatch of fair hair streaked with premature gray.

"Inmay, I can't believe you would come here!" Kirian said. "Do you know I was stopped by armed guards on the cliff path? Take your friend and leave here. I want nothing to do with this."

Inmay came out of the room, followed by a woman clad in plain gray trousers and tunic. The woman looked straight at Kirian and Kirian caught her breath. She had never before seen anyone so beautiful. The woman had large, soft brown eyes fringed with thick lashes in a face that would have suited one of the gods. Her skin was honey-colored and smooth. Even through the stiff folds of her tunic, her graceful curves were apparent.

Inmay took the woman's hand and smiled at Kirian with pride. "This is Eyelinn. She and I are escaping together."

Kirian put her hand to her head. It had begun aching. Inmay's pride in his companion was so totally inappropriate that at first she did not know how to respond. Ruthan broke the silence.

"Then you had best escape faster, young one. I'll not call you a Healer anymore, since you've caused harm to another."

"I have hurt no one. Lord Tilonar was simply ill. Their talk of poison is nonsense. Is it not, Eyelinn?"

Eyelinn's glance flicked downward, hiding her eyes. "Yes. They made it all up." Her voice was as smooth as her skin. Kirian could almost understand, even in those few words, how Inmay could have got trapped in it, like a fly drawn to sugar. She cast a quick glance at Ruthan who sat staring at the slave with her all-seeing blind eyes and a frown on her wrinkled face.

"I fear that what you do not know has hurt you a great deal, young man," Ruthan said. "You will undoubtedly get what you both deserve. Well, Kirian? These are your friends "

"Friends? I think we are no longer friends."

Inmay said, "Now, Kirian…"

"You were once a friend of mine," she said. "We all stumbled all over ourselves to help you when you got into trouble in Sugetre—and yes, you got off easily compared to Hass, didn't you? Hass died for it! You have learned nothing. I don't know whether this woman manipulated you or you seduced her. Either way, I will offer you no aid. One of you is a murderer. You are putting me and Ruthan in danger just by being here.

What do you suppose Lord Alkiran will do if he discovers you? Or Hon Jiriman, if he thinks I lied about not knowing where you are?"

"Help us anyway, Kirian. Do it for me. For us. I love Eyelinn so much." Inmay came closer as if he wished to take Kirian's hand, but she stepped back.

"I have had my fill of helping you," Kirian said.

"We will manage without her," Eyelinn said to Inmay in her low, sweet voice. "We will stay the night and go our way. Perhaps this woman can show us the way to Two Merkhan—a way that will keep us away from any search parties. Jiriman knows me well, Inmay. He has followed me back at home, watching me. If he finds me, I will not see Fortress Mount again; even to stand trial before Lady Mia Lon."

"You see?" Inmay's frantic glance caught at Kirian's. "How can you resist that, Kirian?"

"I find myself quite able to. I have been caught in your toils before." Kirian sighed. "Ruthan, may I give them some fruit and the hard cooked eggs from this morning?"

The old woman nodded. "They can go up the cliff path— but take the fork, to go up to the caravan road. The way you came in, Kirian. The sooner the better, I say."

"And run right into castlefolk? We'll wait until nightfall." Eyelinn sat on one of the dinner chairs, drawn up to the table.

"If you wait until nightfall, you'll drive Ruthan into a nervous fit. And me, too. You'll go when I say you go, or I'll send a messenger to the Castle. That would save my skin, wouldn't it?"

Inmay's eyes were sorrowful. "You've become so cruel, Kirian."

"Consider yourself fortunate that you're getting food and directions. I am really tempted to give you neither." Kirian brushed past Inmay into the pantry area and shoved the eggs and some apples into a cloth sack. As an afterthought she threw in a loaf of bread.

When she emerged, Eyelinn was still seated at her ease, but Inmay stood fidgeting near the door.

Ruthan spoke up from her chair. "Kirian, my girl, I believe I hear horsemen on the path."

Kirian peered out the window and saw that there were indeed four horsemen just leaving the steep part of the trail. She thought she could see that one of the riders had a black beard. Her ears caught the faint sounds of hooves on the small rocks at the foot of the path.

"They could not have spoken to Lord Arias already?"

"Get us out of here, Kirian!" pleaded Inmay. Eyelinn showed no signs of panic. She stood, and her fine eyes narrowed. Inmay clung to her hand.

"Kirian!" Ruthan said, pushing herself forward in her chair. "You must not allow those men to find them here. Lord Arias has a temper, like Mikati. Your life will be in danger!"

"My *life?*"

Ruthan hoisted herself out of the chair. "You do not know what these lords can do. A Collared Lord can do anything, Kirian, anything. And no one will call him to account."

"I realize that, but I have committed no offense."

Ruthan, unusually agitated, waved Inmay and Eyelinn away. "Girl, you don't know. Neither did I commit any offense years ago when I told Lord Mikati I wanted to go back to my family after serving here for years."

"I thought he valued you. I thought he gave you your eyes of many col—"

"He did, child. He gave me these eyes, a miracle they are! But first he *took my own eyes*, and left me blind for months before he realized I could not serve him thus." Ruthan gasped for breath in her agitation.

Kirian felt her mouth drop open. "He blinded you?"

"Where are those men?"

Kirian looked. "They have stopped at Elder Hame's house."

"Get these runaways out of here! You must pretend to no knowledge of them, Kirian."

"What about you?"

"I am safe. I am old, and I am under no suspicion. But you — you have helped this idiot before. I fear for you, Kirian." Ruthan's voice cracked.

"All right, I hear you. Inmay, you and Eyelinn are to leave. Now!"

"We have no idea where to go." Eyelinn's voice was still calm. "The cliff path is apparently out."

Kirian thought fast. The couple could indeed no longer use the cliff path, since that would mean walking directly past the search party. "Go through the village, out along the strand. Those rocks over there hide a sea cave—the entrance will be exposed now, at low tide. You can hide there until Jiriman goes, and after that I care not what becomes of you. Ruthan, calm down, or you will take ill. Remember this Lord Arias is not his father."

"They are all the same, Kirian. All of them, the Collared Lords and their get. Where are those men?"

"They are at Hame's house. They are inside. Inmay, Eyelinn, go!"

Inmay pulled at Eyelinn's hand. "Let us go, my dear. They are too close."

She did not budge. "We know not where to go. This woman can show us."

Inmay looked pleadingly at Kirian. She cast a look up to the ceiling.

"Gods above, how can he be so helpless? Ruthan, I will take them to the cave and leave them."

"No! Kirian, I have come to care for you . . ."

"The fastest way to get them out of here is for me to take them. You had better follow me like my shadow, you two. And I don't care where you go, but do not trouble me again! Because I aided you in Sugetre doesn't mean I am an endless source of self-sacrifice, Inmay."

"We can see that," said Eyelinn.

"Come, then!" Glad she still wore her berrying cloak and tough shoes, Kirian gestured to the pair and peered out the door. The guardsmen were still in Elder Hame's house, horses held by one of the village boys near the wooden walkway in front of the house. The boy's back was to her, but one of Hame's windows was unshuttered and stared directly at Ruthan's house. Kirian said, "We will go out the window in the kitchen. Then, we go between houses until we reach the open strand. Then you run. Can you run, Eyelinn?"

"She has been a sheltered house slave," Inmay said. "Running will hurt her feet. She may fall behind."

Kirian almost hissed. "Then you stay behind with her. Once I start you off, you are on your own! Stay overnight in the cave—get far enough back and up to avoid the high tide. It opens in the back, up into the rocks—the village children hide there sometimes. In the morning, make your way to the Two Merkhan road. It is due north from the Castle; you cannot miss it."

Kirian opened the shutters and felt the cold air blow into the house. She climbed over the sill, scraping her thighs against the weathered wood, and dropped to the ground outside, out of sight of Hame's house. Inmay followed her and stopped to help his lover, who, as far as Kirian could see, needed no assistance at all. Once they were all outside, Kirian led the way from house to house, staying alongside the gray, paintless walls. She saw no villagers; between the wintry day and the earlier search by Jiriman's men, they were staying indoors where they were safe and comfortable. After a few minutes she heard voices and realized the guards were leaving Elder Hame's house and mounting. She waved the others into a shed—it was a pig shed, she noticed—and waited to see what the guardsmen would do.

Eyelinn made a face. "Must we go in here?"

"Shhh!" Kirian glared at her. For a slave, the woman seemed remarkably spoiled. Although considering her good looks, her duties were probably more of the bed than of the kitchen and field.

Inmay looked out over Kirian's head. In a choked voice, he said, "They are fanning out to check between the houses."

"Let's go, then—while we can!" Kirian took off out of the shed, running low to the ground past the last house, a tumble-down affair belonging to the village's least successful fisher-man, a single man who drank most of his good fishing days away. Their good luck ran out as they passed the ramshackle house. A male voice rasped, "Hey! Here they are!" It was Gremwar, the fisherman, probably hoping for a reward from Jiriman's men.

"Go! Run!" Kirian said. She shoved Inmay forward, toward the open strand. The low tide had exposed the smooth, gritty slope of beach that should allow for easy running. The tumble of rocks that concealed the sea cave lay before them, only a few minutes run across the strand. The rocks shone in the winter sun, their feet dark and wet from the receding tide.

"Hey!" shouted Gremwar again, coming out his front door and waving to the guardsmen.

Inmay and Eyelinn were running, Eyelinn's feet swift on the strand. Inmay pulled her by one hand, the gray strands in his hair reflecting the sun. Kirian stepped back into the pig shed, hoping to remain concealed in the odorous warmth while watching the escapees. A guardsman urged his horse between the houses.

"Hey! You!" Gremwar yelled, clutching his jug of ale. "They're getting away!"

Then the guardsman saw Inmay and Eyelinn and shouted for assistance. He spurred his horse away from the village. Water left in little hollows from the receding tide splashed up under the horse's hooves.

Eyelinn stumbled as she ran, falling to her knees. Inmay turned and looked behind, saw the galloping pursuer, and released Eyelinn's hand. He ran, sandals slipping in the damp. Eyelinn screamed after him, but he kept running for the sea cave.

Kirian saw two more guards riding hard after Inmay and Eyelinn, but they were too far behind to catch the runaways before they reached concealment in the sea cave. The first guard was the danger. He caught up to Eyelinn, reached down from his horse as he slowed to a walk, and grabbed a fistful of her tunic. Eyelinn twisted away, but the guard grabbed her by the hair and one arm and lifted her up off the gravelly strand.

Eyelinn shrieked and tried to kick him.

The guard laughed. He pulled Eyelinn to him, one hand now around her body under her arms, the other hand dropping his reins and grabbing at her breasts. He turned to his fellows, riding hard to aid him, and shouted: "I have a big catch here!"

The guard stopped short. He sagged, his mouth open wide though Kirian heard no sound. He released Eyelinn and clasped a hand to his chest. A red stain grew there, blood dripping through his fingers as he clutched his wound. His horse smelled the blood and shied so that the wounded guard swayed. The guard's face was as white as the sea foam. Eyelinn dropped to the ground, crouched down, and put the dagger back into its sheath, under her tunic. Then she ran for the sea cave, her hair flying.

One of the trailing guardsmen had caught up to the first. He stopped, slid off his horse and pulled the injured man down. Jiriman and the remaining guard rode hard after Eyelinn.

"Gods above," Kirian whispered. She saw the wounded man slump to the ground. There was blood everywhere. Eyelinn had clearly known where to strike. Kirian stifled an urge to run to the man's aid; she had no skill that would heal a wound to the heart. She slipped out of the pig shed and between the houses, heading back to Ruthan's house.

Halfway there she was met by Cam, the small boy who had been injured by Miri sennights ago. He carried her Healer's bag. He stopped her and whispered, "Hon Ruthan says not to go back, Hon Kirian. It's not safe. They saw you. They know you helped the man and the slave."

Kirian's heart sank. Jiriman must have seen her lead the pair between the houses. She gave the boy a quick hug and said, "Thank you, dear, and thank Ruthan for me. Tell her I will be safe."

Cam handed her the bag. It was heavier than usual; Ruthan must have stuffed some extras in. *Curse Inmay*, she thought. The man's selfishness had dragged her down with him, this time. She thought of Lord Arias as she had last seen him, cold and grim with his new Collar at Lord Mikati's funeral. Indeed, Ruthan knew these people better than she. If Ruthan thought Lord Arias was as cruel as the Collared Lord who had blinded her—who was she to disagree?

Kirian bid the boy goodbye and watched him scamper off. Then she returned to the welcome shelter of the pig shed.

Cracks between the wide boards allowed her to watch the activity going on down the strand. Apparently they had not yet caught Inmay and Eyelinn. Jiriman had returned from the chase to crouch near the fallen guardsman. One man still pursued the pair; he had apparently entered the sea cave, since his horse stood riderless near the rocks.

As Kirian watched, the two men on the strand stood, heads bowed, looking down at the wounded man. The gravelly sand around the fallen man was soaked with blood. Jiriman mounted his horse and began riding back to the village at a slow pace. Kirian supposed that the man Eyelinn had stabbed was dead and that Jiriman probably rode to get something to bring him back on.

She waited in the pig shed until they took the fallen man away. The horsemen climbed the cliff path back to the Castle. Inmay and Eyelinn were still free. The village remained still and empty; people did not want to get involved in this mess. A young woman came to feed the pig around dusk; although Kirian knew she could see her sitting against the interior wall of the shed, the woman said nothing to her, walking away when she was finished without a glance to show she knew Kirian was there.

When it was full dark and the tide was high, Kirian began walking along the strand toward the rocky outcrop. She could make her way in the dark through the rocks until she met the path that would join the road to Two Merkhan. Her mind was still in shock; she could not take in that her life at Seagard village was over, at least until she could contact the Healer's College and ask them to intercede for her with Lord Arias. Perhaps, too, they would not intercede – she was a charity student and had no noble family to agitate for her. Perhaps Lord Arias would not listen. These *righ* all stuck together, and an attempt had been made on Lady Mia Lon's husband, a *righ* lord.

She stumbled over some rocks. Travel was difficult; it was getting hard to see, and the mountain trails were hazardous at night. She felt she must press on in spite of the danger. At least the moon was full. She would find shelter at Two Merkhan, and consider her options.

Chapter Six

A groom jogged up to take Miri to the stables. Callo's hand dropped from the mare's bridle as he stared at Arias in astonishment.

"You just gave those men permission to turn the village upside down," he pointed out. Arias, who had just mounted his gray mare when Callo and Jiriman's group arrived at the Castle stables, raised an unfriendly brow.

"I will not deny access to Fortress Mount. They are seeking a murderer, after all. Do you think I will hide a criminal?"

"No. I just thought we should handle it ourselves."

Arias gave a humorless laugh. "I have other priorities than rifling through the village's closets and spare rooms. Let Jiriman do it."

"He is impatient. He'll get the village upset, and find nothing. A search party of your own men would have been wiser. Anyway, Hon Kirian told me she has not seen this man Inmay since she has been posted here."

"And you believe her?" Arias' gloved hands were tight on

the reins; the gray bobbed her head, pulling. His face was harsh, stern as his father's had been.

Callo said, "Yes, my lord, I do."

Arias did not object to the formal mode of address. In the old days, Callo remembered, calling him *my lord* would have sparked a quick, sarcastic reply. Or a laughing challenge.

"You ought to know better. A pretty face is not always an innocent one. Jiriman said she had dealings with this Inmay before."

Callo had worked hard in the little clearing to work away his anger and regain the god's gift of calm. In spite of his struggle, Jashan had not granted surcease from the crawling irritation—no, if he were honest, it was far more—a suppressed rage that had possessed him ever since the King had told him the secret of his parentage. He had been powerless to stop his anger from informing his actions on the cliff path. Now, he felt it rise up again. Hearing Arias—*Arias!*—cautioning him about being seduced by a pretty face was the last straw.

He said, with a growl in his voice that even he could hear, "I am glad you know best. Be on your way then, my lord."

Arias' eyes sparked red. "You'd better understand I do know best. Accept it, or leave."

"I barely know you since you got that damned Collar. I'm not going to suddenly bow down before you. You aren't any wiser than you were two weeks ago, my friend."

"This Collar," Arias gritted, "Means you'd better speak with more restraint!" His hands on the gray's reins were wreathed with color. The gray felt the energy; her eyes showed white.

Callo's temper flared in instinctive response. Then he took a deep breath and quelled it. Anger would not help resolve this regrettable scene at all.

He took a step backward and bowed. "My lord."

"Good to hear you acknowledge it!" flamed Arias. He spurred the gray into a nervous trot and proceeded across the open area. It looked as if he were riding out to the caravan road.

Callo stood and looked after him, then took a deep breath. It could have come to blows, or worse; and since color magery could subdue even the most skilled swordsman, he knew he wouldn't have made it alive out of that encounter unless Arias came to his senses and remembered that Callo was his lifelong friend. That seemed unlikely, given Arias' demeanor since he had learned of Callo's parentage.

Callo missed the old, carefree Arias. This new man was too like Mikati. The Collar had completely changed him.

He proceeded to the stable to check on Miri. The groom had cared for her well; her tack was off, and she was covered with a blanket and nosing into a bucket of oats. As he stood and stroked her glossy neck, he heard the sound of a throat being cleared.

"Yes?" he said without turning.

"My lord," said Chiss' familiar voice, "This boy has been looking for you."

Callo turned to see Chiss with one of the village boys, a young man of about twelve years old with a thatch of dirty brown hair. The boy gave an awkward bow. Callo sighed and gave the boy his attention.

"Lord Callo, Elder Hame sent me to tell you the ship was sighted at noon today, just off the High Rocks." The boy was breathless, either with his news or the climb on foot up the cliff path.

"At noon? When will it make port at Two Merkhan then?"

"Should be tonight, or by dawn latest, my lord."

"Good. Good news at last, Chiss! Show this boy into the

kitchens, will you? Cook will get you something, boy—what is your name?"

"Linle, sir—my lord."

"Linle, then. Here is something for your trouble." A coin changed hands and the boy bowed, thrilled. "Give Elder Hame my thanks. Chiss, when you are done . . .?"

"Yes, my lord. I'll be back."

Callo watched them leave and turned back to Miri. She nickered at him and he smiled, his heart lifting. The wintry sun reached through the open doors of the stable and sent tiny specks of floating dust and hay spinning like gold in the air. The bulk of the Castle was hidden from this angle, and the Watch tower, with Forell or Uncle Eamon on the interminable Watch, was high above them, likewise invisible from the comfortable horse-smelling stable. He felt a sense of freedom he had not experienced since he and Arias had been with the military in the south. After a few minutes he began to hum an old tune, and heard Chiss stop short as the man returned to the stable.

"Chiss!" he said. "I have news for you."

"Yes, my lord?"

"I will be leaving a message for Lord Arias regarding the Leyish ship. He should be back in a candlemark or so—enough time to organize a party to greet the diplomats. Will you see he gets it, please?"

"Of course, my lord." Chiss looked at him with his narrow head cocked, as if trying to figure something out. Then he said, "I am glad to see you feeling better."

Callo smiled. Chiss, who had been his friend and mentor since Callo's ninth birthday, would certainly have noticed Callo's uncertain state of mind over the last few days. He probably knew the cause of it too, though Callo had not shared that story with anyone.

"I am feeling better. I have reached a decision and that has cleared my mind. Chiss, after you have delivered that message, I want you to consider yourself free to do whatever you want. Go back to my estate if you wish, or to Sugetre. It is your choice. I release you from your oath."

"And you, my lord?"

"I am taking unauthorized leave."

"May I ask . . .?"

"Where I am going?" Chiss nodded. "To Ha'las, Chiss, on that Leyish trader if they'll take me. I think I'd like to find some things out for myself."

He gave Miri a last pat on the nose and walked out of the stable. He would have to pack some things, and make sure he carried ample coin and convertibles for the Leyish, who certainly wouldn't transport him out of charity.

He heard footsteps behind him. Chiss stopped him in his tracks by saying, "I would come with you, Lord Callo."

"No. I can't ask that of you."

"You are not asking it. I am offering. I have been with you for near twenty years."

"I know it. Don't think I would dispense with your aid lightly. I know very little about Ha'las, but I do know it's dangerous. I don't know when I'll return. Why would you want to join me?"

Chiss shrugged. "There is nothing else I want to do. I would be bored to death waiting for your return. In Sugetre my services would likely be commanded by the King."

"And you would not like that."

"I wouldn't care for it, no," Chiss said.

"So you want to come along and tend me in Ha'las."

"I have enjoyed doing so the last twenty years."

"Have you! I don't remember you always thought it that enjoyable." Callo paused. The thought of having Chiss along on this foray into a strange land was very reassuring. "I shouldn't allow it."

Chiss, knowing him well, said nothing. Callo looked at the narrow face and dark eyes, remembered Chiss' quiet support during his troubled years as a child in the King's palace. Chiss had taken it upon himself to search for a warrior-priest who would show the boy how to use the ancient forms to channel his inconvenient emotions that seemed to spark unrest around him. He smiled at Chiss.

"Thank you," Callo said. "I hope you don't regret it later."

"Go then and write your message, my lord," Chiss said. "I will pack our things."

A candlemark later, message delivered, and belongings packed with Chiss' usual efficiency, Callo and Chiss rode down the road to Two Merkhan. There were only two bags strapped onto the horses and an additional pack wrapped around Chiss' shoulders, but Callo knew Chiss would have thought of everything. The Two Merkhan trade road split off from the caravan road and wound through mountainous terrain, looping to minimize the slope of the road. Miri, prancing in the cold air, pulled at the rein as if she wanted to run, but Callo held her in.

They passed two farm carts on the way into Two Merkhan. They carried burlap-covered loads, probably stored hay. A lone man on horseback rode in the opposite direction; apparently unarmed and dressed as an artisan, he nodded at them and went on. There was very little traffic; Callo found himself thinking back over the events of the last two sennights and of Arias' increasing hostility. Every now and then a memory of his estate would intrude, or he would recall his steward (a man he had always considered a friend as well as an employee), or he would think of some friend in the capital like Lady Phoire. Twice, Chiss' voice startled him out of deep thought and he had to ask the man to repeat his words. After that Chiss left him alone.

After a while, the sun sank behind the peaks and the road fell into a dank early dusk, then night lit by a full moon. They saw a cloaked figure walking on the side of the road. Callo recognized the moss- stained cloak and the spiky hair. He spurred Miri forward, ahead of the walker, and then turned back to face Healer Kirian.

"You!" he said. "What are you doing here?"

The healer looked up at him. Even in the monochromatic quality of the light from the full moon, it was apparent that her face was red from the cold. Her hands, holding her bag, were bare. It was easily a couple of hours from the village on foot. Suddenly the road looked very lonely indeed. He could not reconcile her presence here on this unwelcoming winter road, alone, with what he knew of her. There were enough inconsistencies in his life lately, he thought with a twist of annoyance; he needed no more.

"I am travelling to Two Merkhan, my lord."

"By yourself? At night? With not even a donkey cart?"

"Donkeys are not numerous in Seagard Village," Kirian answered. "I will be fine, my lord. Please continue on. It is not much farther."

"Was this a sudden decision?"

Kirian ignored his question, looking up at him with those soft brown eyes, now shadowed by a frown. "It is late, my lord, and I am tired. I would like to get in to Two Merkhan sometime before midnight. Must we hold this conversation now?"

"Chiss! Have you room on that nag of yours?"

"Yes, my lord."

"Take the Healer up, will you?"

"Yes, my lord."

"I will take the extra pack, and her bag," Callo said, reaching for the brown-wrapped bundle.

Kirian waved the manservant off. "Now this is ridiculous! I don't want to ride in with you, Lord Callo."

"Why not? Chiss said he would take you up. It is getting cold, in case you hadn't noticed. And I couldn't swear to there being no bandits on this road at night."

Kirian's shoulders slumped. She looked very cold indeed with only the thin cloak wrapped around her, especially now that the winter sun was gone. She said, "I will ride in with you. My thanks, Hon Chiss."

"Just Chiss, Healer. I am a servant." Callo dismounted and helped Kirian up, behind Chiss. Chiss handed Callo the bags and waited while Callo fastened the bags down behind his own saddle. The manservant found a blanket in their possessions, and gave it to Kirian to wrap around her shoulders before they continued on. Miri pulled at the bit, wanting a warm stable. Callo murmured, "Almost there, Miri, my good one."

There was no conversation between Chiss and Kirian on the other horse. Callo felt his weariness slam down on him as if he had been hit with a board. There was no one else on the road, and he had just spotted the lights of Two Merkhan in the valley below them, when there was a muted rumble behind them. Callo stopped and turned, hand on the back of his saddle, listening; he could hear the jingle of a bit, the sound of someone calling.

"Off the road!" he ordered. He dismounted and led Miri off the road. There were big boulders clustered where they had tumbled at the foot of a steep slope, and a couple of stunted evergreens with roots winding between the rocks. The bright moon lit the area well enough for them to find concealment. It would have been easy for Miri to put a foot wrong in the jumble of rocks; he took care. "Shh, Miri, my girl," he whispered, and the mare stood silent. Chiss led his horse in and pushed the stolid gelding near Miri. Callo thanked Jashan that the gelding was so calm in temperament. He saw Kirian climbing up the rocks, her feet slipping against the stone, and wondered what the Healer thought of all this. The thin ever-greens provided very little cover, but he knew the emissaries from the Castle were riding to greet the Leyish dignitaries, and would not be looking for them.

The small, fur-cloaked group of riders carried Arias' banner and two torches to light their way. Their horses wore gold at throat and chest, caparisoned to honor the Leyish dignitary. The group rode past. Not one of the riders even glanced to the side of the road. Callo watched them continue down the road, and then stopped as the sound of quick hoof-beats came from behind.

The fast rider caught up with the escort and pulled up his horse. He spoke to the men, speaking fast and gesturing. Callo could hear only a few words here and there, but the gist of the communication was enough to make him frown. After they rode on, he led Miri from their hiding place to the road, turned and frowned at the Healer. "Hon Kirian, you owe me an explanation."

The healer flushed. "Lord Callo, if an explanation is the price of this ride into Two Merkhan, I'll leave you now. It is not your concern."

"I defended you on the path this morning, and believed you when you said you knew nothing of the criminals. But here you are, alone and on your way out of the village, on the same road where they are being sought. You don't appear to be on a feastday jaunt, Hon Kirian. I defended you to my bro — I defended you, when he would say you could not be innocent."

"My lord, the Healer was alone," Chiss offered.

"Thank you," Kirian said. "Do you see any fugitives with me, my lord?"

"Obviously not." Callo controlled his temper with a quick flash on Jashan's ritual. "Then what is going on, Hon Kirian? Why do you travel here at this hour, with no baggage?"

Chiss had led his gelding out of the rocks and back to the road. Now he nudged Kirian, directing her to re-mount. With a frustrated sigh, she let Chiss help her up, and then sat glaring at Callo like a queen would at a recalcitrant servant. Her spiky hair showed her ears, which were red from the cold.

"I cannot tell you," she said.

Callo swore. Miri fidgeted under him. Chiss mounted behind Kirian. It seemed Chiss wanted to proceed as before into the port city, regardless of the argument between his lord and the Healer.

"I did not lie to you," Kirian went on. "My lord, I told you I had not seen Inmay. That was true."

Miri snorted irritably and tried to sidle out from under him. She wanted a warm stable and her feed, and here they were standing on a dark road at night arguing. Callo felt his stomach rumble.

"Perhaps you have seen him since," Chiss said.

"I was blameless in this affair," Kirian said. "But I was seen with Inmay in the village after you took Jiriman to the Castle. I gave them supplies and told them to leave. My mentor told me of Lord Alkiran's wrath. She said my life was in danger and that I should leave."

"Your life is in danger?" Callo repeated.

"I could not risk it. Ruthan was terrified that Lord Alkiran would punish me. She said my life was in danger."

"From *Arias?*"

She lifted her chin defensively. "I see you don't believe me.

I do not know Lord Arias well. But perhaps he has changed since he was Collared."

Callo reined Miri around and spurred her on. The other horse followed. His thoughts whirled. Yes, Arias had changed. But after the initial shock of his violent binding wore off, surely Arias would regain his old easy ways. Never, never would Arias take a life for no more serious a thing than what Kirian had done.

Then he swore to himself. He was not certain. No matter how he reasoned with himself, he did not truly know what the Collar had done to Arias. The *righ* were a self-protective group, jealous of their honors. He knew well what brutality those in power were capable of in pursuit of their own ends. King Martan Sharpeyes had given him numerous examples, and he knew the Collared Lords were notorious for their brutal punishments. In his experience, those who possessed power cared nothing for those who did not.

He slowed, and Chiss' mare caught up to them. They were on the last slope. The lights of the first inn on the outskirts of the city shone at them. It looked welcoming, warm and loud.

"Hon Kirian, where are you going? Are you expected somewhere?"

"I will call on Hon Ruthan's herb-seller. I'm sure he will let me stay with him for a while."

Chiss made a skeptical sound in his throat. "Where is this herb seller?"

Kirian sighed. "I am not sure, Lord Callo. I will stay at this inn, or another. It matters not. Leave me here, would you, and go on your way."

He frowned. This inn looked welcome enough, for travelers on a cold night, but perhaps it was a little shabby. The sound of loud singing came from the common room. Four horses were tied outside as if their riders had stopped for a quick drink and a meal but would not be spending the night. He would not be at all surprised if there were willing women inside, catering to such travelers. He shivered as the wind picked up.

"Not here," he objected.

Another sigh. "My lord, thank you for your concern, but please spare me your gallantry. I am very tired. I won't be spending any time in the common room drinking, I promise you that."

"Hang on another half a candlemark, Healer. I am not going to leave you here."

"It's not up to you, Lord Callo," she snipped at him, but he saw her look again at the inn and then look down. She made no move to dismount.

"My lord," Chiss said. His voice was dry with the cold. "If I may. Can we take our discussion inside, perhaps at the Maindeck, and warm up whilst we argue?"

He grinned. "Absolutely. Lead on, then."

Chiss led them down Two Merkhan's streets until they drew up at a big old inn near the port itself. The building was large and clearly catered to the upper classes; there were liveried slaves carrying bags, grooms ready to care for their horses, and a courteous steward who made no comment about the way they had arrived but conducted them to two small adjoining rooms with a central parlor as Callo requested. Then the steward ordered food and drink for them and left them alone. Callo lay down on the bed for a moment and dozed off; wakening to Chiss' voice telling him that their refreshments had arrived.

He yawned. It seemed very late, although it was still a candlemark short of midnight. Perhaps the cold air and the long ride had done that to him. He found that Chiss had ordered hot water, so he washed his face and re-tied his hair, feeling better right away. The savory aroma wafting from the parlor drew him in, his stomach rumbling.

Kirian sat at the tiny table with a bowl of stew before her. She looked tired but somewhat refreshed. Chiss was eating, too, but when he saw Callo he rose as if to serve him. Callo waved him away.

"No, you eat," he said. "Feeling better, Hon Kirian?"

She looked up at him unsmiling. "I must thank you for all this, Lord Callo."

"You are welcome." He spooned stew from a tureen into a bowl and pulled off a piece of bread. He sat and took a deep draft of the ale that Chiss had poured. "Ah," he said, relaxing. "This is very good." The bread, made with little red seeds in it, was warm and comforting. After chewing a piece, he took a generous spoonful of the thick stew. There was a brief silence as they all indulged in the excellent fare.

Then Kirian said, "My lord, may I ask a personal question?"

His brows went up. "I suppose."

"Where are *you* going, so late at night?"

He considered his answer. Before he could speak, she added: "You also are traveling alone, and packed for a journey. I thought you were on some mission for the King or Lord Arias, but I am not so tired that I'm stupid. You hid from Lord Arias' men."

He couldn't help but grin. "I thought that little fact wouldn't escape you. Thank you for holding your curiosity in check until we were warm."

"Well?"

He smiled at her. Full of stew and ale, tired but warm, he began to be amused by her lack of proper social conventions. Perhaps she was too tired to remember that she should not question a *righ* lord – even an outcast like himself—like this. Or perhaps it was ingrained. They did teach etiquette and diplomacy at Healer's College, did they not?

"You needn't answer, my lord," Kirian said, but she looked unhappy.

"It is as you have guessed," he said. "We are on no mission but our own. In fact, Lord Arias may send men after me. When King Martan discovers I have left, he will seek to punish me as well."

She frowned. "This does not sound good, my lord."

He shrugged. "It is as Jashan wills. I am taking unauthorized leave."

"Where are you going?"

He didn't know why, but he wanted to tell her. "To Ha'las, Healer, on that Leyish ship if she'll take me."

"Ha'las."

Another sip of ale went down like silk. He could almost forget Arias' face this afternoon as he threatened him with color magery. He looked out the parlor's little window and said, "I would appreciate it, Hon Kirian, if you would keep this information close."

"Of course." A pause. She was watching him with those acute brown eyes. "Do you know anyone in Ha'las?"

"Not a soul."

Chiss regarded him for a moment and said, "If I may, my lord."

"I think we need not burden Hon Kirian with all my reasons for this journey," he said to Chiss. She did not need to know that Callo had discovered that his life had been a lie, and that he had decided he could not live this way, a supplicant to an uncle who was using him only as a tool.

"I only ask because, well," she hesitated, "I wondered if I might come with you."

He almost choked on his ale.

"I beg your pardon, Hon Kirian?" Chiss asked.

She sipped at her ale. Callo noticed a rather becoming flush on her cheeks, from warmth and ale and possibly a little embarrassment. "I wondered if I might accompany you."

"No," Callo said. "This is not a pleasure trip, Hon Kirian."

"I realize that. I have only two choices, as I see it. I can remain here—in an inn—or find employment somewhere, but not as a Healer for a while, so that if Lord Arias is seeking me, his men will not find me. Or I can join you."

"Then you have only one choice," Callo said.

"Hon Kirian," Chiss interjected, "This will be a dangerous journey. We have no experience of Ha'las, other than to know the ku'an are hazardous. Our return is uncertain. It is not safe. Why by the Unknown God would you want to come to Ha'las?"

She shrugged. "A sense of adventure. I don't know."

"You can return to Sugetre," Callo told her.

"I don't think so. Remember I am thought to have aided someone who threatened the nobility. The *righ* will seek me everywhere, and they may demand aid from the King. Sugetre is unsafe."

"The *righ* don't care about you," Callo said. "You exaggerate your importance in all of this. And Arias would not have you slain."

"And Lady Mia Lon, and her husband who was the target of their attempt at murder?"

"I suppose I can't speak for them. Tilonar is a fool, always was." Callo thought a moment. Clearly he would not convince her that her life was not at risk. He wondered what the other Healer had told her, to make her so afraid. "Then if you must hide, hide here. What about staying with this herb seller?"

"I have met him only once. I have been thinking that it is

very likely he will turn me over to Lord Arias' men for a reward."

"Then you must hide elsewhere."

"I suppose that is what I must do." Her hand was at her belt, unfastening her purse. There was a jingle of coins. She was counting. "I see I have sufficient money to stay in Two Merkhan for some time. I will say farewell then, my lord, and take my leave in the morning. Thank you for listening." She pushed back her chair and rose.

"Wait." Callo frowned. "How much money do you have?"

"That's not a problem, my lord. I can easily support myself for a sennight or two."

He felt his temper flicker. "That's not what I asked."

"It's not your concern."

"Chiss, will you get my purse, please? I want to give Kirian some additional funds."

"I will not accept it," Kirian said.

"Because you have enough, as you have said." He rose and began pacing to discharge some of his tension. The woman was as irritating as sand in the eye. Why could she not accept a little money? What if she starved here, stubborn as an ox until the end?

She eyed him. "I am sorry you are upset. Look, I'll show you." She took the purse and spilled the coins into her palm, then onto the table. Ten silver kels rolled onto the table top.

Chiss coughed.

Callo said, "Ten kels?"

"My savings. This is really quite a sufficient amount. I will be fine, as you see."

"Kirian. You cannot think you can feed and house yourself in Two Merkhan for—several sennights—on ten kels?"

"I am certain I can, Lord Callo," she replied with some surprise. "Not here, of course." She gestured at their comfortable surroundings and the remains of their meal. "But this will feed me for quite a while. But now that you have put the idea in my head, I may just try to buy passage to Ha'las for myself."

"Ghosian wouldn't take you. It's illegal."

"You must think he's willing to circumvent the law, or you would not be here."

"Can you not go somewhere else—anywhere else?" Callo snapped.

Chiss added, "There are many places in Righar that might be safe for you. Have you no family—no friends elsewhere?"

"None. I am alone. How much do you suppose passage to Ha'las would be?"

"Jashan's eyes!" swore Callo. "You try me. All right, then. You have beaten me down. Come with us to Ha'las, then, if you must. At least you will not starve in the streets."

Her face lit up. "Really?"

"I said so," he said, knowing he was glowering at her.

She made a quick instinctive motion, almost as if she wanted to put her arms around him then stopped herself. Her smile brightened the room. In spite of himself, he felt his shoulders losing their tension. "I can't wait!" she said.

Chiss made a motion of protest.

"Chiss?"

"If you will forgive me, Hon Kirian. You should not approach this as a vacation. It is possible that none of us may live through this adventure."

"Oh, I know that, Chiss. But right now, with this terrible day behind me, and a journey ahead of me to *Ha'las*, of all places—I'm thrilled. It's much more exciting than sitting in some inn hoping to be overlooked for a few sennights."

"You said you have no family to miss you. Have you no one to wonder where you are?"

"No one. This is the first time I have ever been glad of it, since they cannot forbid me." She smiled at Callo again. He was charmed, his tension gone. He smiled back. Perhaps she would be a good companion on this journey.

Then she yawned, and watching her, he did as well. Chiss' narrow face creased in a smile. "If I may, my lord," he said, "I will order you both to your beds."

"I will help clean up," Kirian offered. "There is no reason Chiss should have to stay working while we sleep."

This had never occurred to Callo; Chiss was a manservant after all, and paid well to do exactly that. But he could not allow Kirian to stay cleaning up the room while he retired. He was not sure why, since she was in fact of common birth and, as a Healer, was used to physical work. But whatever the reason, he could not. He began to set his bowl onto the waiting tray when Chiss said: "The house servants will do that, my lord. I am off to rest. I bid you good night." Chiss bowed and retreated to the room he would share with Callo, where he would sleep on a servant's cot near the door.

"Good evening," Callo said. Kirian covered another yawn and bid him a polite good night, vanishing into her room. Callo returned to his room and changed into the sleeping clothes Chiss had packed, feeling the day's stresses melt into weariness. He lay on the bed, almost asleep already, aware, through his exhaustion, of Chiss fidgeting with their packs, searching for something. Then he sighed and sleep took him before he could even acknowledge Chiss' good night.

Chapter Seven

Daylight reached its pale fingers under the shutters. Kirian curled tighter under her wool blanket. She listened hard; there was no sound from the adjoining bedchamber.

She smiled. In spite of everything, she felt good, charged with anticipation at the adventure ahead. It had taken no small amount of persuasion to convince Lord Callo to allow her to go with them to Ha'las. Showing him her savings had been a stroke of genius. Ten kels would have kept her in relative comfort for a sennight or two until she could find a way out of Two Merkhan; but he was accustomed to a different style of living, and she had guessed it would look insufficient to him.

She stretched and grinned. She couldn't account for it herself, but after Callo's brief statement of his destination she felt a powerful urge to go with him. The thought of Ha'las, dark and dangerous, had taken possession of her. For the first time in her life, she would do something on her own, without being directed to it or expected to do it because she was a charity student.

The thought of betraying her oath was shrugged aside with barely a thought. There were people in Ha'las who could use the services of a Healer. She could serve the sick wherever she went. There was no need to abandon her Healer's oath simply because she was leaving Righar.

A muffled sound in the next room told her someone was awake and moving around. She threw off the blanket and hurried into the spare set of clothing Ruthan had stuffed into her Healer's bag. She dragged a comb through her hair—thank the Gods for short hair that required no time at all to make presentable. A brisk swish of lukewarm water from the washing jug served for her teeth since she was in a hurry. Stuffing her old clothes back into her bag and donning her cloak, she was ready to go. She intended to dog their steps today until they were all safely on board the trader. Given a chance, Lord Callo might leave her here after all, and she didn't intend to give them a chance to get out of her sight.

She peered into the hall twice, but saw no sign that her companions were up and about. By the time she heard a tap on the door she had re-brushed her teeth properly, opened the shutters to let in the cold morning sunshine, and been bored for a while. Once, she imagined that they had departed without her, and she was about to leave a whole kel on the nightstand for payment and take off after them. She wrenched open the door to see Chiss, who held a tray with a steaming cup of tea.

"Good morning, Healer. Would you like some tea?"

She stared at him for a confused moment while she rearranged her expectations. A corner of Chiss' mouth twitched. He said, "My lord is still asleep, Hon Kirian. He will not leave without you, now that he has agreed to take you with us."

Kirian sighed. "I have not been raised to expect honor from the nobility, Hon Chiss."

"Indeed. You can believe me in this, however. Have some tea while you can. The servants will bring up breakfast in a few minutes."

"Thank you." Kirian took the mug and inhaled the sweet aroma.

The first sip scalded her tongue. She said, "Have you a moment to have some tea yourself?"

"I will wait for breakfast, thank you. I must go awaken Lord Callo."

"When do we leave? Do you know?"

"I assume we will visit the ship this morning. Lord Callo will want to wait until the emissaries have gone. I have no idea when her captain will plan to leave port."

"How do we know they are going to Ha'las?"

"I know of this ship, and her captain. They frequently make secret runs to Ha'las from here, since we are the closest port to Las'ash." He paused, looking at her. "That is the capital of Ha'las, and the only port of any size."

"Thank you."

After Chiss left, Kirian took some time to go through her bag. Ruthan clearly expected her to stay away from the village for a while. The old woman had packed a change of clothes, tooth powder, a comb, a cake of soap. There was a crumbly oat cake and some dried fruit wrapped in a dish cloth at the bottom of the bag. As expected, there were her Healer's supplies: bandages, a few essential herbs in pouches, and the precious Healer's knife which had been presented to her at graduation. Kirian packed everything away again, blessing Ruthan. She hoped the old woman would not worry.

Kirian took the bag with her to breakfast. As she entered the parlor, Chiss was reading something by the light of the window. It appeared to be a message, scrawled on quality paper. He started and stuffed the paper away in his pocket as she came in. Kirian gave him another good morning and settled in to eat. There were boiled eggs, and bread with cheese, and more tea, as well as a jar of ale. On a plate sat three huge pastries, filled with gooey sugar and butter and cinnamon. She smelled them across the room. After yesterday's cold, hungry walk, it seemed a feast.

"Where is Lord Callo?"

"I believe he went out to look around." Chiss sipped his tea.

There was only an egg and some fruit on his plate.

Kirian rose and went to the tiny window. She looked down at the street, watching the passers-by. A carter drove his horse toward the back of the inn; his cart held hay for the inn stables. "At least I know he will be back, since he left you here."

"He will not leave without you, Hon Kirian, even if perhaps he should."

She shrugged. "He doesn't want to take me. If he's like every other nobleman I've met, he won't let a silly thing like a promise stand in the way of his wishes."

"You have met so many of the *righ*?"

"Second or third sons and daughters, at the College. Sometimes family, come to visit. They were not promising examples of their class."

"Maybe they felt they had something to prove—since their families sent them away, and as Healers they could no longer lay claim to *righ* status."

"Very likely," she said. "It was still no excuse for treating others like the dirt beneath their feet."

Chiss nodded. The rest of the meal passed in silence. After she finished eating, Kirian walked down the hall to the inn stairway and was about to descend to the public rooms when Lord Callo's deep voice stopped her.

"That's not a good idea if, in fact, Arias' men are looking for you. I have no way to control who comes to this inn or what they might tell others." Callo wore a plain, dark tunic and breeches, unadorned with any decorations of rank. His cloak, slung over one arm, was trimmed with valus fur. His fair hair was caught back in its tail. He looked every inch the nobleman.

"I understand," she said. "When do we leave?"

"Chiss has ordered the horses. Are you ready?"

"Yes." She hoisted her bag. She did not tell him that she had been ready for hours.

There were three horses waiting in the yard. Kirian sighed in relief; she was grateful for last night's shared ride, but she was not used to being in such close contact with a man. Miri nickered at Callo, and he smiled. Kirian turned her attention to her own horse, and found herself looking at a little lady's mare, slender of leg and bright of eye. *What a beauty*, she thought.

Kirian remembered the docks from her trip to Two Merkhan with Kin and Rashiri. Then, she had sat on deck while they sold their catch, and ventured onto the docks only long enough to buy a meat pie for lunch and to meet Ruthan's herb seller by the gate. Now she was amazed by the press of people. There were men who slung huge sacks over their shoulders, carrying them from ship to shore. Other men, on board ship, slid crates down an ingeniously-made, slippery ramp to a cart on the dock. There were food vendors, trinket sellers, and women, always accompanied by other women, carrying baskets as they shopped amid the wares laid out on blankets. A spicy, meaty smell hung in the air as they passed the sausage vendor; next to her a sagging table was loaded with fruit, imported on one of these ships during this season, the dead of winter, in Righar. Two men in the furs of mountain herders argued with raised voices. A merchant in a fur-trimmed, red cloak walked past, accompanied by a young man with a ledger. Kirian was so fascinated by all the activity that she almost forgot that Lord Arias' men were seeking her—and Lord Callo as well.

Watching for signs that anyone was interested in their progress, she nearly kept going when Miri stopped. Lord Callo dismounted at the foot of a sort of swinging, wooden walkway that led to a ship. With Callo halfway up the walkway, she turned to Chiss. "Aren't we being very public about this?" she asked. "Lord Arias' men are looking for all of us—surely they will know exactly where we have gone?"

"Hon Kirian, there is no use asking my lord to be secretive about this. I believe he would draw more attention if he were to try to sneak aboard."

She sighed, scanning the docks now for guardsmen who might be suspicious of her. "I hope they do not come for me before this ship sails."

"There are no Seagard men here to see us, and the people on the docks are pretty close-mouthed," Chiss said, starting up the walkway after Lord Callo. "Once we do sail, no one will follow us to Ha'las."

Kirian grimaced, hoping he knew what he was talking about. She gave the rein to the boy Callo paid to hold their horses, and followed Chiss and Callo up the walkway and onto the deck of the trader.

The ship's name was painted on her bow: the *Fortune.* An excellent name for a ship that would carry her away from everything she knew. A dark-skinned man wearing not one, but two earrings in his right ear directed them to the captain's cabin. They entered, stooping under the low lintel to find a heavyset, dark-eyed man seated at a wooden table. The man stood as they entered; he wore a rich blue tunic over another of red, and black seamen's trows. There was a ring in his nostril, and a huge red stone in a ring on his thumb.

"My Lord!" he said instantly. "Welcome to the *Fortune*. You are too late for the emissaries; they went with Lord Alkiran's men at first light." He grinned, and his teeth shone white in his sunburned face.

Callo looked around for a seat; the ceiling was too low for his height. He sat on a trunk, and Chiss gestured to Kirian to sit beside him, but she shook her head.

"Captain Ghosian, well met," Callo said. "I am not here to meet the emissaries."

"Indeed I guessed not. Do you have business for me? Does one of your companions require passage?"

"Your next port?"

"Since it is you, my lord, I will tell you. It is Ha'las, of course. We depart for Las'ash at evening." Ghosian looked round his cabin. "Refreshments? Smoke?"

"Neither, thank you. Ghosian, I require passage for all three of us to Las'ash.

Ghosian's eyes narrowed. "Ah! Lord Callo, I will be honored. We have space—just barely, but space enough. I am sure we can come to some accommodation. But what shall I say when Lord Alkiran's men come galloping back—or even King Martan's, on my next call here at Two Merkhan—and ask why the Royal Bastard has flown to Ha'las?"

"They are more likely to be seeking an escaped slave and a young Healer of noble descent, one Inmay, who are fleeing Fortress Mount's justice."

"They have already mentioned this Inmay." Ghosian paused. Kirian watched the captain scan each of them with those large, calculating eyes. She wondered what he made of her.

"The woman," Ghosian said with a polite nod at Kirian. "She will be with you in Las'ash?"

Lord Callo nodded.

"She may be a problem," Ghosian said. "They guard their women against the ku'an. Unmarried women must be accompanied by a male relative, or some other woman. Otherwise, she may be taken from you by their priests."

Kirian stared at him. This sounded very unpleasant. She wondered why it was necessary to guard young women against the ku'an in particular. She was about to speak when Lord Callo said, "She is a Healer."

Ghosian shrugged. "That may make a difference. I do not know. I simply warn you. As a friend."

"We will deal with it later," Callo said. "For now, Ghosian — your price for passage?"

Kirian let the negotiations fade from her attention as she pondered the role of women in Ha'las. She had not thought through what she wished to do in that foreign land, but she hadn't intended to be tied to her male companions. The thought of remaining in Two Merkhan crossed her mind; perhaps she could wait for Kin and Rashiri to make their next visit and return with them on the *Homebound*. Perhaps the villagers would hide her.

The idea of hiding, perhaps for months, oppressed her. She looked out the porthole and saw the bright sun glittering off the sea past the clutter of ships in port, and grinned to herself. She would find a way to remain independent, even in Ha'las. She returned to the conversation to find that Lord Callo had negotiated passage for all of them and their horses — the little lady's mare as well, Kirian exulted—for the exorbitant price of thirty kels.

"My lord," protested Chiss when Callo nodded his agreement. Callo waved his manservant's protest aside. Ghosian, red-cheeked and grinning, extended a hand to shake Lord Callo's.

"It is done!" Ghosian said. "You will not be sorry, my lord. The *Fortune* will give you every comfort due to you. Your horses will be treated like the best Southern racehorses! Our cook will provide you with dinners worthy of your station. And I will make my best store of Smoke available to you and your companions."

"That last won't be necessary," Lord Callo said. He rose and then ducked his head, recalling the low ceiling just in time. He quirked an eyebrow at Kirian, and she laughed.

On deck, while their cabins were being made ready, Chiss said, "My lord, thirty kels? Remember your funds must last us a long time now."

Callo shrugged. "I bought more with our thirty kels than passage, Chiss. I bought conditional silence."

"He does not strike me as a secretive man."

Callo laughed. "No, but Ghosian has an eye open for the best chance. He will do his best not to inform on us. Remember, Ghosian has no wish to lose his favored position between the Leyish government and King Martan. He doesn't want Sharpeyes angry at him."

Kirian's cabin looked more like a servant's closet. It was barely big enough for the cot and herself. It was dark, with no porthole. There was a hook on the wall, holding a candle enclosed in perforated tin. But the blankets folded on the cot were thick and soft, and she rejoiced that at least she would not have to share a cabin.

Chiss knocked on her door after a while to tell her they were going to check on the disposition of the horses. He sneered at her cabin and offered to talk to Ghosian about obtaining a larger one, but she refused. When he left, she wrapped the old cloak around herself and set off to look around the ship.

It was nearing dusk now, and the *Fortune*'s crew was preparing to depart Two Merkhan. Hatches were tied down and crates on deck made fast. Ghosian must have succeeded with his bribery of customs, since there was no sign of any inspection. Kirian stood at the deck rail and looked back at the docks. They looked different now, not as safe, inhabited by different people. The shopping women were gone. There were no merchants trailing clerks with ledgers. Instead, the docks were sparsely lit with oil lamps on pegs outside shops that looked like taverns. Their doors hung open and the murmur of men's voices came from within, along with a shout of song here and there, and the clatter of pottery. On the dock were only seamen at leave, and guardsmen, one mounted, two on foot, keeping the peace. The row of docked ships stood cloaked by the progressing dark, and shadows pooled on the dock where there were no taverns trying to attract business. To the west, except for several mage-lit markers in the crescent harbor, was only darkness.

She sighed and stepped back from the rail. It was time to go back to the cabin. Perhaps there would be food soon – the wondrous dinners Ghosian had promised them. She smiled as she realized Ghosian had been delighted with the passage fee Callo had agreed to. My Lord Callo was not a bargainer, but who should expect a nobleman to be good at such a thing?

Walking back to her little cabin, she heard a hatch thud closed as she passed. A cold draft blew under her cloak, chilling her lightly- clad legs. Surely there had been a murmur of voices there, just a moment ago, and then silence. She looked around and saw darkness filling up the corners of the ship, deepened rather than eliminated by the yellow lanterns on the rail. She hesitated, looking at the hatch cover again, then heard a creak as if a door eased open. She spun, and saw a cabin door ajar, and in its opening a face she knew very well.

"Gods above," she whispered.

The face looked downward, the pale and gray hair ghostly in the dusk. Then the cabin door closed. Inmay had said nothing.

She walked on, to her cabin, where she changed into her other set of clothing. Kirian was pleased to have something to make her feel appropriately dressed for the Captain's dinner. She slipped her ten kels into a pocket. She combed her hair and tried to banish Inmay from her mind. She tried hard to convince herself she had not seen Inmay at all.

Ghosian's table was almost as good as he had promised. She sat at table next to Lord Callo, himself wearing a valus-trimmed tunic that proclaimed his status but must have been unbearably hot in the close quarters of the Captain's cabin. There were two other guests of the Captain: a young Leyish lady who was draped in colors as rich as Ghosian's, and her companion. The lady wore two earrings in each lobe. Kirian had thought that was a seamen's style, flashy and outrageous, but now she realized it must be common in Leyland. The lady's older companion also wore them.

Chiss stood behind for a while, and served them; this bothered her. After a while Callo enquired what was causing her terrible frown, and she asked why Chiss was not seated with them.

"Oh, he prefers it this way," Lord Callo said.

She doubted that, but said nothing more. After a while, when she saw Chiss and the captain's servant step outside for a breath of fresh air, she envied him.

Kirian did full justice to the baked fish and buttery potatoes offered them. The drink filled her mind with clouds; she was not used to such strong wine. Ghosian dominated the first candlemark with tales of his latest journey from Leyland to Two Merkhan, and the sea monster that he said had delayed them for more than a sennight while they debated how it could be killed or avoided. The Leyish lady, who had glimpsed the monster from deck, described it in a breathy, frightened voice. Kirian hoped they encountered nothing like that on the way to Ha'las, but Ghosian said: "No, Hon Kirian, these creatures stay to warmer waters."

The Leyish lady began talking politics over dessert. She had heard of a new group at a southern Righar port, an unbound color mage and his followers, who were talking up the overthrow of the King's mage-supported rule.

"I saw a drawing of him," the lady said with wide eyes, shaking her head. "A scary man, all wild hair and eyes. You can tell he has no binding; he looks half crazy."

"An unbound mage is not invariably crazy," Callo said.

"I have heard that the magic drives them crazy, if they are not taught and Collared," the lady said, her eyes avid. Her companion ate dessert beside her, seeming to pay no attention. "I have been told they are unmanageable, and can't control their impulses."

Ghosian said, "I fear you are misinformed, my lady. Though I also hear there have been some cases of madness, Lord Callo?"

"Occasionally. The color magery is hard to control. But only the *righ* lords are Collared, my lady, and some mages are even left unbound. Not many, it is true, because His Majesty prefers it that way."

Ghosian gave a huge belly laugh. "King Martan knows how to protect himself, eh? Bind anyone who can cause him trouble. I have heard of worse ways to ensure one's security. Now, my lady, would you like more wine before you leave us?"

The lady's companion spoke up. "No, Captain, thank you anyway for your gracious hospitality. I will conduct my lady to her cabin now."

The lady giggled in a way that made Kirian think she had enjoyed far too much wine already. Her companion rose and stood by her until the lady rose, complimenting Ghosian extravagantly. As she pushed her chair back, her eyes laughed into Ghosian's. The Captain and Lord Callo rose, too, bowing, and Ghosian's eyes swept the lady's slender form as she left the cabin. Kirian wondered if the companion slept in the same cabin as the lady, and if not, whether Ghosian would find his way there later that night.

When they were gone, Lord Callo asked her how she liked her cabin.

"It is comfortable," she said. "I cannot wait to see Las'ash."

"It is a grim place, Las'ash," Ghosian said. "But all I can speak of is the port area. It is restricted, you know, my lord—we are not permitted into the city itself."

"How will we enter then?" Kirian asked.

Lord Callo shrugged. "I hadn't considered it."

Kirian stared at him. How like a *righ*, to assume all barriers would be cut down before him. "Well, we must do so. What if we end up deported, or imprisoned even?"

Ghosian grinned. "I have been putting in at Las'ash, legally or not, for a decade. I've made some few connections there. I think we can get you in, my lord. It may require a little . . . incentive."

"Of course. So no one comes out of Las'ash either?" Lord Callo asked. He sat back, sipping his wine. His broad shoulders leaned against the tall chair-back.

"I did not say that," Ghosian said. "Thrice I have been able to bring Righans out of the city—and my predecessor brought more than one. Find them and you may unlock the stories of the ku'an. I myself have never seen one."

"Not one ku'an? In ten years?"

"Strange, is it not? And the ku'an so talked about. They protect their women from them. They say that the ku'an can infect them with a powerful desire, so that the women beg to go with the ku'an." Ghosian sighed, as if he wished he had this power over women. "They say the ku'an can pull the life from men's minds, so that the people so attacked go about their days with deadened minds, like the fish before a Black Tide. And yet—no, I've never met even one."

Callo fell silent as Ghosian himself poured more of the wine into both their cups. The Captain turned his red ring on his thumb, watching Lord Callo, and then gestured at his manservant. The servant brought a tiny brazier and set it in the center of the table. He lit it from a candle. The grassy substance in the brazier burned slowly, releasing a fragrant smoke into the close air of the cabin.

"Captain, when do we leave port?" Kirian asked, trying to think of a way to leave politely. She had no desire to breathe the Smoke.

"We have left, Hon Kirian, unless my second is asleep on the job."

Kirian listened for a moment. There was only a slight difference in the rocking motion of the ship, but the distant sounds of Two Merkhan that had infiltrated the Captain's cabin were gone. She shivered, realizing there was no turning back.

Lord Callo seemed to awaken from his consideration. "Are you cold? I have a cloak, back in the cabin. Chiss, would you . . ."

"No, no need. I am fine." She hesitated. "I am very tired,

however. Captain, if I may be excused, I would return to my cabin."

Callo's golden eyes glinted with sudden humor. "I cannot imagine what reason you have to be tired, Hon Kirian."

"The last few days have been exhausting. I'm sure you are tired too, my lord." She grinned, looking back into the intriguing eyes. "Perhaps you, too, should retire early."

Ghosian gave a bray of laughter. "An invitation, my lord! And from such an unusual piece."

Just like that, Lord Callo turned cold as ice. She saw his face set, his shoulders square. Before he could speak, Chiss said, "I will escort Hon Kirian back, my lord."

Silence filled the room. Ghosian watched Lord Callo like a specimen. After a moment, Lord Callo said, "Thank you, Chiss." And then, looking at Ghosian, "Hon Kirian is a Healer and a respectable woman, Captain. I ask you to remember it."

"My very deepest apologies, Hon Kirian and my lord." Ghosian rose and bowed, the lamplight glittering on his jewelry. "Indeed I meant no insult."

Kirian made a courteous rejoinder and left the Smoke-filled cabin.

"Do not take offense," Chiss said as he walked her back through the chilly night. "He is only a seaman, after all."

"Of course," she said.

Chiss left her at the door to her little cabin. She lit the candle and replaced it in its tin cup; it cast a dim and febrile light on the walls. Kirian sat on the cot and fished her old nightgown out of the bag Ruthan had packed. The cabin felt chilly, but rocked her like a pair of comforting arms. She heard movement in the larger cabin next door and knew Chiss was preparing Lord Callo's things for his return. She thought of Lord Callo's eyes, smiling at her, and told herself not to be foolish. After changing, she lay down and pulled the big soft blanket over herself. It wasn't until she was almost asleep that she remembered Inmay's pale face staring at her from his own cabin on the *Fortune*.

After a few minutes, she threw back the blankets, wrapped one of them around her, and left her cabin. She could not let this wait. She had to talk to Chiss.

Chapter Eight

Callo excused himself soon after the Healer had gone. Waving away Ghosian's offer of wine for his cabin, he pulled his valus fur closer about him and stepped outside.

The night air was very cold and carried a taste of salt. Callo walked over to the deck rail. The sea was calm; the gentle rocking of the ship was little greater than it had been in port. There were lanterns at bow and stern, and a seaman visible at the bow.

He looked east, towards Two Merkhan. The mage-lit beacon in the harbor had fallen behind, its reddish glow blending into the lights of the port. At night, Two Merkhan was a collection of lights, sparse around the hills, growing thicker in what he supposed was the dock area. The docks would be active all night, he knew. Farther South, although he could not see it from here, were the few dim lights of Seagard Castle on its promontory, the village at its feet.

To the west he saw only the black of night.

The breeze stirred his hair, but did nothing to dispel the

cloud of Smoke in his brain. He leaned on the rail, looking into the impenetrable dark. The *Fortune* sailed into the unknown.

Only now, passage safely gained and with his goal before him, did he have a moment to reflect. It had been bitter, these last days, to see his oldest friend turn against him. The knowledge that Arias was to some degree at the mercy of the dictates of his Collar eased this bitterness very little—for surely if he wanted to, his half-brother could overcome that. Surely one binding could not erase the friendship they had shared.

He wished there was something he could do to free Arias from the Collar. He even wondered if the blunt edge of Arias' hostility would have eased had he stayed to remind Arias of their friendship with his constant presence. But Callo could not stand the thought of staying at Seagard Castle, where he was a pariah, reminded always of the myth his life had been. In the end, every time Arias had met him, his half-brother's hatred had seemed sharper.

He must accept that there was nothing he could do about Arias. Only King Martan bore the responsibility for that. Perhaps time would make a difference, and someday he would return to Righar and be welcomed by his old friend.

The Smoke is making you stupid, he told himself. *Arias will never welcome you again. If you show up, he'll kill you himself.*

Callo knew that there was no going back for a long time. Whatever his reasons for traveling to Ha'las, he was going to an enemy land which had only recently attacked Righar through the Black Tide. Even worse, he had disobeyed the King; Sharpeyes would have his head as a traitor if he ever saw him again.

With a wrench he realized that his little estate near the Leyish border was lost to him. Sharpeyes would seize it immediately. The manor house, the stables, the valley where his tenants raised his crops—all gone. His steward, a man of integrity who had always treated Callo with respect, would curse his name as a traitor. The nobility of Sugetre would raise their brows and whisper behind their hands and say that breeding did tell. He hoped his men and Drale, his second, did not reap any ill effects from their commander's rebellion.

Callo put his head into his hands. He'd had too much of Ghosian's excellent red wine. Even worse, that cursed Smoke filled his mind with evil shadows. The tops of the sea's gentle swells gleamed as he stared down at them.

A seaman had joined the man at the bow. Raised voices drifted back to Callo on the night breeze. They were arguing. He ignored them, but became aware that a sense of misery hung over the ship. Behind him, from one of the cabins, he heard someone cry out, a sound of distress that plunged him deeper into pain.

Someone cleared his throat behind Callo. Callo did not react; he did not care who it was.

"My lord."

It was Chiss—Chiss, who had come along on this desperate excursion for love of him or for lack of other alternatives. Either way, he owed Chiss something. He tried to push away the murkiness claiming his mind so that he could respond.

"My lord," Chiss said again. "Come inside."

"I'm fine out here," he said, and stared west again, toward Ha'las.

"It is very late. You have been out here for some time."

He didn't respond to that. He had never been in so gloomy a mood, so dispiriting that it was hard to keep his attention on Chiss. There was a crash of dropped pottery in the galley and someone swore. He let his mind drift out into the night again.

"Surely you are cold, my lord."

He twitched the valus fur cloak at Chiss. Why would the man not leave him alone?

"It would be best to come in. I have something I must say to you, my lord. Besides, there is an evil mood on the ship."

"No worse than my own," he said. He straightened and sighed. The stiffening wind tugged at his hair. Whoever had cried out was silent now, but he heard the shouts of some argument coming from the seamen's quarters, along with the thud of fists. There was more noise from the galley, as if someone had dropped dishes. It was late, but those who were awake did seem to be in the grip of a foul temper. It seemed a different ship by night, as if Ghosian's insidious Smoke had claimed all the vessel's inhabitants.

"Must you?" he asked.

"It is important."

Callo remembered he did owe Chiss something—at the very least, his attention for a while. He turned and nodded, leaving the blackness of the sea behind, and headed for their cabin. Chiss followed.

In the cabin, two shielded lamps hung from hooks and the beds were made up and piled with blankets. It looked very comfortable, but Callo felt closed in. He looked back at the deck railing, but Chiss followed him in and closed the door. Then, wearily, he sat on the edge of the bed and reached for the mug of wine that Chiss had prepared.

"Where is the Healer?" he asked, trying not to think about the danger he was taking her into.

"Abed, hours ago. There is no one to hear us."

"What is it, then?"

"My lord." Chiss paused, as if he was having difficulty putting his thoughts into words. "You should not have the Smoke."

"I had little chance to refuse it," he snapped. "Why is this your concern?"

"My lord, Callo. I have known you for many years. Will you trust my words?"

"I have no reason not to. You joined me on this wretched journey. You have never failed me. What would you say?"

"The Smoke. It is not good for the ku'an."

"What?"

Chiss said: "You are ku'an, my lord."

Callo stared at his manservant. The Smoke would not release him; he felt dull, with depression still clinging to him. "Nonsense."

"It is true. You know you are the son of a ku'an. You have his yellow eyes. And now, this ship is caught in some blight of the mind because of it."

"You say that I have—somehow infected this ship with my black mood?"

"That is what the ku'an can do. They cannot read minds or force actions. But in the realm of emotion they are supreme. A ku'an can induce any state of mind. When he is under the influence of Smoke, his barriers come down, and the whole world shares the state of his emotions."

Callo stared at Chiss. The manservant's narrow face was side-lit by the lamps, so that it looked strange to him. He shook his head, trying to dislodge the wisps of Smoke. It was true that the stuff had invaded him, turning his thoughts dark in a way it never had before. But for his grim thoughts to cast such a pall over the ship—no. He searched within himself for the wall of restraint Jashan's discipline had helped him build and maintain, and found it wavering, almost transparent. He snapped alert, shocked.

"Your sword forms, my lord," Chiss said. "You should worship Jashan as soon as you may. The discipline will help."

"Jashan has turned from me since Lord Mikati's funeral," Callo admitted, remembering the forms he had done in the clearing near the cliff path where Kirian had interrupted him. "My control has gone."

Chiss poured him some water and he gulped it. It was fresh and cool. It chased away the stale taste of wine and Smoke. He sighed, looking at his old servant. "A ku'an, am I then?"

"It seems so, my lord."

"Then I go to the right place after all."

Memories flashed—his bewilderment when, as a child, his own moods seemed to blow events around him out of proportion. How his childish tempers fueled anger in others, including his old tutor, who had beaten him in an inexplicable fury. How his rage at the other children, who taunted him as a bastard, made their teasing warp into violence. He had learned early, never understanding, the consequences of lack of self-control. He had tried to suppress his moods, without success. That is, until Chiss was hired for him, and told the King that Callo needed the discipline of Jashan's worship. It all clicked.

Questions nagged at the edges of his mind. Most refused to come clear. He sipped again, staring at Chiss, and began to frown as suspicion grew.

"Chiss. How the hell do you know all this?"

Chiss stood straighter, his chin up. "I hoped you would not ask me that, my lord."

"Am I supposed to accept that you are the authority on the ku'an—without asking why? That is asking a lot."

"It is indeed. I will explain—it is very simple. Before I came to you, I served a ku'an in Ha'las. I left him, came to Righar – on this very ship, in fact, before Ghosian was her

Captain. I went to Sugetre, and being in need of a position, applied to His Majesty for the position of your manservant."

"And he welcomed you with open arms, never knowing your history."

Chiss smiled.

"It is just a coincidence, in fact, that you were chosen to be the closest servant to a ku'an's bastard son. The only one in Righar, and the King's nephew."

"I would tell you so if you were a fool, Lord Callo."

"Hah!" Callo drank more water, emptying the mug. The smothering depression he had felt earlier was gone. He still felt odd, a little elated, but suspicious of Chiss. "He knew, did he not? And chose you for that reason?"

"He must have," Chiss agreed. "I hid nothing from him, not wanting to end up strung up on the castle walls when he eventually discovered it elsewhere."

"And you left Ha'las—why? Gods above, Chiss, you know what I'll be walking into there, and never told me."

"I left Ha'las for reasons of my own, my lord."

Callo stared at Chiss. "That's all?" The man's narrow face, so well known and trusted through the years, was as closed as ever. He no longer felt disposed to trust it. He hoped Chiss was not Martan's tool as well.

"It has to be."

"You hide this from me for nigh on twenty years, and that is all?" Callo felt anger boiling up inside him now, his moods changing with a speed engendered by wine, Smoke, and betrayal. He stood. "When were you planning to inform me of this? Never?"

Chiss was watching his face. The man stepped backwards, putting his back against the cabin wall. His eyelids drooped, hiding the expression in his eyes, but Callo saw his jaw muscles clench, and noted his hand was shaking. Chiss was afraid of what he might do. That astonished him.

As soon as he realized that, the rage was gone. "Chiss? Why in the world didn't you tell me this until now?"

"My lord. It is indeed personal, the reason I left. I never even told King Martan. As for why I did not inform you of my history sooner – King Martan forbade me. After all, we did not know for certain that you had any ku'an talent."

"That's not true. You knew damn well, when you took me to Jashan's priests."

Chiss' head bent.

"A ku'an's servant, were you? Who was it? What was he like?"

"He was an arrogant man, my lord. They are all arrogant and most of them are corrupt. They believe their ability and their station in life gives them rights over others. They use their abilities without concern for those around them. They think they are raised above others by their god Som'ur, and don't care what pain they cause. What else do you want to know?"

"For one thing, can I expect to be thrown into prison for showing my face there?"

Chiss laughed. "Oh, no. I don't think there's any risk of that."

Callo frowned. "You sound very certain."

"I am, my lord. You have the ku'an's eyes. As Captain Ghosian told you, there are very few ku'an. They will be desperate to know where you came from."

"Except the one who already knows." Callo had so many questions he did not really know what they were, or how to ask them. Chiss stood before him with his head lifted and his shoulders back, as if he expected punishment. Callo knew he should send Chiss away; any other man would, when presented with such deceit from a servant. But for some reason, he could not think Chiss a fraud. The man had been his loyal servant for a very long time. Chiss was the only thing he had left, the only relationship not destroyed by the revelation of his parentage.

"Chiss. I don't know what to make of all this yet. But you may stop standing there as if you expect me to slay you. Have a mug of this excellent wine Ghosian left for us."

"It is very good wine," Chiss agreed. His shoulders relaxed, and he sat on the foot of his cot and poured himself a mug from the nearly empty jar. He slugged it down as if he felt he needed it.

"I will have questions for you, Chiss, as soon as my head clears." Callo stood and yawned, stretching. The cabin walls moved around him, and he did not think it was from the rocking motion of the ship. "Jashan, Chiss, but I think I may be drunk."

"I would not be surprised," Chiss said diplomatically.

"But the Smoke is gone from my head, at any rate. At least I think it is. So you can tell me about the ku'an?"

"I have told you what I can, my lord. I was very young, and I was only what you would call a footman."

"But you know your way around Las'ash. You know what Kirian will have to deal with there."

"Yes, my lord. A little."

"I'll expect you to share that."

"I will do whatever I can to aid you, my lord. You know I always have."

"I do know that."

"And that recalls another thing to my mind, my lord. The Healer came to me after we left the Captain this evening. She was troubled because she has seen the fugitive Healer Inmay aboard this ship."

"This is the Healer sought by Fortress Mount?"

"Yes, my lord."

Callo sighed and rubbed his forehead. The seed of what was likely to become a massive headache was growing there, behind his eyes. "Chiss."

"My lord?"

"I really don't give a kel—hell, I don't give a *copper* for Inmay and his problems. I care nothing where he is or where he goes. Why in the world would Kirian think this was of concern to me?"

"I suppose she is afraid you will think her involved in his escape somehow."

"Well, I don't think it."

"I shall tell her, my lord."

"Or I will, if I remember. Truly, the adventures of some miscreant Healer matter to me not at all. Does she not think I have other concerns?"

"I think she has been through a lot lately, Lord Callo. I think she wants you to trust her. Remember, she knows nothing of your own concerns, since you have not favored her with them." Chiss had stopped standing there so stiffly and was now going about his usual evening activities, taking Callo's cloak from his shoulders and then pouring water into a bowl for washing. Things began to seem more normal, and Callo's incipient headache eased a little. He sighed. He really wanted things to be normal again, if only for a few hours.

Chapter Nine

Kirian pulled her cloak tight against the stiff wind and closed the door of her cabin behind her. The day was in sharp contrast to yesterday's wintry brilliance—overcast and gray, the sea white-capped and choppy. The ship's deck moved uneasily beneath her. She was glad she had eaten little for breakfast.

Not that she wanted to eat much anyway, after the evil dreams that had assailed her half the night. She rarely remembered her dreams at all; yet, she recalled every dark moment of last night's visions, each one dripping with guilt. She wondered whether such odd dreams could have been sent by a god—perhaps the Unknown God, deity of those like herself who had nothing.

As she approached the bow, she saw Lord Callo. He was doing his form alone on the deck, intent on the disciplined moves of his body and his sword. He wore only a belted tunic and breeches against the bite of the wind, but seemed unaware of the cold. He moved with restrained grace; the movement of the deck did not seem to impede his skill at all.

She knew of this ritual; warriors practiced it to reinforce the discipline of training. Jashan's devotees among the *righ* said it gained them divine favor.

Callo seemed more than just intent on the minutia of his moves; he seemed exalted, somehow, infused by light. Kirian watched, holding her breath, as he completed a form, his sword held above his head in a stylized salute. The sword seemed to flare with light, although the sun was occluded by heavy cloud. Then he dropped his arms, pausing for a moment before returning the sword to its sheath.

She stepped forward. "Lord Callo, that was beautiful."

He turned and looked at her without surprise, as if he had known she was there. "Thank you. It is a form of worship, you know."

"To Jashan, yes, I know. But I have never seen it done." *Apart from that day near the cliff path, when he had seemed so distraught.* Then, his face was pulled into lines of worry; now he appeared eased, as if the form brought him peace.

"Are you settled in well?" Callo asked, leaning back against the rail.

"I am. I wanted to ask you though, my lord…"

He raised a brow when she hesitated.

"Did Hon Chiss tell you that Inmay is here on the Fortune? And I assume the slave Eyelinn is here as well, though I didn't see her."

Callo smiled. "He did. Thank you for telling him—I'm glad you trust us enough to do so. But Healer Kirian, I must tell you I care nothing for Inmay and his troubles. I have other concerns."

"I thought so. Even though you haven't told me the reason for your journey, I know you hid from Lord Alkiran's men on the road." She saw his brows draw down at that unhappy memory. "And you purchased Captain Ghosian's silence."

He laughed at that. "I would be delighted to purchase Ghosian's silence, but it can't be done. Ghosian is a law unto himself. I encouraged his silence only. He will keep it as he may, but break it when it pleases him."

"You informed me before we left Two Merkhan that you flout the King's will. Something of large concern must drive you, to go to an enemy land in the teeth of the King."

The smile left his face. "I do not see why I should burden you with my reasons, Healer."

He was offended—and rightly so. She had not meant to pry—well, she had, but she hadn't thought he would mind. "Of course not, my lord. I was just hoping for something to guide me. Will you tell me where you mean to go, in Las'ash? Or at least if you intend to remain there long?"

"I have left everything that is mine back in Righar. The King will surely have me killed if I try to return. He probably has taken my lands already—and Lord Alkiran will aid him in the effort to find and destroy me. So no, I do not intend to return soon unless I am forced to. I will be of no use to you when you return to Seagard Village."

"I fled for my life from Seagard, so I am glad you allowed me to come with you," Kirian said, remembering how long it had taken to convince him. "But what is so serious it made you give up all that?"

"Just that I found my life was a lie." The blunt words surprised her. "I am seeking something dangerous, Healer. I really don't have any right to take you into Ha'las without telling you what it is. Even I have not really taken it all in yet." He paused. After a moment she shivered in the wind and cleared her throat. His eyes met hers again.

"It's all right," she said. "Don't tell me now, then. But don't expect me not to ferret it out in the end. I have a pretty strong urge for self-preservation."

He grinned. "You do. I can vouch for it."

"And also, my lord, please call me Kirian."

He gave a little bow. "It is a beautiful name."

She felt herself blushing. "Thank you, my lord."

"We will be together quite a bit from now on. Please call me Callo. There is no need for all this formality between us." She had not expected that. He was a *righ*, bastard or not, and the *righ* were so jealous of their status they guarded every syllable of title, every outward show due their rank, as if it were diamond. She nodded, unable to think how to respond.

"Kirian, please join Chiss and me in our cabin after the noon meal. I understand we will be docking near first light tomorrow. We need to discuss our options. That is, if you don't want to go your own way."

"It's my understanding I can't. Isn't there some law about a woman being accompanied by a man at all times?"

"We'll talk about that. But if you decide you would rather stay on the *Fortune* and go to the next port of call, you may. I have funds for your passage."

"I have funds as well, my lord. Callo."

"I remember. Ten kels."

Kirian laughed, remembering his appalled look as he saw the sum total of her funds to support a stay of a sennight or more in Two Merkhan. She supposed he would have little reason to know how cheaply one could survive. His needs were supplied by his servants, out of the produce of his land, or gifted by his powerful uncle, and she was very sure he had never bought linen in the market or a ticket on the Sugetre caravan. Let alone survived on bread and beans in the charity orphanage, as she had before she was taken in by the Healer's College.

"I am more than content to disembark with you at Las'ash."

"Good." His golden eyes were glinting down into hers. He was standing very close now, his broad shoulders blocking out the view of the bow. She caught her breath and stepped back.

"I will see you after the noon meal, my lord. Thank you." She retreated, smiling at him so he would not see her confusion. He grinned back and turned to grab his cloak from the section of railing he had tied it around, and she fled—there was no other word for it. The wind chapped her cheeks, but they were hot with something else; she could hardly believe the sudden attraction, the heat she felt when she was near him. And he a lord of the land, the King's nephew, no matter in what disgrace! He was everything she had always despised.

As she left the bow, she looked up. The Leyish lady, who had giggled so much at dinner last night, stood on the upper deck, her bright robes fluttering about her. She watched Lord Callo. The lady called out a greeting, and Callo looked up. Kirian kept walking.

She walked fast, ignoring the sea and the gray sky and the beauty of the sails and the men who climbed in the rigging like spiders from one strand of web to another. Her thoughts were in confusion. Then, as she passed a row of cabin doors, one creaked open and a voice said, "Kirian!"

She recognized the voice instantly. She knew it well, from the years at the Healer's College. She looked towards the sound and saw his peaked face peering at her.

"What?" she hissed.

"Come in here, Kirian. We need help."

Kirian hesitated, but as a Healer, she could not ignore those words. She slid through the narrow gap of the open door and saw Inmay, pale and tired-looking by the door, and Eyelinn reclining on the single cot. The cabin was as small as her own, and lit by a single candle in a tin holder. The light from the open door illuminated Eyelinn's deep brown eyes, fixed on Kirian like an adder's.

"What now?" Kirian asked.

"We need help. We need to disembark at Las'ash, but we can't let anyone see us. There's a lord on the ship from Two Merkhan."

She could not believe what he was asking. "Is anyone hurt?" Kirian asked. "Ill?"

"Hurt? No. We need your help distracting the cursed nobleman. I don't know how many men he has with him, or why they haven't searched the ship yet."

Kirian stared at him and wanted nothing more than to be rid of both of them. She shook her head and turned toward the door.

"Kirian!" Inmay pleaded.

"You can get yourself off the ship. I am not being dragged any further into this. I'm in trouble myself because of you."

"It was your own decision," Eyelinn drawled from the bed.

Anger flooded her veins. She did not trust herself to speak. Without another word she slipped back out the door and proceeded to her own cabin. There she sat on the bed and covered herself with the blanket against the chill that invaded the boards of the cabin. Eyelinn and Inmay could rot, for all she cared—Inmay with his helpless desire for beautiful women, Eyelinn with her scorn and selfishness. She owed them nothing. She had already given up her life at Seagard Village for them. If not for Inmay, right now she could be sitting with Ruthan before the fire, healing someone in the village, hiking one of the mountain goat-trails through the winter terrain. Or she might be at the Castle, ministering to one of the spoiled *righ*.

She smiled, thinking about all that, and wondered if Inmay had not done her a favor after all. Because right now she felt free for the first time in her life. She would not be anywhere else.

———

Day dawned cold and wintry as the *Fortune* docked at Las'ash. Kirian had been awake for an hour at least, mulling over her conversation with Chiss and Callo the previous day. Callo had excused himself from Ghosian's table at the first appearance of the Smoke brazier, and they had gathered in his cabin to discuss what they wanted to do in Las'ash. Or rather, what Kirian wanted to do. She still had no idea what Callo sought there.

She was beginning to wonder whether it was wise for her to stay with Lord Callo. Again last night, as they discussed plans, she was aware of every motion Callo made, responsive to his every change in mood. She realized she was infatuated with him. She thought Callo, absorbed in his own concerns, seemed unaware of her interest, but twice she had noticed Chiss watching her.

Chiss had an unsuspected depth of knowledge about the role of women in Ha'las. She wondered how he came by it, but when she asked, Chiss evaded the question. He told them that women were guarded with single-minded determination, always accompanied by another woman and frequently a male relative. Those who had no protector were taken in by the priests. Those who broke the laws— especially broke them in such a manner as to offend the public sense of morality—were punished.

"Punished, how?" Kirian asked.

"That varies," Chiss responded. "The woman could be imprisoned. She could be given to some man in the priests' favor to protect from that point on." Kirian grimaced at that. "Or she could be executed."

"Serious about this, aren't they?" Callo said, frowning.

"Very serious, my lord. It is a concern for us."

"Kirian is a woman of knowledge, a Healer. Won't that make a difference?"

Chiss shrugged. "I do not know. I know of no such women in Ha'las."

"I will not hide in some room waiting for one of you to have time to escort me about," Kirian said. "We are foreign. They must make allowances for foreign ways, surely."

"I would not count on it, Hon Kirian. It is a religious matter, you see. Matters of religion tend not to be so flexible. And I know the priests are jealous of their status. They will defend their laws."

"Jashan's eyes," Callo said impatiently. "How do we get around this? Perhaps you would rather choose to go on, Kirian. Stay with the *Fortune* until her next port. I think the Leyish lady is returning home. You have a sense of adventure. Do you want to see Leyland?"

She made a face at him.

"It is not so bad, Leyland. My estate is near there. I go into Leyland sometimes when I am there."

"I am not going to Leyland. I do have a sense of adventure, my lord, and I have decided I want to see Ha'las."

"My lord," Chiss said. "Perhaps when we arrive we could introduce Hon Kirian as a blood relative."

"No." Callo's tone was abrupt. Surprised, Kirian looked up, but Callo was frowning at Chiss.

"It will not solve the problem, but it will make things a little easier for Hon Kirian," Chiss argued.

"Nevertheless. If the ku'an have any knowledge at all of

the Righan royalty, they will know there is no young woman anywhere in the family tree, let alone a Healer."

"Then she could be a relation of mine," Chiss said. He looked at Kirian. "Let me be clear, Hon Kirian, this will not eliminate the need for a chaperone for you. But it will allow us to see each other, at least."

Kirian was not going to allow herself to be isolated from the only link she had to Righar. "That would be fine, Chiss. Thank you. A cousin, perhaps."

"So be it," Callo said. "You must have a veil. Chiss said all the women go veiled."

"All the respectable women go well-covered, yes," Chiss said.

"I can arrange a veil," Kirian said. Then she flushed. "Although, it occurs to me, Lord Callo. I left the village suddenly, and without time to pack. I may not have suitable clothing after all."

"Is that all? I have funds. We will take care of that in Las'ash city. I am getting tired of seeing that cloak anyway." He waved at her only cloak, which she had been wearing since they had met on the road.

She wanted to make a rude comment about that, but was stifled by her appreciation for the generous offer he had just made. She did not look at him as she said, "Thank you, my lord."

Then there was a finger under her chin, raising her chin so she would look up and meet his eyes. "You are lovely even in that old cloak," he said. She caught her breath and looked away.

The next morning, after the horses were offloaded, she bid a polite farewell to Ghosian, who stood on deck with a pipe in his mouth. She descended the ship's walkway to the dock. Callo was already mounted; Miri was dancing a little with pleasure at being out of the ship's hold. Three ships were at dock along with the *Fortune,* their rigging ghostly in the morning fog. Moisture dripped from the ship's rails and the hawsers. Smaller craft bobbed on the choppy sea nearby.

"Good morning," she said. She mounted her mare, and fumbled with the bit of cloak she and Chiss had turned into a makeshift veil, making sure it covered the lower part of her face.

"Good morning to you, Healer," Chiss said. "It's a bit of a gray one though."

"Good luck to you!" Ghosian called from deck.

Callo waved, and they set off down the dock. Kirian cast a last look behind, wondering if Inmay and Eyelinn were still aboard or had already stolen onto the docks. Even at this early hour there was some activity on the docks as men began to offload the *Fortune's* cargo from her hold. Dark-skinned sailors on one of the other ships called across to the *Fortune's* men, but the fog muffled most of the sound.

Las'ash city was apparently in the middle of a winter thaw. Heaps of dirt-crusted snow stood here and there, off to the side or behind small structures, as if there had recently been a snowstorm that had been cleared. Everything on the docks— cloth banners, tabletops, ropes, roofs—dripped with moisture. The horses splashed through occasional puddles as they made their way past the docks.

Two food stands were open at the end of the dock. The indistinct shapes of several people stood near them in the fog with their hands full of tea or bread and cheese. There was a spicy, fatty smell that made Kirian's mouth water—sausage, she thought, but different from that in Two Merkhan.

The dock was walled off from the city proper. The wall, a weathered wood structure, allowed glimpses between slats of the houses and streets of Las'ash, but permitted no exit from the public dock area. Kirian followed her companions along the wall until a tall gate came into view. It was chained shut and guarded by two armed men. More men stood at lazy guard near a structure a few yards away. A flag showing a golden eye on a black background drooped from a post atop the guard house. Kirian braced herself for trouble.

The men had been watching them for some time. As they approached the gate, one guard called: "Names and business?"

Chiss dismounted and approached the guards. He ran down the list of their names. Then he said, "My lord's business is with the palace."

The guard snorted. "I've heard that before. We've received no word of you or your Lord Callo. You'd best get back on the tub that brought you and count your blessings."

Callo urged Miri closer to the guardsmen. "It would be in your best interest to admit us without delay."

The second guard, his interest caught perhaps by Callo's mild tone, looked up and into Callo's face for the first time. He paled and said, "Uh, Ja'lar…"

"What do you think you're going to do to make us let you in?" jeered Ja'lar, hand on his sword. "In case you don't know, Las'ash is closed to foreigners, lord or slave. King Ar'ok don't want foreigners cluttering up the place. What in the hell do you want, Sa'jal? Why are you jabbing at me like that?"

Sa'jal, bowing very deeply in Callo's direction, said: "My lord ku'an."

Ja'lar's eyes widened. He looked up, at Callo's face, into Callo's eyes. After one horrified moment, he was bowing even deeper than his companion. Kirian looked at both of them, her jaw dropping in disbelief. Then she looked at Callo.

He frowned at the men's reaction, and was silent.

After a moment Chiss said, "We will need an escort to the palace."

"Of course, great Lord," babbled Ja'lar. "I didn't know—please forgive my, uh, mistake. I myself will escort you to the palace. You will want to see the Ku'an'an, Lord Si'lan. What do you want done with your woman?"

"What do you mean, what does he want done?" Kirian demanded. "I accompany Lord Callo and Chiss."

The two guardsmen had seen no sign of anger from Callo other than a frown, so Sa'jal had the temerity to speak up. "It is not allowed, my Lord Ku'an, to take a woman into the public rooms without a female companion."

"I'll deal with that at the palace," Callo said. "This is no ordinary woman. She accompanies me."

Sa'jal and Ja'lar peered up at Kirian, trying to see what made her so out of the ordinary. She looked at Chiss, who smiled at her and shrugged. Kirian checked that her makeshift veil was in place; she hoped it met the local standards for modesty.

Ja'lar actually left his post to escort them. Calling another guardsman to relieve him, he led them through the city.

The journey through the narrow streets of Las'ash was uneventful. Kirian guided Lady after the others along streets slippery with half-melted snow and ice. Wood-smoke from chimneys clouded the air. They passed many small buildings, houses, and little shops, most of them just showing signs of life as Las'ash awakened. In one small open area, veiled women, cloaked against the cold, gathered around a community well, drawing buckets of water for household tasks. A shopkeeper threw up his front shutter, startling Lady, who shied and neighed. The shopkeeper's dark eyes met Kirian's for a second before the man looked down and away.

Then they were in an area with no houses. A slightly larger building sat to the side of the street, doors decorated with a colorful mural showing some bloody scene from Ha'lasi history; Kirian caught a glimpse of a larger-than-life being—a god perhaps? —with a red anatomically-correct heart painted on his chest, and a screaming woman, unveiled and terrified. Perhaps the building was a temple, dedicated to the ku'an god Som'ur. Kirian shuddered. The scene on the door was barbaric, and gave her no faith as to the kindness of the people of Ha'las.

They rode up a walkway to a large stone building, surrendered their horses into the care of a groom, and were politely detained at a wide double door by a unit of guardsmen. Ja'lar stepped forward and conversed with one of them in a low voice. A moment later, the other man strode off and came back accompanied by his commander.

When Ja'lar presented them to his commander, Kirian was once again amazed as the man bowed low to Lord Callo.

Callo's face was expressionless. From her vantage point seated on Lady behind him, Kirian could see his shoulders set.

They dismounted and gave the horses into the keeping of a groom. The commander led them into a windowless receiving chamber. There, a golden tray laden with dried winter fruits and nuts was set before them, and a heavily veiled servant brought wine in cups to match. They were left alone while the Ku'an'an was notified of their presence.

"Well!" Kirian said. "I'd avoid the wine, if I were you."

Lord Callo set down his cup. "You are the voice of reason."

"You may need to stay sharp. What is this ku'an business, Lord Callo?"

After a moment passed during which Callo showed no disposition to reply, Chiss said: "My lord is a ku'an by birth, Hon Kirian. They know when they see his eyes."

Callo looked tense to the point of breakage. Kirian ignored his grim face and, lightly, said: "Thank the gods for that, or they'd have dropped us into the sea when we refused to go away."

"Very likely," agreed Chiss.

"As it is, we have a favored status," Kirian went on. "And I have not been thrown into some women's hermitage somewhere, my lord, because you vouched for me."

"There is that."

"Ah, but we are not done with you yet," said a deep voice.

The new arrival was a man in his vigorous middle years. His hair was mostly silver, but had once been the color of straw. His lined face was still handsome, and his eyes were the color of amber. He wore a long robe caught up with a gold sash, slit to show the scarlet tunic beneath. Authority was written all over his face.

Callo was staring at the man's eyes as they all rose and bowed. "Yes, you have my eyes," the new arrival said. "I am Si'lan, the ku'an'an—that is, the lord of the ku'an, the psychic mages. An unknown ku'an is a rare thing. They called me immediately."

"You said I have your eyes."

"A ku'an's eyes, I mean," said Lord Si'lan. The half-smile on his lips struck Kirian as malicious. "You came in on the *Fortune,* they said, from Righar."

Callo nodded. "I am Callo ran Alkiran, and my companions are Chiss and his cousin, Healer Kirian."

Si'lan scanned each of them, slowly, returning to Callo. His eyes seemed very golden in the enclosed room, as gold as the platter with the fruit and nuts. Kirian began to feel odd. Suddenly she felt her shoulders pressing against the wooden chair-back, the backs of her knees ticklish with sweat against the seat. The chill air began to have texture; it scraped against the skin of her face and neck. The sweet fragrance of the fruit and wine mixed with the brown scent of nuts, overwhelming her. The sound of everyone's breathing was loud as coughing, and when she touched the fabric of her cloak, she almost cried out from the pain of the contact with the worn fabric. Confused and frightened, she blinked back tears against the sensory onslaught. Her stomach heaved in reaction.

Then the ku'an'an swayed back, hand to his head. Callo came to his feet, reaching for his sword.

"Stop!" Callo ordered.

"I have. I have. Sheathe your sword," Si'lan's voice was hoarse, and he blinked his eyes as if they teared. "I have stopped."

Kirian took a deep breath. The world was back to normal again, her nerves only a little raw from the overload. Chiss, behind her, drew an audibly ragged breath.

"What was that?" Kirian asked.

"That was an attack," Callo said, glaring at Si'lan. He had not yet sheathed his sword.

Si'lan shook his head. "Please, Lord Callo, sheathe your weapon. It was not intended to be an attack but rather a test. I had to be sure, you see, that you were in fact what your eyes advertise you to be."

"And you are certain now?"

"I am." Si'lan had recovered, Kirian saw, and there was a calculating look in his eyes. "You shoved my magery back at me. I am surprised you knew what to do. You have great strength, for a half-breed."

"You know who I am, then."

"Oh, yes. We have been aware of the yellow-eyed Royal Bastard for some time."

Callo slid his sword back into its scabbard. He showed no reaction to the slur, which he must have been well used to hearing. Kirian took a deep breath and wondered what she had gotten herself into.

"I am here to talk to you, or some other ku'an," Callo said. "My intentions are honorable. I do not expect to be attacked, or to have my companions attacked, just because you have the power to do so."

"We will not do so. Be seated, Lord Callo, until I can have a slave show you to the rooms we are having prepared. Later, we will present you to the King. This man, I take it, is your manservant? Yes? And this woman, you are not related to her — she must go into the women's quarters." Si'lan's voice was calming. Kirian wondered whether he was exerting a calming psychic influence as well, and if Callo would notice it if he were.

"I would prefer not to, Lord Si'lan," Kirian said.

Callo said, "She is my manservant's cousin. She must stay near us."

"Indeed? We can provide a room near your own but she must accept a female companion to be assigned by the Queen if that is so. Our customs, you see—in fact our gods—require it."

There was no brooking the dictates of religion. Kirian sighed. "All right, then."

Chiss was looking at her. "Are you sure?"

"I have no choice. It is better than the women's quarters, wherever those might be. My thanks, Lord Ku'an'an."

"And you, Chiss, stay with your employer of course, as I know well," Si'lan said, looking at the smaller man. Kirian thought the wording of this was odd and looked at Chiss, but there was no expression on the man's face.

"I will allow you to settle in before I begin asking questions," Si'lan said. "I have many."

An hour later, looking around the small suite that was provided for her, Kirian wondered if she had been wise to accept the female companion. The woman Sara'si was heavily veiled and completely silent except when advising Kirian how to wear the Ha'lasi dress and veil that had been provided. Kirian's attempts at friendly conversation fell unheeded into the chill air of the chamber. After donning the clothing, Kirian found her stride restricted by the narrow robe and her vision partially blocked by the veil, which she found annoyingly opaque.

The suite itself was more than sufficient for her needs. It had a small window that looked over the city from a height of two stories. A narrow bed was pushed against one wall, blankets and one fur piled atop it. There was a little table and a wardrobe for her clothes. A curtained alcove to one side contained a small bed and table for Sara'si, who was expected to be with her at all times.

When she opened the door of her suite, intending to go next door to confer with Callo and Chiss, she found a guard outside.

"By the gods!" she said. "Am I a prisoner here?"

The guard, a rotund man wearing an insignia of a golden eye, kept his eyes averted from her as he replied. "Healer Kirian, Lord Si'lan says your status allows you to remain outside the women's quarters. But you must be guarded."

"Both inside the room and out?" Kirian said, looking back at the silent, veiled woman folding her cloak away behind her.

"That is our custom. Lord Si'lan said I should explain if you asked. I beg pardon for speaking."

"You need not beg pardon. Are you not usually allowed to speak to me?"

The guard cast a glance into the room at Kirian's companion. He turned to place his back to her again.

"Good gods," Kirian said. "Guard, what is your name? Will you tell me where Lord Callo is? I need to speak with him."

What the guard's response would have been she did not know, for just then a liveried messenger dashed around the corner and came to a stop in front of the open door, breathing hard.

"Hon Kirian!" he said. "Her Majesty the Queen has been told you are a Healer in Righar."

"Yes."

"Her Majesty the Queen requires your attendance immediately! Please hurry, Healer!"

Kirian grabbed her bag from the table and hurried after the messenger. Her companion followed, a dark shape reminding Kirian strongly of some brooding Fate. The messenger urged her to go faster, but her stride was restricted by the narrow skirt of the robe. It was several minutes before two uniformed armed guards opened an ornate door and another attendant announced her into the presence of the Queen.

The Queen was wrapped in robes so that Kirian could not tell much about her, but from the bony hands, she guessed the woman was very spare of frame. The Queen's fingers were loaded with rings that sparkled in the reflected light of the fire, and her reddish-gray hair was threaded with diamonds. The woman's face was coated with powders beneath a veil that was not much more than a drift of netting, and her gold eyes glittered through the fabric into Kirian's. She looked alert and perfectly healthy at first glance.

Kirian bowed respectfully before the Queen. The Queen said: "A Healer, are you?"

"Yes, your Majesty. Are you ill?"

"A real Healer? Not a witch or a midwife?"

"I attended the Healer's College in Sugetre, Your Majesty. I was assisting the Healer at Seagard just before I came here."

"He may not accept a woman Healer," the Queen said to

one of her attendants, a robed figure also wearing a mostly symbolic veil.

The attendant said: "He is in great discomfort, Your Majesty. He will try anything. If you send her, he will accept her."

The Queen looked hard at Kirian. Her eyes glittered. Kirian felt a tremor of fear run down her spine.

"If you harm His Majesty, I will see that you die a most miserable death," the Queen said. "But it is worth a try. Have you treated anyone with the breathing disease?"

"There is more than one kind of breathing disease," Kirian said. "I have treated two different kinds."

"The King has attacks," said the Queen's attendant. "He is fine for days, then he wheezes and cannot breathe. At the worst he cannot walk or lie down, and must sit hunched over until the attack eases."

"It is getting worse," the Queen said. "Our Healers have done nothing to stop these attacks. They mutter together and try concoctions and fill the room with noxious smoke. Our priests ask the mercy of the gods. What can you do that is different?"

"Your Majesty, I must consult with your Healers. I do not know if they have tried the leaves of the sart plant. This plant, when used in a tea, eases one form of the breathing disease."

"Take her in to him," the Queen ordered. "Tell him it is by my wish. You, Righan Healer, if you harm him, you and yours will not see the end of your suffering, ku'an or no ku'an. Do you understand?"

"I am a Healer, Your Majesty. I will not harm any person brought to me for my aid. I will be glad to see if I can help the King."

The attendant went to the door and called two guards from the hallway outside the Queen's chamber. The guards, the attendant, and Kirian walked two doors down the hallway and were admitted into a guarded room that was, indeed, filled with "noxious smoke." Kirian detected a fragrance of charred roses, and grimaced.

The room was dense with servants and guards. King Ar'ok sat on a low chair, hunched forward, his head down. He was a slight man with the straw-gold hair that seemed to belong to the ku'an males in this land. Then he raised his amber eyes, and she realized he was not a man yet at all, but a boy in his mid-teens. His face was pale and unlined, and his eyes shadowed with the strain of the breathing attack. A male slave stood behind him, rubbing some ointment into the bare skin of his back.

"Your Majesty," she said, bowing. The attendant did the same.

"Gods help me, can you not tell that I am ill?" the boy King gasped. "I have no time for my mother's fancies now. Go away."

"Your Majesty," the attendant said. "The Queen has sent you this woman, a Healer from Righar. She may be able to help you."

"A woman! And from Righar." The boy King stopped speaking and drew a difficult breath. Kirian heard the rasping of his breath from where she stood, and she knew the burnt-rose smoke could not be helping.

A tall man in green robes approached. She cast a quick look at his face and was relieved to see that he did not have ku'an's eyes—finally, someone here in Las'ash city in a position of power that could not influence her mind without her permission.

The man introduced himself as Yun'lar, lord of physicians in Las'ash. He said, "You are a real Healer? You have completed the training in your capital city?"

"In Sugetre, yes." She smiled at him, hoping that this fellow Healer could be an ally in this strange place. But Yun'lar sneered at her.

"A woman cannot be permitted to examine a man's body. Particularly that of our great King."

"It's up to you, lord physician. I see you have been burning roses."

"It has had no effect," the physician said.

"Sir, my experience is that this irritates the lungs even more," Kirian said. "Will he not do better with clean air?"

Yun'lar frowned at her. "You do ill to think a slip of a girl knows more than a physician of many years standing. The outside air is cold. It will freeze the swollen passages in his lungs."

Kirian shuddered inside, but let that comment go. "I have twice eased the breathing disease in Seagard. If His Majesty has the same type of illness, the leaves of the sart plant, made into a tea with just a little mellweed for relaxation, will stop the attack. Have you tried this?"

"I have never heard of the sart plant," said Yun'lar.

Kirian looked around for a table, saw none, and bent to lay her bag on the floor. The narrow robe made it hard for her to bend. She opened the bag and withdrew a little paper twist with writing on it. Inside were a few dried leaves, gray-green in color, with nubby surfaces. They were still whole, but very dry. Yun'lar peered at the leaves. He looked at the hunched figure on the chair and shook his head.

"I do not recognize this herb," the lord physician said.

"It is up to you, Your Majesty," Kirian said in a clear voice. "I believe I can help you."

"She must not examine you, Your Majesty!" said Yun'lar.

"Gods, I don't care right now. Let her come near. You, Healer, what do you need to do?"

"I must listen to your breathing, Your Majesty."

Yun'lar hissed. Ar'ok, struggling for breath in a way almost painful to witness, gestured Kirian near. Two guards on either side of the King's chair stiffened, hands on weapons.

"Relax," she said. "I'm sure you can defend your King against me without the weapons. Now, Your Majesty…"

Kirian bent close. She placed her ear against the King's back, where it stuck unpleasantly to the smelly lotion the slave had been applying. "Please breathe, Your Majesty," she told the King.

The King took a breath. The wheezing was very loud. He did not seem to be able to draw a complete breath. Sensitive to his quivering tension at having her so near, she stepped back immediately.

"I must have hot water and a cup, for tea," Kirian said to Yun'lar. "I will crush just one of these leaves and steep it in hot water. Then I will add a pinch of mellweed, and the King may drink it."

There was hot water on a side table. One of the slaves drew Kirian over to it while Ar'ok watched Kirian with narrow golden eyes. Kirian crushed one of the leaves, steeped it in hot water in a delicate cream-colored cup, and stirred in the mellweed. Bits of the leaves floated on the surface of the liquid, and the whole thing looked slightly oily. When she presented it to King Ar'ok, he looked at it with disfavor.

Yun'lar made a face when he saw it. "Your Majesty, I cannot vouch for this plant. It may harm you."

"Am I to suffer this misery forever? You can provide no relief. Maybe she can. Though it looks most evil." Ar'ok tipped the mug back and forth. Green grains drifted back and forth in the murky depths. The tea smelled faintly of grass.

One of the guards said, "Your Majesty, we do not know of this woman. She is foreign, and accompanies a foreign ku'an.

Do not drink the tea." The man reached out to take the cup. Ar'ok withheld it. He lifted his ku'an's eyes to her face.

"Ku'an'an," he said.

Kirian lifted her head in surprise. Si'lan, the ku'an whom they had met when they first arrived, was there, standing in the back of the group. At the King's call, he came forward. "Your Majesty?" he said.

"If this concoction kills me, see that this one dies a painful death. And the new ku'an, too."

Si'lan bent his head in agreement. "Yes, Sire."

Ar'ok tipped the mug to his lips and drank down the whole thing. When he thrust the cup away from him, his eyes showed tears and there were green stains at the corners of his mouth. He bent over, making grunts of disgust.

"Ah, that is foul. Perhaps she has tried to harm me." Still wheezing, the King looked pale and miserable.

Kirian said to Yun'lar, "My lord, please check his heart rate. The leaf will tend to speed it, but the mellweed should keep it under control."

Yun'lar approached the King and said, "With your permission, Sire." When Ar'ok ignored him, he bent and held Ar'ok's wrist, counting silently. "Fast, it is fast," he said. "But not fatal."

"For this reason the leaf cannot be taken more than once in a day," Kirian said. "It's hard on the heart."

"And has no effect!" Yun'ar objected.

"Wait, my lord physician," Kirian said. "Wait, for half a candlemark at least."

For Kirian, the half a candlemark progressed in extreme discomfort. She bent and put away the unused sart leaves, watched Yun'lar take the King's pulse again, and look worried. The Ku'an'an watched her. The King's guards stayed very close to her, and had a tendency to let their hands rest on their weapons. Before the time had passed, she noticed Ar'ok was sitting straighter on his chair. A moment later, he snapped at a slave who was applying more lotion on his back. Kirian said, "I think you will find, Your Majesty, that you are feeling better."

Ar'ok's golden eyes narrowed at her. "I am breathing better. Where did you learn of this plant?"

"At Healer's College, Your Majesty."

"Are there many women Healers in Righar?"

"Yes, there are quite a few."

"And you examine men's bodies?" Ar'ok's eyes were no longer exhausted. His expression was lascivious. Kirian shuddered inside.

"We are Healers. We examine the bodies of men or women when they come to us for healing, yes. As do your own physicians."

"She is a heathen, Your Majesty," said Yun'lar. "She knows no better."

Ar'ok looked her up and down. "She did know something you did not know, though, lord of physicians."

Yun'lar bowed low and did not speak.

"This unpleasant leaf is a wonder," the King continued. "I breathe as usual. Yun'lar, learn about this leaf from the Healer."

"Your Majesty, if I may," Kirian said. "Remember that the sart leaf cannot be taken more than one time in a day, because it speeds your heart. While it is working, you must have your slaves clear this room of smoke. A little fresh air will help your lungs. If you do not do this, you may find yourself suffering another attack by evening."

"Do what she says." The King turned to the ku'an'an, and began discussing something else, apparently forgetting Kirian.

She bowed and retreated from the room with the Queen's attendant and the lord physician following close.

"I will call upon you to learn about the sart leaf," the physician said. He had a sour look on his face, but Kirian thought he was attempting to be polite. "It is more appropriate for the King's own physicians to be administering it."

"Lord Yun'lar, I thank you for allowing me to treat the king," she said. She could tell the lord physician was not her friend, but she had no wish to alienate him further than her gender, her profession, and her success at treating the King had already done.

Kirian nodded and followed the attendant back to the Queen's parlor. The attendant whispered admiring congratulations to her, to which Kirian responded politely, but Kirian was exhausted. The stresses of the morning had worn her out. The boy King's narrow ku'an eyes bothered her; she had discerned no trace of benevolence in them, in spite of their youth. She remembered how many dried sart leaves there were in her bag, and wondered what would happen when she ran out.

The Queen, still sitting spiderlike in her chair, gave Kirian stately thanks and told her to ask for whatever she needed to be comfortable in Las'ash city. Kirian thought about asking to be rid of Sara'Si, but simply bowed and thanked the Queen.

Back at her room, the rotund guard was about to let her in when Chiss' lean face appeared in Callo's open door.

"Come in here," he said.

The guard looked as if he were about to protest. Kirian's veiled chaperone followed her into Callo's room. Chiss frowned at the woman, but she ignored him.

Callo was pacing up and down before an unshuttered window, looking out at the city. A bitter wind gusted into the room, making the fire snap and waver.

"Gods! It's cold in here," Kirian said. Callo turned on one heel to look at her.

"Who is that?"

"My companion, Hon Sara'Si. She goes with me everywhere."

"Not here," Callo said. "You may await the Healer in her chamber."

"Yes, please go," Kirian said. "I will be fine here."

Sara'Si bowed and said, "My lord ku'an, I have been ordered to accompany Hon Kirian wherever she goes."

A muscle worked in Callo's jaw. "I am ordering you to leave. You can await Hon Kirian in her room, or you can go to hell for all I care."

The veiled woman clearly felt it wasn't wise to argue with an irritated ku'an. She bowed and retreated.

"I will have to pay for that later," Kirian said lightly.

"What can she do to you?" Callo said dismissively. Kirian did not know the answer to that, but she feared she would find out if Callo kept disregarding the customs of this land.

Chiss closed and shuttered the window, casting them into a shadowy gloom. He brought wine and nuts from a side table. Callo poured himself some of the wine and drank, and then gestured at the jar, which prompted Chiss to pour some wine for Kirian and then for himself. The wine tasted dry and strong.

No sooner had she felt its taste on her tongue than Callo said: "Where were you?"

"I was called to help with a healing." Kirian could have said more, but his tone annoyed her. "What concern is it of yours?"

"You could have told us where you were going. I am responsible for you."

She couldn't believe her ears. "Since when, my lord? The

last I heard, I asked to accompany you to this place, not marry you."

Callo flushed. His eyes glittered in a disconcerting way. She almost thought she saw a spark. "As far as these people are concerned, you are of my household. That makes me responsible."

He was worried, Kirian realized, as she sipped the wine again. Most of her annoyance vanished. "I will try to do better in the future," she said. Out of the corner of her eye, she saw Chiss go into the little alcove reserved for the servant's cot and belongings. She looked up at Lord Callo, a smile beginning to light her eyes. She was charmed by his worry.

He stood very near her, his eyes on her smiling ones. His face was expressionless. He did not speak, yet Kirian felt as if he were under the influence of some strong emotion.

"I thank you for your concern," she said in a soft voice.

He raised his hand and with one finger traced the line of her jaw. She stood motionless, hardly breathing. He seemed very tall and warm, standing so close. She saw his eyes on her mouth. Her breath came faster.

Chiss dropped something in the alcove. The sound made Kirian jump. Chiss pushed aside the curtain and returned to the main chamber. Lord Callo stepped back. Kirian flushed and looked away.

"The Queen called me," she said, hurrying into words. "The King has the breathing disease, and was in the middle of an attack."

"King Ar'ok? The boy king?" Chiss asked.

"A strange boy." She remembered the look in his eyes after he recovered, when he was watching her, and shivered.

"Did he do something to you?" Callo asked, noting her reaction.

"No. He's just—older than his years. Not really a boy after all," she said lightly.

"All that power doesn't make for normal individuals," Callo said. "Look at Sharpeyes. It's why I can't get around this ku'an business."

"Surely there are people who use power benevolently," Chiss said. "King Ar'ok is most definitely not one of them."

"What have you heard, Chiss?"

"He uses a ku'an's power to get what he wants. Nothing unusual in that – most of them do, here. But he is very young to be so ruthless. He has a bad reputation with women."

"So did you cure him?" Callo asked.

"Temporarily," Kirian said. "There is no cure for the disease, but sart leaves taken as a tea will ease the attacks. They don't seem to know of the sart plant here, so I am Ar'ok's only source of it until their physicians can locate some."

Callo smiled. "Good."

Chiss took the empty wine jug from the table. "It will make them think twice before they do anything hostile towards you, my lord."

"I will not withhold my aid for any kind of political reason, my lord," Kirian warned.

"It doesn't matter. They will *think* you will, Kirian. And they'll be as accommodating as they can to me because of it."

Chapter Ten

Callo stood outside the ornate wooden door. The door was carved with figures from Ha'lasi myth or history — the god Ur'brok siring his son Som'ur, the first psychic lord of Ha'las. Callo examined the carvings as he waited. The human woman Ur'brok had settled on as the vessel of his legacy looked pained, almost agonized, as Ur'brok ravished her. Ur'brok, he thought with a startled smile, bore a strong resemblance to Jashan.

The door swung open to reveal a bowing guard and a veiled woman, probably a noblewoman of some sort from the quality of her robes and jewelry.

"Lord Callo?" the woman said. "You may enter."

Callo nodded and entered the room. There were guards and servants, but only three occupants of status. One was an older woman dressed in ornate robes that hung on her bony frame. Jewelry glittered in her red-gray hair, on her hands, stitched into her robes. As Callo entered, she was splaying her fingers in front of her, admiring the sparkle of multiple rings on each finger. An adolescent boy sat near her, looking sulky as if forced to an unwelcome duty. His face was peaked in the light of the fire. Behind the boy stood Si'lan, the ku'an'an of Ha'las.

All three of them had eyes the same amber color as his own. Callo made a formal bow to the King, then to the Queen.

"Your Majesties," Si'lan said, "This is the ku'an I told you about. Callo ran Alkiran from Righar."

"I am most honored, your Majesties," Callo said.

The boy king's eyes slid over Callo. His eyelids dropped. "You must know how this half-a-ku'an came to be. Mother?"

"Your royal father did not share as much with me as you might have thought," the Queen said. Her eyes were avid as she evaluated Callo. "But he makes a fine addition to our ranks. Perhaps you would honor me with your presence at dinner soon, Lord Callo?"

"He is accompanied by the young woman Healer," murmured Si'lan. "Shall she be invited as well?"

The Queen pursed her lips. "No need for that, Si'lan. You may entertain her, if she is worth entertaining."

Callo stiffened. "I understand Hon Kirian has performed a great service for His Majesty."

"Indeed," Si'lan said. "And he is grateful. Are you not, Sire?"

Ar'ok grimaced. "Yes, yes. Though a woman Healer is an abomination. What is she like, Lord Callo? In bed?"

Anger flashed through his veins. Si'lan, watching him, said: "Excuse His Majesty, Lord Callo. He derives pleasure from prodding you thus."

Callo's speech was frozen by the exigencies of his awkward position here. He could not reply.

Ar'ok laughed. "You do not behave like a ku'an at all," he said.

"I came here to discover the Ha'lasi part of my heritage," Callo bit off. "Thus far, it does not please me."

Si'lan said, "Calm down now, my lord. You don't know us well enough to make such a judgment. And you! Your Majesty. Please guard your tongue."

Ar'ok's eyes narrowed. "You overstep yourself, ku'an'an." The lazy smile was gone from his face. His stare was malevolent. He sat up and transferred his stare to Callo. "You are but half a ku'an. What use you are I do not know. But Si'lan has asked me to accommodate you, so I will, for a while. Talk to Si'lan. Go to Som'ur. Maybe you will learn how to be a ku'an."

If you are an example, then I will not wish to. Callo was furious. He choked down his first rash response. Chiss had warned him against this boy King, and had advised him to keep a firm hold on his temper. When he spoke it was with rigid control. "I cannot agree with you, Your Majesty, but I can only be appreciative of your hospitality. I hope you will discover the error in your opinion of us."

Ar'ok laughed again, then his eyes slid away from Callo towards a slave girl who approached with a tray of refreshments. Callo decided he would not touch the offered food if his life depended upon it. The Queen watched him, eyes flirting from under her ridiculous veil; he knew her admiration would turn in a blink to antagonism if he insulted Ar'ok. He bowed and took his leave. Si'lan was just behind him as the carven door closed behind him.

"I would offer my apologies," Si'lan said. "But there is no point. It will happen again whenever you see him."

"Jashan's eyes. What have I done to that . . .?" He stifled his words, aware that Si'lan was no friend either.

"There is no need for you to have done anything. His Majesty is a young King with great personal power, and has never been subject to much discipline. You must remember you are the adult here, and draw upon your patience."

"No doubt." Callo let Si'lan draw him along the corridor. His thoughts swirled, as the conversation with the King replayed itself in his head. Then he realized he had no idea where Si'lan was taking him. "Where are we going?"

"To Som'ur's temple, as His Majesty commanded. To be introduced to the god. All ku'an worship Ur'brok's son Som'ur."

Callo sighed and withdrew his arm from Si'lan's hold. "You are rushing me along as if I am a steer going to slaughter."

Si'lan's answering grin was malicious. All Callo's defenses snapped into place.

"If you wish for me to instruct you, as a ku'an, you must be accepted by Som'ur. He weeds out pretenders and false motivations."

"How does he do this?"

"The new ku'an stays in his temple overnight. Som'ur comes to him. If the ku'an is free of impure motives, he lives."

"And that boy—excuse me, His Majesty—has been through this procedure?"

Si'lan nodded. "He would not be King, if he had not been accepted by Som'ur. None of us could rule this land without his sanction, especially as few as we are."

Callo wondered how stringent the god's requirements were, if such an idiot as Ar'ok had lived through the test. "I have worshiped Jashan since I was ten. Why would Som'ur let me live, since I owe my life to Jashan?"

Si'lan began walking again. Callo followed. "If you do not complete the vigil, we will have no choice but to assume your purpose here is espionage. Why should we give up our secrets to a foreign ku'an that is not vouched for by our god?"

"I don't want any of your damn secrets. That's not why I'm here."

"Then, why? To find your father?"

"I'd like to know who he was. Why a Ha'lasi mage went to such trouble to sire me. I most certainly am not here as a spy for King Martan."

"But King Martan is your uncle."

"Yes."

"Surely you must understand we cannot simply trust you. You have no choice, Lord Callo. I will escort you to the temple – there is one here, in the castle, and a priest to pray over you."

"I will not go. It is suicide." Callo stopped, began to turn around. Si'lan gestured and Callo was surrounded by armed guards. He reached for his sword, but, of course, he had not been armed in the King's presence. He took a deep breath and met Si'lan's expressionless gaze.

"I think you will go," Si'lan said. "After you have recovered, we will discuss what you need to know."

The guards escorted Callo down the hallway. Si'lan stood in the corridor, watching him go.

The guards left him at the door to Som'ur's temple, closing and locking it behind him. The temple was a small room with six chairs spaced in a circle around a small dais. The dais, covered in gold leaf, held what looked to Callo like a live human heart, but much larger than he would have expected such a thing to be. The organ hung suspended above a polished base, pulsing. He stood there looking at this improbable centerpiece, then reached out to touch the plinth, but a barrier he could not see stopped his finger before it could come anywhere near.

The heart beat. Callo frowned at it. Why was such a thing on the dais? Was it something to be venerated? Or was it simply a focus for meditation? It looked real. Could it be Som'ur's heart?

He did not know why he had expected a temple of Som'ur to be large, for the only worshippers would be ku'an, and there were few of those in Ha'las. According to legend, all descended in some way from the god, similar to the way the *righ* all claimed descent from Valotnor. He looked around; the walls were covered with freeform curves in more gold. The ku'an had spent a fortune on this tiny room, money he knew the poor island kingdom could not afford. The overall effect was both rich and barbaric. He looked up and around and saw, partially hidden among the gold-leaf decorations halfway up the tall ceiling, a gap. It was a spy-hole. From the space on the other side of that hole, the ku'an'an, or anyone else, could observe what happened to him here.

He sighed and sat on one of the chairs. A long night lay ahead. He had no idea how Som'ur would manifest himself, but he doubted a man who had sworn oaths to Jashan would survive the night.

The lock rattled. He turned to look as the door opened. Callo tensed, ready to use this entrance as an opportunity to escape what he expected to be certain death from a jealous Ha'lasi god, but the man who entered was flanked by three of the armed guards. They were taking no chances.

The man who entered wore the gold eye insignia of the King. He sat next to Callo, looking at him curiously with the ku'an's gold eyes.

"Another ku'an," Callo said. "You are everywhere."

"There are actually very few of us," the man answered. "If you survive this night, we will welcome you very gladly indeed. I am Wan'tal, Som'ur's priest."

"Callo ran Alkiran."

The priest nodded. "I am to tell you what to expect. You

will spend the night here. At some point Som'ur will come to you. He will put you through some kind of ordeal – it seems to vary from ku'an to ku'an, and I would not try to guess what it will be for a foreign half-blood like yourself. If you survive, you will be accepted here."

"What is the significance of the heart, up on the dais?"

"That is Som'ur's heart."

"It is . . . very lifelike," Callo said.

"It is not a representation of Som'ur's heart. It is the god's heart. It was cut from his body on the battlefield and has been guarded by the ku'an ever since."

"I see."

"Do you have any more questions?"

"No. I would appreciate it if you informed my man Chiss and Healer Kirian of where I am."

"Of course." The priest stood and drew his robe about him. He stepped toward the door.

"No prayers, then," Callo said.

"They would mean nothing to you, worshipper of a foreign god that you are. And Som'ur himself requires no prayers from us, just dominance in his name. Good fortune to you, Lord Callo. I hope to see you in the morning." The priest bowed and nodded to the guards. They walked out behind the priest, hands on weapons, eyes never leaving Callo until the door locked behind them.

Callo stretched and leaned back in the chair. It was hard and uncomfortable. He did not know how the ku'an worshipped Som'ur, but he was sure none of them fell asleep in these chairs while doing it. After a while, he got up and began pacing the perimeter of the tiny room, practicing the controlled breathing he had learned from Jashan's priests.

There were no windows for him to tell the passage of time, but the candles had burned down a couple of marks when he felt the first intimation of danger. He sat in one of the chairs, waiting.

The air around him turned cold. In a flash he felt the heightened sensation he had felt when Si'lan had tested him—the rasp of air on skin, the pain of the hard chair pressing into his back, the intense unbearable aroma he had not even noticed before. He rose, unable to keep touching the chair, but the pressure of his feet on the floor almost made him cry out. He closed his eyes for a moment against the searing light from the two candles. All his senses were on fire.

He sat back down, gritting his teeth against the rough sensation.

Then the heightened sensitivity vanished.

All was quiet. He opened his eyes, wincing, but the candle-light was once again just a dim glow. He waited.

Then two amber eyes opened in his mind, and he lay back across two chairs, dismayed.

The eyes scanned his mind, sweeping back and forth across the expanse of his memories from the earliest childhood when he had let his anger spill out onto those around him. The gaze saw into every dark corner. Callo lay there sweating as his mind opened up its possessions to the god. The wall he had built to contain the ku'an ability vanished under Som'ur's eyes. The eyes burned where they looked, leaving his mind feeling raw and sore. This was miserable, but if all Som'ur was going to do was look, Callo thought he could make it through the night.

Then the god started testing him.

The first feeling was joy—an explosion of it, so white-hot that his muscles stiffened, and he gasped. He had never felt joy like this, so intense it was almost pain. Then the joy was swept away as if the god tired of it, and lust took hold, only for a few seconds of exquisite torment, before it vanished. Then came fear, and the fear did not let go.

The fear turned his muscles rigid. His heart raced; his breath came fast. He felt as if he was going to black out. Was this what a ku'an did, what Som'ur let them do—cause this agony? Was he supposed to accept the god's intrusion somehow, let Som'ur in? He could not do that—Jashan was his god, who had guarded him from himself for decades. He could not accept this brutal invasion; there was no way he could assimilate it, although he thought that was what Som'ur expected of him.

He tried to shove Som'ur away the way he had the ku'an'an when Si'lan had tested him, but his will was in shreds, his barrier wall gone. Som'ur was inflicting misery on him that he thought would kill him. His heart beat rapidly, and so hard he almost thought he would be able to see his chest vibrate with it. All his muscles were clenched, and his breath came fast, yet he could get no air. He slipped from the chair into a heap on the floor. His vision began to blacken, and a sharp pain slammed from his head through his body. His heart spasmed.

Then something hot ran from his tormented heart down his veins into his hands. He felt Som'ur hesitate; he was able to draw a deep breath. He opened eyes that felt as if they were rimmed with salt, seeing fire in the room—color magic. Jashan's magery raced into the room as Jashan responded to his call and defended him from the other god. Surely it was extraordinary that Jashan would come to fight for him in the very temple of Som'ur. Even more astonishing that the god's fire came from his own hands.

The fire died. His heartbeat eased. The pain subsided until he thought he could sit up. His arm almost gave out as he pushed himself up into a half-sitting position. The gold eyes in his consciousness closed and Callo's mind was his own once more.

He was alone. No gods lurked in his mind. He looked up at the spy hole and thought he saw movement, then shrugged to himself and dragged himself to his feet. Swaying, he took a quick inventory and found his body weary, shaking, painful, but whole. His mind was seared but seemed to contain everything it should, including his protective wall, which loomed stronger than ever somehow. He looked up at the plinth and saw the god Som'ur's heart still there, still beating. To his exhausted eyes, it looked a little scorched.

He gave himself a few minutes to recover, then stood in the center of the tiny room, swordless, and did the most basic of his rituals, turning without his usual grace in the small space available. The familiar motions seemed to ease the raw feeling in his mind. He thanked Jashan for his aid.

Som'ur had left no influence in his mind that he could detect— just pain. He wondered how it was for the other ku'an. He knew he dared not ask. After a few minutes, he lay down again across the chairs, put his hand across his forehead, and fell into an exhausted slumber.

Neither the rattle of the locks nor the opening of the door awakened him in the morning. He startled awake to the odor of bad breath and the sight of a looming red face a few inches away from his own. The ku'an priest peered at him.

Callo raised a hand and pushed the man back, grimacing. What a way to wake up, he thought, and after such a terrible night. He could trace the path of each of his muscles by the pain.

"He's alive," Wan'tal announced. "Som'ur has accepted him."

Callo sat up, then stood. His body was one big ache, but his mind was clear. He said, "I can go now?"

"Yes, my lord. I will inform the ku'an'an of the results." He looked at Callo. "May I say I am pleased, Lord Callo."

There was a small commotion at the door. Chiss shoved past the two guards. He glared at them, straightening his tunic as if they had tried to restrain him.

"Chiss, I am very glad to see you this morning!"

"Lord Callo, thank the gods you are all right!" There was unaccustomed emotion in the man's voice. "When they told me where you were, I tried to convince the Lord Ku'an'an this was a mistake. I regret I failed. Are you well?"

Callo stretched carefully. He coughed. His throat and mouth felt like sandpaper. "Very well, Chiss, considering."

"I assume my lord may go now?" Chiss said to Wan'tal frostily. "Or must he run some other gauntlet?"

Wan'tal said, "He may go. I will send Lord Yun'lar to you if you wish, Lord Callo. He is the King's physician."

"No need," Callo said. If he needed a Healer, there was one he would far rather consult. He shouldered past the curious guardsmen and walked with Chiss to his chamber. Inside, Chiss brought him wine and food. He sipped the wine, closing his eyes briefly as the tart liquid went down his abused throat. He could not remember why his throat was so sore. Had he screamed, during Som'ur's ordeal?

Chiss moved about ordering hot water for a bath. After a while he said, "Lord Callo, shall I call Hon Kirian? You look— ill. And you have some cuts, I see."

Callo looked down in surprise. There were indeed shallow cuts on his hands and forearms, cuts he did not remember receiving. The skin on his hands felt stretched and hot, as if singed. When he got ready for the bath, he would see what other wounds he had.

"Not now," he said. "I need quiet. Let me see, after the bath."

"I did not think you would survive it," Chiss said. "I am very glad to see you well, my lord."

"I didn't think I'd make it through either."

"Then—Som'ur actually came to you?"

"Oh, yes. Not gently, either." He began to take off his tunic and winced in pain. Chiss stood at his side, helping him as if he were a boy again, needing help to undress after a tiring day.

"Are you his man then now?" Chiss stared at him, eyes narrowed.

"I am Jashan's sworn man. But, I think—maybe Som'ur claims me also, in some way."

———

Kirian fumed as she walked down the crowded street toward the market. She would have liked to defuse some of her tension by taking longer strides, but the long robe wrapped too tightly around her to permit such freedom of movement. Even if she could have walked faster, she was forbidden to leave Sara'Si behind.

She had never seen Sara'Si without her veil, even in the privacy of their own chamber. This veil was nothing like the ornamental affair the Queen and some of the other older women wore when there were no men present—it was so thick that Kirian wondered how the chaperone could see. She had no idea what Sara'Si looked like. Kirian also knew nothing about Sara'Si's personality, since the other woman kept this as veiled as she did her face. She had tried to be friendly with Sara'Si when she had first arrived in Las'ash, but her overtures were met with a blank hostility Kirian did not understand. All she knew was that Ha'lasi custom required her to keep Sara'Si with her always. She had flouted that custom once, when they were newly arrived in Las'ash city. On that occasion, Lady Min'dou, one of the Queen's ladies, sat her down for a talk about what was expected of women in the King's court. If she could not acquiesce to this arrangement, Lady Min'dou said, she would be required to stay in the women's quarters.

Kirian tried to acquiesce. She was a guest in this land, and bound to try to follow their customs. She could envision few things worse than being kept a virtual prisoner in a place with a lot of other women, under guard, with nothing to do.

For her first sennight in Las'ash city, Kirian held to the prescribed behavior, feeling more desperate every day. Ha'las was more restrictive than even the charity orphanage she had been raised in, which was run along strict lines. Here, she knew there were people with different customs, strange gods, and lives she knew nothing about. Here were ku'an—people in Righar scared their children into obedience with tales of the ku'an, yet the only one she had met for more than a few minutes was Lord Callo, who hardly counted, being Righan by birth after all. Here were new treatments she could learn, to broaden her Healing skills. Although she had not been impressed by the treatments they used for King Ar'ok's breathing disease, surely there were other things she could learn from them.

She was held back, restrained, almost imprisoned. None of these things were open to her. Even Lord Yun'lar, who seemed to respect her proven healing ability, would not discuss his art with her.

In the Queen's chambers, she met a number of other women of the court. Most were frivolous creatures, interested in nothing beyond the palace walls, as they had been raised and educated to be. But Kirian knew there were intelligent women there, too. Lady Min'dou introduced her to Lady Yas'hira, wife of one of the city lords, who impressed Kirian with her sharp wit and knowledge of the outside world, which far exceeded Kirian's own. Another woman, the Queen's companion, discussed Righan healing with her, and told her about the political factions that fought each other behind a screen of subservience to the ku'an. These were intelligent women, used to influencing the world from their traditional positions in the women's quarters or in their husbands' homes, but worthy of respect nonetheless.

Now, walking toward the market, Kirian clutched her cloak tightly about her against the cold. This was not the stained cloak she had worn berry-picking, but a new one, lined with rabbit fur, that she found in her chamber one morning. Lord Callo (or actually Chiss) had provided it when he realized how cold it was here in Las'ash city. She had thanked both of them. Recalled to her situation, Lord Callo gave her Ha'lasi coins and told her to get what she needed. She stifled her embarrassment and sent one of the servants out on a shopping excursion since she was not permitted to go herself. Then she found Lord Callo in the library and tried to return the change to him.

"What's that?" He looked up at her, his eyes a little unfocused from prolonged reading.

"This is your money. I bought what I needed—my thanks, Lord Callo. There are several coins left."

"Really? Out of that little I gave you?"

"Here they are. Thank you for your generosity."

He shrugged, took the money, and put it on the table next to him. "You are welcome, of course, but I hauled you out of Righar with no chance to buy anything. It's the least I can do."

"You weren't the reason I had to leave so suddenly."

He put the book aside. His mind back to the present, he smiled up at her in such a way that she caught her breath. He had that effect on her; perhaps it was a good thing she did not see him so much anymore. He said, "We have had no chance to talk. How has His Majesty been?"

"He is fine, Callo. No more attacks, for now."

"And yourself?"

She shrugged, looking away from him. His brows drew together in a slight frown.

"Kirian? Is all well?"

"Nothing is wrong. It's just—there's nothing to do. It's terribly boring."

"Boring?" He looked surprised. "But there's a city to explore. People to heal, I am sure."

"Perhaps you have not noticed how it is for the women here at the palace, my lord." It would be just like a nobleman, in fact, to be blind to the situations of everyone but himself. She must not forget that Callo was a nobleman, and thus self-centered. Though she had to give him credit: he was most generous with his money. And he had brought her here in the first place, at her urging, against his own wishes.

"The women here?" He glanced at Sara'Si, a shadow near the door. "Of course I have. They can't do anything on their own. It's a terrible waste. But what has that to do with you?"

She stared at him. "What do you mean, what has that to do with me?"

He stood up, gestured her to the chair he had been sitting in, the only chair in the room. "Why do you need to keep the Ha'lasi custom?"

She remained standing. "I would much rather not keep the custom! My lord, I have been told it is a religious matter, and I may not flout it without severe consequences."

"Oh, the chaperone, yes." He bowed towards Sara'Si. "Of course. But why can't you take her with you? Go learn from their Healers, explore the city, whatever. You'd best take a couple of guards along, though. Maybe Chiss will go as well. Parts of this city are dangerous."

"My lord, I have no status to request such a thing. Lady Min'dou would never relay such a request from me. I have tried. I am pretty much stuck here."

He was getting upset. He began pacing, the frown deepening between his brows. "I did not realize you were sitting here bored out of your mind. I can't imagine you cooped up—well, enough. What have you been doing for the past sennight?"

She sighed. "Nothing, Lord Callo."

"What do you mean, nothing?"

"Exactly that. I have been forbidden to leave the palace in case His Majesty needs me. I cannot explore the palace itself, because I am informed there are soldiers here and other rough men, and a respectable woman cannot be seen near them. I cannot—oh, gods, I won't go through it all. It is enough to say I am cooped up like a chicken. And guarded, too, my lord."

She could see the tension in his shoulders. "Chiss has said nothing to me of this."

"I have not mentioned it to Chiss."

"Or to me. Why did you not come to me for help? Perhaps a request from me will meet with more cooperation."

"You have been occupied." She had seen Callo at meals and around the palace occasionally. He had asked after her welfare, and sent Chiss to ask what she needed. But the easy familiarity they had enjoyed on the *Fortune* had faded a little, due to her forced seclusion. Also, he had been closeted with the ku'an'an, or training in the practice ring, or studying in the extensive palace library, and who knew where else. He was taken up with the questions that had brought him here. She had not wanted to disturb him with such a trivial thing. She said so now.

"It's not trivial!" He glared at her. "You are a virtual prisoner here. This is not what I agreed with the ku'an'an. I will see him."

"I think he will tell you the affairs of the palace's women are not his concern. It is Lady Min'dou, or perhaps the Queen, who rules us. I doubt she is susceptible to demands from foreign supplicants like ourselves." She was pleased, though, by his willingness to act on her behalf.

"I don't care whose concern they are! You are not a hostage. You are to be given your freedom, as long as you agree to a chaperone. I will see the Lord Ku'an'an now. You, Sara'Si! If Hon Kirian wants to visit the city tomorrow, you will accompany her, is that clear?"

Kirian had noted before Sara'Si's reluctance to gainsay Lord Callo when he was annoyed. The woman simply bowed, but later in Kirian's chamber she made her opinions heard about how a male, even if he were a ku'an, had no say in the life of a woman he was not married to.

Nevertheless, it had worked. Faced with an irate Lord Callo, the ku'an'an did what he needed to do to make sure Kirian was allowed freedoms not typically permitted women in Las'ash city. The very next day, she was allowed to go to the city's market with several other women of the palace and three chaperones. She walked along the wide aisles, her cloak wrapped about her, and enjoyed the sights and sounds of the city. The day after that, she discovered the hospital.

Kirian approached the market, Sara'Si lagging behind her. In spite of the general poverty of the city residents, the market was full of noise and life. The place was enclosed in canvas and heated with small braziers in the vendors' stalls. The market sold flowers, vegetables, and fresh meat in the summer. Now, in winter, it held baked goods stalls, sellers of pins and needles and used, mended pots and pans; as well as a weaver, candlemaker and other craftspeople. There was a furniture maker with chairs and cradles stacked along the sides of his space, sawdust coating the ground. It was a crowded, loud place. Exploring on that first visit, with Sara'Si's gloomy shadow behind her, Kirian had ducked out of the market proper and, following a group of women and children, had found the hospital. It had now been three sennights since she had discovered the hospital. She walked in to talk with the midwife who ran it and made arrangements with her to start working there, thus allowing herself to fulfill her Healer's oath as well as to fill the hours.

The hospital was in an abandoned shop; the midwife had divided it into rooms by using cloth and canvas. The place admitted only women and children. Two heavyset men guarded the place; Kirian later learned they were eunuchs. The midwife ran the hospital with strict propriety. Kirian had tried to get Sara'Si to leave her at the hospital for a candle-mark or two, but the chaperone refused. Instead, she stayed in the hallway, seated on a bench with the people waiting to see a healer, a silent and watchful presence.

Kirian went into the hospital and greeted the midwife. Jhan'ko was a round, middle-aged women with early wrinkles in her parchment-fair skin. She looked like a shopkeeper's wife in her white sash and veil, and that is indeed what she had been until her husband's death had left her childless, financially well-off, and bored with the shop and her occasional midwifery. Jhan'ko took advantage of the relative freedom afforded a widow to start this hospital for women and children. Still, she was accompanied to the place each day by a chaperone and her eunuch guardsmen.

Kirian went into one of the makeshift rooms and waited. Jhan'ko's chaperone started sending people in. Kirian left her veil on. In Healer's College she had been taught always to make eye contact with her patients, but here in Ha'las an unveiled woman made people nervous. So she tried to use her voice to put them at ease.

In her time here, she had seen babies with ear pain and colic, the babies crying, and the young mothers exhausted and needful of reassurance. Sometimes a patient complained of menstrual pain, or an inflammation of the throat that lasted for weeks, or of a cold—the same maladies that plagued women in Righar. One grinning girl of about seven came in with a broken arm, and watched the setting and splinting procedure with great interest. Kirian wished the child would not have to don the veil in a few years when she reached puberty.

She also treated a woman who had been battered around the face, and another who had blood in her urine, the result of a severe beating by her male protector. These cases made her furious at how helpless women were in this land. After she treated them, Jhan'ko calmed her down and warned her against reporting the cases. "It will only cause them worse trouble," the midwife said.

Kirian bowed to the other woman's knowledge of her own culture. "I wish I could help them, though."

Jhan'ko placed her plump hand over Kirian's. "You are. We have been treating many more women here, since you began to help me. They know we have a real Healer here now —an even better one than they have up at the palace."

"Oh, I'm sure the nobility have excellent physicians," Kirian said, though she remembered Lord Yun'lar burning rose leaves in the King's room and wondered.

Jhan'ko shook her head. Her white veil rustled as it moved against her rough-textured robe. "No. I have heard stories about the Healers in Righar. You are trained in a college, for years, and you serve an apprenticeship, is that not so? And you can call upon a god to heal through your hands."

"There is no god that heals through us. We are human, and have no godly help. As for the rest, though—the Healer's College is the best in the world."

Jhan'ko sighed. "I wish I were only young enough and rich enough to attend there. Is your family very rich, to pay for you to learn at such a place?"

Kirian smiled. "No, Hon Jhan'ko. I was a charity student. The Healer's College is required to take one in, every two years, according to the rules set by the noble who funded the College many years ago. I lived in a house for orphans before that. The Unknown God was looking out for me the day they chose me."

"I can see why they chose you. You have something I have not seen in our physicians here. It is not just your knowledge, Hon Kirian—though it is good to know of the herbs and the way the body is put together. You have something more. It is why the line in front of this place stretches back to the marketplace even now."

Kirian rose and looked out the front of the shop, past the eunuchs who guarded the entrance. A line of cloaked and veiled women, many with children, snaked past the other shopfronts. "It is not always like this? I thought the women of Las'ash came here because they could get no treatment elsewhere."

"There are midwives. Most women see them, for most complaints. We do our best. But you have a different touch. I learn from you every day."

Kirian could feel her face heating. "I'm—thank you, Hon Jhan'ko. I am honored."

Jhan'ko lowered her voice. "You came here with a ku'an, didn't you?"

"Uh—Lord Callo, yes."

"And he does not forbid you to come to the hospital?" Kirian smiled. "He encouraged me to come here."

Jhan'ko paused. Kirian looked up to see an odd look about the woman's eyes.

"You are fortunate," the midwife said. "But the ku'an are a capricious lot. If he changes his mind, do not feel obligated."

"I make my own decisions," Kirian said.

"I have never heard of a lady from the palace being out in public, in such close contact with ordinary people. I hope it does not come to the Queen's ears."

"Let us hope it does not," Kirian said lightly, and rose to go back to her treatment room. She was eager to see that line in front of the hospital start moving again.

Jhan'ko's chaperone began sending patients in as soon as Kirian returned to her room. The first one was a veiled mother drawing her son behind her. The boy was probably ten, really too old to be permitted in the hospital, but Jhan'ko had admitted him. The boy slumped in his chair and stared at the floor. When she spoke to him, he did not reply, and when she lifted his head to look at his eyes, they were dull and unfocused.

"What happened?" Kirian asked the mother, frowning. The reply shocked her.

"It was a ku'an," the woman said. "From up at the castle. The lord ku'an was in the city on business, and told my son to hold his horse. My boy—well, he is not always very responsible, always looking at the birds, or drawing in the dirt, or daydreaming . . ." The woman stopped, cleared her throat, and then resumed. "Well, he was the gods' gift, but not good at staying with a task, you understand, Healer?"

Kirian nodded. The boy's eyes were looking at the canvas

wall but were unfocused, paying no attention to anything going on in the room.

"Me'lar—that's my boy—wasn't paying attention. The horse was taken, and Me'lar couldn't catch up to the thief. The ku'an came out of the building where he was, and…"

"Did this?"

"My husband says the ku'an was just punishing the boy. Using his magery, making Me'lar feel guilty, just for a while, to teach him a lesson. My husband says the lord ku'an would never do this on purpose, that he was just too heavy handed."

"Where is the lord ku'an?"

"Gone. He took another horse from the stables and went back—to the palace, I suppose."

"Does he know about this?"

"No! No, we would never dare try to tell him."

Kirian looked at the boy, sitting slack and empty on the chair. She looked in his eyes, checked his reflexes, and gave him some simple directions which the boy did not respond to. "Who was this ku'an, then?"

The woman shrank into herself and said nothing.

"You know his name," Kirian said, sure of that from the mother's reaction.

"No. Can you help him or not?"

Kirian sighed. "I wish I could. Illnesses of the mind and of emotions are not simple to treat. There is nothing I can do. As time passes, maybe he will come out of it."

"Time! It has been a season already. The ku'an burned out his mind."

"Who was it, then?" Kirian demanded.

The woman rose and grasped her son's limp arm, drawing him to his feet. "Things are bad enough for us already, Healer. We do not need to go accusing a ku'an. Gods, he would destroy all of us. Leave it alone. I am sorry I came."

"As you wish. Look, if anything occurs to me, I will tell the midwife here. You know Jhan'ko."

The woman paused a moment. Her voice was softer when she spoke again. "Yes. I will check back. I thank you, Healer."

Kirian saw the woman out, her mind whirling. A ku'an had abused his talent so as to destroy a boy's mind, and nothing was done? It fit in with what she had begun to learn about the ku'an—that they were corrupt, and above the law. In this way they were no better than the Collared Lords of Righar. She wished Callo did not have this psychic magery that seemed to corrupt those who used it. Although, remembering Callo with the injured boy back in Seagard village, she could not imagine him doing anything like this.

Her next patient was a single woman. Her veil was an uncommon affair that covered her down to her knees. A row of beads weighted its hem. The veil, draped over the woman's floor-length robe, disguised everything about her except the woman's ease of movement, which led Kirian to think that she was young.

"What may I help you with?" Kirian asked. She looked into the woman's eyes through the veil and was surprised to see them sharp and bright, staring back at her with none of the timidity she sometimes saw from these women, who knew she was a foreigner of strange beliefs.

"You are the Healer who came to Las'ash City with the foreign ku'an?" the woman asked.

"Yes."

The woman lowered her voice to a level that would not be overheard in the adjoining areas. "Then you have been here long enough to know that the ku'an are evil."

Kirian started to reply, but the woman waved her to silence. "They are corrupt, all of them. For the first time in memory—in several lifetimes—their numbers are few. There are not enough of them to rule. Only a dozen ku'an hold this land in their fists; did you know that?"

"That's all?"

"They cling to power. They are afraid. That is why they are becoming more brutal, to keep the people down through fear. Not that they aren't always self-serving bastards."

"I am no supporter of the ku'an. But…"

"Help us, then. This foreign ku'an—bring him to us."

Kirian wondered why they wanted Callo. Would they kill him? Use him for bait of some sort, to draw in other ku'an? She said, "He is not like the rest."

"Oh, no?" The other woman laughed. "He will be. The more time he spends here, the more they will teach him to be like them. He will use his magery to force people to his will, no matter how trivial a matter it is. He is not a priest, is he, to resist that? Is he not what they call a *righ,* a man of noble birth in his own country?"

Kirian rose. "You know, I think you'd better go."

"I will tell you where to bring him. There will be no blame for you – we'll arrange it that way."

They'll kill him, and then the ku'an here will kill me, she thought. "Go, please," she said.

The woman walked toward the door. "I will see you again," she said. "Look around you, until I come again. Watch him—watch all of the cursed ku'an. You will see what I mean."

Chapter Eleven

The surface of the practice ring was dirt, worn smooth and hard with the pressure of many feet. It was surrounded by a rail where observers leaned to encourage the participants—or sometimes to howl their derision at an ill-done maneuver. Callo had heard both, in the season he had been at Las'ash, but neither was ever directed toward him. He was usually unobserved; when men did watch his forms, they were silent, gauging his skill with eyes that gave back nothing of their reactions.

Today, he had come to the ring before breakfast. He waited his turn behind a clump of armed guardsmen and warriors waiting for their chance to hone their skills. He stood there only a portion of a candlemark before the waiting group dissolved, men moving away here and there in so casual a manner that, if he hadn't been watching for it, he might not have realized their disappearance was because of him.

Interestingly, he had seen only a few ku'an since his arrival, yet everyone seemed to know what a ku'an looked like, and no one seemed to trust one. The power of this land was crammed into the fists of the ku'an. They were feared, so Callo thought they had used their power to ensure their wills were followed many times before. He despised the boy King, with his lust for women regardless of whether they were willing. He thought the Queen valued her comfort and her status above any natural feeling of affection for her son. He had met the First Warlord, a brutal man who mistreated his servants. And then there was Si'lan, lord of the psychic mages. He could not make up his mind about the ku'an'an.

Looking at Si'lan, he could not help but notice the fair hair turned silver, the amber eyes. There was a certain structure to the face that seemed familiar, the body type that seemed an echo of his own. Si'lan was complex, sometimes malicious, and unwilling to provide much information about the capabilities of the ku'an. In spite of this, Callo had never seen in him the overt misuse of power common to the other ku'an. He hoped that Si'lan had honor, because he thought Si'lan might be important to him.

Now the ring was empty. There were still contestants in the smaller rings, but this one stretched smooth and dusty before him as if to welcome him. Callo lifted his sword in the traditional salute to Jashan, god of light and war, and began the form with slow fluidity, stretching, welcoming the contracting and loosening of his muscles.

Long ago Chiss had found the Jashanite sword instructor, and he had seen to it that Callo had been taught the forms. "Focus on this," he had said. "Learn what the master has to teach you, and the god will help you keep your anger to yourself."

Even then, Chiss had known he was ku'an.

Now everyone knew. He had not had a decent match since he had been here. No one would contend against a ku'an.

Just as the prescribed motions of the first form drew to a

close, Callo heard the clang of the bell at the entrance to his ring. Someone craved a contest.

Callo saw a lean, brown man of middle years. His face was seamed with a scar under his eye, another along his jaw. The man carried a huge sword and a scarred shield.

"I am Ha'star, newly back from the front. I wish a match."

"Welcome," Callo said, and meant it. The prospect of a match against a man honed by battle pleased him. It could be a good match, a challenging one. He remembered when he and Arias had returned from duty on Righar's fronts, tired but sharp and strong, dangerous to those who were soft from life in Sugetre. This man might be equally dangerous.

They took their positions in the ring. Ha'star leaned his shield up against the wooden rail support. He and Callo exchanged their weapons for blunted training swords which were resting against the rail.

Callo measured the other man as he took his stance. Ha'star weighed the training sword, gauging its feel. He handled the weapon as if it were the real thing, and Callo thought Ha'star would fight in deadly earnest, training match or no. Callo found himself grinning in anticipation as he lifted his own sword. He nodded at Ha'star.

The other man gave the order—"Hai!"—and they swung into motion. Callo found himself at an immediate disadvantage, blocking a surprisingly fast cut to his left shoulder. He stepped inside Ha'star's reach, blocked the blow arm against arm, wishing he had a shield. Ha'star leaped back. Callo turned on his heel and struck back, and Ha'star's sword knocked the move aside. The blow was so strong, the sword with Ha'star's strength behind it so powerful, that Callo staggered a little.

Callo's arm tingled with the shock of Ha'star's block. The man was as strong as a horse. He focused tight as they circled each other for a moment. Even these training swords were capable of delivering a powerful blow when wielded with strength, and although blunted, could break bones.

They moved back and forth across the ring, slowly weighing each other's skill. Packed earth slipped under Callo's feet. His sword scraped against Ha'star's as his opponent blocked another cut. Ha'star moved faster than he thought possible, his sword blocking Callo's like a wall. Used to depending upon a shield or even a left-hand dagger, Callo found himself leaving his side open too often. He was sweating, and the air around him seemed hot.

Ha'star sliced at his arm, and Callo moved sideways, aiming for an opening at Ha'star's chest. He thought for a moment he would succeed, but at the last moment, Ha'star evaded the thrust, awkward as he twisted away. From the corner of his eyes, Callo saw a flash, and then Ha'star's sword was there, brought out of nowhere to point like a splinter of steel at Callo's unprotected throat. At that moment Ha'star looked into Callo's eyes and grinned—a real smile, without antagonism. Callo stepped two paces back, wiped his forehead with the back of his arm, and bowed.

"Your contest," he said, out of breath, grinning with the pleasure of the battle.

"An even match, I'd say, my lord," Ha'star allowed. He was breathing hard, too, and his brown cheeks were flushed with heat.

Callo nodded. He was regaining his even breath. "Thank you for the match. None other has given me one."

"No, they wouldn't. I'm the only one who don't care, being as how I've got no kin. I must say, you fought fair, ku'an, and didn't use those yellow eyes to foul my arm."

Callo looked into Ha'star's brown eyes. "And is that what the others said I would do?"

"No need to say. It's what ku'an do." Ha'star looked around and Callo realized there was a silent line of men, hanging on the rails. They had been watching the contest of arms in complete silence. "You'll get a match next time you want one, I'll warrant."

Callo walked out of the ring. There, a starry-eyed boy of about ten years galloped up to Ha'star and begged to take his sword, and get him a drink. Ha'star ruffled the boy's hair, growling at him in an affectionate way not to treat him like a weakling. Watching them walk together into the arms room, Callo jogged to catch up to Ha'star.

"Ha'star."

The brown man turned.

"You seem like someone who would be willing to talk to me about the ku'an."

Ha'star spat off to the side. "Beggin' your pardon. I've got no wish to talk about the fiends. Ask the ku'an'an—you're one yourself, after all."

"You know I am not from Ha'las, and many things are new to me. I am looking for a different opinion. I think I could trust yours."

"You can trust it to piss you off. No, you seem like a decent man for a ku'an, but I'd be stupid to risk your temper for speaking the truth. Here, boy—get me water after all." Ha'star waited until the boy had run off, then stared into Callo's eyes for a moment. He shook his head.

"Gods help me, I must be crazy. Here you are with your demon's eyes, and I'm still going to do what I'm going to do. I'd swear you're not influencing me." It was half a question.

"No." Callo let the single word hang between them. Further protestations, he felt, would only damage the frail connection he felt building between himself and the scarred warrior.

Ha'star sighed. "I believe you. I'm still as leery as I should be. I go to the Black Duck, in Seaside. I'm frequently there evenings. You show up there, you make it through Seaside safe, I'll talk to you some. You gave me a fair fight after all—no ku'an magery about it."

"Thank you." Callo stepped back to let the man disarm and get back to his day. There was hope in his heart for the first time since he had met Si'lan. Returning to his chamber, he cleaned up and dressed in unusual good humor, until Chiss commented on it.

"You are in a fine good mood for a man who's missed breakfast," Chiss said.

"Missed completely? No, I see you've saved me something. I had a match, Chiss, a good one. I feel great."

Someone knocked on the door and Chiss went to answer it. Kirian's veiled figure rushed into the room, followed by her ever- present guardian Sara'Si.

"Lord Callo," Kirian said. "I must speak with you."

"Good morning," he said, smiling at her. "Have some breakfast— stale bread, right Chiss? And ham. What did you want to talk about?"

Kirian did not respond at once, and Callo's eyes flicked to the shrouded Sara'Si. The woman did seem a dour presence, and he had no doubt that she reported on Kirian's activities to someone. He said, "Sara'Si, please leave us for a moment."

The companion bowed. "My lord ku'an. It is inappropriate for her to be alone with you."

"Great gods, I traveled in a ship from Righar with the man," Kirian said. Callo grinned at her exasperation.

"We will be but a moment, Sara'Si; this I promise you. I will leave the door open, and I will remain." Chiss took over and escorted Sara'Si out. When he returned he said, "My lord.

Hon Kirian. There is no reason they could not be listening anyway, although the woman is out of the room."

Callo looked around. "Do you think so? I see no signs of it."

"We might see no signs."

"It doesn't matter," Kirian said. "I'm tired of caring what they think of me." She slipped her veil off to reveal her lovely brown eyes and short hair, ruffled now from the veil. Callo felt an urge to stroke that spiky hair but restrained himself.

Chiss said: "I don't think you understand, Hon Kirian. You need to care what they think of you. These restrictions are a matter of religion, remember "

"After being here a while, I've become quite sure that enforcement is a matter of politics," Callo said.

"So, then, Chiss," Kirian frowned. "What is the penalty for being alone with a man in a room with his servant?"

"A ku'an's servant is considered nothing but an extension of himself. Any woman alone with a ku'an is considered to have broken the laws of modesty. The penalty for this…"

"I remember," Kirian sighed.

"Perhaps the rules may be a little relaxed for you, since you are a Healer and since the King needs you." Chiss shrugged.

"I have been a little more assertive than they like. And Sara'Si does not like my visits to the hospital. She says it is not fitting. But Lady Min'dou has said nothing to me about it."

"They are treating us with caution," Callo said. "It has been almost a season we have been here. Our lives have been at risk since we got here. I wonder if this makes much of a difference."

"Not to you," Kirian retorted. "You are a ku'an, able to do whatever you want. There are no barriers for you."

"Nor, perhaps, for those who are of my household." Callo shrugged. He knew they had several times violated the Ha'lasi religious law in what he considered to be minor ways, but as of yet there had been no repercussions. He said, "We have no doubt made another mistake. Let us be quick and minimize the damage. Why are you here, Kirian?"

She came close to him, looking up into his eyes. "My lord, the King has taken a concubine. It is someone I know."

Callo frowned. "How could that be?"

"Her name is Eyelinn. She was a slave in Righar, in Fortress Mount. Do you remember the men who came to search that day, for my friend Inmay and the slave he escaped with?"

He did remember. He remembered how even Jashan's rituals had not calmed his anger, how the power had writhed free of his control there on the path, almost sparking a fight which would have proven fatal to at least one of them. The ku'an'an had not taught him much since he had been in Ha'las, seeming reluctant in spite of his acceptance by the god Som'ur—but he had been quick to show him the way to contain the psychic magery to keep from unconsciously influencing others around him. Callo had been working daily to strengthen his internal walls, without much success he feared.

"I remember," he said, his mind on his own problems. Then Kirian's guilty glance broke through his memories. "Wait. This is the slave? Eyelinn, you called her. You know this woman?"

"She came to Las'ash city with Inmay, on the *Fortune*."

"I remember you saw the man aboard. So this woman is Ar'ok's concubine now. Is she unwilling?"

Kirian sighed. "No." She paced away from him, frowning as she spoke. "As a matter of fact, when I was there to treat him, she seemed—eager. But the ku'an can do that, is it not so."

He nodded. "Where is the man? Inmay?"

"I have not seen him."

Callo moved away and sat down at the table. "You are not going to ask me to do something about this."

She made a soft, unladylike snort. "I don't know. On the one hand I don't care if they go to hell. On the other . . . I hate to see her enslaved—no enthralled—against her will."

He mulled it over, sipping from the cup of tea Chiss had left at the table. "I don't see what I can do. Our position here is uncertain. I have no influence to waste on asking favors of that snake Ar'ok. And this Eyelinn—she has committed a crime, Kirian."

"I know, I know. If she were back in Fortress Mount, she would be dead, for I am fairly sure she tried to kill her master there."

Callo made a dismissive gesture. This woman Eyelinn sounded as if she deserved Ar'ok. "Leave it alone—that is my inclination. This is the end of the path she chose for herself. You will get yourself in trouble by taking responsibility for everything."

Kirian flushed. "There speaks a nobleman."

Anger flared. From long habit, Callo forced it down. As quickly as she had spoken, she waved a hand in a gesture of repudiation. "I am sorry," she said. "You did not deserve that."

He nodded at her, but his nerves were on edge now.

Kirian continued. "I am wondering, though, about Inmay. He never would have left her. He was more than in love with her—more like possessed by her. Will you watch for him, Callo? A slight man, my age, with light yellow hair—with a fair amount of gray in it."

"I will not promise to rescue him from the consequences of his own stupidity," Callo said.

"I understand."

Callo nodded. "I will watch for him and let you know if I

see him. I will be out in the city this week. You never know what I might see. Now Kirian, is there more? Or should we call the chaperone back?"

Kirian sighed and rolled her eyes "If you had a chaperone following your every step, you'd sympathize."

"I sympathize already. I cannot imagine someone always at my back, watching everything I do." Then he allowed his eyes to rest appreciatively on her face, her slender form. "And Kirian—I would like to be rid of her for other reasons, as well. I miss your company."

She flushed. "I will go," she said awkwardly. He laughed. "Chiss. Call in Sara'Si, will you?"

She cast a fuming glance at him and pulled her veil back over her face. Sara'Si entered, a dark gloomy figure, and took up a position behind Kirian. Together, they left the room.

"My lord," Chiss said.

"Hmmm?" Callo was still thinking about Kirian.

"How long do you think it will be until the local physicians will have their own supply of the sart leaf?"

"I have no idea. We don't know if it even grows here."

"I only ask because that may be the limit of the King's tolerance for Hon Kirian's unusual ways."

Callo lifted an eyebrow and looked at Chiss. "Then we will have to be ready," he said.

Later that day, called to wait upon the King's pleasure as sometimes happened, Callo entered the room to find Si'lan just leaving. The ku'an'an nodded his head without smiling. Callo was familiar by now with these sessions where the boy king conducted business while keeping him waiting—sometimes asking a pertinent question, but usually seeming to delight in just keeping him kicking his heels. Callo had learned to stop showing his impatience with these tactics and Ar'ok had lost interest in his continued presence—until now.

He entered, was announced, and made his bow to Ar'ok. The boy king sat on a dais, in rich robes and a coronet. He narrowed his eyes at Callo and said: "I hear you had a match in the ring today with the great Ha'star."

Callo nodded. "Yes, Your Majesty. A most worthy fighter."

"With dangerous opinions, I hear. It is not wise to follow up that acquaintance—other than a thrilling contest in the ring, of course."

"As your Majesty says." Callo wondered who had heard them in the arms room. The King gestured him away, and Callo went to stand with some other men near the wall, resigned to standing for hours while Ar'ok conducted business, drank wine, or otherwise entertained himself while demonstrating his power over the time of others. This King was young, but that alone was insufficient to explain his spiteful actions and the pleasure he seemed to take in his ku'an powers. Callo feared it was the psychic magery alone that warped him.

As he waited, he noticed a young woman, the only woman in the room, standing to the side of the throne. He was caught by her face, which was mostly visible through the very light fabric of her veil; she was the most beautiful woman he had ever seen, dark of hair, smooth of skin, and by Ha'lasi standards, practically displayed for all the throne room to see. Her robe was cut low and belted to emphasize her breasts. She seemed to Callo to be heavily under the King's ku'an influence; far from showing any shyness at her situation, she clung close to the throne, bending near to caress Ar'ok's face, and allowing him to peer down her robe. The King reached out to fondle her breasts, and then cast a sly glance at his assembled court. Then Ar'ok pulled the woman onto his lap before them all, spreading his legs to settle her between them.

So this was the reason he and the others had been called to

wait upon the King; to witness his manipulation of this woman. Perhaps this was the slave woman Kirian had told him about. Regardless, he was sure Ar'ok had her well under his psychic control—'eager', as Kirian had said. He felt the foulness of the King creeping toward him. No doubt the boy would show off his influence over her for a while, then take her up to his chambers. It would be nothing but a rape. He looked around the room; there were no representatives of Som'ur's priesthood present, and he knew the sycophants in the room would keep silent about what they saw here. Guilt filled him, just by association, at having the same abilities as the King. Too angry to be sensible, he stalked out of the room.

———

The door to the Black Duck was unadorned; only the banner hanging above with the figure of its name painted on it let Callo know this was the right place. Chiss stared at it with disfavor, then looked around at the men moving alone and in small groups through the dockside streets. Two other blank doors looked out on the same wet alley.

"This is a hole," Chiss said. "You have no idea what awaits you in there."

"I never said it was safe," Callo said. In fact, the entire excursion to Dockside had been fraught with tension. He had noticed men watching him from the alley a block down, and had let his hand drift to his sword hilt; however, no attack materialized. Some children had peered out of a window two streets back, calling harmless taunts at the foreigner. Then, someone had whispered something to them, and they had vanished from the window, leaving the street cold, empty, and ominously quiet. The gloom of the early spring day added to the psychological chill until Callo was on edge. He realized his hand had drifted to his belt again, checking the presence of his sword and backup knife. Chiss had been trying to get him to return to Ar'ok's Castle for the last several minutes.

"And how do you know this Ha'star won't have laid a trap for you, Lord Callo?"

"He could have killed me in the ring. He had the skill."

"And there would have been no doubt who did it. Much better to lay a trap, lure you in with promises of information."

"All right, all right," Callo snapped. "I'm going in, Chiss, whatever you say. Maybe if you don't try to frighten me out of my wits, I'll be more alert."

"I'm sorry, my lord."

"Don't worry about it. Look, you stay out here." At Chiss' motion of protest, he raised his hand. "Keep watch for Ar'ok's men. Let me know if you see any threat. I'll be out in a candle-mark at most—less, if Ha'star's not here."

Chiss nodded and took up a position in the shadows of the opposite wall. He looked out of place there, with his lean, refined face and thin hair; but he would be safe enough, and Callo was glad to have an ally on the outside.

The door to the Black Duck opened as he approached. He entered and it swung closed behind him. His heart leaped. The room was completely dark, so black he could not move in any direction.

"What ha' we here?" rasped a voice. "One only, is it? Blind as a bat you are. All right my man, your weapon first and then in you go."

Callo unbuckled his sword and handed it over. It was not unusual for a tavern keeper to insist his patrons be disarmed before entering. He was glad he had a weapon in reserve in this unknown place.

Callo saw a glow as a curtain or some other barrier parted before him. He moved toward it then into the yellow light of the tavern. As he left the darkness, the outer curtain swung closed. It was intended to make newcomers pause until the old man inside had judged them safe to enter. It worked well, he thought, limiting entry and allowing the guard to shout a warning if necessary.

He looked around at a tavern like dozens of others he had seen. Men sat at wooden tables or on benches around the fire, drinking ale or eating bread and savory stew. A veiled woman delivered mugs of ale to a group of seamen near the fire.

When Callo entered, everyone went still. He looked around for a seat at an empty table. An older man with wisps of gray hair adorning a shiny scalp approached. He had the arms of an old seaman, lean and ropy, and wore a tavern-keeper's apron.

The keeper looked straight into Callo's face and blanched. Callo could see the change even in the flickering yellow light.

"Ku'an!" the man whispered.

Chairs scraped against the floor as men rose. Callo turned his back to the empty section of the room and reached for his knife. His hand closed on empty air. His knife had been detached from his belt, so neatly that he had felt nothing. There was only one place it could have happened. He looked around for another weapon.

"No, no, my lord ku'an, be at peace," the keeper said. "You men, sit down."

"My knife," Callo said evenly.

"Yes, yes. Gri'nel, come out!"

A gnarled man came out of the curtained entrance. His grin showed missing teeth.

"Missed something, ha' we?"

Callo did not feel like smiling. The men at the fire had begun to sit down again, no longer on alert, but they were still watching. The tavern keeper looked at Callo's face and said, "Gri'nel, get my lord ku'an's knife. And his sword as well."

"Isn't that a choker? A ku'an, in here! Too dark t'see the cursed yellow eyes," Gri'nel explained. "Or I wouldn'a taken it, Fal'ar."

"I'm sure," the keeper said. "Just get it, would you?"

Gri'nel reached back into the alcove and brought out Callo's weapons. Callo took them and buckled both weapons back on, never looking away from the old man's face.

"Little pissed off, ain't ya'?" Gri'nel asked.

"I apologize, my lord," Fal'ar said. "Sit, please. Gri'nel is employed to watch the entryway. He is supposed to warn us if he thinks someone is a risk. Sometimes he goes too far, you hear me, Gri'nel?"

The old man shrugged. "It were a nice knife, Fal'ar. Couldn't keep my hands to my own self."

Callo looked around the tavern. The men were still watching him, but there was no further attempt to rise, no intimation of threat. The tavern keeper seemed eager to placate him. He drew a deep breath and felt his shoulders relax.

"That's right, my lord," Fal'ar said. "Please be seated. Mostly we just have ale for the seamen, but I could find some wine for you."

"Ale is fine." Callo sat at an empty table, his back carefully to the wall. He said, "I am looking for one Ha'star."

"He said he challenged a ku'an. Just like the wharf rat not to tell me you might show up here. Be at ease, my lord." Fal'ar bowed.

Callo sat back and looked around the room. The other men turned and resumed their various conversations or activities. The veiled woman brought him a large cup of ale, but shook her head when he put coin on the table.

"Fal'ar says no payment is necessary, my lord ku'an."

"Just the same, here it is," Callo said. He left the coin on the table. The woman bent her head and retreated.

Several minutes later, he decided that Ha'star would not be at the Black Duck that evening. He rose, about to take his leave. Then he heard Gri'nel's cackle from the security door, and the curtain blew aside to admit the warrior himself.

Two men by the fire who were much the worse for drink shouted, "Ha'star!" He waved at them and then his eyes widened as he saw Callo.

"My lord ku'an," he said, pulling a chair out and sitting down across from Callo. "You are very quick."

"I have questions, as I told you. I did not want to wait to have them answered."

Ha'star lifted one eyebrow. "Well, my lord, I know ku'an want everything right away. I never swore to answer every question, though. Wouldn't be safe. If you're going to lose your temper over me refusing to answer now an' then, tell me now, and we'll go our ways."

Callo sighed. "I apologize. It's been an odd day. Have an ale. Of course, I will not lose my temper if you don't answer every question. Really, I just want you to tell me what you know about the ku'an."

The veiled woman brought ale to the table. Ha'star lifted his mug in a silent salute to her. She nodded, then turned and went away. Callo stared after her.

"I thought women could not work in a place like this in Ha'las," he said. "Is it safe?"

Ha'star snorted. "Safer than bein' in the public places, where any yellow-eyed bastard could see her," he said. "Begging your pardon. Fa'lar is her uncle. It is allowed. No one here would touch her."

"All right."

Ha'star sipped. "I'm a damn fool to be talking to you. I

don't know why but I've taken a liking to you. If you go and pull some ku'an foulness, I'll know I was wrong."

"I will do my best not to prove you wrong," Callo said.

"The ku'an? Demons, all of them, saving your presence. They use their foul powers to get whatever they want. They can see a woman they like on the street, and a sennight later she's living at the Castle being a whore to some bastard. If you get a chance to take her away, she won't go—the ku'an 'mag-icked' her to think she really loves him." Ha'star spat on the floor. "No man is safe around a ku'an. They say they can't put thoughts in your head, just emotions, but emotions are strong, damn them. They can put false courage into a man's head so he'll charge an enemy of thousands, all full of the glory of the fight, and when he's cut to pieces, no help for the family he left behind."

"You sound as if you have seen these things yourself."

"Some. There was a ku'an with the army in the south. He was a right demon, he was. Jol'tan, cousin to the King."

"How many ku'an are there, then?" Ha'star shrugged and drank his ale.

Callo said, "I have heard of only four here, at the palace, and this Jol'tan. That's five. That is few to have a nation in their grip."

"I hear the King has relatives, in the north. But I've not seen another. Just Jol'tan. And you. I'm not sure you count."

Callo's mouth twitched. "I hope not, from what you say. And these few ku'an can send a Black Tide against Righar?"

"Ah, so that's it." Ha'star's eyes narrowed, making his scar draw tight. "You want to find out about the Black Tide. You are a spy for Righar."

"No. I am sure I have been exiled from Righar."

"Ar'ok took you in at the Castle. The ku'an'an talks to you. Maybe you are right, and you are no spy. You ku'an are beyond me. You seem to despise the ku'an, yet here you are, one yourself. How do you justify that? Now I talk to you, and for all I know, I'll be sent to prison tomorrow for it."

"Not by me," Callo said. He sensed Ha'star's cooperation waning, the man's bitterness growing. He should draw this talk to a close before Ha'star turned against him. He drained his mug and stood.

"You have my thanks," he said. "You will not lose by talking to me. You have courage."

"I'm a fool," Ha'star said, but he was grinning again. "But I know you did not influence me, my lord. Mayhap you're different."

"I hope to be different." Callo nodded to the warrior, tossed another coin on the table, and walked out through the curtained section.

Gri'nel was invisible in the dark. Callo stopped a moment, waiting for his eyes to adjust. "Damn if I know how you can see in here," he said.

"It's a gift," Gri'nel said. "No hard feelin's now?"

"No, I suppose not." Callo began to walk toward the outer door, visible now as a faint gray line of light.

"Beggin' yer pardon, ku'an," Gri'nel said. "Ha'star seems to like ya, more fool he, so for his sake, I'll tell ya. There's men outside, waitin' for someone. Could be you."

His heart leaped. He grasped his sword, unsheathing it with a faint hiss of steel. "My thanks," he told the old man. Then he eased open the door, just an inch, and peered out.

Chiss no longer leaned against the opposite wall. There was no one within his field of vision. The alley had grown dark, lit only by a torch at the nearby intersection. The paving stones were still wet, as if it had rained again while he was in the Black Duck; they reflected the torchlight in a wavering shine that made visibility even more difficult. The hush outside seemed odd for a dockside alley with three taverns in it.

For just a second the thought of re-entering the Black Duck occurred to him; perhaps there was another door. Then he decided it would be better to get this over with. Assuming the men were along the wall beside the door, he bent low, sword at the ready, and leaped through the door, out into the alleyway. He slammed up against the wall on the other side and braced himself.

The men were there, backed up hard against the wall next to the tavern door. His low profile and fast exit caught them by surprise. The first man leaped at Callo, swinging his sword.

Callo easily countered the wild swing. His knife hand stabbed at the other's wrist. His attacker's sword clattered to the ground. The man grabbed his wrist and ducked back out of Callo's reach as Callo kicked the sword away.

"My lord! There are six of them!" It was Chiss' voice, shouting from farther up the alley. The men must be restraining him, Callo thought—no easy task, for Chiss was ready with a weapon.

Callo balanced on the balls of his feet, centered, ready. He knew he had only a breath before the next attack.

A man with a red beard, built like a barrel, lunged from the doorway. His sword was bigger than Ha'star's. His strike came down like a boulder as he tried to crush Callo by mass alone.

Callo barely evaded the blow, slashing for the man's sword arm. Their swords crashed together, ringing loud in the wet alley. The other men stood back, waiting for Redbeard to subdue Callo, staying out of the way of the man's huge sword.

Redbeard raised his sword again, then swung into a powerful downstroke. Callo barely blocked the hammer-like blow.

Callo blocked the next strike, but his back was against the wall and he had no room to fight. His sword was no match for the massive battle sword. His arms ached and he knew his time was running out. The next time Redbeard drew up for a strike, Callo stepped forward and slammed the heel of his boot into Redbeard's knee. The man screamed as his kneecap shattered. He fell back, sword dropping from his hand.

Two more were on him before he could catch his breath. Callo backed against the wall, trading strikes. One of the men swung a heavy mace. Callo had no choice but to block the blow on his upper arm. Then he struck back hard, slashing into the man's shoulder. Blood spurted from the wound.

The mace was gone then but Callo's shield arm—if only he had had a shield!—would not move as it should. Pain raced up to his shoulder. He wished he could protect it, but the first man, the one he had disarmed, was back. He and two others came at Callo in a semi- circle. He tried to attack without leaving himself open but knew it was impossible.

He tried to move, to gain some advantage. His feet slipped on blood, and a sword that would have sliced open his neck flashed over his head as he stumbled. Another sword flashed in his peripheral vision as he scrambled to rise. He struggled up, dodged the strike, and cut hard to the left. He was rewarded with a spurt of blood from the other man's arm. But he was out of breath, and this newly-wounded man kept fighting; the wound had not disabled him.

Nearby, Redbeard still screamed with the pain of his shat- tered knee.

Callo was struggling now. Three men still pressed around him. One stood by, ready; the other two fought. If his attackers were not impeding each other, he would be dead by now, Callo knew.

His nearest opponent, a lean man with a black raven tattoo

on his cheek, still pressed him. That one moved fast and Callo felt the bite of steel into the upper part of his sword arm. The blood came, fast but not the spurt of an artery. Nevertheless, it flowed down his arm and slicked his sword hand. He felt light-headed, and his left arm was now refusing to move at all.

"My lord!" shouted Chiss, sounding alarmed. And well he might. All at once Callo felt as if he might fall to exhaustion and the shock of his wound. Forcing himself to stand, he took one desperate action.

Still warding off blows with a weaker arm, Callo reached for the barrier in his mind that he had built to keep himself from using his ku'an ability. For the first time in his life, he consciously dropped it. Then he let his own sense of desperation fill him, gave it free rein until it loomed like a monster. He sent it like an arrow into the minds of the men around him.

When he had a breathing space to work with, he reached for the worst thing he could think of, something that would stop his attackers cold. He remembered what the fear of a child's nightmare felt like, added it to the mix, and forced it away from him, hoping it was enough to stall the attack. Then he released the terrifying pressure.

The blows stopped. No more swords whistled about his head. He staggered back against the alley wall. Two men had fallen to their knees on the paving stones, arms clutching themselves as if they were trying to protect themselves from something. One man—Raven Tattoo—ran off down the alley, arms windmilling, moaning. He had dropped his sword. Two lay in limp postures that suggested they were dead or uncon-scious. The last was nowhere to be seen.

Callo slumped against the wall.

A hand gripped his shoulder. "My lord, stop now," Chiss said. "Please stop." His voice quavered.

"You feel it too?" Callo asked. He closed his eyes and

pulled the emotion back into himself, then buried it deep. He built the wall again, stone by stone. It took a few moments but felt much longer. When he reopened his eyes, Chiss leaned against the wall beside him, pale as an egg. Callo thought he saw tear tracks on the man's lean cheeks.

"I'm sorry." Callo moved his left arm—the one that had been struck by the mace—and tried to use his left hand to hold onto the bleeding wound in his right. The arm moved slowly, shooting pain up into his neck and back. He put his head back against the wall. Things seemed to be very dark in the alley, as if the torch at the corner had gone out in the rain.

"My lord." Chiss' voice sounded stronger. "We must get you to the castle. I will tell one of these tavern people to go for a carriage."

Chiss left him. While the man was gone, Callo decided he'd best sit down if he didn't want to fall. The blood flowed faster than he had thought, slicking his fingers. He found himself incapable of looking around to see what had become of the two kneeling men. They were still there, hugging themselves on the paving stones. He supposed they could strike him down whenever they wanted, now that he had withdrawn the fear. When Chiss returned, he asked, "Where are the other men?"

Chiss looked aside and said, "No need to worry about them. They're gone."

"Good."

"A carriage is on its way, my lord. Hold on."

Callo closed his eyes. Chiss' hand was on his shoulder, giving him strength. He thought of what he had done to the attackers and how Chiss had seemed affected by it too. He said, "Chiss. I am sorry."

Chiss said, "Here is the carriage, my lord."

"I did not mean for you—" Then Chiss and someone else

had hands under his arms, lifting him, and he forgot what he had meant to say in the wave of pain.

When he recovered his equilibrium, the carriage was moving. Chiss was wrapping something around his upper arm, where he had taken the sword cut. The cloth was torn from something blue-gray; he thought it was part of Chiss' cloak.

He put his head back and looked out the window at the rain-swept streets. The carriage jolted and pain washed up his arm. He looked out, trying to distract himself, as they approached the castle walls. Guards stood before the gate. They strode forward to stop the carriage from entering the walls.

Callo heard voices—the coachman and the guard—then saw a face peer in at him. He looked at the man but said nothing. The guard made a slight bow, then shouted to someone to admit them. Callo kept looking out the carriage window in spite of the rain that now spattered his face. He could see the muddle of makeshift camps where people awaited admittance for an audience. Far above, and away from the main gate, he saw spikes on the top of the castle wall. A few of the spikes wore the severed heads of capital criminals, displayed for all as a warning. Through the haze of pain he saw that one of the fresher heads had pale yellow hair threaded with streaks of gray.

Chapter Twelve

Kirian was eager to get Sara'Si into her adjoining alcove and out of her sight for a while. She tried to follow the rules of this place, but the woman's constant, judgmental presence annoyed her. Neither the King nor the Queen required her presence, Lord Callo was out on the town somewhere, and there was not a book anywhere. Kirian curled up on the bed and closed her eyes.

She had no idea how much time had passed when she heard tapping on the door. Sara'Si emerged from her alcove, pulling her veil over her face. How odd, Kirian thought, that she had spent all this time with the woman and only now for the first time saw her plump, attractive face.

The guard outside spoke to Sara'Si in a low voice. Sara'Si gave a heavy sigh and turned to Kirian.

"The ku'an's man wants you. There is some crisis."

"I'll go," Kirian said. She scrambled out of bed and pulled on a robe, belting it over the tunic she had worn to bed. She ran her fingers through her hair, pulled the veil over her face, and grabbed her Healer's bag.

Her chaperone waited. The guard stepped back and looked away as they walked the few steps to Lord Callo's chambers.

Chiss opened the door on her knock, as if he had been waiting right there. There were weary circles under his eyes and lines in his face Kirian had not noticed before. The room was lit by a good fire and several candles.

"Hon Kirian, I am glad you brought your bag," he said. "It is in your Healer's capacity we need you. Sara'Si, please come in."

Kirian's heart started beating hard enough that she felt it in her throat. She said, "Who is hurt? Is he all right?"

Chiss nodded. "The physician has been here. I thought it would be advisable to have you look at him as well."

"Not having a high opinion of the physician?" She took a deep breath and forced her heart rate to slow. *What a reaction, for a Healer!* She ignored Sara'Si, who stood like fate near the door, guarding Kirian's virtue. "Where is he?"

"In the chair over there," Chiss said. "My lord was in a fight. He has quite a few scrapes, but it is both arms and the area near his collarbone that you will particularly want to examine."

Callo was leaning back in a large soft chair, his feet up on another chair. His head relaxed against the high back, and his eyes were closed. He wore a loose gray tunic and breeches. The arms of the tunic had been slit, and one arm was wrapped in white cloth bandages. A mug on the table next to him held a small amount of liquid—originally wine, she thought, but from the milky swirls and the distinctive aroma she knew it had been mixed with mellweed. He had not drunk it all.

"Lord Yun'lar was here? Or was it someone else?"

"It was Lord Yun'lar. He gave my lord the mellweed. He

said he would not work with an injured ku'an unless he was sedated—too dangerous, he said."

Kirian remembered trying to help Lord Arias, in Seagard Castle, after his violent Collaring by King Sharpeyes. She recalled how, as Arias' feverish dreams had intensified, he had lost control of his color magic. She supposed a ku'an in pain might be even more perilous.

"I am surprised he drank it." She sat down next to the drowsing man. "Still, I suppose it is for the best. My lord? Callo?"

"Hmm?"

"It is Kirian. I have come to see how you are doing. Where are you in pain?"

Callo opened his eyes and smiled in a sleepy way. "No pain."

Perhaps Yun'lar had given him more mellweed than she had thought. She said patiently, "I must examine your arms and chest, my lord. That is where Chiss said you were wounded. Will you let me help you?"

Sara'Si hissed from the other side of the room, but Kirian ignored her. With unexpected gentleness, Chiss helped Callo withdraw his arms from the loose tunic and pull it off. Callo's chest gleamed in the candlelight. There were bruises and cuts, but nothing serious there. His left arm, the one not wrapped in bandages, was already purple and swollen from shoulder to elbow. She probed with gentle fingers.

"He has had the mellweed, so I'll not ask him to move it around," she told Chiss. "Did Yun'lar do that?"

"He checked my lord's range of motion. It wasn't a pleasant experience. Lord Yun'lar said the arm was not broken."

Kirian unwrapped the bandage on Callo's right arm, trying not to disturb him as he had closed his eyes again. The stitches closing the wound were crude but adequate. The thick brown stuff coating the cut would protect the wound from any infection. She rewrapped the arm and let Chiss draw the tunic back over Callo.

"My lord?" she said.

Callo looked at her. His eyes were slightly blurry in the candlelight. "I feel fine," he mumbled.

"Yes, indeed. I will have them bring ice for Chiss to put on your left arm so it does not swell so much you cannot use it. I will also have the kitchen send you blood broth to help restore you. You lost a fair amount of blood, it seems."

"My sword arm," he said, frowning a little.

"We shall see. If no infection begins, your arm should be fine. You must rest and recover. You look as if five men tried to beat you."

"Six," he said. He looked up at her and gave her an unusually sweet smile. "Thank you for coming. Yun'lar . . . was afraid."

"Well, you have been very cooperative," she said. He reached out and took her hand, drew it to his lips, and kissed it. She felt a shiver go through her at the sensation, even as his eyelids dropped over the amber eyes. His grip loosened as the mellweed took over, and she withdrew her hand. Callo's breathing slowed and he slept.

She avoided Chiss' glance as she gathered up her bag. "Blood broth, Chiss, and ice for the left arm. I have never seen such severe bruising. I assume they have an icehouse here?"

"Yes, and much fresh ice, Hon Kirian."

"Good. Yun'lar will examine him for infection."

"My lord does not care for Lord Yun'lar," Chiss said.

"He will have to do," Sara'Si said from the doorway. "Hon Kirian cannot continue to visit Lord Callo here in his rooms.

She has been immodest in the extreme. You see, it only causes my lord to take liberties!"

"He is wounded and drugged," Kirian said. "I am a Healer, Sara'Si, and you are here, after all." She said in a low voice to Chiss, "We must talk. Who attacked him, Chiss? You must call for me tomorrow after Lord Callo awakens. I expect he will be in some pain."

"You will not set foot back in this room while I am your chaperone," Sara'Si objected. "I will call the lord high priest. It is wrong for you to be with a ku'an in his room!"

"Sara'Si—nothing happened," Kirian protested. The chaperone continued her complaining on the way back to Kirian's room. She went to her alcove and snapped the curtain shut behind her.

After Kirian was in bed and the candle doused, she lay awake, remembering the feel of Callo's lips on her skin. He was not himself tonight, she reminded herself. She should forget the sweet smile, the kiss. It was all due to the shock, the drug, gratitude for her care. But she thought about his lean swordsman's body, his amber eyes so full of light, his deep voice . . . and she wanted him.

Sara'Si left the room after breakfast. Kirian was left alone for the first time since she had been in Las'ash. Foreboding plucked at her nerves; she remembered that modesty was a religious matter here. Pacing in the room, she welcomed the messenger sent by Chiss around noon.

Chiss opened the door. "Hon Kirian," he said. He looked behind her and frowned. "Sara'Si?"

"She has abandoned me," Kirian said lightly, ignoring her own apprehension about this very subject. "How is Lord Callo?"

"He will not take Yun'lar's mellweed, so he is in no very pleasant humor. Will you come?"

She nodded. She could no more refuse than she could stop breathing. Her eyes craved the sight of him, unpleasant temper or no. She gathered up her bag, slid on her shoes, and followed Chiss next door. Her guard was still there; he said not a word as she passed him.

Callo paced up and down in front of his window; it was unshuttered, and the noon light, fresh with the beginnings of Las'ash's late spring, beamed in. The sunshine lit his fair hair and gave an unearthly glow to his eyes. It took the dazzled Kirian a moment to notice his pallor, the tension in the set of his shoulders.

"My lord. How are you this afternoon?"

"Well enough," Callo returned shortly.

"I think you must be in some pain. Has Yun'lar been here?"

"With his mellweed, yes. I won't take it. I won't lie around in a stupor while Ar'ok tries to kill me."

Kirian was about to reply when Chiss held up a hand. "Wait, my lord. I thought you realized—those were not Ar'ok's men."

"Whose, then?"

"I fear they were King Martan's men. Did you note one of the attackers wore a raven tattoo? That is his private guard's emblem."

Callo sighed. "I had forgotten. Yes, the raven, from Alghasi. I remember now."

Kirian frowned. "Surely anyone might have such a tattoo?"

"Perhaps. But I think these were Martan's assassins."

Callo asked, "How in hell did Sharpeyes get six men through the port?"

"It would be easy enough to simply arrive at some other

place. A small town, perhaps. If you had your own boat, your own navigator— why not?"

"I am slow today." Callo tested his left arm, wincing as it pained him. "I cannot think."

"You lost much blood," Kirian said. "Your body takes time to repair that. Also, Lord Callo, mellweed would ease some of that pain."

"No!"

"It need not send you to sleep. Yun'lar used a heavy hand. He was afraid, I think, that you would use your psychic magery if he caused you pain while examining your arm."

There was no response to that. Callo gave her a level stare, then turned and looked out at the golden sunlight illuminating the rooftops of the city two stories below. Chiss gave his lord a look out of the corner of his eyes, then began to tidy the room; he poured fresh water and wine, disposed of a clump of bandages lying on the floor near the soft chair, and freshened pillows. Kirian stood, not sure what to do.

After a while, Chiss said: "My lord, I will request luncheon from the kitchens. Please allow Hon Kirian to examine your arms. The left arm in particular has swollen a great deal, and the ice does not seem to be helping."

Callo sighed. "All right."

Chiss left the room. Callo turned away from the window. "Where do you want me?"

"The big chair will be fine. Tell me, honestly now, how you feel."

"Like I've been dragged by a wild horse." He didn't smile when he said it. He sat on the chair and with much tugging and awkward twisting, managed to get his left arm out of the tunic.

Kirian touched the arm as gently as possible, probing around the shoulder and elbow joints, evaluating the swelling.

Callo sat through this with a muscle twitching in his cheek as he clenched his jaw. When she was finished, she sat back on her heels and looked him in the eye. There was perspiration on his forehead.

"Mellweed would…"

"No, I said."

"Do you think I would knock you out?"

He was silent for a moment.

"I must still examine the right arm."

He sighed. "All right. A little."

She mixed it in the wine cup so that he could see how little she used. He drank it down fast and then sat with his eyes closed. After he had taken it, she went through the things in her bag while she waited for the drug to take effect. She said, "My sart leaves grow fewer."

"They have not found it here yet?"

"Lord Yun'lar said they had found it in Leyland. They have sent someone to obtain some and bring it back to grow. It must be grown indoors; it will not withstand the winters, I hear."

"So it will be a while until they have a supply."

"Yes."

Callo sighed. She thought he was relaxing a little. He said, "Be very careful, Kirian. When they have their own supply, or when you run out of yours, I think they will have no more tolerance for the freedoms they have allowed you."

"I know."

Yes, he had clearly relaxed against the chair. The mellweed was working. She readied herself to check the sword wound in his right arm. He said, smiling, "I would miss your visits."

She unwrapped the bandage. As he waited, she checked the condition of the sword wound; then she used cool water from the wash basin to clean it, and slathered more of the brown wound dressing over it. The injury was well stitched and would need only careful cleaning and dressing to heal well; only if signs of infection developed would the other herbs in her bag become necessary.

He sat in silence throughout, holding still with obvious determination. The mellweed must have kicked in then, because he closed his eyes and let out a long, slow breath in relief.

"Better now, my lord?" she said.

He smiled and opened his eyes. "Much. But what is this *my lord*? I thought such formality between us was over long ago."

He laid his hand over hers on the armrest. Her pulse quickened. A tingle ran up her arm from the warmth of his touch.

"Kirian, you have the most beautiful eyes. I have meant to tell you for some time."

She wanted to object. His eyes, lit by the golden daylight, were warm and inviting and as beautiful as the light itself. *This is just mellweed and gratitude*, she told herself. *Or more likely, a bored nobleman, amusing himself during his illness.* But she could not really believe it.

She said his name. His hand caressed hers, sending an exquisite sensation up her arm, then lifted to caress her cheek.

All the longing she had suppressed over the past season rose up to overcome her. All her doubts vanished. Totally charmed, she felt her lips curve into a smile. She leaned forward, eager to taste his lips.

The kiss was warm and sweet. His mouth had a faint, alluring taste of mellweed. The kiss set off shivers throughout her body. Her heart beat faster. Callo's breathing came faster as he reached up with his right arm—apparently pain free— and pulled her closer. She smiled up at him. Their lips met again, and she let herself relax into his body.

Then he jerked away from her.

She looked up at him, startled at the sudden change. Had she hurt his wounded arm? He was still breathing fast, but his eyes had gone grim. He stared at her, but she could tell he was no longer connecting. His arm released her. He pushed her away.

"Callo? Is it your arm?"

He shook his head, frowning. His muscles were tense now. Kirian stood up fast—hurt and beginning to feel angry at his sudden coldness. She tried to calm her breathing as she straightened her robe, which had come loose at the front. In an attempt to regain her dignity, she ignored his gaze on her fingers as she pulled the robe closed. She stood and began to gather the contents of her Healer's bag.

"You should go," he said. His voice was strained. He got up from the chair and moved away, toward the open window, as if he could not bear to be near her.

She was too shocked to be tactful. "I hope I have provided you . . . entertainment, my lord ku'an."

His hand lifted toward her, and he started to speak, but then stopped himself.

"I meant no insult," he said. She noticed through her distress that his words were a little slurred, as if the mellweed affected him. *Too bad*, she thought. *He is just like all the other nobles. Inmay was right.*

"What else would you call it, my lord?" she said. She grabbed her bag and stalked towards the door. She opened it on the startled Chiss, who was accompanied by a veiled servant girl holding a tray. She walked past him, head held high. It was not until her chamber door closed behind her that the stinging tears came to her eyes.

———

For the next two days, Kirian lived in a world of her own where everything seemed dull and without life. Spring had taken hold at last in Las'ash, and golden sunlight poured in her window each day; she walked in the courtyard with the other women, feeling the sun on her back, hearing the other women gossip and laugh, and said nothing, felt nothing. She was not called to check Callo's progress, and resolutely kept herself from hoping his sword arm was healing without infection. The birdsong in the open courtyard reminded her of spring back home. She wondered how Ruthan was feeling, and the people she knew in Seagard Village, and her friends back at the Healer's College in Sugetre. When she thought of her future, all seemed closed to her; she could not stand life here in restricted Las'ash, but could not imagine how to get out of the place.

She thought back to her flight from Seagard Village, and of how the chance for adventure in a foreign land had opened her eyes to many possibilities. Now it seemed she had forgotten the first rule of working with the *righ*: do not trust them. She felt betrayed—not just by Callo, who had followed a moment's impulse and clearly regretted it, but, even worse, she felt that she had betrayed herself. When had she given up her self-respect to become just another servant in Lord Callo's dependency? When had she become so sensitive to his opinion of her?

She tried hard not to think of Lord Callo's rejection. She had known since she had met him that she had been attracted to him; she had thought him better than his kind, too honorable to toy with her and then push her away. She could not understand it. When she remembered his face at the moment he had pulled back from her, she remembered blank shock, almost a look of realization—and then had come the frown, the silence.

Sara'Si did not return. Another chaperone made an

appearance and followed Kirian around, as ubiquitous as Sara'Si, but not as outspoken.

On the third day, she was awakened before dawn by a servant calling her to the King's aid. She collected her bag and went to examine the King, finding him in distress because of a recurrence of his breathing disease. She mixed the curative drink under Yun'lar's eye and watched the King drink it down, complaining of its taste as usual. After the remedy took effect, the King returned, sleepy-eyed, to his curtained bed.

Kirian returned to her own room. She sipped her tea and realized it was full daylight now, so she dressed in a loose tunic and veiled herself for a walk in the garden. In spite of herself, her misery of the last two days dropped from her; it was a glorious day, with the earth welcoming Jashan's return. It made her soul sing. She decided to forget about Callo for the day; the man did not deserve her misery. After spending most of the day outside, she returned to dress in her best for her daily audience with the Queen. Putting on the jewel-toned blue tunic made her remember the day she had purchased it from a seamstress near the market. Lord Callo had been generous with his funds, paying for a wardrobe for her since she had arrived with very little. He never said a word about it, just admired her taste when she showed off what she had bought, and waved away her words of gratitude. She could not reconcile that man with the one who had toyed with her.

There was a knock at the door. She finished dressing her hair, which had grown long enough to need a traditional comb. Then she pulled the veil over her hair and opened the door. Her chaperone stood against the far wall, watching.

Chiss stood in the hall, small and lean. At the look on her face he said, "No, don't close the door, please. My lord sent me with a message, but for myself, I ask how are you doing?"

"I'm fine."

She could see he wanted to ask what had happened. Apparently Lord Callo had not been forthcoming with details. "You are going to the Queen? Will you hear the message first?"

She nodded. But first, hating herself for asking, she said, "How is he, Chiss?"

"Improving. The blood broth is helping. He is regaining his strength, but Yun'lar frowns when he looks at the right arm. I hope it has not become infected." Chiss paused. "Apart from that, he is as ill-tempered as an ice tiger. Even getting out into the sun has not helped."

She kept her face expressionless.

"The message," Chiss said, as if he had just remembered his errand. "May I come in?"

"I'm on my way out."

"You will want to hear this."

She stepped back into the room. Her chaperone made a stifled sound, then subsided. The guard in the hall ignored the man entering her room. She felt a wave of affection for the rotund guard, who put up with her unconventional ways with no criticism.

"I am the bearer of bad news," Chiss said. "I am sorry for it. My lord meant to tell you this when he remembered it yesterday, but this morning he ordered me to come here and inform you."

"All right. What is it?"

"Your friend, the fugitive Inmay?"

"Yes?"

"He is dead." Chiss looked at her, his dark eyes sympathetic. "I am sorry."

"Dead? How do you know?"

"We have confirmed it with the ku'an'an. He says it is true. Inmay was executed three days past."

"I don't understand," Kirian said. She was surprised that she felt no sorrow at Inmay's passing, but she sensed something was being withheld from her. "Lord Callo has never seen Inmay. How did he know to ask if he had been slain? What are you keeping from me, Chiss?" He paused a moment, then nodded to himself. "My lord did not want to distress you any more."

Kirian snorted at that.

"When we brought Lord Callo back after the fight, my lord saw a head on the wall spikes. He recognized it from your description—I think it was the unusual hair. I am sorry, but in the stress of his injury, he did not remember until yesterday. Then he confirmed it with the ku'an'an."

Kirian sighed. She did not feel greatly shocked; Inmay had been doomed to a bad end ever since he escaped with Eyelinn. She wondered if the King had ordered him slain to free Eyelinn of any attachments, or if Inmay had actually broken the law in some way.

"Thank you, Chiss. I appreciate you letting me know. Now I must go; the Queen wants me."

He bowed and left, and she collected her chaperone and walked to the Queen's chamber.

"At last!" said the Queen. Kirian sank into a bow. The Queen sat near her closed chamber window, red-gray hair once again threaded with glittering gems, powder creeping into the lines on her face. Her ku'an's eyes were cold and accusing as she stared at Kirian. "What took so long? The King is in distress. He needs the remedy."

"Your Majesty? Just this morning..."

"I care nothing for this morning. Get your bag and go to him."

"I cannot give him the sart leaf, Your Majesty. He had it just this morning... It makes his heart beat too fast. "

The Queen rose to her feet and flung a bony arm out at Kirian. "Go to him!" she shrieked. "Guard! Take her to the courtyard."

A guard she did not know took her by the arm and pulled her from the room. She had never seen a Ha'lasi man take such liberties with a respectable woman's person. Suddenly she was afraid. She yanked her arm free. "I will go myself," she said, but the man remained at arms-length behind her the entire way to the courtyard.

The unmistakable signs of revelry surrounded her the moment she entered the courtyard. Wine jugs and mugs cluttered a stone table. There were several young men present, one in the process of vomiting into a flowerbed. The women who were with them were unveiled; the sun lit their hair and faces in a way Kirian was surprised to notice she found objectionable. One of the women was Eyelinn, who had loosened her outer robe to better display her body. The aroma of Smoke hung heavy even in the outdoor air, and a pipe lay broken on the tiles.

The King was in distress, bent forward in the effort to breathe. He coughed and clutched at his chest. She heard the rasp of his breathing as soon as she entered the courtyard. Apprehension gripped her. This was a serious attack, and the King had already had sart leaf once that day.

Lord Yun'lar entered the courtyard after her. "Good! Here you are. The King needs the leaf."

"My lord, you know I can't give him more."

Yun'lar looked grim. "I know this is a dangerous attack. Listen to him."

"He has had Smoke. What was he thinking?" She saw Ar'ok notice she was there. His narrow ku'an's eyes were on her. "Your Majesty, we must treat this attack in other ways.

Using the sart leaf twice in one day is too dangerous for your heart."

"Get the ku'an'an," Ar'ok wheezed to a guard. "You, Healer, I need the tea."

"Your Majesty, I cannot. Here, Lord Yun'lar, please order someone to clear the courtyard. The crowd does his Majesty no good." She watched the King struggle for breath. His lips were not blue, she noticed, so maybe there was time. Thoughts whirled through her mind as she tried to figure how best to treat this serious attack. Yun'lar called for a servant to bring a chair, and asked the King to sit. Slaves drew near, ready to carry the chair indoors. She said, "The air is clean out here. Better out here, Lord Yun'lar."

The ku'an'an strode through the gate, authority personified. He took in the disorder in the courtyard in one sharp stare, then ordered, "Everyone out! Everyone but the King and the Healers. And you slaves—we may need you."

"I want to be with him," crooned one of the women— Eyelinn, Kirian realized.

"Out, I said," Lord Si'lan snapped.

Moments later, the courtyard was blessedly free of extraneous babble.

"King Ar'ok," Si'lan said.

"Ku'an'an. This foreign Healer will not help me."

Si'lan looked at her.

"Lord Ku'an'an. The King has already had the sart leaf tea once today, just before dawn. It is very dangerous to give it twice in a day. It is a strain on the heart."

"I want it," Ar'ok rasped. "Can't breathe."

"It could kill him?" Si'lan asked.

"I doubt it," said Yun'lar. "But the lack of air may if he continues unable to breathe."

"It could, in fact, kill him." Kirian glared at Yun'lar.

Fear grabbed her by the throat until she could barely breathe herself. Her hands started to shake. Her teeth chattered. Terror twisted through her mind, and she wanted to run. Forcing her quivering legs to stay put, she gasped, "Your —Majesty!"

"She cannot help you if you frighten her like that," Si'lan rebuked the King. "Let her go."

The King released her from the psychic magery, and the terror left her. She took deep breaths, trying to cleanse her mind of the aftermath. Her muscles felt weak with reaction. She realized she had dropped her bag and it lay half-open on the tiles.

"I will have it!" Ar'ok said. His alien yellow eyes glared at her. Even as ill as he was, he could control her. She wanted to leave him to his own misery.

"You may decide, Your Majesty," she told the King. "You and your advisor. You have heard the risks." Let the boy King make his own decision. She knew he could order her slain without a second thought if she did not follow his orders.

"Now," Ar'ok said. Si'lan shrugged. Kirian nodded and called for tea, pulling the little twist of sart leaf from her bag. It broke into pieces and dissolved under the hot water, releasing its grassy aroma. She mixed the mellweed in, just a pinch, aware that Ar'ok had recently had Smoke. She gave the grainy stuff to the King, and he grabbed it, almost spilling it, and drank.

Kirian watched. It did not take long before the mellweed in the tea helped relax Ar'ok's tension. As his anxiety eased, so did his cramped posture. Yun'lar stood beside him, fingers at the King's wrist, checking his pulse. The King's labored breathing gradually grew slower, and he breathed freely.

"So what's the problem with that?" Ar'ok asked. "I can breathe, and I still live. You wished only to prolong my illness."

Si'lan cast an impatient look at the boy King. His eyes moved to Yun'lar. "Well?"

Yun'lar said, "It is fast."

"It will grow faster," Kirian said.

Yun'lar grimaced. In a few short minutes, Ar'ok said, "I want to lie down."

Kirian went to him and helped him recline on the bench. A slave brought a cushion for the King's head. She noticed the King's chest rising and falling fast and shallow. He coughed. Yun'lar took the King's pulse again, frowning. He said, "Your Majesty, how do you feel?"

"Sick. Faint. My body trembles. The foreigner has poisoned me." His voice was weak.

"What do I do for this?" Yun'lar said.

"I have no idea," Kirian said. "He has had alcohol, Smoke, mellweed and sart leaf. I wouldn't dare give him a sleeping draft. This is the danger I warned you about. All you can do is wait and help him relax, and pray to your god for the best."

"Yun'lar! My hands are tingling."

The lord physician's eyes looked desperate. "You learned at the Healers' College in Sugetre. I have heard what success you have had, treating the city women down at the hospital. Do you say there is nothing even you can do?"

"I know of nothing. I did warn you, Lord Yun'lar. But the King is young and strong. If he can relax, perhaps he will win through this."

"Yun'lar!" Ar'ok's voice trembled. "My hands are shaking now!"

Si'lan said, "Get a blanket, and get his slave in here."

Kirian looked at him.

"I mean for her to massage his neck and shoulders; this may help him relax. It may also take his mind off his discomfort, so he does not add to his stress by needless worry."

She looked at him with more respect. "Very well." She sent for Eyelinn and intercepted the young woman at the door. "Look," she said, "No games. The King is really ill. If you can relax him, make him sleep, it will be well. Can you massage his neck and shoulders?"

Eyelinn nodded. Her beautiful eyes were on Ar'ok. "I love him. I will do anything," she said.

Kirian wondered if she knew about Inmay, but decided not to muddy the situation with complications. The slave hurried to Ar'ok's side, showing more concern than Kirian had ever seen from her. She was clearly still under the King's ku'an influence. She bent over him, caressed his face until the King snapped, "Leave my face alone!"

Eyelinn knelt by the bench. A moment later, she began moving her hands along Ar'ok's neck, using slow, smooth strokes. Her long fingers wound up through Ar'ok's hair, down his neck, over his shoulders. The King's frown slipped away. A slave brought a cloth soaked in warm water and placed it on the King's forehead.

Si'lan said, "Will it answer?"

"It is better than nothing. It may work." She looked into the amber eyes, so like Callo's, in the lined face. "It was creative. Thank you, Lord Ku'an'an."

The King still breathed fast. But his eyes were closed and the long, gentle strokes of Eyelinn's hands soothed him. After half a candlemark, Yun'lar again took the King's pulse.

"A little better. Still very fast. We will need to keep vigilant. How long will this effect last?"

"Candlemarks, perhaps. Stay close, Yun'lar." She turned to the ku'an'an as Yun'lar returned to the King's side. "My lord, may I speak with you?"

They went aside so as not to disturb the King. She said, "I must ask you about the Righan foreigner that was put to death a few days ago."

"This Inmay? Lord Callo asked me about him."

"Why was he executed?"

"He would not accept reality."

Kirian feared she knew what that meant, but said, "What do you mean, my lord?"

"The King wanted this woman Eyelinn. He saw her in the city, unveiled. Inmay would not accept it. First Ar'ok ordered him imprisoned, but during the transfer the young man escaped and went to her in the slave's quarters, trying to entice her to escape."

She sighed. Inmay had been besotted far beyond common sense. "And he was found out."

"No, Healer. The woman gave him up to the guards."

"Eyelinn did?" She looked at the concubine who knelt patiently on the hard tiles by the King's side, kneading his shoulders. "She owed Inmay a great deal, my lord. I am not sure how she could have done a thing like that."

"You know how. His Majesty has used his ku'an influence on her. She loves him more than breath itself, would do anything Ar'ok asks. That is how it works." There was a note of warning in the ku'an'an's tone.

And Ar'ok, of course, wanted only one thing from Eyelinn. Kirian wondered what the King would do when he tired of Eyelinn's body. Where would she go, and what would she do? Certainly the future did not look promising for the slave.

She checked with Yun'lar about the King's condition and found it unchanged. It would be some time until the sart leaf ceased to affect the King's heart. At least the boy was as relaxed as possible, enjoying the sensation of Eyelinn's hands soothing his muscles.

Yun'lar settled into a nearby chair; he would remain, watching and monitoring, although Kirian had no idea what the lord physician could do to help if the King's heart began to race out of control.

She left the courtyard, returning to her rooms. There she found three guardsmen waiting to remove her Healer's bag from her and deliver her to the cells under Las'ash Castle.

Chapter Thirteen

Callo was sick with self-disgust. He wanted to go work off his misery in the ring, but couldn't move either arm well enough to even take a few jabs at a practice dummy. After Kirian left, he found himself drinking wine in his chair by the window until he could no longer feel the pain in his arms or in his heart. When Chiss came to remove the wine jug and get him to bed, the servant asked no questions. Callo slept the sleep of the deeply inebriated, but the next morning he still felt awful.

Now, with his left arm beginning to move normally, he was free to go where he wanted. He felt that not all was right with the other wound. He followed the physician's instructions with care, but knew his recovery was in Jashan's hands. He refrained from watching Yun'lar's face when the man checked the status of his wound, and snapped at Chiss when the man suggested they have Healer Kirian in to look at it. He held it firmly against his side to ease the pain and refused any more mellweed.

He went to the ring very early the next day. There he stood

weaponless and asked Jashan to guide his ku'an magery so he could never use it for ill. He did not complete the form, and did not know if the god heard him.

The memory of Kirian's face, after he had pushed her away, was bitter to him. It played over again before his mind's eye, heedless of his misery. He remembered his delight in her face and body, the pleasure of her voice, her humor, and care for him. He had known for some time he desired her. He remembered the urge to touch her, to kiss her, the thrill of the urge to bed her. Then he would remember her face, lips welcoming him, eyes shining. It seemed he was fortunate, and she desired him too.

He remembered his shock as he realized what he must have done, how he must have influenced her. Images of Ar'ok's uncaring manipulation of the slave girl Eyelinn rose before his eyes. He could see again his attackers fleeing in the alley outside the Black Duck, infused with fear by the power of his psychic magery. How powerful emotions were! How easy it was to wish upon others what one wanted them to feel—even without realizing it.

The mellweed might have weakened the guard he always kept on that part of himself. Even now he did not quite know how he had done it. But one thing he knew: all his life he had seen those with mage power use their wills to get what they wanted, without thought, without care, and sometimes without purpose, other than self- satisfaction. He would not be one of those.

He would keep the shock and shame of Kirian's reaction to remind him.

Now, wandering in the Castle with no clear place to go, he knew his errand here was done. He had learned enough about the ku'an to realize he would never be comfortable using their power to advance their goals. That way lay corruption. He had been manipulated too often by King Martan during his youth, and he had seen the shrewd and suspicious king use others without compunction. He would not become like that.

He could barely stand to be here in Ar'ok's palace, walking the halls, seeing the common people look away when they accidentally looked into his eyes.

Maybe somehow he could make restitution for what he had done. He would do it obliquely. He dared not address Kirian on this issue. Perhaps, now that he understood better what he could accomplish as a ku'an, there was some way he could at least help Arias. The Collar worked by compulsion; maybe the ku'an magery could ease that compulsion somehow.

He was in the weapons room, working on his sword, when he heard the ku'an'an's deep voice hail him. Si'lan was the only one of these people he had never seen try to exploit another human being, the only one he might, someday, come to respect. But he still knew little about the man. He knew his distrust was obvious in his voice as he responded to Si'lan.

"I have news for you," Si'lan said, "Which I give you for nothing, for reasons of my own. The Healer, Hon Kirian "

"What of her?"

"She has been taken and imprisoned by the King. No, don't rush to her rescue—she will be well treated." An amused note came into Si'lan's voice. "And put away that sword, please. You look very martial, but that will not help."

Callo took a deep breath. He sheathed his sword, his right arm protesting. "What happened?"

Si'lan told him. Callo sat through the story, his eyes on the ku'an'an's face. Then he said, "So her usefulness to the King is done. He has the sart leaves, and Yun'lar, the fool, knows how to use them until they can obtain more. They had best treat her well!"

"She is in the cells. I will have someone take you to her, so that you may assure yourself."

Callo frowned. "Why did you bring me this news yourself?"

"I felt I owed you that. And Kirian, as brave a soul as she has turned out to be."

"Owed us? A noble concept, for a ku'an."

"I am aware you think poorly of us."

Callo laughed, a bitter sound that felt as if it came from his heart. "Why do you care?"

Si'lan sat down, pulling his cloak around him. "It is irrelevant now why I care. The world has changed, and things are not as they were planned to be."

"So even a ku'an cannot always have things…" Callo stopped as Si'lan's words caught up with him. He frowned, looking at the older man's face as if for the first time, seeing again the strange similarity.

Si'lan's mouth twisted in a bitter smile. "No. A ku'an cannot dictate the movements of time or of kingdoms—as much as Ar'ok would wish otherwise. And when he tries, time mocks his plans."

Callo tried for a moment to figure out the meaning behind the older man's words; he felt as if they had a very personal import. Then, strained by days of pain, Callo lost his patience. "Out with it," he said, knowing he was being rude. "What do you know of the circumstances of my birth?"

Si'lan rose, shaking his head, the malice back in his smile. "Was I there at your birth? My duty to you is done, and more than done, and my message brought to you personally out of respect for the Healer. Ask no more of me."

"You do not feel you owe me an explanation?"

"I have none to give. I will send someone to show you to the cells. Once you have satisfied yourself that she is being treated well, pay heed to me and forget her. You will be better off learning the ways of the ku'an you profess to despise, for you are one after all, however it came about." Si'lan walked off, leaving Callo staring after him in a state of anger and confusion.

The slave who came to show him to the cells was not talkative. Callo followed him, taking careful note of the turns in the passages, the stairs they took. This was a maze of a place, and he wanted to be able to find his way back to Kirian. They exited the castle proper and went down a roofed passageway, dirt-floored and open to the weather through big arched windows that lined the walkway to both sides, until they came to a gate that led to underground rooms. A cloaked man in Ar'ok's insignia came to admit them, then accompanied them into the stone-walled tunnel that took them to the cells.

There were prisoners in almost all of the cells. Callo could hear their sounds, the mumbling to each other through the walls. He saw an occasional face through the tiny, barred windows. One cell held a group of women, veiled even here in prison. In another cell a bearded man with a pale face yelped "Ku'an!" and the warning echoed in a dull fashion down the passageway, stilling all the voices for a moment. Then the warder brought them to one door, no different from the rest, and said, "Here she is."

Callo looked through the little window and felt his pulse jump. The cell had no external window, so Kirian was lit only by the wavering lamplight from the hallway. She paced back and forth, but did not seem in undue distress. She seemed in deep thought, her gaze on the floor.

"Kirian!"

She looked up at the window. "Lord Callo!" She smiled. "Thank the Unknown God, you are here. I wasn't sure they would tell you what happened."

"The ku'an'an told me. He respects you, I think. Are you all right?" In spite of his fear for her, he felt a rush of relief that she was glad to see him.

"I am perfectly well, except I am forced to be here. I should have expected it sooner."

"What happened?"

She told him what had happened that morning. "But whether that was why they decided to arrest me, I don't know. I think they've been ready to do this since the day we set foot on the docks."

"The ku'an'an told me you are being treated well. Is that true?"

"Well enough. I have food, and water, and a blanket. No one has hurt me or even spoken to me rudely." She moved aside so he could see a water jug and some bread on a wooden tray on the bench behind her. "What do you think will happen next?"

Callo's mouth set. "I have no idea. It could be almost anything. I'll get you out of here, Kirian, I swear it."

"My thanks." There was no distress in her voice; it was even a little soothing, as if she were trying to keep him calm.

It did not work. His blood was boiling.

The warder took care on the way out to show Callo the room of guards, currently sitting around a table playing dice, but clearly armed and available to quell any attempts at escape or rescue. He pulled the big gates together with a crash and locked them, nodding at the two men standing guard there before he bid farewell to Callo and vanished into his rooms.

Callo went to Ar'ok's audience room and demanded admittance. "My lord ku'an, the King is not here," said the guard.

"Then where is he?"

The guard did not know. Callo tracked down the ku'an'an

again, this time in his office, and said with no greeting: "Where is Ar'ok? I need to see him."

Si'lan raised his eyebrows and dismissed the clerk he had been meeting with. "You'd best calm down before you find him, or you will likely be in the cell next to the Healer's."

"How could he do that? She saved his life, Si'lan. Gods curse him."

"Ar'ok follows only his own inclinations."

"As do all of you ku'an," flashed Callo.

"You came here. You are subject to our rule. If you don't like it, you should not have come here! The woman is out of your reach. Accept it. It was too late when she went to that hospital, flouting the modesty laws in public. There is nothing you can do. She will be treated well until…"

"Until—what?"

The ku'an'an stared at him and did not reply. Callo felt a pressure inside his mind and shook his head viciously, seeing to his internal wall, making sure it could keep away the man's influence. "No, you don't. Don't you dare try to calm me down. What do you think I am, a fool, to let you do that twice?"

Si'lan's mouth curled in an unpleasant smile. The pressure ebbed. Callo swore and stalked out of the room. When he got back to his own room, he found Chiss sitting on the floor, sorting through a pile of clothing and other items. He strode past Chiss without a word of greeting and began pacing back and forth in front of the open window, trying to plan through his rage.

"My lord," Chiss said. "How is Hon Kirian? You have been to see her?"

"She is well enough, considering what that fool King has done to her." He turned and looked at Chiss where the man sat in a welter of fabric, and some things that looked like veils. "What is that stuff?"

"Hon Kirian's clothing, my lord. I saved it from her room. I'm packing some of it."

"Not her bag though? I am sure they took that?"

"They searched it, then threw it away. I know they took the sart leaf from the bag. But I saved what I could. Here it is."

Callo opened the bag and looked through the few items remaining in it. Kirian's Healer's knife was gone, of course; anyone would want a fine knife. The precious sart leaf was gone. The bag still held a few vials and bags of herbs, jumbled from hasty handling. No doubt the searchers had no idea what these were, and had abandoned them with the bag. "I'm surprised they left anything at all behind."

"They are fools," Chiss said. "They took only what the King ordered them to take, and maybe the knife out of greed."

"I imagine the King or the Lord Physician will send them back for the rest of the bag's contents as soon as they know it was left behind. My thanks for rescuing it, Chiss." He handed the bag back to Chiss. "What do you think they plan to do with her? Execute her, perhaps?"

"My lord, there is no way to know. I have tried to get some information out of some of the other servants here. I think she could be executed. She could be handed over to one of Som'ur's priests. She could be branded and freed—but she is a political prisoner too, and I think they do not plan to free her under any circumstances."

Callo felt his face flush again with temper. "They will not do any such thing while I am here to do something about it."

Chiss looked up at him, his eyes gentle. "My lord, they will have you watched."

"They may watch me until their eyes fall out. They have

already tried to soothe me by showing me how well they are treating her. Jashan's eyes! They are planning to kill her! Do they think I am so self-involved as to not protect my own?"

"They do not expect you to do anything, since they would do nothing in the same circumstances. What is your plan, then, my lord?"

Callo looked at the man's lean face and grinned. The helpless anger receded. He said, "I do greatly value you, Chiss. I don't know what I would do without you, my friend."

Chiss folded another rectangle of fabric and added it to his pile. "What then?"

"It looks as if we are going to have to leave this place. I hope you have not grown too attached."

"I left Ha'las once before. Remember? I am not at all attached to it. There is a feeling of desperation about the people here in the palace that I will be grateful to escape."

"Comes from being around all these ku'an," muttered Callo. "Damn Ar'ok infects all of them with his cruelty."

"I think the King is very young to have such power. It is more likely that he is a product of others' intentions, don't you think?"

"I don't know. I never saw a boy of that age so . . . warped. It is the psychic magery that corrupts him. I won't be one of them, Chiss, I have resolved it."

"I think it is the man who shapes how the power is used, rather than the power that shapes the man."

"Hah! My experience indicates otherwise." Callo paced a few more minutes as his anger wound down and his mind began to function better. "Chiss, we must pack. We must leave this place immediately."

"My lord, I am willing to go wherever you say. But have you accomplished what you wished to, when we abandoned your life in Righar?"

"You know I have not. I have my suspicions about who my sire might be, but they won't be confirmed. And as to finding out more about the ku'an, I am no longer interested in the brutal fools."

Chiss began to gather the pile of veils together. His eyes still did not meet his lord's. "If you leave, there will be no chance of ever finding out more."

"I no longer care. Kirian is in prison, and if not for me, she wouldn't even be in this cursed land. It is my fault. I find she is more important to me than what may or may not have happened thirty years ago."

"My lord, there is no foreign ship in port—no way to buy passage."

"How do you know this?"

"It seemed a good idea to know when Ghosian or some other foreign captain was in port."

"Well done. So we must find a way out of this city and head overland, to the east. If those assassins got in, we can get out." Callo stared out the window again, not feeling the warm breeze. His mind struggled with plans and contingencies. His thoughts suddenly felt muddled, as if he were ill. "We need to pack light. Just what we need to get us back. Also, some Ha'lasi coin."

"Some food and water would be even more important than extra coin. My lord, we must have our horses."

"And an idea of the lay of the land. How did you leave last time, Chiss? Have you any idea of the land between here and —say— Anha'lin? That is on the east coast, according to my maps."

"I left on a ship from Las'ash. I grew up in the northern countryside until I was brought here to serve."

"A farm boy," Callo said, only half his attention on the

man. "So, do you think you can help us live off the land until Anha'lin, if I can find the way?"

"Not unless the gods set out a table of meats for us every evening, Lord Callo."

Callo laughed. "I think we need a guide."

"My lord," Chiss said in alarm. "Whom would you trust? Telling anyone our plan is likely to have us in prison next to Hon Kirian, and hanged the next morning in front of the boy King."

Callo made a calming motion with his hands. "Don't worry, Chiss, I know of a man who might help. I will track him down if you will pack—very light, all right? And for Kirian as well." His eye caught the tunic he had just purchased, one of gold-threaded amber that looked like the sun in spring, and he sighed. "It is too bad about the new clothes, but one can always get more of those later, I suppose."

"Indeed. My lord, do we go armed to the cells?"

"We will have to. I am glad you can carry your part of a fight." Callo took a quick sip of the wine on the table to quell his growing headache. His face felt flushed, yet he shivered a little in the breeze from the open window. He ignored the deepening ache from his right arm as he turned to leave. Chiss stood before him, looking grim.

"What?"

"You cannot wield a sword, Lord Callo."

"I will do my best. I have no choice."

"You must consider that you will need to use your ku'an magery to get Hon Kirian out of the cells."

"With Jashan's aid, I will not. My arm will hold."

Chiss gave him a level look. "I remember something you said when you and Lord Arias commanded a unit in the South. It comes to mind just now."

Callo crossed his arms. "Well?"

"You told Hon Drale that if he were not honest with his men, he'd deserve the failure that would come to him."

Callo sighed. "I remember."

"Then take your own advice, my lord."

"I have asked Jashan to bind that magery. It is cursed, Chiss. It brings only shame."

"It will not bring shame if used with honor and care." Chiss shrugged. "I will do as you say, as always, Lord Callo. But if you go in unprepared, we may not get out again."

Callo did not want to think about using the magery again — even if the god Jashan, whom he had asked to bind him, permitted it. Each time he had used it, he had regretted it. But he supposed he would do anything to get Kirian safely out of Ha'las.

"I will consider it. Let me go, Chiss, or I'll be unable to find my guide."

Chiss bowed very slightly. His unusual courtesy puzzled Callo all the way to the Black Duck. He rode Miri to the tavern, his head swimming a little from the pain of his wounded arm. The mare was skittish, and she pranced in the spring dusk. The poor mare had not had enough exercise, Callo thought. "My good Miri," he said, and she flicked her ears back at him. "I have missed you, my beauty. Soon we will be on our way again."

He tied Miri to a rail under the eye of a city guard and, for good measure, tucked a coin into the guard's hand to make it worth his while to keep the mare safe. Then he walked down the alley and entered the Black Duck. As the door swung shut on the early dusk, blackness enveloped him, and he said, "Gri'nel, is it you? You know I cannot see you."

"Ha, is it you?" came the raspy old voice. "Ku'an's ass, I don't believe it. You lived, did ya?"

"I did. Will you let me keep my sword?"

"Hell yes, and your belt knife too. Don't want no ku'an pissed at me again, do I?" The inner door opened and Callo entered the tavern proper.

Fa'lar, leaning against the bar with his ropy arms crossed, came alert when he saw who had entered. "Welcome, my lord ku'an. You'll be bringing no more trouble with you now?"

"The trouble was never yours," Callo said. "I am looking for Ha'star."

"Sit down and have some ale. He'll be along."

The veiled young woman brought the drink, and Callo sat sipping it until the door opened and Ha'star came into the tavern.

"Lord Callo," he said. "What brings you here again? I've told you what I know." He sat next to Callo and accepted a mug of ale.

"I need help," Callo said. "I thought of you first, since you are no friend to the ku'an in the Castle."

"No friend to any ku'an."

Callo nodded. "That's as may be. I thought to ask you, since you acted as a friend to me."

"So what is it? You'll not use your ku'an magic on me if I say nay?"

"You know I will not." Callo eased his arm, which was throbbing now, and noticed Ha'star follow the subtle movement with the keen eye of a swordsman. It was just as well; Ha'star should know what he was getting himself into, and what the risks were, especially that he could not necessarily count on Callo's aid in a fight. "I need a guide. A guide who knows his way to Anha'lin or some other place where myself and two others can secretly take ship back to Righar."

"This isn't court-approved, or you'd be leaving from Las'ash." Ha'star shook his head and looked doubtful. "You being a noble and all, I doubt you know how to manage 'til we get there. You need a woodsman."

"That's right."

"Someone who can avoid troops sent to follow."

"You understand, I see." Callo took a great slug of ale and called for more. His arm burned. It etched a path of pain from his shoulder to his wrist. This was a bad time for it to grow worse. "You said you have no kin to take the brunt of the King's anger. I will not lie, however—you will be putting yourself at great risk if they ever discover who aided us." He wanted to mention reward, the coins Chiss was packing even as they spoke, but he felt, if Ha'star agreed to help them, it would not be because of money.

Ha'star grunted. "I hear the woman Healer is in prison."

Callo nodded.

"Wasn't her place to be healin' folks, you know my lord ku'an."

"In Righar…"

"Doesn't matter about Righar. You're here now. I suppose you know what they'll do to her."

Callo forced down the anger. The King had used Kirian for what he needed, and then disposed of her. He knew he hadn't helped, joining Kirian in her disregard of the modesty laws. "I don't mean to wait to find out. What do you say?"

Ha'star evaluated him with narrowed eyes. Callo stared back, wondering how much of his pain the other man could see. He was beginning to feel odd, too. He held on to his expressionless look as Ha'star thought.

"You're one of the decent ones," Ha'star said. "The only decent one by my lights. I'll do it. I'm on leave now, so I've got time. This be my chance to strike at Jol'tan."

"What did he do to you, this Jol'tan?" Callo asked.

Ha'star made a savage cutting motion with his hand. "None of a ku'an's business, is it? Not friend or foe."

"My apologies." Callo stood, held out a hand. Ha'star took it, but did not smile. "Meet us in the woods to the east of town, just to the east of the tanneries?"

"When?"

"Gods know. What is it now, full night already? We will try to be there by dawn. If we are not there—we could be delayed, I do not know what we go into. Use your judgment."

"Nothing else," Ha'star said. "I will be there, horsed and packed."

"My thanks. You will not regret it, Ha'star." Callo put all the sincerity of his feelings into that phrase.

"Not for you to guess what I'll regret," Hastar said in a voice that held more than a little warning. "Nor to do anything about it either, my lord ku'an."

"As you say." Callo nodded to him, and to the keeper, and left. In the security hole, he exchanged a few words with Gri'nel, who informed him that unlike last time, there were no assassins waiting outside the tavern. Wishing the old man the luck of the gods, Callo left.

———

The horses waited near a vacant part of the stables, hidden in the shadows of new-leafed bushes and the tumbled gray stone of the old buildings. Chiss had tied the packs so that all they needed to carry was their weapons. The packs were small, Chiss had cautioned several times, as if he thought Callo did not realize that one could not bring valus fur and extra pillows on a flight for one's life. Callo had chosen a time when most residents of the castle would be asleep— except, of course, for the King's companions, who attended a late party, and the servants who were kept scurrying to attend to their wishes. But that was on the other side of the hulking building, and also in the kitchens. Here near the cells, all was quiet.

They crouched near the arched walkway that Callo had traveled with his guide earlier that day. It seemed a different world now. The moon was a slender crescent, lighting very little. The torches set by the gate for the guards burned snappishly in the unsettled breeze, so that the shadows wavered about under their feet. Callo remembered that there was no outside window in Kirian's cell; he thought of her alone in the dark, and moved restlessly, anxious to get in.

Callo crept forward until he was hidden from the gate guards only by the lower half of the arched wall. Then he moved fast, sliding behind one of the men and smashing his sword hilt into his head. The guard crumpled.

Callo looked for the second guard. The man lay on the ground unconscious, with Chiss leaning over him, pulling a key from the man's belt. Then Chiss dragged both men out of sight while Callo kept guard. In a few minutes he appeared again, breathing as if he had been fighting, but he only waved at Callo to continue on.

The gate opened smoothly and without sound. As they entered, clinging to the wall to avoid making an obvious silhouette, Callo checked for more guards. The lamps were lit in the center room, and he could hear the rumble of voices coming from it—and also the clink of pottery. It seemed Jashan was with them, and they had happened to arrive at the guards' mealtime. Callo could see no one in the dirt- floored passageway at all.

They crouched low to avoid being seen through the tiny windows, and moved down the hall. When Callo thought they had arrived at the proper cell, he lifted his head and peered inside.

He could see Kirian by the light of a torch set at the end of the hall. She sat on the low bench in deep shadow. A tray with a bowl on it lay on the bench beside her, but she did not seem to be eating. She put her head in her hands, and her hair swung forward to cover her eyes.

"Kirian," Callo whispered.

Kirian looked up, eyes wide, and saw Callo. She jumped up and almost knocked over the tray, but caught it as it tipped. She settled the tray safely on the bench, then hurried to the door.

"Get ready," Callo whispered, and set the big metal key they had taken from the gate guard into the lock, and tried to turn it.

It would not turn.

Jashan aid us, he thought, and tried again. The thing would not turn. He looked over his shoulder at the guards' common room, wondering which one kept the key and how he could get it. Just then a burly man stuck his head out of the guardroom and glanced up and down the hall. His eyes caught on them where they crouched before Kirian's door.

"Ware intruders!" he yelled in a voice like a lion's roar. There was a clatter of overturned pottery and a slam as something wooden went over hard. Five men ran out of the guardroom, arming themselves as they went. There was nowhere for Callo and Chiss to go. Giving up on secrecy, they stood. Callo pushed the dizziness and the pain to the back of his mind and readied himself to fight.

"Ku'an!" yelled one of the prisoners. His shout echoed down the passageway, a dull underground reverberation that mixed with the metallic clash of swords as Chiss engaged with the first guardsman. Callo saw another man race forward to strike and raised his own sword, blocking the cut full on his weapon and shaking his wounded right arm to the bone.

Chiss disposed of the first attacker; the man lay on the floor, blood pumping out of a wound in his gut to soak into the dirt floor. Callo's foot slipped in the blood and he almost went down; his attacker's swing flew over his head, striking the door behind him. Callo hauled himself upright with his left arm in Kirian's window and stabbed with his sword as if it were a knife, piercing his opponent's leather shirt and his heart. The man gurgled horribly and went down, only to be replaced by a fresh and angry guard.

Callo wanted to look around for Chiss but dared not turn his eyes from this new man. He heard Kirian shriek and wondered if Chiss had been wounded. His attacker swung at his unprotected neck, and Callo ducked then lifted his arm to strike back.

The pain swept up his arm into his shoulder, into his neck. For just a moment, every bit of will Callo had would not move his arm. He felt someone grab him by his left arm and pull, hard, moving him away while his vision shaded from red to black and back to normal.

Kirian's voice, behind him, warned: "Beware, there's another!" Callo raised his left arm, hoping to get inside his opponent's guard and block his arm at very close range. He knew he had failed when there was a blur of movement and he felt the agony of a fresh sword cut on his already wounded arm.

The pain screamed up his arm and felled him. He realized he was on his knees on the dirt floor, with Chiss standing in front of him trying to defend him against the three guards that remained. Someone shouted from the entrance, and the gate guards they thought they had disposed of loomed in the hall-way, ready to join the fight.

"My lord!" gasped Chiss.

Callo dropped his sword. He ignored the sick, swimming

feeling in his head. He forced his shoulders to relax, and fought behind the barrier of his pain. He found the source of the ku'an magery, searched for the essence of the emotion he needed, and shoved it out into the hallway in desperation, hoping this would work. There was no time to finesse the effects of the magery. He said "Sorry" to Chiss and Kirian under his breath as he felt the energy leave him, and heard the sudden silence as the fighting stopped.

"My lord, thank you—I knew you could do it," Chiss said as he helped Callo to his feet. Callo did not look at him; he didn't want to see the false trust in Chiss' familiar eyes.

"Lord Ku'an!" said one of the guards. "Why—I mean, are you all right? I do beg your pardon! Forgive us!" The man actually knelt in shocked repentance. He had dropped his sword; it lay with its tip in a pool of blood on the hard-packed dirt floor.

"Just—give me the key," Callo said, holding his right arm with his left, trying to fight the dizziness that wanted to bring him down. Blood leaked between his fingers. One of the guards opened Kirian's door and she rushed out, prying at his fingers to see between them.

"Let me see that," she said.

"No time," he said, because the effort to keep all the guards in a trusting frame of mind was tiring him. Between the wound and the strain of the magery, he did not know how long he could keep this up.

Kirian let go his arm and looked up at him. The contrast between the glowing trust in her eyes and the stunned look he had seen days before was too much for him; he looked away.

"My lord, let us help," said one of the guards. He motioned the other guards back, directed them to see to the fallen men, and accompanied Chiss, Callo, and Kirian to the gate entrance. "I am sorry we did not realize who you were. Let me call a physician. You are bleeding."

"No, no! I have access to a—a Healer. Go back and take care of your men."

"We have two dead. Can you send someone to help take them to the priests? We should not leave the prisoners," the guard said, then added, "I regret the disturbance. We did not know, my lord."

"Yes, yes. I know. Go back. Go to your men." The ceiling began to make large, slow circles around his head. He staggered a little. Chiss supported him with an arm under his left shoulder. "Go! You know you can trust me to say nothing."

"Of course, I trust you absolutely. I will do as you say." The guard bowed and vanished.

"In about two minutes he will remember I'm not so trustworthy," Callo said raggedly. "Chiss, Kirian, the horses "

"I knew I could depend on you to get me out of there," Kirian said.

Callo ignored her words, knowing they were the product of artificial emotion. They were out the gate, up the arched walkway in full view now, since no one was suspicious—to the side of the stable, to the horses. The night sky swung wildly about him. Callo felt himself lose the magery. He felt the wall seal him in and the others out, dropping on him in massive finality. He cried out in pain, exhausted and sick, no longer sure where he was.

"All the gods," Chiss muttered next to him. "You did it, didn't you? Are you still with us, my lord?"

Callo could not reply.

"What *was* that?" Kirian asked, sounding shocked.

"A ku'an at work," Chiss replied. "Here, help him up. Jashan aid him to keep the saddle until we are out of reach."

"I'll—stay the saddle," Callo gasped.

"Good, Lord Callo; now let me wrap that arm." Kirian had found something long and soft—a strip of cloth from somewhere about her person—and she wrapped it around the wound with precise, impersonal movements that comforted him in his misery not at all. Although how he should expect comfort from one whose mind he had subverted, even briefly, he did not know. All he could do now was stay in the saddle. He determined he would do that if it killed him, to try to make amends for the wrong he had done both of them.

The night careened about him as he was helped to mount, and Miri moved uneasily under him. "Miri, now go gently, guard him well," he heard Kirian say to the mare, and he remembered that he had, after all, saved the Healer from whatever foul execution they had been going to inflict on her, and perhaps she would remember that. Then he had to devote every ounce of attention to staying on Miri, as Chiss, on his own gelding, led Miri through the night. He held on through the twists and turns of the city streets, seeing occasional torches like bleary beacons in the late spring night. They stayed away from dockside, went through the merchants' square, through a twisted alley crowded with leaning houses, through dank, wet spring streets with water pooled in gutters too clogged to drain. He gave up any effort to keep track of where they were. Once he heard Chiss say, "My lord, we are almost there," but he felt too dizzy to respond. "Are you all right?" Kirian asked, and Chiss said, "We cannot help him until we are there."

Then the stink of the tannery pierced his haze, and he lifted his head. Miri plodded along under him like a child's pony; they were keeping their pace easy for him. He looked around, saw the tannery looming ahead, and smelled the bitter stench that drifted east on the wind.

"In the woods," he told Chiss. "Someone is waiting."

"Your guide," Chiss agreed. "You told me, my lord. Easy, we are almost there."

Callo subsided into confused pain. The tannery stench abated a little, freshened by the fickle spring breeze. His mind felt as if it were filled with wool, and pain enveloped his arm. He devoted himself to hanging on until they had left the scattered environs of the tannery and entered the eastern woods.

The woods was a small patch of wilderness close to Las'ash, free of houses or the makeshift settlements of traveling bands that clustered near the city to the north. The tannery smell no doubt had something to do with the lack of habitation here. As the deeper darkness of surrounding foliage claimed them, Callo felt the difference in Miri's gait as she began walking on the leafy detritus of a trail. The slim moon vanished behind spring's new leaves, and he could see nothing. Miri stayed in line with the other horses, and Callo thanked all the gods that he had to do nothing.

He thought he had lost awareness for a while; time seemed to have passed, and Miri stood still in the pitch blackness. A pinpoint of light appeared before them and grew larger. It moved then lit a brown, scarred face.

"Better be who I'm expectin'," said Ha'star's voice.

Callo tried to respond, but felt himself swaying in the saddle.

Darkness claimed his consciousness at last.

Chapter Fourteen

Kirian was a little afraid of the scarred Ha'lasi warrior at first. He stood by, frowning, as Lord Callo slumped, then swayed in Miri's saddle. Chiss nudged his gelding to Miri's side just in time to keep his lord from falling. Lord Callo kept his seat, but he had clearly reached the end of his endurance. They would be staying here, wherever the Ha'lasi warrior could find for them to camp.

"Great angry gods," Ha'star swore. "Night is the time to move. Are you sure he can't?"

"I'm sure," Chiss said in a clipped voice that was quite unlike him. "They will be expecting us to head for the port. If we don't rest a while, we may lose more than a few hours."

Chiss and Ha'star helped Callo down from the saddle and onto a blanket, where the ku'an lord slumped with his hair falling forward to hide his face. Kirian could barely tell one man from another in the dark woods, but she wanted to see Callo's arm. His old wound, plus the new cut he had received in the same arm, seemed to have drained him of strength;

unless it was the ku'an magery that had done so. She asked Chiss.

"I have no idea," Chiss said. "I assume the psychic magery takes strength, just as color magery does. But Hon Kirian, he was already ill before tonight. There is something wrong with the wound in his sword arm."

"Then I must have a fire," Kirian demanded. "I have to look at it."

Chiss glanced over his shoulder at Ha'star. "He will not want to build a fire. Too dangerous."

Ha'star did indeed swear when she asked about a fire. Then he sighed, and muttered something about nothing being easy where a ku'an was concerned. Soon after, he had a tiny flame burning in a hole cluttered with small sticks, and was stalking about the clearing collecting better fuel. "A very small fire," he insisted, staring at Kirian with his hands full of branches. "Or we will all be in prison by daybreak."

Chiss assisted his lord to sit near the fire, and helped him to remove his cloak and loosen his tunic. Callo had said nothing since they had made camp. He shivered noticeably as Chiss bared the wounded arm. Kirian put her hand to Callo's forehead and sucked in her breath as she felt the fever radiating from him. Then she turned to his wounded arm.

The first wound site was swollen and burning hot to her touch. The new wound was still bleeding a little after she removed the makeshift bandage. She looked up and saw Callo's exhausted eyes on her face.

"What in the name of all the gods did you think you were doing, ignoring this wound?" she hissed. "Do you want to lose your arm?"

Callo shook his head and dropped his gaze to the fire. Kirian felt ashamed of herself for berating a sick man, but she felt overwhelmed. These were not the best conditions under which to treat a man as ill as Lord Callo. From across the fire, Ha'star looked on, clearly displeased. Kirian hoped he would not lose patience and leave them to find their way on their own.

Chiss said, "I think you will be needing this, Hon Kirian." He passed a familiar bag to her. She breathed a prayer of thanks to the Unknown God and opened her Healer's bag. She was not surprised to find the sart leaf and her knife gone, but the herb she needed was still there in its cloth pouch. She began to clean the infected wound. Callo turned his head away from her work and sat holding his arm rigidly still.

Chiss handed a leather flask to his lord, who took it and sipped. "What's that?" Kirian snapped.

"Wine," Chiss said.

Kirian reached out and took it from Callo's hands. "No wine. Lord Callo, you are feverish."

"I brought water also," Chiss said.

She told Chiss to grind some of the herb she gave him and soak it in water. The tea would help to chase the infection from Callo's blood. Then she poured some of her own water over Callo's arm. In a perfect world, she would be able to apply a topical treatment to the wound, then order rest and broth and plenty of tea with honey.

Ha'star had gone off to rummage in his pack. When he returned, he handed her a little jar. She looked up at him, eyebrows raised in inquiry, and he said, "Liquor from the south." She opened the jar and smelled it, nodded, and gave Callo a considering look. Then without warning, she poured a good slug of it over Callo's wounds.

Callo jolted and sucked in air. Kirian could see the muscles tighten as the shock slammed through his system.

"The pain will ease," Kirian said. "Now drink this tea. Eat

something. Then, go and rest for a while. Ha'star says we have to move on soon."

"If you want to get out of Ha'las alive," Ha'star said.

Callo nodded. He rose without help and went to the bedroll. Chiss brought him the tea. Kirian took a deep breath.

"You're no fool," Ha'star said. "You'll do. No hysterics about being alone with men out here in the night?"

"I'm perfectly safe."

Ha'star nodded. "Yes, you are, thanks to him. Not your ordinary ku'an, that man."

She smiled. "I think you are right, Hon Ha'star."

They rested for a candlemark, then Ha'star doused the fire, and they mounted again. Callo did not respond to Ha'star's call and had to be shaken out of sleep, but he was able to mount Miri on his own. They plodded along after Ha'star, keeping the horses quiet, until they were forced by the brightening dawn to find shelter in an empty herder's shed. The sun was rising earlier every day; they would have plenty of time to rest in the barn until nightfall.

Kirian sat with Callo near some missing boards that let in the daylight. She cleaned away the infection and poured more of Ha'star's liquor over his wound. Callo took the treatment in grim silence. As she re-wrapped the wounds, he caught his breath and relaxed a little, leaning back against the gray wooden wall. She looked up after a moment to see his eyes on her face.

"I am sorry about your friend." His voice was low, tired.

"Inmay?" She sighed. "I am too, of course, but it was to be expected. He has courted such an end for longer than you know."

"And about the little slave."

"Ah. Yes, she does not deserve to be Ar'ok's plaything. Even as unpleasant as she is."

She pulled the bandage tight and he winced. After a moment, he said, "Yesterday I went in the ring and asked Jashan to bind my ku'an abilities. I did not wish to use them again."

"That resolve didn't last long, did it?" She grinned and then looked up to catch an unguarded look on his face that surprised her. "I am sorry. You are not well enough to tease. In fact, I have not thanked you yet for freeing me from that prison. I am not sure where I would have been by now if you and Chiss had not come after me. You have my deepest thanks, Lord Callo."

He made an impatient gesture. "I thought you gave up *my lording* me."

"If you still wish it." She watched him lean his head back against the wall and close his eyes. His hair, loosened from its tie, fell back in a wave of gold. She wanted to smooth it, but stayed her hand, instead waving at Chiss to bring a cup of the herbal tea. "But I'm glad Jashan did not grant your wish. Where would I be now, if you had not used your psychic magery to help free me?"

"I did the same to you and Chiss as I did to the guards. Made you feel something false, something I forced you to feel. It is an invasion. I've spent most of my life trying to repress it, even before I knew why."

Kirian said carefully, "It is true that you should not use such power for only your own pleasure. But I am glad you chose to use it yesterday. If you had not, you and I, and Chiss would likely all be dead or imprisoned."

There was a brief silence. Then Callo's lips curved upward. "Now we are pursued by the kings of two countries. Ar'ok has all of Ha'las hunting us, I am sure. Our escape will have enraged him. And it seems Sharpeyes has not forgotten me in Righar. All in the space of a season or two. What might we accomplish in another year?"

She laughed. Looking up, she saw Chiss standing there holding two cups. She took hers and sipped, tasting sweet red wine. Callo sipped his and gave a great sigh. "This tea tastes like grass, Kirian."

"Do not complain. It will likely save your life. It is the only remedy I know for an infection that has already gone into the blood. You will be drinking a lot of it for the next few days."

"My lord. Hon Kirian," Chiss said, holding out a slab of bread and cheese. Callo said, "Chiss, you are a wonder."

"I raided the kitchen before we left," Chiss said. "I have dried fruit as well."

Callo devoured his bread as if he had not eaten for days. Kirian smelled the sharp cheese and felt her mouth begin to water. Ha'star slipped in and accepted bread and cheese from Chiss. He sat near them and sipped from a wineskin.

"I have not had a chance to speak with you, Ha'star," Callo said. "My thanks for your aid. Without you…"

"Ye'd be lost in the woods," He shrugged. "Don't like to see someone else crushed by the damned ku'an. Even if he be ku'an himself."

Kirian smiled at that. "So," she said expectantly, "what is the plan?"

"We return to Seagard," Callo said.

There was a moment's silence. Then she said, "You just finished telling me how King Martan still searches for you in Righar."

"Not to mention, he sent six armed men to kill you in Las'ash city," Chiss added.

"I don't intend to have the servants announce me at the main door to Sugetre Palace. I do not plan to see King Martan at all. But I have something I need to do in Seagard." He looked around at three faces which were carefully blank. "You need not accompany me, you know. Once we arrive, you may go your own ways."

"My lord," Chiss said. "Have you accomplished what you wished in Ha'las?"

"Priorities change," Callo said. He looked at Kirian. "I came here to find out what my heritage was, but I have found the whole class of ku'an to be corrupt beyond my imagination. I don't wish to be any part of them."

As she finished her food, exhaustion swept over Kirian. She was glad they had the whole day ahead to sleep before riding again at dusk. With a weary smile, she moved away from the others, found a corner where she could wrap herself in a blanket, and fell asleep.

———

Two more days found Kirian almost used to living roughly. Their travel was curtailed as the early summer days grew longer, and their night progress was slowed by the waning of the moon. Ha'star and Callo fretted and edged their riding time further into the daylight hours, but this was risky; they were always on guard for King's men who might be seeking them. Kirian felt sure Ar'ok's men were looking elsewhere, in the city and at the port, and rode with a sense of pleasure she had not felt in some time. She delighted in the gait of her little mare. She enjoyed the spring sun on her face, and even smiled when the weather grew fickle and windy, forcing her to draw her cloak tightly about her. Chiss and Ha'star treated her with uncommon courtesy—more, she thought, than that customarily due a Healer, and certainly more than a Ha'lasi woman riding alone with men was due. She began to think them her friends, even the scarred warrior who led them.

She did what she could to ease Callo's injured arm. It did, in fact, seem to be improving, but the change was slow, and she feared that the infection would return with serious consequences. He was no longer feverish, but he still grew tired easily, and spent much of their rest time sleeping. When they rode, he was alert for pursuit, and tended to be short about interruptions. The time they did spend together, awake and at ease, was the best Kirian had ever spent in her life.

It took her two days to realize that this feeling was more than affection, more than lust. She had hoped for some time that he was not the typical thoughtless nobleman she despised. She had begun to respect him when he calmed little Cam back in Seagard Village. She had admired Callo's looks, as well—his broad shoulders, his lean swordsman's body, his golden hair, and amazing eyes, which she had not known were ku'an's eyes. She thought of his quirks with affection and his struggles with his ku'an abilities with exasperated respect and a touch of unease. But now, when he turned to make some laughing remark, with his eyes warm when they met hers, she knew she loved this man. In fact, she realized she had loved him for some time.

How inconvenient! she thought, puzzling over the situation as she rode. This man was the bastard son of King Martan's sister and some unnamed ku'an, still a *righ* in spite of his disgrace. He was a member of a class she had always despised, and now unwelcome in his own land. This man was so conflicted about his abilities that he had asked his god to take those abilities away.

Callo was not a great prize in spite of his status and power. Yet, even all his troubles had not brought him low enough to be her equal. Not to mention that he couldn't stand the thought of going to bed with her.

Her mind occupied with this unexpected problem, she

went in unaccustomed silence about her small duties as they camped for the last time before reaching Anha'lin. This camp site was just a clearing deep in a wood, with no shelter but the overhanging branches. Tomorrow, they would sleep in an inn, she hoped, and Ha'star would go out searching for an independent-minded captain who would take them to Righar. She thought of a real bed, and hot food from a tavern with longing. Then she remembered that she would have a separate room from the men, and felt a sense of loss that surprised her.

Callo provided for Miri. He unpacked her tack and bags, watered her, and tethered her in a loose fashion so that she could move about to graze. Ha'star roamed about on horseback, checking the area to make sure they would be secure. Chiss was occupied with their meal, so Callo collected Chiss' gelding and Kirian's mare Lady to care for them as well. As he began to lead Lady away, he hesitated.

"Is everything all right?"

She turned, startled out of her confused thoughts. "Yes, of course. I just…" She could not continue.

He nodded. "The town will be welcome. Yet I'll miss this odd journey."

His eyes held warmth she had not seen for more than a sennight. Her heart began beating faster. He was still for a moment, looking at her as if he were about to say something, when Lady yanked at the bridle and pulled his attention from her. "Well then, you are anxious, my Lady?" he said to the mare. "Come then." He led the horses away to care for them. Kirian looked after him with a longing in her heart so deep it hurt.

Ha'star shouted from the woods. Metal clashed. Callo dropped the bridles, leaped onto Lady's back, and raced in Ha'star's direction, unsheathing his sword with a hiss of metal as he rode. Kirian stood with her mouth open; then she grabbed Chiss' horse and pulled the resisting gelding to its master. "Here!" she said to Chiss. "Go with them."

"I cannot leave you alone."

"He needs you!"

"He has Ha'star. He will be furious if I leave you alone here." But Chiss went to Miri where she stood, ears pricked and neighing after her master, and began to resaddle her, fast, in case they needed to run. Kirian threw some supplies into a saddlebag and had just begun to mount the fidgety gelding when she heard someone approaching on horseback through the trees. It was Ha'star, leading his horse, with a bound man thrown over the saddle. Callo followed close behind.

Ha'star pulled the captive off his horse, letting the man fall to the ground. There, the man knelt in his stained riding leathers, hands tied behind him with a strip of cloth. His dark hair fell in sweaty strands around his face. The captive spat at Ha'star, and Ha'star cuffed him. Callo dismounted, and Chiss ran up to take the horses.

"What happened?" Kirian asked.

"A search party. We surprised them. There are two dead back there." Callo went to Ha'star and the captive.

Kirian followed. "Did any of them get away?"

"No, we got them all." Blood began to show at Callo's upper sleeve, as if he had torn open the old wound. He ignored it. "Who sent you?" Callo asked the captive.

"Where is the rest of your unit?" added Ha'star.

The captive spat at him again. Ha'star hit him, harder than before, and the Ha'lasi man sagged back into the dead leaves and mold on the ground, staring at his countryman. "Traitor," he said, "I'll tell you nothing." Then he saw Callo, looked into his face and paled, dropping his eyes to stare at the ground.

"He thinks," said Ha'star, "That if he don't look at you, you can't use your ku'an influence."

Callo started and looked at Ha'star, shaking his head.

"I know this man," Ha'star said. "He is a King's man. He served in Jol'tan's unit in the south. Don't you know, man, this ku'an can make you want to tell us everything?" The captive did not look up. "You are on the wrong side, idiot. This man is nothing like Jol'tan. You should be aiding us."

"What's he paying you?" The captive growled at Ha'star. "What's your price, for aiding a spy?"

"No spy here," Ha'star said, "just a man trying to escape Ar'ok's grasp."

Kirian saw Callo frowning at the captive. "Ha'star," he said. "I don't know."

"What's the use of being a damned ku'an then?" Ha'star said. "If you are too fussy to do it, we'll have no choice but to slay him. For our own good."

"It will do no harm, surely?" Kirian said.

Callo looked grim, but after a moment he nodded. "I suppose I must. He might have a troop with him. Jashan, I get sucked deeper and deeper into this—all right then." Kirian observed Callo's face as he fell silent. She did not know what she expected—perhaps sparks from the eyes, like a color mage in a temper? But Lord Callo's face showed nothing other than a small frown as he stared at the captive.

Instead of becoming at once amiable and trusting, like the guards in the prison, the captive bent over on the ground and wrapped his arms about himself like a protective shield. "No!" he shrieked. "I won't look at you, spawn of evil." His hand fumbled at his belt, but his knife was missing from its sheath.

"He resists," Chiss noted, looking surprised. "I didn't know it was possible."

Callo swore and turned away. "Apparently it is." He motioned at Ha'star.

"Well, isn't this a mess o' worms," Ha'star growled, hand on a long knife Kirian didn't remember seeing before. Before anyone else could react, he slashed through the captive's throat. Blood spurted and they jumped back, too late to avoid being sprayed. The man fell back, a horrible gash in his neck.

"Unknown God, gather him in," Kirian prayed in a whisper.

Chiss said, "I assume we must move on right away. Where are their horses?"

"Tied up ahead. Let's get going," Callo said. He brought Lady back over to Kirian.

Ha'star said, "I never saw someone resist a ku'an's influence, but I've heard tales of such."

Kirian took Lady's rein and mounted. "Isn't it odd that we would just happen to meet with such a one?" Kirian said.

"The ku'an'an's behind this," Ha'star said. "I have heard stories—but not now. We shouldn't be takin' our sweet time like this, Lord Callo."

Callo nodded. "We ride for Anha'lin now. No more resting."

Chiss handed them all some bread and cheese after they were mounted, and they ate as they rode. Ha'star rode at point, and they stayed close behind. Callo took the rearguard, holding his right arm close to his side as if it pained him again. Kirian remembered the stain on his sleeve and resolved to check his arm carefully at Anha'lin.

The first they saw of Anha'lin was a clutter of low, gray sheds that turned out to be chicken coops, and then fields bright green with the first growth of spring. Cows grazed in sloped pastures as they rose to steeper mountains to the north. Farmhouses presided over their acres for a short while, the road winding from house to house so that they rode under the eyes of whomever chanced to be outside. Two barefoot boys raced out to the road and pestered them for a short while with questions; they replied as casually as possible, and Callo kept his eyes down. They waved at a veiled woman who sat on a low bench in front of a house, cleaning something in a low-sided tub. Kirian, reminded of the proprieties, pulled her cloak over the lower part of her face to form a makeshift veil. Chiss called a short halt, rummaged in his bags for a moment, and emerged with a russet veil edged with amber stones, fit for court. He presented it with a bow, and she accepted it with a compliment on his efficiency—and a sigh of relief.

After a while, the houses drew closer together, and the street more crowded, and then they were in the town of Anha'lin itself, looking out over a blue and cream-frothed sea. The streets behind them sloped up, to the gentle hills and eventually the mountains. Before them, they eased downward, dropping into the sea. There were no big ships here that Kirian could see—nothing like the *Fortune*— but little fishing craft bobbed amongst mid-sized vessels that ranged from fishing boats to pleasure craft, and she was sure some of them were large enough to dare the sea back to Two Merkhan.

If it had not been such a serious matter, she would have laughed at their attempts to appear inconspicuous. Ha'star slouched in an unmilitary manner in his saddle, his reins slack. Callo tried to keep his ku'an eyes down, but curiosity drew his gaze up again and again; and Miri was obviously a nobleman's mount. As for herself— certainly, the jeweled veil was not something one wore everyday. Kirian knew they stood out like birds in a fishnet, and hoped they would arrive at the inn before too many people took note of them.

The little inn had its own stable, and windows that stared

at the sea. It looked bare of company as they drew up before it. "I wonder if it has three rooms to spare," Callo said.

"I thought we were trying to avoid notice?" Kirian said. "The innkeeper will certainly wonder at such largesse."

"What do you suggest, then?" Callo said. "It can't be more than a few Ha'lasi coppers?"

Ha'star snorted at that. "I'll set it up. The Healer must, o' course, have her own room, rather than sharing with the maid or some such."

"Gods, yes!" Kirian said, aghast at the notion.

"And we three will share. If ya' don't mind, my lord."

"Of course I don't mind! Do you think we had separate rooms in cozy inns on campaign in the South? But if the place has bugs, we find another inn." Ha'star dismounted and vanished into the dim interior. A few minutes later, he emerged, trailed by a skinny young man in dusty leggings, who smelled of horses. The boy took all four of the horses and led them around to the stable yard. Callo stood looking after them until Chiss said, "My lord, we can check on Miri later. Let us go in."

"Yes, yes," Callo said absently, and Kirian took his arm and led him inside.

The inn had very little custom. There were only two drinkers in the dusty common room. The keeper led them upstairs to two rooms at the end of the hall, remaining attentive as Ha'star and Chiss lugged the bags in and dumped them on the floor. The room had two cots spread with straw-filled mattresses, and a scarred, wooden table next to the unshuttered window. The keeper promised to bring a third cot and a chair, and said his wife would have supper in a candlemark. Then he showed Kirian to the next room and watched as she bowed and closed the door gently behind her.

When the keeper had gone, Kirian knocked on the other

door. Chiss opened it and bowed to her as if they were in Court in Las'ash Castle. She grinned. "What now?" she said. "We've been riding since dusk last night. I'm exhausted. Can we do anything tonight, do you think?"

"We must," Callo said. He stood at the window, looking out at the sea. "The ku'an'an's men could be near. They'll miss their friends."

"Chiss and I will go," Ha'star said. "After we eat. This place ain't no Las'ash, but still it's bound to be easier to get something illegal done after the decent folk have gone t'bed for the night."

Callo laughed. "Can't I help?"

"You and your ku'an eyes?"

"I suppose not."

"I need some supplies, if there is time," Kirian said. She went to Chiss and named a few herbs she thought she could use. "An herbalist will have them. Maybe a physician."

"Won't that draw attention, Hon Kirian?" asked Chiss. "It will be only a few days until we are back in Righar."

She sighed, aware that Callo favored his sword arm as he looked again out the window at the sea. "Can you get me just one, then? You can get it even at a grocer's. It is oil of biscan; cooks use a few drops in pastry. It will ease stiffness if worked up with some grease. I think it would be better to have it."

Chiss understood. He looked over at Callo, who seemed unaware of their conversation as he observed the activity on the dock. "I will obtain it, Hon Kirian. Thank you."

They left, promising Callo to look in on the horses on their way. Kirian said a rather shy farewell to Callo and returned to her lonely chamber.

When the door opened on the men's chamber next morning, Callo was the only one there. He greeted her, courteous enough, then paced over to the window and stared out as if he would be able to see Chiss and Ha'star. His hair was tied back, and he wore a fresh tunic with gold thread in the sleeves, and looked very noble, if a bit distracted.

"When did they leave?" she asked him.

"Not more than a candlemark ago. Jashan send, they are fortunate—the King's men are not far behind us. Chiss saw signs of newcomers at the Anha'lin lord's fort when they were out last night."

"That is not good news." She put down the small bowl she had carried in. "Come here, please, Callo. I have something that may help your arm."

He walked over and looked at the gray paste in the bowl. "What is that? It smells terrible."

"It may smell terrible, but it's going to help the mobility in your sword arm." She gestured to him to slide his arm from his sleeve, and scooped up a glob of paste on her forefinger.

"Is this the stuff Chiss got for you? I suppose I'll smell like a trussed pig after this."

"The odor goes away," she said. "I think. This is oil of biscan, mixed with grease. I've used much more than bakers use, though. Come here." He sat and extended his arm. She noted that the bruises were starting to fade, and the wound itself was closed except for the small section he had torn open in yesterday's fight. There was no further sign of infection. "This is looking better. You seem to be feeling better, too." She began smearing the stuff all over both sword cuts, avoiding the open part of the wound.

He wrinkled his nose. "Wonderful. And I have to keep this on how long?"

"All day would be best." He laughed and shook his head,

not turning his eyes from her hands as they worked on his arm. "Have you ever seen a wound that healed so tightly with scar tissue that it would not let a person move?"

He nodded.

"Your wound goes here, and here—into the elbow. If you hold it tightly, as you have been doing, it will heal that way. Notice you tore it when you tried to use the arm yesterday. This preparation will keep it soft, and if you move and flex it —gently, mind you—it should heal well."

She finished smoothing the grease. As she wiped her fingers on a towel, he pulled the tunic back over his arm then began moving. He stretched his arms before him, turned his wrists, and slowly pulled his arms back. She slid closer to the table to give him room.

The sun came in the window, and his face eased. He began to move with more grace, a touch of an old rhythm of movement, as if he began one of his ritual forms. He moved slowly, extending an arm as if he held a sword, pivoting on his feet, centered and graceful. She saw his eyes grow distant. He lifted his face, seeming to have forgotten her. His right arm made a supple arc, moving without hesitation.

"Lord Callo," she said.

He stopped as if startled, coming back to himself. He dropped his arms and laughed. She thought he seemed a little embarrassed.

"It feels good to move again," he said. She remembered he had probably been in the ring every day since childhood, keeping his skills honed.

"We've been on the move for days," she responded. But she knew what he meant. She stood and began collecting the bowl and his old bandages, ready to return to her room. When she looked up, he was there, inches away from her.

"Your hair is growing," he said. "It looks soft." He tipped her chin up, looked into her eyes. She smiled into his eyes.

"Gods, Kirian, you are beautiful." His fingers stroked along her jawline.

Greatly daring, she reached out, touching him back—his jawline, his hair, wanting to touch his mouth—but he caught his breath and started to look away.

"Please don't," she whispered. "Don't stop."

His eyes caught hers again, and he smiled ruefully down into her face. "I must. It isn't fair to you."

"To hell with fair." Her vehemence had startled him. "I know you think this is all your doing—that I'm—under your power somehow."

"Is that what I think?" There was no expression in his face.

She kept going; she might never have another chance. If she offended him, so be it.

"You haven't influenced me to want you. Trust me. I've felt a ku'an's influence, as you know, since you were the ku'an. This isn't it. You have more control than that—you have to trust yourself."

"I have only the control Jashan grants me. Sometimes— that's not enough. It gets away. Kirian, you know I think you're beautiful. I admit it—I desire you. But I can't risk…" His voice trailed off, and he took a step back from her.

She sighed. She was losing the battle. Losing *him*. "You care enough about me to want me to make my own decisions."

"Yes, well, *everyone* should make their own decisions!" He stepped away from her. One hand went up, ran through his hair. She reached out and put her hands on his arms and stopped him.

"I can't be inside your head, Callo. I know what's in mine, though." If she was going to have to expose her feelings, he was worth it. She would have to trust what she knew of this man, that he would not ridicule her for what she was about to say. She braced herself for his reaction. "I started caring about you when you helped with little Cam. I've wanted you since the Fortune, that awful night when everything went wrong, remember? I think I came to love you before we made port in Las'ash. I know *damned* well you weren't trying to influence me then. You barely knew I existed."

He only looked at her. She looked down, away from his gaze, feeling a little raw with what she had revealed about herself. She knew he only desired her, but did not love her. If she had to take this risk to be with him a little, she was willing to do it.

"So, see? What I feel—it isn't what you feel at all. You didn't create this in me. Don't take responsibility for things you can't do. You're not that powerful." Quite suddenly she had had enough of him and his conscience. She turned away.

"Kirian." His voice was low.

"What now?" Her voice broke. She reached for her veil, pulled it over her face, hiding her eyes. His hands drew it away, gently in spite of their strength. He tipped her chin upward until she looked into his eyes again.

"Gods. I dream about those eyes." He paused a moment. "Thank you, Kirian."

She didn't say anything for a moment, then sniffed as her nose began to run. "It wasn't easy."

"No. It wouldn't be." He drew his finger over her cheek, wiping away a tear. She was appalled. How could he want her now, when she was weeping all over the place? He added, "You are right. I take too much on myself."

"Well, it's very honorable of you to guard your ku'an powers like that. The other ku'an are despicable. Perversions. I'm glad—Gods, I'm glad you aren't like that. But don't start thinking you always know what's going on in everyone else's head." She knew she was babbling, but could not seem to stop.

"I know." He gathered her into his arms. There was no urgency about his embrace, just comfort. She put her head on his shoulder and closed her eyes, steadying her breathing, beginning to rejoice in the nearness of him. His arms were strong and warm, and he showed no sign of favoring his injured arm. Her eyes opened wide as she realized what she was doing, and she snorted.

"What?"

"Nothing. I am always a Healer."

"You probably can't stand that smell," he frowned, letting her go. "Must I really wear the stuff all day?"

"If you can. I'll put more on tomorrow."

He sighed and sat down on one of the beds, pulling her down next to him. He stared at the door. "They could be back at any moment."

"Yes."

"Or the ku'an'an's men—they could show up."

"They could indeed."

"There is no time." He sighed. "What am I thinking? You need a chaperone."

"I am very grateful you didn't see fit to bring Sara'Si."

He laughed aloud. "She would have been a ray of sunshine on our journey. Kirian, my sweet, we should not seize this moment. As much as I want to . . . ." His voice faded, and she leaned over and kissed him. He responded with no shadow of reluctance, and she began to melt against him, his arms going about her again, hands caressing her back. His lips were on her neck, trailing fire down her nerves. She let him pull her closer. His hands slipped under her tunic, caressing her bare skin. His mouth was soft yet firm; she opened her mouth for him and felt, more than heard, him groan as his hands reached her breasts.

She spared a thought through the thrill of anticipation for whether they had locked the door when she came in. Well, she thought, Chiss won't let Ha'star come in without knocking—and then she forgot the others, forgot where they were, let Callo seduce her with his hands and mouth until she forgot everything.

Until, near the last burst of feeling, she opened her eyes to see a swirl of golden color wrapping them. An amorphous coalescence of energy, much like color magic, shot with light.

Chapter Fifteen

They led the horses through the steep streets of Anha'lin, guided by a few street lamps and the occasional dim glow from a second-floor window. Moisture hung in the air, rain mixed with salt spray, reminding Kirian of Seagard Village. She peered ahead, following Callo and Miri, shivering under her cloak. Chiss rode behind her, guarding the rear.

Callo had scattered a few coins on the table before they left. Ha'star insisted that they hurry; the ku'an'an's men were searching the town. The captain he had found was anxious to get his bargain over and done with, and there was no time like the present. None of them protested.

The houses and businesses of the town dropped behind them. Kirian looked ahead and saw a clutter of wooden docks and hulls bobbing in the sea. There were no gates, no taverns, and no prostitutes waiting for seamen on shore. This was no Two Merkhan, nor even Las'ash port, but a small town. A lone, rickety table, naked of any goods, had a sign offering "Hot Sausage, Warm Bread" but there was no sign of anyone around at this hour. The gentle slap, slap of the waves against the dock lulled Kirian's ear.

They turned away from the main dock and followed Ha'star down a dirt path that edged the smaller docks. The horses' hooves made little sound on the damp earth. The darkness covered the boats at the main dock as the group left them behind. The captain Ha'star had found must be waiting away from the main group so as to avoid drawing attention.

Just as she thought she could make out a darker patch of hull ahead of them, someone shouted from behind.

"Stop!" The shout rang loud in the moisture-laden air. Kirian's mare startled and Chiss' gelding neighed in alarm.

"You there, stop! By order of the King!"

"Mount! Let's go!" snapped Ha'star. Kirian jumped onto Lady and went after the others as fast she could in the near-dark. Callo pulled Miri back, letting Kirian go ahead as he looked back over his shoulder at their pursuers.

"I think there are several." She heard him say to Chiss. "Go!"

The horses' hooves hit the wood planking of a dock, and clattered as they picked up the pace. Kirian saw a boat drawn up by the end of the dock, not much bigger than Kin and Rashiri's *Homebound*, from what she could see in the dark. A single lamp flamed on her rail. A sturdy gangway was laid between the ship and the pier—only a few feet long, and not very high, yet Kirian's heart quailed at the idea of riding Lady over it with the dark waters below.

Ha'star pulled aside. "Go up," he said. She could hear the clash of metal behind her. Chiss and Callo were defending their rear until they could get aboard. Holding her breath, she gripped Lady's sides with her knees and urged her on. The mare stopped with her front hooves on the gangway, trembling.

Kirian slid off, clinging close to the mare as she slid by, and went to Lady's head.

"Come on, Lady," she whispered. "They're coming. You can do it." She looked down at the swirl of dark water to either side of the gangway. Then she slid her veil from her face and wrapped it around Lady's eyes. She backed up the gangway, encouraging the mare, while alert to the sounds of battle behind her. The mare followed her lead, ears laid back, and stood on the rocking deck, trembling.

"I didn't like that either," Kirian whispered to the mare. "Ha'star, I'm aboard!" She looked back over the rail to see that Ha'star was riding back to Callo and Chiss. A bearded man wearing a rain-slick oiled coat grinned at her from the deck.

"Just you, eh?" he said. "No reason I should wait here to be boarded, is there?"

Kirian turned and yelled through the dark and the clash of arms: "Now! Get here now! He's leaving!"

The man swore and pulled her back, covering her mouth. She jammed her elbow into his gut. He grunted but still held her firmly. "A handful, are ye," he said. "Thamsa—get up here, get this horse out of our way! We're casting off!"

"No, you're not," came a menacing voice. Kirian sagged in relief in the seaman's grasp as she recognized Ha'star's scarred face weirdly shadowed by the lamp on the rail. "I paid for all of us, and all of us you'll take." He had left his horse on the dock so as to get aboard fast. He faced the captain with unsheathed sword.

"All right, then, we'll wait on ya!" the captain said angrily. He released Kirian. She ran to the rail and looked into the lamp-lit darkness.

There was a clatter on the gangway and Miri came up, eyes showing white as the planking trembled beneath her hooves. Callo had been able to ride her aboard, but Chiss had to practically drag his gelding onto the ship.

"*Now* go," Ha'star yelled, waving at the seamen. Then he grabbed bridles, moving the anxious horses to the center of the boat. He threw their reins around some projection and ran back to lean over the rail and peer out into the dark.

Callo said, "Four men, mounted. Swords only, I think."

This was rapidly proven wrong as something hissed past Ha'star's cheek, the air singing behind it. All four of them hit the deck, crouching low. The ship's captain swore. "And arrows," Callo said. "Stay down, Kirian. Chiss are you all right?"

"Just grazed, my lord," Chiss said, as calmly as if he were serving tea in Seagard Castle. He held his hand to his cheek in a dignified way. Kirian felt an urge to laugh hysterically, but she quelled it with a silent prayer instead. The arrow lay spent on the deck, and the boat slid away from the little pier. It moved terribly slowly. The mounted men were up at the pier, flinging themselves off their horses, racing for the boat. One of their pursuers leaped, hands grabbing the boat rail as his feet scrabbled at the hull for purchase. Callo shoved his hands off the rail, letting the potential boarder splash into the sea.

The boat moved farther away, the wind picking up in her sails, and the pursuit fell behind. Three, now powerless men stood frustrated of their goal on the pier. Then the darkness drowned their faces, and Kirian could no longer see any of them.

"Now, for that bastard Modjho," said Ha'star, and he started along the deck toward the wheel.

"Ha'star! Let him alone." There was a ring of command in Callo's voice. Ha'star, conditioned to years of obeying the ku'an, stopped.

"The fool almost left you," Ha'star bit out, glaring at Callo. "You want him to think he can get away with it next time?"

"No. But I need him well-disposed to us for now." Callo went to Ha'star and turned away with him, so Kirian could see only their backs as the two men talked. She could hear nothing.

Chiss stood, hand still on his cheek. She said, "Let me see that please, Hon Chiss."

He removed his hand. "I think it is nothing much, Hon Kirian." She saw a shallow scrape across his cheek. There was no more bleeding.

"You're right. All the same, when we get settled, remind me, and I'll take care of it."

He nodded and looked at the sail billowing above them, visible as a gray wing in the dark.

The man who had seized Kirian—Captain Modjho, apparently— was at the wheel. He turned and called, "There's no navigating in this muck. After we hit the Out Island, we'll rest 'til dawn."

———

A full night and day of crossing a choppy sea in a glorified fishing boat was tough on Kirian's stomach. Never actually seasick, she continually fought a queasy feeling that left her unable to eat. Although, judging from Callo's reaction to the fare on board, she wasn't missing much.

"Tripe," he said.

"Really?"

"As bad as." He shoved his plate across the table, where it slid back and forth against the low, wooden table rail. "It bears no resemblance to any animal I've ever seen."

"You're used to better food."

"Aren't we all?"

"I meant richer food. Prepared by a chef." Kirian hadn't taken anything from the simmering pot on the stove, and now, as the boat rolled, she was glad. She grabbed the table to steady herself.

"I'm no spoiled courtier, Kirian."

"I didn't say that." She sighed. "You know perfectly well what I mean. Chiss brings your food. Do you know where it comes from?"

"Sometimes. As long as he knows, I trust it's safe."

"What do you mean, safe?"

"Safe to eat. Not poisoned." He stood and wandered over to Chiss, who stood at the door to the mess. Returning with a thick slice of bread and a mug, he said, "I trust Chiss absolutely with that."

Kirian was shocked. "You mean people have tried to poison you?"

"I'm not popular in Sugetre, Kirian. I am a *righ* bastard. If I'd been of common birth, I would not have been allowed to live. And some people get fixated on the idea that I'm in the direct line to the throne."

She stared at him. "You are?"

"I won't inherit. Don't worry about it—I don't." He took a deep drink of ale and grinned at her. "Sharpeyes has a nephew, a child, son of his late brother Yarin. He hates the boy, but Ander is the heir to the throne. A promising color mage, too, I hear. Arias would have been his next heir, as oldest son of his sister, and an unCollared color mage—but Sharpeyes had to go have a fit of jealousy and bind him to Seagard. Takes the Alkirani right out of the succession."

Kirian processed that. "Does Lord Arias mind?"

Callo's grin vanished. "I doubt it. He's Collared now. That

binds him in a way you and I can't understand, to Seagard and the Watch."

"It controls him like a ku'an controls a person."

"No, that's different. A ku'an can project a certain emotion into a person, very strongly if he wants to. Arias doesn't have to deal with that."

"Why not? He's controlled, all the time, at the mercy of this compulsion."

Callo frowned and did not reply.

"How is that different?" Kirian asked, wondering why Callo was distressed at the turn the conversation had taken.

"A Collar is an instrument of control," Callo said, his mouth grim now. "But Arias has his own emotions. He is under a compulsion . . ." Callo stopped. Kirian saw him frowning as he looked down at the table—as though he had forgotten her. After a moment, she spoke.

"It is not so different, I think. Maybe it is even worse, since he is always under this control, every hour of every day."

Callo looked up at her, his face unreadable.

"Do you think there is something you could do for him?" Kirian asked.

He shrugged. "I have been wondering the same thing for a while now. That's why I can't just escape, leaving him there by himself. I owe him, Kirian."

"This is the thing you decided you must do, in Seagard."

"Yes. And then, if necessary, I'll go anywhere else in the world with you, keep you safe from harm. But first I must see Arias."

"He may kill you. He is a Collared Lord now. They aren't known for their gentleness."

"I know. Oh, yes, I know. He was different, after he was Collared—more like Mikati. But he is my brother, and I can't abandon him to that if I think there's a chance I can help.

Arias was always glad he was in line for the throne, you know, since it meant Sharpeyes left him alone and unCollared."

"I liked him," Kirian said. "When we first met, that is, after he recovered from the binding fever. I am sorry he is so changed."

"Hai! Everyone up here!" yelled Captain Modjho from the deck, a few feet away. "We have a problem."

Kirian went to the door. Modjho stood still, staring at the western sea. Bright spring sunlight glittered off the rocking waves, making it hard for Kirian to see what he was looking at. Ha'star came up beside her, and shaded his eyes against the sun.

She looked again, and saw a thin, black line lying on the surface of the sea.

Her heart thumped. Callo, behind her in the doorway, swore. "We're in trouble," he said.

"Is that what I think it is?" Ha'star asked.

The line grew thicker, spreading closer to them. "Black Tide," Callo said. "Jashan curse them."

Modjho yelled at his crewmen and they began piling on the sail, trying to eke every last iota of speed out of the little craft. The deck heaved under them; the waves were growing higher. Kirian grabbed the rail.

"What will it do to us?" Kirian thought back to the Black Tide she had seen on Kin's and Rashiri's fishing boat. They had been terrified of it, trying to tack out of its way. She looked westward and saw the sea covered by a film of black.

"It looks like the ku'an'an wants us dead if he can't have us back," Chiss said. "The Black Tide is a physical manifestation of a ku'an's psychic magery. It usually takes three or four of them to do something so huge."

"Can you tell what it will do?" Kirian asked Callo. He

stood staring out at the rushing blackness as if the Black Tide were a personal challenge.

Chiss answered. "They use it before a military attack. The Black Tide deadens everything in its path. Puts the enemy in a somnolent state of mind. They go to sleep, right where they are. Look at those fish." He pointed at the few tumbling fish they could now see in the front of the low black wave. "They're not dead. They're stunned."

"Then they follow it up with force," Kirian said.

"They'll come in after, to capture us while we can't resist. Or they can simply let us drown."

"Not if I can help it," Callo murmured.

"You can't," she said. "What can one ku'an do, against this?"

"Not a ku'an," he said. He stood gripping the rail, braced against the heaving motion. The black wave rushed forward. He said "Damn them," in an intense voice. He bent his head as if he were struggling with something.

"Get inside! Get inside!" screamed Modjho. The captain abandoned the helm and raced toward the ladders that led below.

"Callo! Come on!" Kirian yelled. The sea kicked up, and a wave crashed over the rail, drenching them. Chiss pulled at Callo's arm, but the muscles corded in Callo's arm as he resisted, refusing to move.

"Don't touch me," he said.

"My lord!" Chiss yelled. "You'll be washed overboard when it hits!"

"Just go!"

Chiss put a hand on Callo's shoulder and, in spite of all the other sickening motion around her, Kirian could see Callo shudder. "Don't touch me!" His voice was low and hoarse.

Kirian said, "I won't go below without you." His head

snapped around when he heard her. "Go in, Kirian, get in there!"

The black wave crashed over the deck.

Kirian saw nothing for a moment but an intensity of dark that blotted out the brazen sunshine and the sea. All the glaring reflections vanished. She could see nothing, not even Callo or Chiss on the deck next to her, but she could feel Callo's arm under her hand. She cried out, but could not hear her own voice. Then a massive peace descended on her, a heavy somnolence that made her loosen her grip on Callo's arm. She took a deep breath and relaxed, then let go. There was nothing she cared about enough to make her move. She closed her eyes and felt her legs give out under her as she sank to the pitch- black deck.

Silence ruled. Darkness, like that behind her eyelids on a sleepy, dark, winter morning, reigned. She felt only a heavy lassitude. Vaguely, she felt water rushing over her, sliding her over the deck. She must be lying down on the deck; it felt pleasant. The water rushing into her ears and mouth was warm, like a womb must be.

Through her closed eyelids she saw an arrow of white light.

It was only one of those things that happened behind your eyelids just after you closed them, she thought, and smiled. Then a starburst of multicolored light glared through her lids. The darkness retreated behind it, just for a second, before swarming in again.

Kirian rested. The wool-soft Tide cushioned her. It became hard to draw a breath past all the sea water, but this was natural and it did not disturb her.

Then, a wall of brilliance hit her. She awoke a little, squinted through tearing eyes, to see that something like the sun was burning through the darkness, a fireball of intense light of all colors, thrusting upward, chasing back the Black Tide, devouring darkness where it rested in layers on the deck.

She looked away from the brilliance. It hurt her eyes. She began coughing up water from her lungs, rolling to one side as her body tried to expel the seawater she had swallowed. Then she saw Callo, standing there like Jashan himself, crashing glory flying away from him at the Black Tide. He stood with his eyes closed, braced against the deck railing. Light of all colors emanated from him like rays of sun through a gap in dark clouds.

Kirian dragged herself to her feet. Water sloshed in her shoes. Her leggings and tunic clung to her skin. She whispered a prayer to the Unknown God. She remembered the Black Tide she had seen before, how the radiant barrier from the Watch tower had defeated the dark. Looking to the west, she saw something similar—a curtain of light, pushing back the Tide.

She went to Callo and stood next to him, but dared not touch him. She saw Chiss getting to his feet, coughing. The manservant stared at his lord with an indescribable look. Then, without a sound, the energy vanished. The light was gone. No smudge of darkness remained on the western sea. The sun shone as if it had never been eclipsed, and the frothy sea slapped up and down at the rolling hull. Callo stood, shaking, on the slippery deck.

Ha'star came running from below deck with an exultant whoop. "Ku'an's teeth, man, what did you do? Was that color magery?" He gave Callo a congratulatory slap on the arm.

Callo bit off, "Don't touch me."

"My lord," Chiss said. "Are you all right?" His face was pale. Callo walked a few steps away and turned away from them.

Kirian saw his hands were shaking, as if with cold. The

skin of his face and forearms was flushed. Violence clung to him; she could sense it. She and Chiss and Ha'star stood staring at him with no idea what to say or do.

Captain Modjho came swaggering onto deck. "What the hell?" he said. "You some kind of mage?" Chiss shook his head in warning but the wiry captain seemed incapable of taking a mild hint. He brushed past them and dropped his weight against the deck rail, leaning next to Callo—too close, apparently. Callo made a muffled sound and jerked around. Then his hands were around Modjho's neck as he slammed the captain up against the rail. Red light crawled over his hands. The rail creaked. Chiss said, "No, my lord!" and Kirian cried out, and Callo's hands loosened, allowing Modjho to tear free and stagger away. The captain hacked over the rail, swearing.

Callo turned away from them. His hands, gripping the rail again, were white. Chiss took Modjho's arm and pulled him away. Kirian thought back to the last Black Tide. Lord Arias and Lord Mikati had required Healer's care after defeating it. Mikati's heart was injured by the strain. Lord Arias, as she recalled, had been full of reckless exhilaration, but shaking and weak none the less. Could this be some kind of shock?

She approached Callo, very cautiously. "Lord Callo," she said in a calm voice. "May I come and see how you are doing?" Ha'star's hand gripped his sword hilt as if he would defend her against Callo should he attack her.

He did not respond, so Kirian took that as a yes. She leaned near him at the rail and looked sideways at him. His amber eyes were unfocused; he stared at the waves without seeing. He still shook, and his breathing was fast, as if he had been running.

"Please sit down," she asked. "It is all over now."

"It's not over," he said. His voice was hoarse. There were

gold sparks in his eyes—beautiful, she thought, but frightening. "Now I have to contain it again."

Chiss returned from his conversation with Modjho. "Perhaps there is something we could do to help, my lord."

There was a short silence. Kirian wondered how long Callo could hold the rock-hard tension before something snapped. Then Callo said, "My sword. Get me my sword."

Kirian glanced at him. He was not wearing his scabbard—why should he, on board? The weapon must be with their things, in the single shed that served as cabin and mess. Why would he want his sword?

Chiss frowned and shook his head in what was, for him, a show of strong emotion. "No! You don't need it, my lord. What would you do with it?"

Kirian first looked at Callo, then back at Chiss. She said, "I'll get it," and walked away from the group at the rail towards the cabin. Ha'star caught her halfway, took her elbow to stop her. "If you give that man a sword right now, you'll be killing him," he said.

"I don't think so," she said.

"He'll kill himself. He's a wreck. All that energy has destroyed him. A ku'an and a color mage—who would'a thought?"

"I don't think he's a danger to himself." She pulled her arm away and went to get Callo's scabbard. It rested against the bulkhead, with their packs, set aside so Callo could access it easily if needed. She picked it up by scabbard and hilt and carried it out to deck. Ha'star walked beside her, grumbling but not stopping her. Even Chiss, who was speaking to his lord in a low voice when she arrived, did not stop her. He stepped back when she gave Callo the sword. She stepped away, and drew the others with her.

"Gods aid he does not hurt himself," Chiss said.

"You know him so well. Do you really think he will?"

"No. I hope not—Ah!" Chiss lost his worried frown as they saw Callo lift the sword to the sky in a ritual salute. Then, with only a shadow of his usual grace, he slid into the first position of the ritual form.

"I remember this," Ha'star said. "He did this in the ring in Las'ash. Often."

Callo lifted his face to the sky. Red fire ran along his arms, and traced the sword. He began the first passes of the form. Kirian took a deep breath and said, "Let's leave him alone." Ha'star bowed to her, an unexpected tribute that broke Kirian's tension and made her smile; then he vanished up the deck to talk to Modjho. Chiss followed her into the mess.

"You have my thanks," he said.

"I didn't do anything. You are welcome anyway. May I ask, you've known him all his life, right? Where did that come from?"

"There were early signs he had some sort of talent—ku'an magery, King Martan thought, not color magery. There were incidents. I doubt he remembers them—he was very young."

"But, color magery?"

"It is in his heredity. His mother is the King's sister, remember.

And the King is the strongest color mage in Righar."

Kirian looked outside. Callo was completing the steps of his ritual form. His movements were smoother now. He looked stronger, and the color magery that had been sparking from his hands was no longer visible. "I know that color mages train for many years to learn how to control the energy. I assume Lord Callo has not had any of that training?"

"No, Hon Kirian," Chiss said. "He has not."

Chapter Sixteen

Callo lay back on his bedroll, spread on the deck in the cabin, and watched Ha'star and Chiss get themselves ready for sleep. His mind was numb.

Kirian was in her private chamber, created by the strategic placement of a big blanket that Ha'star had hung from the ceiling with nails he found somewhere on board. She moved about, preparing for rest. He imagined her removing her tunic and her veil. He closed his eyes and pictured her wavy hair falling free. As for her naked shoulders and her soft breasts— he caught himself up short. Now was not the time to indulge in that sort of fantasy.

Ha'star lay in his bedroll on the floor near Kirian's little chamber. His knife, a big-hilted affair probably used for hunting, lay in its scabbard near his hand. He looked prepared to defend Kirian's honor to the death. Just at that moment Ha'star said, "I'll be here in case there's any need at all, Hon Kirian."

A hand pulled back the curtain, and Kirian peered out,

wrapped in a blanket. "Thank you, Hon Ha'star. I feel very safe."

Safe from *me*, Callo thought, disgruntled. He looked away and turned on his left side, away from them both. Not long after, his wounded arm began to protest this position against the hard deck, and he turned back. Kirian had vanished behind her curtain.

Chiss brought a jug and some cups. Callo hoped whatever it was, was strong. He still felt shaken at the power of what had broken out of him. What had been locked inside him all this time. With Jashan's help he had buried the color magic again, reinforced the wall that kept the psychic magery bound; but now he felt crippled and restrained as if a good half of his mind was beyond his reach.

He slept deeply and dreamlessly, waking when the sunlight streamed into the little cabin to find that the other bedrolls were folded aside. Dust motes spun in an angle of light that looked like late day. The ship must be in calmer waters; it barely rocked. He looked around, feeling disgruntled and neglected. His throat was scratchy, and his shoulder ached. He rose and went about his preparations for the day, cursing Chiss for not being there when he was needed.

The first person he saw when he set foot on deck was the crewman Thamsa, who bowed and scuttled out of his way as a mouse might run from a cat. Callo stared after him. Then he looked in the other direction and saw they had reached land.

The boat rocked in a narrow bay surrounded by bare rock. The southern section of the inlet was green with trees, but the rest rose into a mountainous crag that reminded him very much of Seagard Castle. But there was no village in sight and definitely no Castle. He spun and climbed the ladder to the upper deck, looking for his other companions.

He found Modjho. "Captain!" Callo said. "Where the hell are we?"

"Righar, great lord," Modjho said, with disingenuous respect.

"*Where* in Righar?"

Modjho shrugged. "Should be north o' Two Merkhan. Not sure exactly where. The warrior went ashore to see."

Callo swore, then took a deep breath. He turned to look around, letting Modjho walk away. Returning to the lower deck, he found Chiss and Kirian, sitting near the stern. Kirian dangled her bare feet over the edge of the deck. Chiss, with characteristic propriety, sat a couple of feet away from her with needle and thread, mending a tunic. Kirian saw Callo first and stood, her face aglow.

"There you are! Did you have a good sleep?"

Callo's face softened. She was flushed by the sun, and her bare feet looked soft on the wet deck. "I wondered where everyone was."

"It is almost dinnertime," she said. "You slept all day."

"Jashan! Why didn't you wake me?"

"You needed the rest, my lord," Chiss said.

"I take it we are somewhere near Two Merkhan?"

"Ha'star is ashore. He will find out exactly where we are."

"He's more likely to be imprisoned as a spy," Callo said. He rubbed his temple, feeling a sense of oppression.

"My lord, we didn't know exactly what your plans were. There is no harm, is there?" Chiss set aside the mending and stood. Callo gritted his teeth, full of anger he could not explain. He saw Kirian look at him uncertainly, and cursed himself.

"Are you all right, my lord?" Kirian asked. Her brow was wrinkled; her hair, almost brushing her shoulders now, shone in the sunlight. Her use of *my lord* grated on him.

"Damn it, I'm fine." He turned away. He heard an explosive exhalation of breath from Kirian—she was angry, then, and no wonder—but he ignored it. He stalked away toward the cabin, found his sword, and took it to an open area on deck. There, he lifted it and began the invocation to Jashan, lord of light. Sunlight glittered all around him, half-blinding him. He slid into the first stance, arms holding the sword in its ritual salute. It felt heavy; his feet felt leaden. His feet slid into the next stance, but he felt no balance, no fluidity; he almost stumbled, and the core of rage in his heart grew.

"My lord?"

Startled, he spun around. Chiss stood near the deck rail, watching him. Chiss had dared *interrupt* him, a thing he'd never done before. The sword dropped into his fighting grip, and he caught himself just before it leaped for Chiss' throat.

"My lord, I think you'd better stop," Chiss said.

"How—dare you?" Callo choked. Deep inside he raged at Chiss, at the world, at himself for threatening his liege man with violence. Before he could turn, he saw the red filaments of light tracing his hands. He froze.

"You see," Chiss said. "Something is wrong. My lord—Callo— please come inside with me."

Callo stared at Chiss. His hand would not move; his sword was a part of him, all violence and control, and he could not release it. Then Chiss came and took the hilt from him, and Callo took a ragged breath.

"You will not hurt me," Chiss said. "Will you, my lord?"

Callo shook his head. He followed Chiss to the cabin. Chiss sheathed Callo's sword and placed it in a corner. He poured something into a cup and offered it to Callo.

Callo almost sobbed with the tension of keeping the magery locked up. It wasn't working; he could see sparks out of the corners of his eyes. The words burst out. "All the gods, Chiss, what am I?"

"My lord, you are what you have always been. What they tried to make, I would surmise, all those years ago when the ku'an'an came to seduce Lady Sira Joah. There is nothing new, nothing you cannot handle."

"Gods damn it, nothing new!" Callo gulped the wine. "It won't stay locked up anymore, Chiss, and I can't keep it down. I'm going to go insane."

"You must come up with a better way to control the energy." Chiss poured himself wine. Callo was surprised to see that the manservant's hands were shaking.

He gave a dry, shaky laugh. "You're afraid of me too."

Chiss' head lifted in surprise. "Never, my lord." Callo could feel the sincerity in the reply. He calmed a little. "I am—afraid *for* you, rather. There has never been someone with both the color magery and the psychic magery."

Callo sipped more wine. A gentle fog was forming in his mind, dulling the intensity a little. "What might I do, with such magery? Be like Sharpeyes, who manipulates even his nephews to shore up his power? You know he tried to have little Ander killed—he hates the boy. Maybe I should aspire to be like Ar'ok, the warped little demon. Do you think so?"

Chiss was silent, his eyes on Callo's face.

"Or maybe I'll just go down in a blaze of self-destruction." His head still hurt.

"I pray not," Chiss said.

Callo began to pace. It took the edge off the pain.

"The intensity should dull, with time. Things do, my lord."

There was a shadow in the door, followed by the bulk of Ha'star. He said, "Modjho told me you were in here." He stopped short, looking at Callo. Callo wondered what he saw.

The Ha'lasi warrior made an apologetic motion and backed out of the room.

"Wait!" Callo said. Ha'star turned and looked at him with no expression, just a level gaze. "What's your opinion? You who hate all ku'an. What do you think, Ha'star?"

"I think that you best get this force under control before it kills all of us."

"Tell me how. I will do what you say."

There was a glint of surprise from the scarred warrior. "You always were different. You want my advice?"

"Gods, yes, anything."

"My advice is, quit your whinin' and go see the healer."

Anger sparked in his head, showing red in his vision. Ha'star stood balanced, as if waiting for an attack, eyes narrowed as he watched him. Callo choked a little, fighting down the headache, forcing down the agonizing color magic. Words stuck in his throat.

Chiss said, "Hon Kirian does not know the color magery, but she is a Healer of mind and body."

Watching Callo, Ha'star relaxed a little. "Good. I wasn't sure I'd live through that much honesty." He grinned. "I'll get her."

Callo stood, trying to suppress the violence that threatened to explode from him. Ha'star went away. Eventually he took a ragged breath and was surprised to find Chiss still there. "Still here?" he said hoarsely. "Haven't run?"

"No, my lord, why would I run?" Chiss held up a narrow hand. "Because you are within a fingernail's width of losing control? Trust yourself, my lord. You will not hurt me or Hon Kirian."

The thought that he could hurt Kirian had not occurred to him. He shuddered and ran through the invocation to Jashan in his mind. When the Healer appeared, he had himself under tight control. He let Chiss run through the explanation. Then Kirian sat down on a wooden stool and scooted it towards him. She made no move to touch him.

"Sorry," he said. "Sorry. I was rude."

"There's nothing to be sorry for. You are fighting a battle." She looked at him a moment. Callo wondered if she and Chiss could feel the pressure building up behind his wall, the energy trying to get out.

Chiss nodded at them and began to walk toward the door. "No!" Callo said. "Don't go. You need to stay and protect her."

Chiss looked at Kirian, who shook her head. Chiss said, "You will do that, my lord." He left the room.

"Demons of hell! Don't you realize what danger you are in?"

Kirian said, "You would not hurt a Healer. My lord, relax. Relax your shoulders, here . . ." Her hand soothed his clenched muscles.

He dared not relax. He said so.

"No, my lord," she said. "You cannot keep up this tension. You can struggle to contain a force of that immensity until your strength gives out. The force will win in the end. This rigid control is not the way to handle it."

"You are no color mage."

"Lord Arias, your half brother. He does not spend his life in this strain."

His muscles were beginning to shake. "He's had—years of training. I am just—a container for this magery. Never trained. Just a gods-damned—breeding experiment."

"You have done very well so far. Now, my lord, relax."

Fire etched his hands, and his vision started to tinge red. He felt a compulsion to stand and let it loose, and destroy whoever got near him. Then he remembered who was next to him—Kirian, with her rebellious short hair, who had gone to Ha'las and been imprisoned because of him. He took a deep breath, said a silent prayer to Jashan, and eased his inner barrier, just a little, just a little . . . .

She inhaled a deep breath. "What?"

"The color magery. It's all around you, washing up the bulkhead like it did when Lord Arias was Collared. It's beautiful. Go on. Relax."

He eased his shoulders. Her warm hands, making small circles on his skin—when had she started stroking his skin?—made it easier. He felt the redness in his field of vision ease. Looking around the cabin, he saw it filled with skeins of multi-colored light. Her hands were warm, pressing on his skin, sliding against him. He began to feel another sort of strain as arousal made itself felt. She leaned forward; he felt her warm, soft roundness pressed up against his back. He groaned.

"The color magery is beautiful. There is a sting in the air from it. Can you feel it?" Kirian whispered.

Callo supposed he could feel the sting. Next to the agony he was experiencing, it felt like a gentle breeze. His headache eased. Light writhed in his mind, but it was gentler now, something he could live with. Kirian came around in front of him. She said something, but between the color magery and his headache—and his arousal—he could not make out the words. He leaned forward and kissed her, a rough kiss, his hands pulling her toward him. She smiled at him and kissed him back. He reached for her.

"Now," he said. The fire in his mind and his body echoed and enhanced each other.

"Gods, yes," she said. She embraced him. His hand slid around her, pulling her close, pulling at her tunic, sliding under her clothing to feel the warmth of her skin. The color magery was damped down, yet he felt it fueling his desire. He pulled her down on the bedroll with him, and forgot the rest of the world.

———

It was another full day until Callo felt he could face going ashore. His mind still felt raw, and Jashan's ritual only helped a little. He wondered how he would come to terms with the energies that he would have to live with from now on.

He sat with his three companions the morning of the second day and told them what he planned. Kirian argued with him until she was red in the face and then stalked off in a rage. Ha'star accepted his plans without comment; the scarred Ha'lasi warrior was making plans to return to Ha'las and to his unit. Chiss said nothing. It might be only Callo's imagination that his manservant seemed troubled about something.

He caught up with Kirian after the noon meal. She sat at the stern with her shoes off, looking at the shoreline.

"Still upset?" he asked. "What do you think?"

"It was you who made me see that Arias is just as much a victim as—as Eyelinn, even."

"I'm sorry I said it. You have no business going right into Seagard Castle. You'll be killed. I thought you would meet him elsewhere."

"He won't leave the Castle for that long." He sat down next to her and lay back, looking up at the cloud-studded sky. "You don't have to come with me, you know. I know you fear that Arias will punish you for all of this."

"Lord Mikati blinded Hon Ruthan. They're all the same, these *righ* – they don't brook dissent. Or disobedience."

He ignored the insult. "Don't come, then. I wouldn't ask you to. I can have Chiss get you to safety. My estate—probably is not mine anymore, but I have loyal people there who would shelter you. Or you could return to Sugetre, to the College. You could go to friends of mine, in Leyland – there is safety there."

"No."

The sun emerged from behind a cloud. Callo closed his eyes, seeing for an instant a bright hot afterimage that reminded him of the color magery. "What, then?"

She turned to him. "Don't go. Something will happen." He opened his eyes and looked into hers. He had never heard her sound that way before, even in the prison in Las'ash.

"Sweetheart, don't worry." He smoothed her hair back; it was short again. Ha'star, having acceded to her demands, had cut it the previous day. Callo thought its rather harsh look made her skin appear even smoother, her eyes softer.

"How can I help it? Lord Arias is no longer any friend of yours, no matter what he was before. The Collar rules him. You are a ku'an, Callo. He will slay you."

"I am not completely helpless."

That drew a laugh out of her, but she grew serious again. "He is a trained color mage. And a swordsman, is that not so?"

"Arias is very good with the sword."

"Well, then. Do not go. He also has a castle full of armed men at his bidding."

"I do not remember you ever preaching caution to me before."

"You have not ever been so foolish."

"I don't think that's true. Especially not for the last season or two." Callo sighed and rested his weight on his elbow, his other hand curving around her waist. "Kirian love, I abandoned Arias. I didn't see it that way at the time, but I do now. You yourself said the Collar was like being under the influence of a ku'an."

"I'm sorry I ever said it," she grumbled.

"He was enslaved by the King against his will. He never wanted to be Collared. His family wished it, as do all the noble *righ*, but he was a spirit of his own. He only got away with it because it kept him in the line of succession. So now, he does something foolish and the King Collars him. The least I can do for my half-brother, who is also my friend, is to try to free him from that, now that I have the ability."

There was a short silence.

"He will not thank you for the attempt," Kirian finally said.

"He will if I succeed. I think I have a good chance, Kirian – I am a ku'an and a color mage now too. How can I fail?" His spirits were light, and he felt a vast relief now that he realized what he needed to do.

"You can't even light a fire with your magery," Kirian said. "You have no skill, only raw power."

He grinned at her, trying to pull her out of her foreboding mood. "Many thanks for your faith in me."

She elbowed him in the side and he fell back with a mock grunt of pain. Then she fell back next to him, her arm embracing him, her voice rough. "Callo, I know you do not feel as I do. But I could not bear to lose you."

"You won't lose me. Have courage, sweet Kirian. This is not like you." He caressed her hair as she clung to him, and after a while he coaxed her face nearer so he could kiss her sweet lips, but she buried her face in his shoulder so he could not reach her. Then, lying half in the sun and considering how best to accomplish his plan, he became steadily more relaxed by the sun and the feeling of Kirian warm against his side until he dozed off. When he awakened, she was gone.

———

Kirian knocked on the door and stood there. Ha'star waited in hiding around the corner, not wanting to alarm anyone until Kirian smoothed the way for him. Moonlight silvered the weathered planks of the house and illuminated the froth on the waves as they curled up the strand. There was no activity in the village; it was very late.

Kirian knocked again and eventually heard a shuffling noise. "Who is it?" asked a querulous voice. "Who's ill?" The door opened to reveal Ruthan, clutching a blanket around herself, her white eyes ghostly in the moonlight.

"Kirian!" Ruthan whispered. "Welcome, welcome! Come in here, girl!" She grabbed Kirian's forearm and pulled her into the house. "Are you all right? Where have you been?" The old woman coughed. "Ah, it was a hard winter without you."

"Ruthan, someone is with me," Kirian said. She beckoned to Ha'star, who slid out of the shadows like a cat.

"Not that Inmay, I hope," Ruthan said. "More trouble than he's worth, that one. They combed this area for days, even went into the old caves. Who's this?"

"I am honored, Hon Healer," Ha'star said, bowing like a nobleman.

Kirian's mouth quirked at that but she said, "Ruthan, this is Ha'star, a friend. He is a Ha'lasi warrior, but he helped us get back here."

"If you're my girl's friend, you're mine," Ruthan said, coughing again. "Come in, both of you. I take it that's all? No slave girls or renegade Healers? No armed search party? Just a Ha'lasi warrior? My life had no excitement until you came here, Kirian." The old woman went back into the house, lit a couple of lamps, and sat in her chair. Kirian thought she looked frail, as if the winter had indeed been hard on her health. She knelt beside the chair and took Ruthan's hand, holding it briefly to her own cheek. The gnarled hand was cold and trembled slightly.

"Ha'star, could you light the fire?" Kirian asked. "Ruthan, are you ill?"

"No, just old. Maybe a little ill. The sea air, even in the summer—it's hard on my bones. But you are all right! I can see, you are healthy to your bones."

"May I make you some tea?"

"Yes. You always did take care of me. I am glad to see you —it is a bit of a shock, at night like this . . ."

"I thought I should avoid the Alkirani," Kirian said. "Of course, with Ha'star here…"

"He looks as if he could well protect you." The fire flared up, and Ruthan closed her eyes. "Ah, thank you, Ha'lasi warrior. Sit."

Ha'star sat on the floor, next to the fire, and tended it as the flame grew. "Thank you for your welcome, Hon Ruthan. Hon Kirian told me about you."

"What happened after I left, Ruthan?" Kirian asked, pouring hot water into a cup. "I know one of the search party was killed. Did Lord Arias – do anything?"

"Thank the Unknown God, he spared all of us. It was obvious the slave girl killed the guard—they searched the caves for days but couldn't find either of them. He was down here…"

"Himself?"

"Himself. With sparks flying, angry as he was. Wanted to know where you were—had you helped them—that kind of thing. But in the end, he sent Jiriman back to Fortress Mount with apologies. And left us alone."

Kirian gave a cup to Ruthan and one to Ha'star. "I worried."

"I told you I'd be safe. But I'm glad you ran. If he had found you—I hate to think."

"Lord Callo—have you heard any news about him?"

Ruthan's shrewd eyes were on Kirian's. "I thought you might know of that. He vanished from the Castle right about when you left."

"What did Lord Arias do?"

"I haven't a notion. They were all wrapped up in this other business, about your friend Inmay. And there was a delegation here, from Leyland. I know a fast messenger was sent to Suge-tre, but what happened after…" Ruthan shrugged.

Ha'star poked at the fire, which now crackled vigorously. He stood, still sipping tea. Ruthan looked at his scarred face, at his sheathed sword and the knife at his belt, and shook her head. "You have a story to tell me, I can see." She cackled. "A Ha'lasi warrior! And you know something of the bastard lord; I can see that too."

The term stung. "You mean, Lord Callo."

"Lord Callo, yes. Tell me your story in the morning, youngling. I am weary tonight. Simah birthed her third yester-day, a long battle it was, and the little one weak and blue when she finally was born. And Gru drinking and moaning outside the door the whole time as if he was dying. So I am not up to long stories, although I almost can't wait—you have the look of adventure about you; that you do!"

Kirian smiled. She was glad to see Ruthan, glad to see the firelight warming the old lined face. "I will tell you in the morning. Thank you for your welcome. How are the others, up at the Castle?"

"In a snit again. Too high-tempered, the lot of them. Though this time—the concubine Shala Si has done it after all, Kirian. Managed to get herself pregnant. Gods know how she avoided the herbs I had mixed with her food! Three moons along and just told Lord Forell. He hauled me up to the Castle to take a look at her. She looks like a peach."

"She always did," Kirian said, remembering the round, voluptuous woman she had seen on her first visit to Seagard Castle.

"Sira Joah wants the baby aborted. I wouldn't do it so far along— might kill the concubine, too—so now she wants it exposed after birth."

"Why?" Kirian stared.

"It's half-*righ*, half-common. It will have the color magery —I saw it—but will never be able to be Collared. A half-breed."

"Unknown God, what is *wrong* with those people?"

"They're nobles," Ruthan said.

"Idiots," Ha'star said from the fire.

"Lord Forell has had an attack of fatherly honor—drank 'til he was brave enough and went to ask Arias as the head of the family to let the infant live. Shala Si cried all over his shoulder and refused him her bed, I think—that's why he disturbed his peace. Sira Joah threatened to expose the brat herself."

"Gods, what a mess," Ha'star said, shaking his head.

"So, what did Lord Arias say?" Kirian asked.

Ruthan cackled. "We'll never know. Sira Joah went and referred it to the King, since he was there anyway."

A spear of ice went down Kirian's spine. Ha'star stood up, looking at her. Kirian said slowly, "Ruthan—do you mean King Martan is there *now*?"

"Why, yes—he's to perform young Ewal's Collaring tomorrow." Ruthan's white eyes went from Kirian's face to Ha'star's grim expression. "Why?"

Kirian looked at Ha'star. "He'll see the King's banner. He won't go in if he knows the King is there."

"It's dark," Ha'star said. "He's not going to see any banner at the top of the cursed castle in the dark."

"He'll notice the extra guardsmen, won't he?"

Ha'star shrugged. "Depends. He's not going to parade through the main hall. He'll try to avoid seeing anyone. He's slipping past the guards. I don't think he'll know."

"All the gods," Kirian said.

Ruthan was watching them. "Well?"

"Ruthan, we have to go," Kirian said in a rush. "Lord Callo is trying to get in to see Lord Arias tonight. I think his life is in danger from the King. I am so sorry—but I have to go."

"Mistake. Getting wrapped up with kings and nobles. What's it to us?"

"Oh, I know, I know. I can't help it. Ruthan, I'll be back. Thank you, Ruthan, thank you. Ha'star, I hope you're a climber. This is going to be wonderful, trying to get up the cliff path at night." As she spoke, she tightened her shoelaces and belted her cloak tighter about her.

"Come back alive, now," grumbled Ruthan, pulling the blanket around her. "I won't sleep all night."

Ha'star gave her that incongruous nobleman's bow again, clearly showing her great respect. "I will bring her back. My thanks, Hon Ruthan."

And they slipped out the door, closing it gently behind them, and walked toward the cliff path.

———

Callo remembered the layout of Seagard Castle as if he had lived there all of his life, instead of just those few, uncomfortable sennights in the fall. In the delicate light of the narrow moon, he and Chiss were able to traverse the caravan road from Two Merkhan, leave the horses loosely tethered off the road, and make their way toward the newer wing of the castle. They avoided the main entryway, which was patrolled by an unusually large number of guardsmen. Instead, they made a wide circle around the castle grounds, avoiding any patrols, and found a path that trickled down to the village from the caravan road. After a short distance, they left the village path, and Chiss took the lead as they walked through a wooded area, threading them past two sentries and bringing them to a door in the kitchen area.

The door was unlocked. Chiss had said servants were in and out that door at all hours. Callo's every nerve was on edge as they eased into the building. The door gave directly onto a small room, off the main kitchen, with buckets and tubs stacked and mops leaning against walls. A cupboard door stood ajar, showing piles of linen within— aprons and dishrags and such, Callo surmised.

The scrub room was dark, but as Chiss had warned him, someone was in the main kitchen. A yellow light flickered, and a hushed voice spoke to someone else. Callo wondered what on earth the servants found to do at this late hour of the night. Chiss beckoned. He followed his manservant past the kitchen to a shadowed hallway. In a moment the muted activity in the kitchen fell behind them.

They approached the great hall. There were guardsmen seated nearby, with dice on the table between them. Callo veered into a stairwell before they could take notice. A servants' staircase rose into unlit darkness before them.

They climbed and turned with the stairs and climbed again, guarding their footsteps.

There were three flights to the second floor, to allow for the high ceilings of the main floor. Here Callo stopped short; there was an armed guard at the entryway. The man was burly and mailed, and looked wide awake; he had a shielded lamp, with candlelight poking through holes punched in the tin shield.

Callo sighed. Chiss, behind him, tapped him on the shoulder, urging him on. Callo closed his eyes for a second, long enough to identify the trancelike drowsiness he wished to inflict on the guard. *Boredom, exhaustion, sleep,* his mind urged the lone guardsman. The man shifted his weight; he rolled his head, easing his neck muscles, fighting the ku'an influence. At last he leaned up against the wall, and his eyelids fell, so somnolent he was almost asleep on his feet.

Callo thought that was the best he would be able to do. He wondered what quirk Arias had developed to have an armed guard over the door to the sleeping quarters. Then he and Chiss slipped by the guard, nerves on edge. The man never stirred. Two more flights to the upper level, and then the tower awaited them.

Callo felt sure Arias would be in the tower. There were three Watchers only, now: Arias, Lord Forell, and their uncle Eamon. He could not see old Eamon keeping a night Watch, nor self-indulgent Forell, who would be with his concubine. Arias had always been a creature of the night; he pictured his half-brother in the dark tower, with the long windows open to the sea and the stars, and smiled. They took the last flights faster, no longer worried about guards.

He knew he was right as soon as he entered the large outer room. The couches and tables were deserted. An oil lamp turned low lit the room, but left the corners dark. A narrow doorway lay through the western wall, and through it Callo felt the draft from unshuttered windows, open to the sea air. The Watch Tower.

A figure was silhouetted against the dim light shed by the slim moon. A tangled green glow rose and dissipated in the grainy dark – Arias' mage cloak was showing the patterns of the color magic—and its master's mood.

Chiss stayed by the door. Callo went on, walking slowly in the dark. His feet scuffed, and the black figure in the window turned.

"Who?" asked Arias. A glow rose in the room, reddish so as not to disturb the Watcher's night vision.

"Arias, it's me. Callo."

"*Callo?*" The glow intensified. He could see Arias' face now, burnished by the color of the magery. His half-brother's eyes were riveted on his face; the Collar gleamed red on Arias' neck.

"Hello, Arias."

Arias' eyes were fierce. "So you've come back."

Chiss took the oil lamp from the table in the outer room. As he approached with it, Callo could see Arias' hand playing with his belt knife in its sheath. His own weapon was sheathed; he spread his arms slightly, to show goodwill.

"You! Chiss! Take that light away. You'll ruin my night vision." As Chiss nodded and put the lamp down on the floor outside the

Watch room, Callo said, "How are you to see a Black Tide in this darkness anyway?"

"Not well. So it's all the more important that I don't blind myself." Arias looked out at the night and then back to Callo. "Are you all right?"

"I'm fine. I should not have left you to the mercies of the King's Collar."

"Well, I realize I may have had something to do with your leaving." Callo's heart warmed; Arias seemed his old self again. Then his eye caught the Collar, and Arias' hand still at the belt knife, and he stopped smiling. Arias continued, "I can only blame the early days of my Collaring, Callo. Things were

—all black and white. I pushed you away without allowing you to explain."

"Explain?"

"How you would not be a threat to Righar."

"Ah, Arias. You have known me all your life."

"But apparently I have not."

"When you were Collared, *you* changed—not I. When I found out about my birth, I was angry and shocked, but still the same as I have ever been." Callo saw Arias look again out the windows into the clear cold night, looking for attack from Ha'las. "Now—I must admit, Brother, my recent travels have indeed changed me."

Arias' attention was on him like lightning. The colors in his cloak swirled faster, red and violet. "Have you come to kill me?"

"No!" Callo said that fast, convinced that if Arias didn't believe him, he would strike first. "I have come to see if you would like to be freed from that."

"This?" Arias fingered the Collar. He gave a dry, incredulous laugh. "You are taunting me. Why would I not hear that suggestion as a threat?"

"Because you know me." Callo came closer. "You were attacked by a jealous king and Collared as revenge. You know it. All the imperatives of your binding cannot have blinded you to that."

"No, the Collar hasn't blinded me to that. Sharpeyes is a jealous ass." Arias' hand was no longer on his knife. Now it touched his Collar, almost a caress.

"Would you rather be free to make your own choices?" Callo asked.

"My duty is to Watch," Arias said. He looked out into the night again. Callo followed his stare and saw only black-on-black, an occasional glitter of moonlight on sea, a patch of darker night that might be forest, or clouds, or rocks. It came to him suddenly that Arias couldn't see a thing now, at night. A Black Tide could rush in at them from Ha'las on the breast of the waves and be upon them before Arias could do more than mutter a curse. Arias was no fool; he must know this, too. The Collar was indeed strong, to force a man to bear a useless vigil, night after night, with no hope of success in the event of a real attack. Callo felt a chill that had nothing to do with the night air.

"You can always Watch. You can Watch of your free will, without your King having to Collar you like an animal. Arias – I have changed, I have found some things out—I have realized what you are going through. I think I can release you. Or at least, you and I together can."

"What are you talking about?"

"I have found my Ha'lasi heritage. I have found the gift that comes with my ku'an ancestry. I might be able to help."

Red sparks flew, and Arias drew back, hand on knife once again. "Yes, you are a Ha'lasi bastard. Is that your new allegiance? Tell me no, Callo, for I don't want to hurt you." But energy licked around Arias' hands, and the interior of the small room was now illuminated by a strident red glow.

"No! Arias, I am not here to harm you or anyone here."

There was a clatter from the stairs. Chiss spun and went to the outer room. Arias drew back, haloed in twisting light, clearly on the verge of action.

"I mean you no harm," Callo said. A door slammed in the outer chamber, and three figures scrambled towards him. Callo began to drop his internal wall, ready to defend himself. Then he saw the spiky hair lit by red magery. "Kirian!"

She rushed at him. He saw Ha'star behind her, holding a sword whose blade was black with blood.

"Friends, Arias, friends," Callo uttered as Chiss loomed in

the inner room. He could see his half-brother's hands shaking. "Kirian, what's wrong? Why are you here?"

"The King is here," she said. "We had to warn you."

"Sharpeyes here?"

"Whom have you killed?" Arias demanded of Ha'star. Callo looked at the Ha'lasi warrior who still held the blooded blade.

"Guard, on the second floor," Ha'star said. "He saw us."

"The King's guardsman," Arias said. "Friends, are they, Callo?"

"Yes, damn it, Arias, I realize this isn't as nonthreatening as it ought to be! Look, I still can help you. Do you want to be free of it? Watch if you will, but let it be of your own will, not the King's."

"I can't." The red energies remained, clinging to Arias' hands. His voice was even. "Callo. You think I don't remember our friendship. Well, I do. But it's still everything I can do not to blast you where you stand, right now. Get out of here before Sharpeyes comes, or I lose control."

"Jashan, Arias, I can't leave you now!"

"It's too late anyway." The voice was calm and held a touch of satisfaction. Arias turned toward the door, white showing around his eyes. Chiss swore, and Callo would have echoed him if he had been able to speak.

His Majesty King Martan Alghasi Monteni strode into the room fully dressed, even to a gold circlet around his graying head. Five guards swarmed in around him. One man carried lamps he set on table and floor, so that the whole scene leaped into relief against a background of sharp shadows. The men surrounded Sharpeyes in a protective semi-circle.

Arias whirled and stared out at the night, searching as his binding dictated, then turned back.

"So you are back," the King said to Callo. "I send men the

length and breadth of the land to find you—even into Ha'las — and you turn up in front of my very nose."

"You sent men to kill him," Chiss accused.

"Apparently, they failed." Sharpeyes stared at Callo, his gaze uncomfortably acute. "You could not be allowed to stay in Ha'las, giving the ku'an the benefit of your talents. Your man," he cast an unreadable glance at Chiss, "knows this."

Callo did not understand why the King addressed Chiss. He said, "You have discovered me. Now what?"

"How much have you changed, Nephew?" Sharpeyes, who had not even glanced at the other occupants of the room, flung an arm out in Kirian's direction. Color magery spun from his fingers and seized her, whipping round her arms and body like a snake. Kirian shrieked as her wrists were restrained by chains of magery, and bound tightly to her body.

Ha'star came to life. His sword hissed free of its sheath, his belt knife in his other hand.

"Stop!" shouted Callo, knowing what would happen.

Ha'star ignored him. He whirled into deadly action with all the skill and power of his years of fighting.

"Ha'star, stop!" ordered Callo. There was no way one warrior, however skilled, could prevail against the five guards. The King's guardsmen clashed with Ha'star, and his sword flew out of his hand, blood blossoming on his chest. The Ha'lasi warrior fell back, eyes rolling up, blood still pumping from a deep and deadly wound straight to his heart.

"No!" Kirian cried out, still entangled in magery.

Callo rushed to kneel at Ha'star's side. The warrior's dead eyes looked past him. "Go with your gods, Ha'star. I will miss you." Shock wavered along his nerves; he felt a mighty rage rise up. As he stood and turned to face the King, he almost didn't understand what he heard.

Sharpeyes was laughing.

The King's gaze—in fact, every eye in the room—was fixed on Callo. With the anger came the color magery, running through his veins, escaping from its captivity behind his wall, and flowing visibly along his arms like liquid fire.

"Jashan's eyes! Callo!" That was Arias, his own magery sparking from his eyes as he stared.

"I told you I had changed," he said.

Sharpeyes smiled. "It worked!" he said. "Thirty years of wondering—I am an old man now. But it worked! How Si'lan must have trembled when he knew you were returning here. My nephew, color mage and ku'an! Sira Joah said it would not work."

Callo almost choked with rage, his friend dead on the floor behind him and Sharpeyes gloating. "You thought to gain from — creating me."

"You are angry now. It will become clear in a moment." The King waved a careless hand, and the brilliant bonds fell away from Kirian. She stumbled a little and began rubbing her arms.

"Are you all right?" Callo asked her in a quiet tone, eyes still on the King.

"I'm fine." She knelt by Ha'star's body briefly, then rose and came to Callo. He saw tears on her cheeks.

"The time has come, then," the King continued. "Sira Joah made little of my plans, but she had no choice but to do as I said. You, Callo—you are my heir."

"What?"

"You heard me." Sharpeyes seemed to be enjoying this. For all the rage and pain flowing around the room—and Arias' stunned incomprehension—only the King seemed relaxed, even smiling, as his great plan came to fruition. "You will be King after me."

"Little Ander is your heir," Arias said.

"That can be remedied. As for you"— the King looked at Arias — "you are a Collared mage now, my lord *righ*, and out of the succession. Callo will bring two great heritages to Righar. With him, we can invade Ha'las and destroy the few ku'an that pretend to rule it."

"Under your rule," Kirian said.

"For now. I will not live forever. Then it will be his. Look at him! He can barely stand it, there is so much power."

"The lords will never accept a *righ* bastard as King," Arias said.

"They will accept what they are told to," the King said.

Callo felt himself losing control. "Arias." he said. "Do you want to be free from that thing? I think we can do it if we work together." His hand found Kirian's arm and moved her aside. He decided that he may as well use this embarrassment of magery that had fountained out of him with his anger.

"I don't want your damned throne, Uncle," Arias said. "Nor do I want your Collar, anymore. Callo?"

Arias closed his eyes. Callo dropped his barrier, threw at his half-brother the state of mind he thought would best negate the dominance of the Collar, a sheer recklessness he remembered from Arias' past. Arias, unbelievably, laughed with it, sounding like his old self. The Collar on his neck flamed with a bloody hue as Arias focused all the breaking power of his magery upon it. Arias' face was lit from underneath, casting his eyes into black shadow except for the gleam of magery that lived in his eyes. Callo prayed to Jashan that he could break the Collar without breaking Arias as well; he loosed his control and let fire arc out of his hands to join Arias' magery.

Sharpeyes let out a grunt of pain. Callo had not realized that the King, being the holder of the binding, might be affected by their attempt. There was a sharp crack and the

Collar split in two, glowing within like metal still on the forge, and dropped to the floor. Arias fell to his knees, gasping. Callo released him from the ku'an influence.

Kirian went to him and knelt by him. "Are you all right, Lord Arias?" She took his wrist, feeling his pulse. Callo turned his attention toward the King, wary of what he might be doing.

"Gods, Brother," Arias said, a light in his eyes. "Thank you. That was—exhilarating." As he lifted his head, Callo could see the raw flesh on his neck, where the Collar had burned him. The edges of the wound were blackened. Kirian began examining Arias' neck, speaking to him softly.

"Ha now!" exclaimed Sharpeyes. His face was pale but his expression still triumphant, in spite of the fact that his hands were clutched over his stomach. "Such power! You will do as I say, Nephew, and be glad of it."

"I feel—strange," said Arias from the floor.

"You'll survive yet, to be a curse to me. Damned Alkirani, you all have too much temper. And even that Collar couldn't curb your stubbornness." Far from retaliating for the broken Collar, the King seemed more triumphant than ever at this evidence of his nephew's unprecedented power.

"Your Majesty," Callo said. "I will not help you invade Ha'las."

"Why? Grown to like your father?"

Callo felt uncertain. The color magery died down, receding until it was no longer visible.

"Yes," Sharpeyes said. "We planned it together, Si'lan and I. You would be the heir to both lands, stopping this endless Watch and the unceasing raids. We planned peace, the ku'an'an and I! At least, he planned peace. I planned to take you for my own and raise you as a *righ*, knowing your duty to your king. I knew that one day, when you came to your full potential, you would know how to repay me."

"You betrayed him," Callo said.

"Betray! You will learn that word has no meaning for a ruler. My duty is to guard Righar. I care nothing for that puny, frightened island and its few distorted ku'an—so worried about their private pleasures that they cannot rule the land. Besides, the old King died before his time, and left that travesty Ar'ok on the throne."

Ar'ok was a travesty. Callo agreed on that. He rubbed his forehead with the back of his hand, beginning to feel confused. He was very tired, and the color magery skirled along his veins, making it difficult for him to think.

"So will you join me, Nephew?" asked King Martan, all warmth and support, his hand stretched out to Callo from across the room.

Callo looked at Arias, but Arias sat on the floor with his head in his hands, still battling with whatever the sudden release from the Collar had done to him. The guardsmen were ranged to the side of the King, screening Ha'star's body from his view. Callo felt the color magery curling through his body, seeking release. He shifted on his feet. It was hard to think while controlling the energy, and it would not be forced down with his nerves in the state they were.

"I can help you with the color magery," the King said gently. "You need a mentor."

That rang wrong. A mentor? Sharpeyes? Callo looked away from the King.

Then Kirian was at his side, her hand on his arm. "Callo," she said. "You have done what you came for. Remember?"

He knew she was trying to ground him. Her touch on his arm was warm and comforting. He took a deep breath. "No," he said. "I cannot be your heir."

"What else would you be?" Sharpeyes said. The lamplight gleamed on his circlet and lit his gray hair to dignified silver. The King had always been the only source of stability for Callo, as a child rejected by his mother, as a boy educated in the palace, to a young man gifted with his own holding. It was hard to spurn the King's offer. Then Kirian tugged on his arm, and Callo remembered the King's malicious laughter as he told Callo of his Ha'lasi parentage. He looked at Arias, also Sharpeyes' nephew, and also the victim of the King's manipulations.

"It doesn't matter," Callo said. "I won't do it. Let us leave here, Your Majesty." The magery grew stronger yet somehow less distracting.

"Why would I let you go, to offer your power to another?" Sharpeyes gestured, and the guards moved, shoving Kirian away, circling Callo. One took his sword and belt knife and threw them into the corner of the room. "If you will not come willingly," Sharpeyes continued, "Then you will come by force."

"It will do you no good," Callo said.

"You might be surprised," Sharpeyes said. He smiled, a most unpleasant expression. "We can persuade you, I think." He gestured and a rope of energy flew out to encircle Kirian again, lashing her arms to her body. She cried out in pain; this was no gentle restraint, the King was hurting her, scalding her. Her voice acted on Callo like a spur. He dropped his internal barrier and, fast and powerfully, flung out a stream of somnolence at the five guards, dropping them on the floor in a welter of mail and arms as they simply sat down, drooping against the floor or wall. Perhaps it should have been fear, he thought, and they would have run away—but then the Castle would be roused, and all the other guards upon them, and Callo did not think he could manage that.

With the guards temporarily disabled, he leaped across the floor and grabbed his sword from where the guard had thrown it. Then he waded across the inert bodies of the guards, heedless of treason, to strike back at Sharpeyes and free Kirian from his uncle's powerful magery.

That is, until he felt another sword, hard at his chest, its point pushing into his tunic and stopping him cold.

He looked away from the King, his vision fogged with rage and the effort of maintaining the ku'an influence on the guardsmen.

The sword at his chest was held by Chiss.

Chiss held the sword steady, with no sign of wavering. The point had run through his tunic and broken the skin; blood trickled down his chest under his tunic. Shocked, Callo froze long enough for Chiss to remove his own sword from his grip, and fling it once more across the room.

"Chiss?" he asked. Unbelieving.

"My lord." There was nothing but calm in Chiss' voice, as Callo had heard it hundreds of times—as if the man responded to Callo's request for a new tunic, or to be awakened at a certain time. Except this time he was poised to murder Callo.

Kirian gasped. The King's restraints were burning her. Callo's level of desperation rose. The color magery flickered in the corners of his vision. He felt, more than saw, Chiss grow tense as the other man caught it too.

"Let her go!" Callo ordered the King. He squeezed his eyes shut for a second, trying to suppress the resurgent energy inside him, then re-opened them to see that Sharpeyes studied him with a calculating look.

"I don't think you can do anything about it," Sharpeyes said. "You are mine, Callo. Born by my will, raised by my plan. You are too full of power to ignore it. You have no choice but to use it."

"I plan to use it," Callo said. "If I don't—bad consequences. But I won't use it for you."

"Then what of *her?*" The King gestured. There was an odd limpness about Kirian. She had fainted, but she did not fall; she was held upright by the King's magery. It wrapped around her like a fiery vine, lighting the room.

Of course, Sharpeyes would use her. That was the point of all this. And if Callo refused to acquiesce in the King's plan, Kirian would die. If he tried to break the King's color magery or attack him, Chiss would kill him. Chiss, his mentor, who had protected him during the years when he learned to hide his ku'an abilities.

"All the gods, Chiss. Why?"

Chiss did not answer. The King did.

"He has always been mine, Callo. I hired him with the understanding that, if you were ever to threaten me with your magery, he would kill you."

Callo tried to move away, but the sword moved with him, taking a layer of his skin with it. It seemed that Chiss was serious. Still fighting the color magery lest it force an uncontrolled and probably catastrophic escape, Callo was still.

He saw a movement in the corner of his eye—not the magery. It was a dark and furtive motion. Callo forced himself not to look in Arias' direction. Then a blaze of golden fire arced like lightning and struck Chiss in the chest, knocking the man away from Callo. The sword clattered to the floor and Callo swept it up, leaping over Chiss and raising the weapon to strike at the King.

Fire met his strike. The rope of energy holding Kirian vanished with an audible crack and rematerialized, snaking toward Callo. A shield of energy forced Callo's sword back. He could not touch the King. With a gasp of relief, Callo finally let go the seething color magery and let it escape. It crackled around his hands. He flung it, with no subtlety, toward the King.

The King's hands were glowing with the power in him. He met Callo's color magery. Sweat dripped down Callo's forehead. Somewhere in the room someone shouted, but he could not tell whom. He lost his hold on the five guards, and expected them to join the fray at any moment as they awakened from the ku'an influence. Light flared elsewhere in the room, and Callo realized Arias had set up a shield of sorts around the guards; they were unable to move past the curtain of energy. But he knew Arias would never attack the King— no matter if Callo was dying at his uncle's hands.

Callo moved a little backward and his foot struck a limp form on the floor. Chiss. Anger at his betrayal claimed him again, and the color magery intensified. Sharpeyes flung up his other hand as if to ward it off and staggered back.

Then Kirian was at the King's back, holding a sword. She wavered on her feet, but she gave Sharpeyes a solid club with the hilt. Sharpeyes jerked in pain. His mage shield faded.

Just like that, Callo grabbed onto the color magery with all his will and hauled it back in to himself. It burned coming back in, as if it wanted to be loosed for good, but Sharpeyes was swaying and defenseless now, and Callo would not murder his King.

Kirian stepped back. He could not see her through his fight to restrain himself. Brilliant floaters rotated in his field of vision. The power fluctuated, getting bright, and then faded a little as he struggled.

"Callo! Try harder!" said Kirian right behind him. He could not respond.

"Your Majesty!" called one of the guards, still stuck behind Arias' shield.

Sharpeyes regained his balance. He stood, hand on his head, for one moment with his gray eyes riveted on Callo's struggle. "Go ahead – destroy yourself," he said. "I do not care whether you live or die from it."

The King turned and walked out of the tower room.

Kirian came to him. "Callo, Callo, we must go. He may call more guards. Come now; you can follow me."

"I'll help," Arias said, almost groaning as he levered himself off the floor. He still maintained the shield that barricaded the guardsmen against the wall. One eye still on them, he said, "Chiss, before me." And he drew his sword.

"Don't kill him, Arias," Callo said.

"I don't know why not. But—as you wish." Arias gestured. "He can walk before me, and if he tries to do anything to you, I'll kill him then."

"There will be no need. I will do my lord no more harm." Chiss got up from the floor, wavering on his feet, and placed himself before Arias. He did not look at Callo.

Callo took a deep breath and silently repeated the invocation to Jashan. He felt the color magery become more manageable. His vision returned to normal.

As soon as it was safely buried, along with the psychic magery, behind his wall, he staggered. The world looked dark, the people in it shadows.

"Come on, my love," Kirian said, her hand on his arm infusing him with warmth. "Stay on your feet. Several flights we have, if I remember, and the King may have roused the guardsmen."

"All the gods," Callo said. It was half a prayer, half a curse. He needed rest. His head swam. Kirian, still not recovered from her own ordeal, was his rock. Shame at his weakness threw new steel into his shoulders, and he pulled away from her and lay his hand on his sword hilt. "I'm fine. Stay back. The King will have roused the Castle, and I must be on guard."

"Gods, poor Ha'star," Kirian's voice broke on the words.

Callo went down the stairs first. He knew Sharpeyes would not give up so easily.

Chapter Seventeen

A rias grabbed a sword from one of the fallen guardsmen and held it at Chiss' back, forcing the manservant into the lead. Callo followed, then Kirian. The stairwell plunged down into darkness. Arias used his magery to light a beacon, which floated just above their heads, lighting the way with a red glow.

Kirian sighed in relief. She hated the darkness.

"Arias," Callo said, "The King will have roused his guard."

Arias nodded. "My guess is, we won't see them until the second floor."

They tensed at the bottom of the stone tower stairs, but all was quiet. There was no sign of any attempt to obstruct their way. Kirian began to feel a little seed of hope that they might actually get out of this – but where were the King's men? Surely he would not let them go so tamely, when Callo was so instrumental to his plans. They went faster down the next two flights. Callo hissed a warning at Arias as they approached the door where Ha'star had killed the guard. They rounded the landing with caution, but there were no guards there, and the body of the slain guard was gone.

Kirian had just passed the door when it swung open and men boiled into the stairwell.

She shrieked and ducked, hand fumbling at her belt dagger. Callo struck over her head, and a man dropped his weapon and fell at her feet, gushing blood. Scrambling out of the way, she saw the color magery light the stairs as both Callo and Arias loosed the energies they controlled. Two more men were flung back, screaming as the color magery burned their skin. She saw Chiss standing below Arias on the stairs as if he had all the time in the world, making no attempt to escape while the color mages were distracted. He stood against the wall, watching. Kirian crouched and made herself as small as she could, and winced away from the swords and the sizzling bolts of magery.

Then the noise faded, and five guards lay dead on the landing and top few stairs. Callo leaned over one man and said "He wears the raven. King's man."

"Good," Arias said. He grinned. Kirian decided she could not help but like him, since he was so recklessly happy in the face of this disaster. Arias grabbed Chiss' tunic and hauled him back up and over the bodies. "Back into the second floor," Arias said. "More King's men will be downstairs."

"How many?" Callo asked.

"He brought a score. Some are outside. I have several of mine on this floor, if they haven't run down to see what the fuss is about."

Callo peered through the door and gestured them in. They were in the old section of the castle, with its stone floors and tapestry-hung walls. The long corridor was lined with doors, resolutely shut. A lamp, burning low, sat in an embrasure in the wall. The hallway looked deserted. The nobles here were staying out of it, behind their doors, though they must be well aware there was a battle going on. Kirian saw no guards; she thought they must be downstairs or inside the rooms with the nobles they were responsible for guarding. Arias slammed a hand into one of the doors and said, "Sim, are you in there with Forell?"

The door opened enough for Kirian to see a thread of lamplight, a burly armed man with long, braided hair, and a glimpse of Lord Forell, swathed in a dark robe huddled in an armchair. The guard said: "My lord!" to Arias. Kirian saw his gaze fasten on Arias' bare neck.

"Sim! My brother has freed me from that cursed Collar. I need you to guard his escape."

"Whatever you need, my lord." Sim glanced back at Forell, then opened the door and slid through the gap. Lord Forell began protesting, his voice plaintive, but it was cut off by the closing door. "Good to see the thing gone, Lord Arias."

"I think so too. Now, Sim—collect the men, see to the King's men in the great hall. Just keep them away from my brother as he gets out of here. Try not to kill anyone you don't have to—I have to come back here after this is all over and face Sharpeyes."

Callo made a protesting sound at that, but said no more. He leaned against the wall as if he needed the support. He was exhausted; Kirian was not at all surprised by this. She wanted to take his hand, but restrained herself.

Sim headed for the main stairs, which were more centrally located than the servants' stairs they had come down on.

"We have three flights," Callo said tiredly. "The King's men will be at the bottom, you think?"

"Or they'll be outside, guarding the perimeter. Sharpeyes doesn't want to let you go, Brother."

Callo grinned through his fatigue; it did Kirian good to see it. "It's just nice to hear you say *brother*, Brother."

"You will have to tell me how in the hell you wound up a ku'an and a color mage." Arias took a deep breath. "No one is Watching, did you know? For the first time in a hundred years." He looked upward as if he could see the Tower room. "I hope all is well."

Callo put his hand on Arias' shoulder and gave it a gentle shake. Then his gaze fell on Chiss. Kirian saw the frown come down like a thunderhead. Callo took a breath as if he were about to say something, then stopped himself and turned away. Kirian looked back at Chiss and was surprised to see the distressed look in the man's eyes.

Arias saw the exchange. "You must slay him, Callo." Callo did not respond.

"You can't trust him. Jashan's eyes, he almost killed you up in the Tower! How can you trust he won't have a sword at your neck when you least expect it?"

"I will do my lord no more harm," Chiss said.

Callo shifted, and looked at the central stair. It looked dim and deserted—typical of a castle in the middle of the night. There was no sign of alarm from downstairs.

"I think that's enough time," Callo said. "Let's go."

"Go," Arias said. "Look, send me a message when you are settled. I will come to you, help you with the magery. You will need help from someone who knows how to contain it."

"Arias, you idiot, you can't stay here!" Callo objected. "Sharpeyes will have you slain!"

"No. He won't murder one of his *righ* magelords unless he wants to risk insurrection from the rest. I'm safe, Cal."

"It won't be murder if he thinks you've committed treason, Arias. Not a soul will stand with you. Come with us, I say!"

Arias shook off the insistent hand. "Let me go! This is still my castle, and I will not leave it by dead of night. My uncle will not have me killed. I know him—better even than you, Cal — and I say it is so. Go, now before we are all caught!" From a distance, Kirian could hear sudden shouts and the clash of weapons. Her nerves jumped.

"Callo," she said.

"If you have no other place in mind to shelter, go south towards Fortress. There is a farm just as you come off the mountains, just after the steep decline—it belongs to a friend of mine. Tell Arter I sent you. Now, go!" Arias shouted, as the sound of combat came closer. Callo grabbed Chiss' arm and spun him around in front of them, shoving him forward.

"Jashan's favor, Arias," he said, then said to Chiss: "Go, man — now!"

They ran back to the servants' stair and hurried down the steps. The only light came from the lamp left burning at the second landing. Kirian wondered if Callo was too drained to light their way with magery. They stumbled as the lamplight faded. Kirian put her hand out to guide herself by the wall. Chiss gasped, a few steps below her; he had stumbled, but she heard Callo swear and pull him back up.

The stairs finally opened out onto the first floor. There, Callo peered to the right, where the great hall was a cacophony of shouts and loud noises as Arias' guardsmen fought the King's men. Swords clashed and men grunted and yelled. Some of the men were without their leather armor, clearly awakened from sleep in the hall to the demands of battle. There was a crash as something heavy fell, and a big mailed body came staggering back through the door. The man fell, swearing vengeance against whomever had pushed him back, then hoisted himself back up and barreled back through the door, sword drawn.

"Treason," Callo mumbled under his breath, observing the

chaos in the great hall. Kirian had to agree the King would be unlikely to pardon such open battle against his men.

The fight moved away from the door, and Callo took advantage of that to pull Chiss out of their sheltering doorway. They moved fast and low through the servants' hall, past the deserted kitchen, into the scrubroom where Callo paused for just a moment, checking to make sure they were not followed. Just as he turned his head away, there was a hiss through the air as a blade slashed for Callo's throat.

He ducked to the side, but the blade caught his shoulder. Kirian heard the breath go out of him as the shock hit. Then he flung color magery at the attacker in a haphazard splash. The figure staggered and went down in a clatter of buckets and tubs, kicking at the things that hampered his movement.

The color magery faded. Callo swayed for a moment, his eyes gone dull with exhaustion. The attacker, struggling to rise, flung an arm out and around Callo's legs and pulled hard, and Callo fell. The King's man grinned – she could see his teeth under the line of his helm in the light from the kitchen fire. He stood and reached again for his sword as Callo tried to rise.

Kirian shrieked a warning. Chiss came up from where he had been waiting, grabbed Callo by the arm, and pulled him bodily away from the attacker. Then both Callo and Chiss were on their feet, and the attacker backed off in Kirian's direction. She turned to flee but felt a huge arm pull her close, a hand over her partially open mouth.

"Kirian!" Callo shouted, weapon raised—then hesitated as the King's man held her close as a shield. The stink of sweat and horses enveloped her. Kirian bit down hard on the thick fingers over her mouth. She was gratified to hear the man curse and pull his hand away, but he only wrapped it around her waist instead. Struggling, she kicked and elbowed, but could not get free enough to do any real damage. The man's hand tightened.

"Come with me, little bastard," the man jeered at Callo. "Or I'll slice her wide open."

Callo's eyes sparked color magery. "Go to hell," he told her captor, and focused on him with a furious intensity that made her heart race even faster. For the space of several breaths, her captor held still, seemingly frozen. Then his hand fell away from her as if she burned his skin. She pulled away. She ran to Callo's side and looked back. The attacker's face had gone slack; then he dropped his sword, suddenly screamed into Callo's face, and ran into the darkness.

The ku'an's skill. Kirian sighed in relief. Callo turned to her, grabbed her in a tight embrace. He was breathing hard. "Kirian, did he hurt you? If he hurt you I'll…"

"No," she interrupted, her free hand stroking his arm. "I'm fine. Thank you. Callo, can you do that to the King's men in there?"

"There are too many," he said. "It's beyond my skill—also, I don't have the energy required to do it right now. The sooner we're out of here, the better for everyone. Let's go."

He looked at Chiss, but did not hold him at swordpoint again. "Let's go," he repeated, and led the way out the kitchen door into the darkness outside. Chiss gave Kirian a thin smile and followed her out. A perimeter had been set up for the King's visit, and the guardsmen had been alerted. Kirian could see two of them, backs against a nearby outbuilding, and she was sure there were many more.

She knew the cliff path to the village would be guarded.

Callo took a slanting path into the trees, staying low. She followed, afraid every moment that the guards would see her or hear her boots scuffing on the ground. Callo led them away from the stables, away from the cliff path. The trees enfolded them. Callo stopped and turned, looking back towards the castle. Now that they were under cover of the trees, looking back toward the castle wall, Kirian saw that they were fortunate that they had exited through the servants' kitchen door. Guards paced atop the wall, and more guards stood near the stables and the cliff path. She thanked the Unknown God for watching over them, turned to whisper something to Callo, and found herself staring into a strange face. The guard was mailed and armed. Kirian somehow kept herself from crying out, but Callo must have heard her sharp, indrawn breath, because he was there, looming up behind the guard in the darkness and slamming his sword hilt into the man's head. Chiss caught the man as he collapsed, and they dragged the man into the undergrowth.

———

When they reached the caravan road, Callo and Chiss stayed well off to the side as they backtracked north to recover their horses. At least, Chiss' gelding and Miri were loosely tethered to some branches off the caravan road; Kirian's mount Lady was lost to her, since she had left the mare with Ha'star's horse off the Two Merkhan road before they followed the path back to Seagard Village. At least Lady would be safe—it was a well-traveled road. She was sure the first travelers on the road that day would find the horses and thank the gods, especially, for their good fortune in finding such a lovely mare. It would be a bit of serendipity for them. She hoped whoever it was would be a good master to Lady.

Kirian heard Miri's nicker out of the darkness as the mare recognized Callo. Callo freed her, murmuring soft words into Miri's pricked-forward ears. He turned to Kirian and said,

"You may have Chiss' gelding, Kirian. As for you . . ." He turned toward Chiss and paused.

Chiss just looked at Callo and said nothing.

Callo sighed. "I won't pretend to understand you, Chiss. I should have slain you already instead of hauling you along with us through the castle. But you saved my life when you dragged me away from that King's man."

"I can explain, my lord," Chiss began. Callo made a frustrated gesture, and waved Chiss off.

"I have no time for your explanations. I owe you much, I can't slay you now in spite of your betrayal. We need your horse. But you may go where you will." He turned away and mounted Miri. Kirian mounted the gelding and followed. Callo stared ahead into the darkness, but Kirian looked behind. Chiss stood in the near-darkness and watched them walk down the dark road.

They went with caution, alert for King's men searching for them on the road. They kept the horses to a walk to avoid making noises that would draw the notice of any pursuers. Perhaps the King did not think they could have made it to the caravan road; at any rate, they saw no sign of pursuit as they retraced their steps back to where the Castle loomed up to the west of the caravan road. There, they dismounted and left the road, walking the horses through the undergrowth and between the dark trees. Branches and weeds scraped at Kirian's legs. Miri slapped her tail around her flanks, skin quivering, as she tried to shake off the bloodsucking night insects. Kirian's ears strained for any sound of alarm, but she heard nothing. After the dark bulk of the Castle sank into the general blackness behind them, they remounted and returned to the road.

Less than a candlemark later, she heard sounds behind them.

"Callo," she whispered, but he had already heard. He directed Miri off the road and dismounted, hand on his sword hilt. Kirian waited, holding her breath, eyes straining through the night.

"It's me," said a low voice out of the gloom. "I'm alone." She relaxed.

"Chiss?" Callo's whisper held a note of disbelief. "I told you to go."

"You said go where I willed, my lord. This is where I want to go."

"Som'ur's cursed eyes, Chiss, don't you know when you're not wanted?"

"I know well I am not wanted, my lord."

"Yet here you are." Callo swore again. "I am too damned tired to argue with you in the middle of the road. We will discuss this when we reach shelter, Chiss. Until then I swear, if you make one suspicious move, you had better be ready to greet your gods."

"I understand," Chiss said.

———

Kirian lay wrapped in a rough wool blanket on a mound of straw and thanked the Unknown God she was not in Las'ash city any more. If she were, her reputation—even as tattered as it had been—now would be in shreds, and she would undoubtedly be in prison again and headed for stoning for immodest behavior.

When she had curled up on the straw, finally released from the day's barrage of shocks, her heart had begun to race. She could not keep a loud sob from escaping her. Callo had come to lie down next to her. He had put his arm around her and drawn her close. A few minutes later, he had fallen asleep, his arm still around her. Now she listened to his even breathing in the darkness, luxuriated in the feel of his warm, lean body, loose and relaxed against hers. In Las'ash City this would have been grounds for stoning.

In the darkness she could hear the grunts and small movements of the animals that stayed in this barn, as well as their own horses. Chiss was rolled up in a blanket somewhere near the horses. She had no idea what motivated the man to stay with them after Callo released him. He was an enigma—his action in the tower room at the Castle when he had threatened Callo totally opposed to his lifetime of service. She did not believe that his continued presence was a danger to Callo. But then, she never thought he would try to kill his lord either.

Arter, the landholder here at the little farm, was a woman. She listened stony-faced to their explanation and to Arias' name and showed them to the barn, explaining that she could not let them disturb her children in the farmhouse. Callo accepted that with *righ* manners, bowing to the little woman as if he were in Sugetre. Arter brought them cold roast meat and ale and blankets and left them to rest.

Kirian sighed and stretched carefully, trying to avoid disturbing Callo, but Callo slept the sleep of mental and physical exhaustion and did not stir. Finally, the comforting sounds of the stable lulled her to sleep.

She awakened in the morning to a sense of chill. Rolling to one side, she realized that Callo was no longer by her side. She threw back the blanket and sat up, rubbing her eyes, to see the mousy-haired farmholder standing in the stable door, the light of a glorious summer morning streaming in behind her. The cattle were gone. A gray cat sat next to Kirian, its tail curled around its paws, staring at her.

"You must go on soon, before they begin searching here,"

Arter said. "I will not endanger my farmholding for the affairs of the *righ*."

Callo stood before her with his hair untied, wearing the same rumpled tunic as the day before, yet managed to look as noble as ever. He said, "I thank you for the food and shelter, Hon Arter. I will not forget it."

She surveyed him. "You look a power better than you did last night, I must say. I will bring you some meat and bread, then you must go on. I will tell you how to avoid the Fortress road. My advice is to head for the southeast, and the Sword of Jashan."

Callo drew back, almost imperceptibly, but Kirian saw it, and so did Hon Arter. "I don't know what your choices are, but from here it appears you have few. The Sword of Jashan would welcome you and protect you."

"Does my half-brother know you are involved with the Sword of Jashan?"

Arter shrugged. "It matters not. I won't give you up to the King's men—that's all you need care about."

"It is, indeed, the only thing that matters right now. But I have other concerns. Someone must ride to inform the legitimate heir that his life is in danger from the King."

Chiss said, "Hon Kirian need not go with us, my lord. As a Healer, she could go anywhere—back to Seagard, even, to her original posting. I am sure she knows by now that Lord Arias would take no action against her on that earlier matter."

In the matter of Inmay and Eyelinn, Chiss meant. Kirian thought of Inmay, dead in Las'ash city with his head on a spike, and Eyelinn in bondage to Ar'ok, and then she thought of Ha'star dead on the floor of the Tower Room in Seagard Castle far from his homeland. For just a moment the little stable seemed to spin around her head, and she felt faint. She was a Healer, trained up to cure ills and deliver babies and bind wounds. She could deal with all manner of crises, from babies ready to birth unturned to an epidemic of the swelling disease.

She closed her eyes, aware that Callo watched her. She was tired and hungry. She had no experience of mages and princes and *righ* lords. What in the name of the Unknown God was she doing here at all, let alone considering traveling far from her posting with a renegade *righ* lord with unheard-of abilities? With nothing but the clothes on her back, no less. No Healer's bag, no clothes, no money.

No friends. No recourse, if Callo were to leave her.

"I don't know," she said into the silence. "I have to think."

Callo straightened his shoulders as if he prepared to take a blow. "All right, then. You must do as you think is best for you." He turned to Arter. "Thank you again, Hon Arter. We will be ready to leave as soon as we have eaten."

Kirian turned away from the talk as Callo and Arter discussed practicalities. Callo was the light of her eyes; she did not want to leave him. But she must be practical. He was a *righ* lord, a ku'an, and a color mage, and his life ran in a path hers did not.

And she knew he did not love her.

She had convinced Callo that he was not to blame for her desire for him. Shamelessly, to get him into bed with her, she had told him she loved him. He had thanked her for that openness, seeming to know what it cost her. But he had never claimed he loved her in return.

She shook her head as she felt tears come to her eyes. This was unlike her, to be so weepy. She was still tired, and her belly growled with hunger, and the image of Ha'star lying dead on the floor still hung in front of her eyes. She was not used to being pursued for her life. It had killed her sense of adventure, at least for now.

Chiss went out after Arter. Callo carried bread with ham and ale from a tray that Arter must have brought, though Kirian had not seen that happen. She took it from his hands, and he sat next to her.

"Kirian, sweet," he said, very seriously.

She braced herself for attempts to persuade her, for endearments she did not want to hear just now. She did not look up at him.

He sighed. "Kirian, you must do as you wish. This is not the way your life should be, being chased from nation to nation with not even another woman to bear you company."

That almost pulled a smile from her, but she did not let him see it.

It was so odd, what the nobles thought people needed in life.

"I don't know yet what I will do. I cannot return to my estate or Sugetre. King Martan will kill me if I do not submit to his will. His heir is a boy who will never live to adulthood if I accept the King's offer. I cannot let that happen, yet his guardians might turn me over to the King if I attempt to warn them."

"Lord Arias would shelter you," she said.

"He is much too optimistic about being forgiven by the King, I think. I cannot endanger him further by staying there, another cause for a charge of treason."

She looked at him and saw his amber eyes troubled, a crease of worry between his brows. "You know how I feel about you," she said.

"But you must act for your own good, not for me. You are sweet, Kirian, a brave companion and a good friend and a joyous lover – but I cannot ask you to be a fugitive in the wilds, not for me."

Her heart brightened. He did not say love. She should not let herself hear what he did not say, should she?

"I will miss your lovely eyes every day, but you should stay in Seagard." His hands fidgeted with the straw. He was distressed because he was being selfless. Cheered by this thought, Kirian began to wonder what she would do all day in Seagard Village anyway. Pick and dry herbs, sit with Ruthan, climb the mountain paths for exercise, and miss Callo every minute of every candlemark of every day.

Her emotions calmed like a sea after the gale had passed. There really was no choice. She could heal anywhere she went. People everywhere needed healing.

And now that she had eaten and her nerves were steadier, she realized she really would like to see what the wilderness was like on the way to Lord Ander's home of Northgard. And maybe a chance to see if Callo could love her after all.

Callo said, "I will let you consider it. I will go and see if that damned turncoat Chiss has abandoned us or not." He rose, his fingers trailing along her arm so that she shivered, and left the barn.

A few minutes later, Chiss stepped in and began leading out Miri and his gelding.

"Did Lord Callo find you?" she asked.

He nodded. "I have convinced him he is better off to allow me to accompany him."

She snorted, an unladylike sound that startled Miri, who tossed her head at Kirian. "Gods know how you did that. Chiss, you are fortunate you are still alive."

"My lord knows I am not a traitor."

"I think your lord remembers too well the years when he was growing up. He said you were his mentor. That is why he did not slay you—he cannot forget the past."

"Why should he forget it?" Chiss said, turning to her for

the first time. "It is true, you know. Without me to recognize what he was and find someone who could train him up in discipline, he would be dead. Either the King would have slain him for using the psychic magery or he would have destroyed himself. He owes me much."

"I think he knows that and is paying it."

Chiss' narrow face, usually so self-controlled, was pale with tension. "If so, it is only what I am due. It is none of your concern why my lord sees fit to keep me with him."

Kirian made a helpless gesture with her hands. "It is my concern, because I will be with you. It's my life, too, Chiss."

"I thought you were remaining here. Going back to the village."

"No."

There was a moment of quiet as Chiss pulled the girth strap tight around Miri. "You have not told Lord Callo this."

"Not yet."

"All right then. I swore an oath to King Martan, many years ago, when he first assigned me to Lord Callo. I swore another to my lord, and have kept it all these years while I have grown to love him more than my own son. Nothing would take me from Lord Callo while I can do anything to help him. But I swore that oath to the King, swore it by Som'ur himself."

"The Ha'lasi god? You are no ku'an."

"I swore it nonetheless. I have not been released."

"You will never be released. How is Lord Callo to trust you, when at any moment you might betray him?"

Chiss' face lost its taut look. He hoisted Callo's saddlebag onto Miri's back. "There is no point in my explaining it again."

"By the Unknown God, you are a complicated man, Chiss."

An unexpected smile graced Chiss' thin face. "You say that, who knows my lord Callo? I am surprised."

She laughed. "He is no child's puzzle either. Perhaps you have influenced him."

Chiss bowed to her. "I will see if Hon Arter can find us a horse, Hon Kirian. It will be a pleasure to ride with you again."

"And me again with no baggage," Kirian said. "It is becoming a bad habit. I must find a better cloak and at least one other tunic if I am not to disgrace Lord Callo at Northgard."

"Of course. But you need not be concerned. We may shelter with the rebels after all, Hon Kirian. I doubt they wear the latest styles."

Kirian did not laugh. "But I will be riding with Lord Callo, who is always so well dressed," she said a little wistfully, and knew that Chiss understood.

"I will see what I can do," he said. "Now finish eating, Healer, and I will see what can be done about a horse."

When Callo burst into the barn a moment later and grabbed her hands to lift her up, she grinned at the expression on his face.

"Are you coming with us? You should not do it," he said, but his face was alight. "Chiss thought you said . . ."

She laughed. "I did. All these close calls have ruined me for normal life. In Seagard Village I would pine away for lack of a battle now and then, or someone trying to imprison me, or a daring rescue. With you I shall not be bored."

He laughed. "Oh, no. Never that." He drew her close, and she could see the golden sparks in his eyes. His hands were on her arms, firm but gentle, but she could see a flare of color magery beginning to wrap his hands, reflecting his emotion.

"Calm down, my lord color mage. Did you doubt I would come?"

"Hell yes, Kirian. Who in their right mind would join me on this fool's journey? I am glad you do not seem to be in your right mind. Kiss me, Sweet, to seal us partners on this journey."

"As long as you do not kiss your other partners this way," she murmured. His lips found hers, and she thought she could feel the color magery flow from him to her, but it was only love, and desire, and a looking forward to something she had no right to look forward to.

When their lips parted, he murmured, "I can stand anything now that you'll be with me."

"You may have to," she said. She pulled away a little to hide the trembling that was beginning to take her. She felt his hands slide along her arms as if he was loath to release her, and savored that feeling even while she heard the stamp of horses' hooves and Chiss reentering the barn, making enough noise to warn them of his coming.

"We must go, my lord. We have a very long way to travel, and they may yet pursue us."

"We have a third horse?" Callo asked, over his shoulder, still looking at her.

"Ready to go. It is one of Arter's livestock, a farm horse only, but it will carry us as well as another."

"I will send her two horses, if this one gets us through safe," Callo said. He grinned a little as Kirian pulled him to the barn door. "If she will carry Kirian in comfort."

"The mare is old and fat. Comfort will be no problem," Arter said outside the door. "Speed will be another matter."

"If we follow the hill trails for a ways, speed should not be necessary. Hon Arter, you know well you have my deepest gratitude," Callo said. "If Arias should come asking, please tell him we ride to warn Lord Ander."

"Him and no other, unless you command it," she said. "I have no love for His Majesty Sharpeyes."

"Which Arias must have known, to send us here. What has Sharpeyes done, to earn your enmity?"

Arter made an emphatic wide gesture with her arms. "What has he not done! Ask any of the farmholders of Righar. But you really have no time to stand here arguing politics, my lord. Go now, before it is too late."

Callo bent and kissed the farmer's hand. She stepped back, a little embarrassed, but she was smiling.

"Farewell, then and our thanks," Callo said.

Kirian echoed that, smiling into Arter's eyes. With a lightness in her heart that was wholly inappropriate for their circumstances, she climbed into the mare's saddle. She leaned forward, stroking the mare's thick neck. "Let us go, horse. I know you'll carry me well."

She followed Callo out of the barnyard, Chiss behind her.

About the Author

Anne Marie Lutz is the author of the two Color Mage novels, *Black Tide* and *Sword of Jashan*, as well as the forthcoming fantasy novel *Taylenor*. Her short stories have appeared in several publications including the "For the Road" anthology, Strange Fictions Zine, and Bards and Sages Quarterly.

She was raised in the Youngstown, Ohio area, and currently lives in central Ohio with her family. She is a graduate of the Ohio State University (Journalism and MBA). She enjoys reading and traveling when she can. She is currently working on another novel.

You can follow her on her blog at annemariesblog.wordpress.com, or on Twitter or Facebook.

9 781937 979584